"**From all the shouting, it's safe to assume you got the gig.**"

Despite his objection to her talking back to her elders, Randy smiled at the young lady. She stood at the entrance of the dining room, shoving the last bite of a slice of cake into her mouth. The lines previously marring her brow had disappeared.

"Not officially. Luther wants to hear how I sound with the band." He grabbed his case and hat and stepped off the stage as she sashayed toward the table where she had been sitting earlier. "I guess I should say thanks," he said, extending his hand to her.

"For what?"

"Standin' up for me like you did, though I don't condone you talkin' back to your elders."

"You're the best player to audition," she said, placing her hand in his. Though her tone was calmer, her accent was still thick. "If it meant I didn't have to listen to anyone else murder music, I'd have spoken up for you if you were purple and had walked in here on four legs."

Randy laughed as he released her hand. "Auditions couldn't have been that bad."

She made an unladylike snort and dropped into a chair. "I've heard sick geese that sounded better than some of the cats coming in here claiming they could play."

He would have argued with her had the other sax player not produced sounds Randy had not heard since leaving the farm. "By the way, I'm Randy."

"You mentioned that already."

He placed the case on the table and dropped his hat next to it. "Sassy, aren't you?"

Praise for Ursula Renée

SWEET JAZZ won First Place in the Historical Category in the 1st Annual (2013) Abalone Awards for Unpublished Authors, an event held by the Cultural, Interracial and Multicultural Romance Writers of America Chapter.

Sweet Jazz

by

Ursula Renée

This is a work of fiction. Names, characters, places, and incidents are either the product of the author's imagination or are used fictitiously, and any resemblance to actual persons living or dead, business establishments, events, or locales, is entirely coincidental.

Sweet Jazz

COPYRIGHT © 2014 by Ursula Renée

All rights reserved. No part of this book may be used or reproduced in any manner whatsoever without written permission of the author or The Wild Rose Press, Inc. except in the case of brief quotations embodied in critical articles or reviews.
Contact Information: info@thewildrosepress.com

Cover Art by *Rae Monet, Inc. Design*

The Wild Rose Press, Inc.
PO Box 708
Adams Basin, NY 14410-0708
Visit us at www.thewildrosepress.com

Publishing History
First Vintage Rose Edition, 2014
Print ISBN 978-1-62830-458-9
Digital ISBN 978-1-62830-459-6

Published in the United States of America

Dedication

Sweet Jazz is dedicated to my family,
who inspired me to pursue my dreams.

Chapter 1

October 1938, New York

He reminded her of a banana. A long, fat, overripe banana.

Cass tightened her stomach muscles to quiet a growl. She would have found the comparison amusing if she had not forgotten to pack a lunch on the same day she skipped breakfast. Back-to-back auditions had prevented her from grabbing a bite from the corner diner. With no hope of satisfying her hunger anytime soon, all she could do was dream of food as she watched him swagger onto the stage dressed in yellow wide-legged pants, matching broad-shouldered long coat, and a black shirt.

His right arm swung in time to the nameless tune he hummed. Under his left, he held his saxophone like a side of beef. He stopped at the center of the platform with his back to the dining room, tapped his foot twice, then whipped the saxophone from under his arm as he spun around to face his audience.

Cass imagined he'd practiced the moves in front of the mirror until he could perform them without tripping over his feet. She, however, was not impressed. Experience had taught her flamboyant antics were a cover for a lack of talent. From the way he carried the instrument, she suspected he had never laid eyes on, much less played, a saxophone before that afternoon.

Cass tapped a pencil on the table and waited for the young man to fulfill his promise to play the saxophone as it had never been played before.

He struck a five-second pose before he moved the reed to his lips, stopped, shook his head, and pulled back the saxophone. He performed the same sequence of motions two more times before he finally placed the reed between his lips, took a deep breath, and blew.

His eyes bulged and his cheeks puffed out, like the blowfish Cass had seen at the aquarium at Battery Park. Yet, for all his effort, the only sound he produced was an imitation of a cow in labor.

Cass tossed her pencil across the table to avoid the temptation to jab it into her ear. She would give him credit for being a man of his word. She had never heard a saxophone make a sound like that.

Junior, at the table closest to the stage, shuddered. He leaned toward the woman by his side and whispered in her ear. She threw back her head and screeched. Her laughter, as irritating as fingernails on a blackboard, was more pleasing than the noise from the stage.

Across from them, Luther Hamilton sat back and crossed his arms. His blank expression offered no clue as to what was going through his head, though putting an end to his suffering by selling his share of the club and moving someplace quiet with his wife would be Cass's first guess.

It was an idea she herself had entertained over the past two weeks as one musician after another strolled through the doors of The Big House and tortured management for whatever sins they had committed in the past, were contemplating in the present, or would commit in the future. The only difference in the dream was she would make the move alone.

At the age of sixteen, Cass had stopped believing in the fairy tale of the knight in shining armor whisking her away to faraway places. After she kissed a knight who transformed into a frog, she decided her future would not include a "Prince" unless he walked on four legs and retrieved the sticks she tossed.

"Okay, thank you." Junior's booming voice invaded her daydream and returned her to the nightmare at The Big House.

The young man ended his performance on a high note—a long and sour one that made her ears ring and her eyes tear.

"Whatcha think?" he asked as he lowered the saxophone until it dangled by his side, barely an inch from the floor. "Groovy, wasn't it?"

"That was, umm… It was a very interesting rendition of…well, of…" Too diplomatic to blurt out *What the hell was that,* Luther hesitated, giving the impression he was trying to recall the name of the song.

" 'Carry Me Back to Old Virginny.' "

The four-member audience stared at the stage as if waiting for the punch line of a joke, the delivery too long in coming.

"Well, do I get the gig?"

Junior was the first to recover. "We'll need to talk it over before we can give you an answer." He draped an arm over the shoulder of the woman next to him, leaned over, and whispered in her ear.

Cass suspected Junior, whose fingers grazed the skin threatening to spill from the neckline of the woman's scarlet dress, used the excuse to cop a quick feel. The woman had no more say in the club's business than the cleaning staff. She was merely a decoration for his arm and would be discarded for a newer one when he got tired of her.

"I dig." The young man hopped to the floor, striking the saxophone on the edge of the stage as he did. "Don't take too long. I've another gig lined up."

"Sure, kid, we'll get back to you," Luther mumbled. He bent over the stack of papers he had brought up from his office to work on during the auditions.

Ignoring the "don't contact us and we definitely won't look for you" tone in Luther's voice, the young man strutted toward Cass with a leer that made her skin crawl. "I'll check you out later, sweet thing."

Cass swallowed the unladylike reply on the tip of her tongue. She dropped her head in her hands and massaged her temples in a vain attempt to soothe the headache that had begun forming an hour earlier.

His footsteps faded toward the back of the club. The blare of a car horn and the pounding of shoes on the pavement as Harlemites rushed by drifted into the room when he opened the door. Once the noise from the street was muted, Junior and the woman burst out in laughter.

" 'Carry Me Back to Old Virginny'?" Junior asked. "Someone needs to carry him back, 'cause there ain't no way he's gonna be a musician in this city."

"They probably threw him out of Virginny for makin' that noise," the woman shrieked.

"Only way he'll make money is if someone pays him to stop playin'."

"Someone needs to arrest him for making that

noise," Cass muttered into her hands.

"The worst part is he's the best one we've heard all week." Luther's somber tone silenced the hecklers.

When Luther had announced the auditions for a saxophonist, the city's elite musicians did not line up outside. The Big House's colored-only policy made the club popular with the Harlem residents, who had watched for years as establishments they were barred from opened in the neighborhood. However, the same policy deterred the most talented musicians from seeking employment there.

With the majority of the big shots in the music industry being white, musicians who had dreams of making it big sought out places where they had a chance of being seen by people who would further their careers. That left those who did not have the right look, like Cass, amateurs who had bigger dreams than talent, and those who did not have stars in their eyes and only wanted a chance to perform.

"We need someone to blow, but there ain't a soul with talent comin' up in here," Junior said. "It's gettin' so I'd hire the next cat who walks in and plays one good note."

"I can play."

Cass shuddered. The thought of having to sit through another audition caused the throbbing in her temples to intensify. She considered excusing herself to do something less painful, like bang her head against the bathroom wall, but then Junior cursed.

"Why the hell ain't nobody tell me it's Halloween?" he asked. "First people tryin' to pass themselves off as musicians come walkin' up in here, and now there's a ghost in my club."

Chapter 2

Randy stepped from the shadows of the foyer where he had listened to the previous musician's attempt to play the saxophone. His footsteps echoed through the room that had grown quiet. Four sets of eyes stared at him as if he were an apparition of a long-departed relative.

"Heard you needed someone to blow the reed," Randy said.

The smaller of the two men squared his shoulders and placed his clenched fists on the table. "Yeah, we wanna sax player, not an ofay."

Randy stepped around the tables, stopping at the edge of the dance floor. He had learned about The Big House's reputation the previous evening. Two men stopped him on the way home and informed him of the auditions at the club. They gave him the details, the where and when, then chatted with him as if they were old friends.

After a few minutes, Randy thanked them before continuing toward the boarding house. He had barely made it around the corner before the men joked there was no way a white man would ever work at the club. Or, as one had so eloquently put it, "That ofay ain't gonna get one foot in The Big House before Junior throws his ass out on the street."

Though the warning had been unintentional, Randy

was grateful for it. He preferred to know what he was up against when going for an audition.

"I can play," he repeated, ignoring the insult.

The man's scowl said he was seconds from fulfilling the prankster's prophecy by tossing Randy out of the club. The only thing he was uncertain on was whether the man would perform the task himself or delegate it to the larger man, who, in a polo shirt that showed off his thick biceps, looked as if he could get the job done without breaking a sweat.

"You don't understand. No—"

"What harm will it do to listen to him, Junior?" A soft voice with a slight southern drawl interrupted the man's rant.

Randy glanced at the young lady who sat by herself at the table behind the others. In a loose-fitting blue dress, modestly buttoned to the neck, and ribbons securing the ends of the two thick braids that reached between her shoulder blades, she looked as if she should have been sitting in a classroom, not a club. He estimated her age at about seventeen, though he would not have been surprised if she was as young as fifteen. He had seen hard living age girls so a fourteen-year-old could look like she was in her twenties.

Though he did not believe someone so young would have a say in what went on in the club, he addressed her directly, despite the popular adage that children should be seen and not heard.

"Been playin' for eighteen years. Ten professionally."

She nodded her head as if she approved. "He's got more experience than the other cats who've come through that door," she said, without taking her eyes off him. "Give him a chance."

"Have you lost your mind?" Junior asked.

She turned toward the other table and shrugged her shoulders. "Maybe I have. After listening to that last kid, anything's possible."

"Forget it. No blue-eyed devil's playin' in The Big House."

"No problem." Randy removed his fedora and stepped to the middle of the dance floor. "My eyes are green."

The young lady laughed, earning her a sharp look from Junior.

"Now listen here—"

"What do you have to lose?" she interrupted, ignoring Junior's glare.

"I'm kinda curious myself to hear what the white boy can do," the older woman added.

Junior focused his glare on the woman, who, unlike the young lady, shrank back in her seat. "Ain't no ofay playin' in my club," he snarled.

"It's our club," the larger man said, speaking as calmly as if he were simply stating the weather. "What's your name, kid?"

"Randy Jones."

The larger man waved his hand toward the stage. "Since you're here, you might as well play something."

Junior gasped in outrage before expressing his objection, loud enough for someone two blocks away to hear. Without raising his voice, the other man defended his decision. The older woman leaned forward as far as she could without falling out of her scarlet dress and nodded whenever Junior spoke.

At the other table, the girl dropped her head in her

hands. She rubbed her temples as if trying to soothe a headache. Randy wanted to reassure her everything would be all right, but he did not want to waste time and give the man a chance to change his mind. Instead, he would let his music speak for itself.

He stepped onto the stage and set his case and hat on top of the upright piano. Once he'd assembled his saxophone, he cradled it in his arms like a newborn baby and moved toward the center of the stage. Without waiting for his audience's attention, he closed his eyes and began playing "Smoke Gets In Your Eyes."

Remembering the teachings of his mentor, he pictured the music in his mind. He saw the beauty of each note and knew where there was beauty there was hope.

For Randy, hope was more than the wish for something he did not have. It was a survival skill. As long as he had hope, he saw the possibilities and was able to keep trying. However, once robbed of it, he would no longer be living, just merely existing, going about his day-to-day tasks until death came to claim him.

When he finished, Randy opened his eyes and looked down at his audience, who had quieted and not made a sound since he began. Junior sat up straight with his arms folded over his chest, scowling back at him. The other man leaned back in his chair. The lines on his face had relaxed, and he wore a slight smile. The woman's mouth hung open as she stared up at him.

"That was beautiful," the younger woman, who had raised her head, said. The corners of her full lips turned up in a smile that spread to her doe-shaped brown eyes.

"Thank you," he mouthed. He winked at her before

turning his attention to the men. "Well?"

"Now that you've played, get the hell outta my club," Junior said, pointing toward the foyer.

The young lady slammed her palms on the table. "Have you lost your cotton-pickin' mind?" she shrieked.

Randy's head snapped back in her direction. He frowned and shook his head. Though honored she was willing to speak up for him, he drew the line at her disrespecting an elder.

"What kinda bull is that?" she asked, ignoring his silent chastisement.

"Ain't no ofay's gonna play in The Big House."

"So, what are you goin' to do? Hire that other kid?"

"I'd hire him before I'd hire an ofay."

The young woman threw her hands up. "That'll solve everythin'," she said. Her accent became more pronounced with each word. "One sound from him and no one—white, colored, red or yellow—will come up in here."

Junior pounded a fist on the table. The woman by his side jumped with a squeak. The young lady, however, did not flinch. She sat with her arms crossed over her chest and glared back at him.

"You tellin' me how to run my business?" Junior asked.

"Yes, I am."

The older woman whistled, shook her head, and muttered, "Girl's got more guts than sense," while the other man rolled his eyes upward as if looking for intervention from a higher power.

"He's the best player we've heard all day," the

young woman continued. "In fact, he's the best one that's come up in here all week. And you did say you'd hire the next cat who walks in and plays one good note."

"Next you'll want me to hire high-yella girls for the show?"

"No, I want you to cut the crap and hire the best person for the job."

"I agree with her," the other man commented.

Junior shot to his feet, overturning his chair. "Then you're as crazy as her."

"No, crazy's lettin' him walk out of here without the gig," she argued.

"Who asked you?"

"You did when you asked me to sit through these auditions."

"That was the biggest mistake in my damn life."

"No, your biggest mistake will be lettin' him walk out of here, 'cause if he goes, I'm liable to go with him."

"Don't mess with me, you little—"

"Don't say anything you'll be sorry for," the other man interrupted.

"The only one who'll be sorry is her," Junior said, stabbing the air in her direction with his finger.

The young woman stood, braced her hands on the table, and leaned forward. "Is that a threat?" Her voice was low and steady, indicating she was ready for a challenge.

"Okay, you two," the other man said as he stood up.

Though he towered over them and looked as if he could take on both at the same time, neither one backed down. They stood, rigid, scowling at each other, as if he had not spoken.

"Cass, sit down."

She glared at Junior for another second, then shook her head. "No, I'm through talkin' to him," she said before marching toward the back of the club.

"Cass, come back here."

"You know where I stand on this, Luther," she called over her shoulder without breaking her stride.

"Cass." A rattle from a muffler and the tapping of shoes against the pavement drifted in, indicating his call was in vain.

Luther sighed as he turned back to the smaller man. "Junior?"

"Ain't nothin' to discuss. He ain't workin' here, and that's final."

"I know how you feel, but let's be reasonable. We need a saxophonist—now."

"Not bad enough to sell our souls."

"Aren't you being a little overdramatic?"

"Like hell I am." Junior kicked the overturned chair to the side before storming across the floor and through a door next to the stage. The woman, who had not offered her input during the argument, jumped up and followed him, moving as fast as her tight skirt and high heels allowed.

"That went well," Luther sighed.

Randy stepped down from the stage. He forced himself to hold his head high and shoulders back as disappointment weighed down on him. Though he had been through the same scene more than once over the years, it didn't make the rejection easier to bear. "Thanks for listenin' to me," he said.

Luther glanced down at Randy as if he suddenly realized he was not alone. "After that, I can't blame you for not wanting to work here."

"I've faced worse from men a lot bigger than him."

Luther raised an eyebrow. "You often frequent places you're not welcome?"

"I don't actively search them out. I hear about a gig and show up. Figure what's the worst that can happen? They show me the door?"

"Not the wisest way to go about getting a gig."

Randy shrugged his shoulders. "Maybe not, but I just want a chance to play."

"That's why we opened The Big House," Luther mumbled, more to himself than to Randy. His features became somber, as if he was remembering how it felt to be denied an opportunity because of something he couldn't control. "Something's telling me I'm going to regret this, but do you still want the gig?"

"Yes, sir," Randy said. He pointed a thumb toward the door next to the stage. "But he just said—"

Luther shook his head. "Junior says a lot of things, but when we opened the club, we agreed he'd handle the menu and I'd take care of the entertainment. I don't tell him what to put on his tables, and he's not going to tell me who to put on my stage." He sighed. "This will be a first for The Big House, but it's been four weeks, and I need someone now. I want to hear how you sound with the band. Rehearsals are at five. Can you be back here by then?"

"Yes, sir." Randy extended his hand. "Thanks, Mr., um…"

"You can call me Luther." He grasped his hand in a firm handshake.

"Thanks, Luther."

Luther slapped him on the shoulder before heading backstage. Moments later, Junior's voice cut though the silence as he expressed with a colorful choice of words his feelings about the audition.

Taking that as his signal to leave, Randy climbed back onto the stage and packed his saxophone into its case. He could only hope the reception he received that night would be a bit more welcoming.

"From all the shouting, it's safe to assume you got the gig."

Despite his objection to her talking back to her elders, Randy smiled at the young lady. She stood at the entrance of the dining room, shoving the last bite of a slice of cake into her mouth. The lines previously marring her brow had disappeared.

"Not officially. Luther wants to hear how I sound with the band." He grabbed his case and hat and stepped off the stage as she sashayed toward the table where she had been sitting earlier. "I guess I should say thanks," he said, extending his hand to her.

"For what?"

"Standin' up for me like you did, though I don't condone you talkin' back to your elders."

"You're the best player to audition," she said, placing her hand in his. Though her tone was calmer, her accent was still thick. "If it meant I didn't have to listen to anyone else murder music, I'd have spoken up for you if you were purple and had walked in here on four legs."

Randy laughed as he released her hand. "Auditions couldn't have been that bad."

She made an unladylike snort and dropped into a

chair. "I've heard sick geese that sounded better than some of the cats coming in here claiming they could play."

He would have argued with her had the other sax player not produced sounds Randy had not heard since leaving the farm. "By the way, I'm Randy."

"You mentioned that already."

He placed the case on the table and dropped his hat next to it. "Sassy, aren't you?"

"No, but you're close."

Her devilish grin told him he'd pegged her correctly and any boy who got with her would have a hell of a time. However, her ability to appreciate music, despite the color of the person playing, made her a keeper.

"Cassie Ann Porter," she said. "Cass for short."

He reached into the pocket of his jacket and pulled out a pack of cigarettes. "It's a pleasure to meet you, Cassie Ann Porter." He held out the pack to her. "Do you mind if I ask you a question?"

She shook her head, declining his offer. "You can ask, but it don't mean I'll answer."

"Are you always so sassy…Cassie?"

Cass rolled her eyes at the rhyme even he had to admit was lame. Randy lit a cigarette and took a drag. A cloud of smoke encircled his head when he exhaled.

"Aren't you kinda young to be hangin' out in clubs?" he asked.

"I don't hang out in clubs."

He propped a foot on the chair next to her and leaned forward with his folded arms on his knee. The cigarette dangled from between his fingers.

"What do you call this?"

"Working."

"Doin' what? Runnin' errands after school?"

"No, a couple of kids hang around outside after school. They run errands for us to make a bit of money, and we keep an eye on them to make sure they stay out of trouble."

He smiled at her use of the word "kids" since she could not be far from one herself. Deciding to humor her, he asked, "If you don't run errands, then what do you do?"

"What's this? An inquisition? What'll you want to know next? My birthdate? My parents' names? The color of the mole on my Aunt Rupert's shoulder?"

He cocked on eyebrow. "Aunt Rupert?"

"Grandma swore she was going to have a boy. She couldn't be bothered to think of another name when the baby turned out to be a girl."

Randy shook his head. He couldn't tell whether she was serious or not. "I just want to know more about the kids who hang around the club."

Cass rolled her eyes as she slid a sheet of paper across the table. He glanced down at the sketch of an older woman standing next to a piano. She wore an evening gown, and her hair was pulled back in a bun, with a feather ornament holding the style in place.

"The Big House is proud to feature Cass, with music by The Big House Band," Randy read. He glanced from the paper to her, then back at the paper. He recognized the similarities in the facial features, but it couldn't be possible. "You can't be the same Cass."

"No other Cass here."

"Your momma lets you work here?" Randy asked as he handed back the flyer.

He knew some parents did not care what their children did as long as they were out of the way. However, allowing a young girl to work in a club was beyond neglectful.

"My momma doesn't have much say in the matter, seeing as how she's down south," Cass said, placing the paper on the table.

"Down south?

"That's where she lives."

"What about your relatives?"

"They're down there, too."

Randy lowered his foot to the floor and straddled the chair. He needed to sit down. There was no way she was up there by herself.

"Don't you have someone lookin' after you?"

"I've been looking after myself for six years."

"Six years? Girl, you jokin'? You can't be no older than…what…sixteen? seventeen?"

"I'm twenty-two."

Twenty-two? It explained why she got away with arguing with Junior, but, still… Randy slowly glanced from the ankle socks and canvas shoes on her feet to her two braids. She looked as if she should be playing with dolls or jumping rope, not singing in a club.

The patter of heels against wood filled the room. Cass placed an elbow on the table and cradled her head in her hand as the woman who had sat next to Junior during the audition toddled toward them.

The woman stopped near the table and screeched, "Cass!" as if the younger woman were two blocks away instead of two feet in front of her.

"What do you want?" Cass asked, without looking in the other woman's direction.

"Junior wanna see ya."

"I'll be there in a minute."

"But he wanna see ya now."

Cass slammed her hand down on the table. The other woman jumped back a foot and wrung her hands together.

"Please." She peeped over her shoulder at the door that led backstage. "He just wanna talk to you. I'm sure he's already tired from yellin' and—"

"Okay, okay, okay." Cass sighed as she stood. "I better go see what that man wants."

Randy stood also. "You're not goin' to have problems 'cause of me?"

She dismissively waved her hand toward the door. "Don't worry about Junior," she said before pointing a finger at him. "You just make sure you get back here and wow them tonight, so I don't have to sit through any more auditions."

Randy took a drag off his cigarette and exhaled. Through the smoke that lingered in front of him, he watched her walk off. He shook his head.

A headliner? It was hard to imagine, in that outfit. Though he did not expect her to prance around in silk and heels all day, she didn't look old enough to be up past nine at night, much less headline a show that had her on stage well beyond midnight.

"Man, you don't know what kinda trouble you caused by comin' up in here."

Randy looked down at the other woman, who stood in front of him, her hands on her hips. With Cass and Junior out of the room, she had found her backbone and glared up at him, ready to speak her mind whether he wanted to hear what she had to say or not.

"I was just lookin' for a chance to play," he replied.

"If I were you, I'd look somewhere else."

Randy understood the warning behind her words. He had heard it many times in the past from various people of different shapes, sizes, and colors. Yet he chose to treat her warning like he had done all the others.

"Then be happy you're not me," Randy said, before grabbing his hat and case and walking away.

Chapter 3

Cass knew good news traveled fast and bad news traveled quicker, but she never realized how fast a rumor could spread until that evening.

By the time she left home to return to The Big House, the news of Randy's hiring seemed to have spread throughout Harlem. As she walked to the club, Cass overheard speculations regarding the newest addition to the band. Since Junior had always been vocal regarding his dislike for the fairer race, a couple of people said they would not be surprised if The Big House burnt down before Randy had a chance to play with the band. A few others believed Junior would not go to such extremes and destroy his business. However, they suggested Randy watch his back so he would not fall victim to an unfortunate "accident" before his debut.

No one seemed to consider the possibility Junior had had a change of heart, though a few hinted he had changes going on in his head that would one day find him locked away in a padded room. One woman even proclaimed she was going to spend the night at church because Randy working in the club was a sure sign of the Second Coming.

The excitement was more evident when Cass crossed Seventh Avenue. Two hours before the doors were scheduled to open, men sporting their finest suits and women wearing dresses reserved for special occasions had gathered in front of The Big House. Shaking her head at the spectacle, she pushed her way through the crowd to a tall, husky man who held the door open so she could slip into the club.

She walked past the coat check and into the dining room, where there was just as much chaos as outside. The chairs placed on the tables so the floor could be scrubbed that afternoon had not been set back on the floor. Tablecloths were thrown across tables with hastily folded napkins lying next to scattered silverware. And, with no concern about the mess, employees, representing the various shades of brown from caramel to charcoal, huddled together in small groups in front of the stage.

Cass stopped as Angel's deep bass voice echoed through the hall.

"I'm telling you, Red, there ain't no way Junior would hire an ofay. Hell would freeze over before he'd let one step foot in this joint."

"Then hell must be mighty cold," the club's bandleader replied, "'cause Earline told me she met the man." Cass assumed he was referring to the woman who had sat through the auditions with Junior. Friendly and outgoing, Red made it a point to remember everyone he met, even if the person was only a temporary figure in his life.

"Earline? That chick chasin' Junior? What does she know?"

"Considering she never leaves his side, you'd figure she'd know something about what's going on," Red said, confirming the woman's name.

"Why don't we just ask Flo?" Angel suggested as a

tall slender woman with short black hair strolled into the room.

As Luther's eldest daughter and a dancer at the club, Florence Hamilton was usually the one people sought out to confirm rumors.

"Ask me what?" she asked with a husky voice that could be mistaken for a man's.

"Did Luther hire someone?"

Florence shrugged her shoulders. "All Daddy said when he got home was he traded one headache for another. He then locked himself in his room and was still there when I left."

"I believe Earline," Red said. "You know how big a gossip she is."

"Bigger than present company?"

All heads turned in Cass's direction. Embarrassed at being caught gossiping, a few quickly looked away. Others stared at her, silently pleading with their eyes for her to verify whether or not the rumors were true. Angel, however, stood and walked from behind the drums to the edge of the stage.

"You here when they hired the new cat?"

Curiosity must have gotten the best of Angel, who could go a week without saying a word to her. Tall and lean, with conked hair, he considered himself God's gift to women. Of course, it didn't help that there never seemed to be a shortage of those falling over themselves to be with him. It was therefore a blow to his pride when, a month after she started working at the club, Cass not only rejected his proposition to go out for drinks but did it in front of the other performers. That prevented him from later saving face by saying he was not interested in her. He had never forgiven her for the slight, and since then they had maintained a strained business relationship.

"Yes, I was."

"What's he like?"

Aside from his skin color, she could not recall what Randy looked like. Battling a headache and frustrated by the argument with Junior, she had paid only the slightest attention to him. She did recall him saying his eyes were green, but she knew no one in the room cared about the color of his eyes, only his skin.

"Well?" Angel prodded.

"He was talented and had a good sense of humor," she replied, remembering how he'd made her laugh, despite the ugliness in the room.

"What did he look like?"

Cass shrugged a shoulder. "He looked like a man, but since he was dressed, I can't say for sure."

Angel hopped down from the stage. He strutted across the dance floor until he stood six inches in front of her. "Can't you ever give a straight answer?" he asked as he scowled down at her.

Cass suspected the frown and the invasion of her personal space were meant to intimidate her. It took a lot of self-control not to laugh in his face.

"Yes," she replied. "But only when I'm asked a question I care to answer."

She walked across the room and through the door that led to the kitchen, leaving the gossips with no more information than they had when she walked in.

****

The scene in the dining room was not what Randy had expected when he walked into The Big House that evening. Instead of waiters preparing tables and musicians warming up, a crowd was gathered in front of the stage debating the validity of the rumors regarding the new hire.

Engrossed in their conversation, no one noticed him standing at the edge of the group. He could have ended their speculation but decided to use their distraction to his advantage.

Randy found one of the easiest ways to learn about others was to observe them when they did not realize they were being watched. There were few who were real enough to openly express their disdain for others like Junior had. Most people tried to hide their true feelings behind fake smiles and insincere words.

As expected, his observation revealed a few who would not tolerate his presence. One man, whose hair was slicked back and who wore a sharp beige suit that probably cost two weeks' salary, sneered as he cursed the "evil whites," who could not be trusted and if permitted to "would swoop in and re-enslave us all." His argument was so fierce Randy was surprised the man had not spit each time he used the word "white."

The rest were simply shocked by the rumors, but they did not express the hatred that Junior and this other man apparently felt.

After several minutes of listening to the conversation, Randy decided to make his presence known. He called out "Excuse me" three times before the most vocal man looked past the group to him.

"Deeaamm," he exclaimed, alerting the others to the new arrival.

All conversation ceased as everyone turned and stared at Randy with wide eyes and slack jaws.

"I'm Randy. I auditioned this afternoon," he said,

stepping forward and extending his hand. When no one replied, he added, "Luther told me to come back at five."

When the silence continued, he lowered his hand and looked down at his suit.

"The salesman assured me these threads looked sharp, but judgin' from your reaction, I'd say he lied."

As he had hoped, the joke broke the ice. An older man let out a hearty laugh. With a genuine smile on his face, he stepped forward and offered Randy his hand.

"Name's Red," he said. "On account of my red hair."

Randy grasped the stockier man's hand. He tried to keep a straight face as he glanced at the white fuzz covering the man's head.

Red released Randy's hand and brushed his hand over the close-cut hair. "Well, it was red, until age caught up with me," he joked. "I play piano and do an occasional duet with Cass."

"I hope this gig doesn't require me to sing. The customers are liable to hurt themselves tryin' to get out of here, if I do."

Red smiled. "I'll remember that."

"I brought a suit with me. Thought I'd change here. Is there someplace I can leave it?"

"The dressing room's—"

"There's a dressing room downstairs," the man who'd first noticed Randy interrupted. The scowl that had previously curled his lips was replaced by a grin as phony as the gold watch on his wrist. "Go through the curtain, walk down the flight of steps, turn right and walk to the back. You can use the last room on your left."

A tall woman shook her head as the man rattled off the directions. She stepped forward as if she was going to offer her input, but was stopped by several chorus girls who blocked her advance.

Randy knew when he was being set up. The only question was whether the man would be original or if Randy would end up looking out into the alley behind the club. On more than one occasion he had been given directions to the back door.

Feigning gratitude, he plastered a smile on his face that was as fake as the other man's and extended his hand. "Thanks…um…"

"Angel," said the man, slipping his hands into his pants pockets. "I beat the skins. You know, the hide, the drums."

Randy dropped his hand to his side. "I know what you mean."

"Just making sure. I didn't know if your kind would be hip to the jive."

"Don't worry about me." Randy's smile faded. "I'm hip to your jive," he said, before walking off to discover what he had been set up for.

****

Cass stepped back into the dining room as Florence pushed through a barrier of chorus girls and shoved Angel in the shoulder.

"You're such an ass," the dancer hissed.

Angel spun around, his hand raised, ready to strike out. He held back as Eli Viera, the club's trumpeter and Florence's man, stepped between them.

"Tell your woman she better keep her hands to herself," Angel warned as he dropped his hand to his side.

Ignoring the threat, Florence stepped around Eli. "Why'd you give him those directions?"

"To let him know where he stands. Besides, what are you getting all uppity about? It's not like anyone stopped you from saying something." He glanced over her shoulder and smirked at the dancers behind her.

Cass walked into the center of the group, took note of Florence's frown and Angel's smug grin.

Deciding she would rather deal with the dancer, she gave Angel her back. "What's wrong?" she asked Florence.

"We met the new sax player, and Angel had to be an ass."

"So I gave him a private room," Angel said with no hint of remorse. "He's lucky I didn't give him directions to the dumpster."

Dreading the thought of having to sit through more auditions, Cass hurried after Randy. She needed to find him and soothe things over before a red-faced man returned ready to curse everyone before he stormed out of the club.

Cass knew what it felt like to be denied an opportunity because her skin was too dark. Yet in the four years she'd worked for The Big House she'd never considered how discriminatory the club's policy was until Junior refused to listen to Randy because his skin was too light. At that moment, Randy was no longer a white man but a talented musician who deserved the opportunity to prove himself.

She was not naïve enough to believe others would be as quick to embrace the desegregation of the club. A few would probably be able to look past Randy's color to appreciate his talent and admire not only his confidence and determination but his ability to maintain his sense of humor when faced with ugliness. Unfortunately, others would not be able to differentiate him from the bigots they'd had the displeasure of encountering in the past.

Certain Angel would not direct Randy to Junior's office, she bypassed the closed door to the left of the stairs. After a quick search of the women's dressing room, Cass stepped back into the dimly lit hall. She was preparing to search the bathrooms when she spied him standing, arms crossed over his chest, outside the storage closet at the end of the hall.

"It has its possibilities," he said as she headed toward him. He had the thick drawl of someone who had recently arrived from the south. "With a little imagination and some work, of course."

"Huh?" she replied, too surprised by his reaction.

"And a mirror," he added. "I don't want to be too demandin', but I must have a mirror. Have to make sure everything's tucked in, buttoned up, and, most importantly, zipped up before I step out on stage. Nothing's more awkward than havin' it all hang out in public."

She smiled. "Sounds like you're speaking from experience."

A pink blush tinted his cheek.

"You're not angry about the room?" she asked.

Randy glanced down at her. His short, dark brown hair was slicked back from his tanned face, giving her an unobstructed view of his smooth angular jaw, slightly crooked nose that had been broken at least once, and eyes that were indeed green. His gray suit complemented his tall, lean frame, and the half-smile on his lips reminded her of an impish boy plotting his next prank.

Though she had never been attracted to a white man and wondered why people made a big deal about leading men like Clark Gable and Cary Grant, she could see the attraction white women, and maybe a few colored ones, would find in him.

"I've two choices. I can laugh and make the best of the situation, or I can get upset and quit. I like playin' the sax too much to quit. Besides, I have to give Angel credit for originality. Most times, I'm given directions that lead me out the back door of the club."

"You make it a habit of frequenting places where they prefer to show you the door rather than the stage?"

He shrugged his shoulders. "I've been to a few."

"Why?"

"I want to play, so when I see the chance I take it."

"And everything works out in the end?"

"As you saw this afternoon, gettin' a gig, it's not without a few challenges. And, once I get the gig, well…" He nodded toward the storage room.

"So, how do you keep such a positive attitude?"

"With my music. I don't simply play the sax, I make music. I once heard a story about a man who said he could teach a monkey to play."

Though surprised by the change in the subject, she was curious enough about the outcome to ask, "Did he?"

"He taught the monkey how to put the sax to its mouth and move the pads," Randy explained. "He even got the monkey to play a song, but that's all it could do. It couldn't make music, 'cause it didn't put its heart into what it was doin'." He glanced down at the case resting by his feet. "When I pick up the sax, I put my heart into my music and forget about everythin' else around me. I guess that sounds kinda silly, but that's how I deal with people."

Cass shook her head as she thought about her shows. She similarly put herself into the songs she sang, pouring her heart out in ballads while expressing her joys through livelier numbers.

"It doesn't sound silly, but does it always work?"

"Most of the time."

"What about the other times?

"I see you found your dressin' room," Junior said.

Cass jumped at his sudden appearance. With all her attention on Randy, she had been unaware of the stream of people making their way down the stairs to get ready for the evening's performance.

Junior sneered as he stood near them. Her earlier meeting with him had lasted ten minutes, nine of which was spent listening to him rant about the injustices whites had subjected coloreds to for centuries.

While he carried on, he rearranged the office he shared with Luther. He sent a waste pail flying from the room and carpeted the floor with papers that had been scattered across his desk. Though Earline cowered in the corner, Junior's outbursts had not fazed Luther or Cass, as he knew better than to strike out at either one of them.

Striking out at Luther was as good as signing a death warrant. The other man was a head taller, outweighed him by at least fifty pounds, and was solid. Even if Junior had managed to get in the first punch, it would have been his last. On more than one occasion Luther had kicked the crap out of someone causing trouble at the club. He then brushed his suit off and walked away like he was going on a Sunday stroll.

Going after Cass would have been just as foolhardy. From the first day she walked into The Big House, Luther took it upon himself to watch over her as if she were one of his daughters.

Luther had tried to reason with Junior, reminding him the club had been short a saxophonist for four weeks. It was the only words he managed to get out before Junior stormed from the room.

Cass, under no illusion Junior would see things differently once he calmed down, did not lie and tell Luther everything would be all right. She simply patted his shoulder before gathering her belongings to head home and deal with her headache.

The loathing in Junior's eyes confirmed Cass's suspicion. He would not have a change of heart regarding Randy. If anything, she swore she saw his brain plotting a way to get rid of him.

"I'm sure the room's to your likin'. If not, I have a suggestion on what you can do."

"It has its possibilities," Randy repeated.

Junior waited for a minute. When Randy did not take the bait and lash out, he added, "If you plan on stayin', the band performs upstairs, or do you expect us to move the show down here to accommodate you?"

Without a word, Randy gave Junior a slight nod. He laid his suit on a box in the corner of the closet and grabbed his case.

"Also, in the future, use the back door. The front door's reserved for the right kinda people."

"Other times I just grin and bear it," Randy muttered under his breath as he passed Cass.

Placing her hands on her hips, she faced off with Junior. "Give the man a break," Cass said, though she knew her words would fall on deaf ears.

"Why should I? Ain't like ofays ever gave me a break."

"'Cause you know how it feels," she answered before she stalked off.

****

It was four in the morning when Randy made his way back to his dressing room for the final time that night. After the show, Luther had asked him to wait a second. An hour later, after speaking with the patrons who had lingered and offering constructive criticism to individual musicians, Luther handed Randy several papers. Once he'd read and signed each page, he was handed a business card for the tailor who provided the musicians with tuxedos.

Exhausted, Randy accepted the card with less enthusiasm then he felt. It had been several weeks since his last gig, and he had to get readjusted to playing into the early morning.

The evening had gone better than he'd expected. After his confrontation with Junior, he'd returned to the front of the club, where preparations were underway for the evening's patrons. Though they were no longer dawdling, the employees gave him a preview of the rest of the evening by gawking at him.

Once the doors opened for business, the crowds packed The Big House. Red explained the club did its best business on Friday and Saturday nights. Only a special occasion, or what some people considered a miracle, would pack the place on a Wednesday night.

Since Randy was considered the miracle of the

evening, every eye in the audience focused on him. The stares of awe, suspicion, and outright disgust lasted through the opening acts. Once Cass stepped onto the stage at nine o'clock, the focus shifted to her. Or at least he assumed it did.

When she appeared, he no longer noticed anyone but her. Gone was the innocent young woman, and in her place was a beauty in a sleeveless black dress that emphasized previously hidden curves. The hem of the full skirt ended mid-calf to show a modest amount of her shapely legs, accented by short black pumps. Her hair had been pulled back in a French twist, and aside from the red lipstick she wore no make-up. A pair of pearl teardrop earrings, a string of pearls around her neck, and a gold watch with a bracelet band finished off the simple but elegant outfit.

He had not gotten over his shock at her appearance before she began singing "Lullaby of Harlem," her lively rendition of "Lullaby of Broadway." And, though he knew the line would not win him points for suaveness, he mentally agreed her outward beauty was only surpassed by her voice.

For two hours, Cass performed upbeat tunes before turning the show back over to the dancers. At midnight, she returned to the stage and performed more mellow ballads until two.

The band played for another hour before calling it a night. Though he had been the center of attention throughout most of the evening, after the show it was as if he disappeared. Aside from Red and Eli, who apologized for the earlier prank and complimented him on his performance, he was ignored until Luther finally had a chance to speak with him. Their meeting lasted less than two minutes before the club's co-owner hurried away to talk to his daughter, who had hung around.

Randy's footsteps echoed through the empty basement. As he reached his dressing room, he noticed the cleaning supplies, which he had not had time to remove from the closet, were sitting in the hall. Expecting another prank, he slowly approached the closet and examined the door. He did not find anything out of place, but to be on the safe side he braced himself for whatever would spring out at him.

He opened the door, pulled the string hanging from the overhead light, and smiled. The street clothes he had left folded in the corner of the closet were neatly draped over a hanger hung from a hook nailed into one wall. A full-length mirror, with a slip of paper taped to it, had been mounted to the opposite wall. In addition to his one request was a chair.

Randy removed the note and read the message scrawled on the paper.

Welcome to The Big House.

Chapter 4

Cass balanced a shopping bag on her hip as she inspected the apples outside the grocery store. It had been more than a month since she'd been able to make anything other than quick meals to get her through the day. Auditions had occupied all her free time, and once Randy was hired, she spent her afternoons catching up on chores that had been neglected. But, as she passed by the stand, the apples caught her eye and she decided she could worry about the hem on her new dress another day.

She tested the firmness of one apple and examined it for any blemish that would deem it unfit for her pie. Her mother had taught her not to settle for anything less than the best when it came to her ingredients. She had taken the lesson to heart and was rewarded whenever she sat down to the table to eat. It made her wish she had realized the older woman was just as knowledgeable regarding matters of the heart, before she had learnt her lessons the hard way.

Engrossed in her activity, Cass did not hear the metal striking concrete or notice the pedestrians making way for the boy hurtling down the sidewalk on skates. By the time she became aware of her surroundings, it was too late to step out of the way.

"Oh, sh…sugar!" she exclaimed as he slammed into her side. She lost her grip on her bag and watched her groceries drop to the sidewalk.

Despite barely reaching her shoulders with the roller skates on, the boy grabbed hold of her arm to keep her from falling.

"I'm sorry," he said.

"That's okay, things happen," she replied, though she wondered why they always happened to her. She patted his hand, indicating she was fine.

"I'll help you pick 'em up." He released her arm, bent over, and reached out to grab a can before it rolled away. As he straightened, one foot rolled forward. With his arms out, he tried to regain his balance. Yet, despite the frantic flapping of his limbs, he fell back, sitting, on top of her loaf of bread.

His startled expression was priceless. Cass doubled over in laughter, ignoring her groceries as they rolled off in different directions. As she held her side and tried to catch her breath, two hands reached under the boy's arms.

"You know, there are safer ways to meet pretty ladies," Randy said, as he set the boy on his feet.

"Ladies?" The boy scrunched his face. "Why would I want to meet a lady? All they ever do is boss me around."

"I guess they can be a little bossy at times."

"A little bossy? My sister nags me all the time, and she's just a girl."

"They have to start young. They need years of practice to perfect the art of naggin'."

Cass, who had finally regained her composure, cleared her throat.

Randy glanced from the corner of his eye at her. "But, you know, not all ladies are bossy," he quickly added.

"Sure they are," the boy replied. He jerked his thumb at Cass. "I bet she'll even be bossy when she grows up."

Randy's cough failed to disguise his chuckle. "Of course, ladies can be good for other stuff."

"Like what?"

"Yes, like what?" she asked, eager to see how he'd handle a conversation not suited for children.

He looked at her, a silent plea for help in his eyes. With a smirk and a slight shake of her head, she communicated just as quietly that he would have to find help elsewhere.

"Well?" the boy asked, impatient.

"We're waiting," she said, placing her hands on her hips and tapping her foot.

Randy frowned and mouthed, "Thanks a lot," before looking back down at the boy, who was staring up at him as if he were about to reveal the meaning of life. "Well, um…" He stumbled for a second before coming up with, "Cookin'. They can cook for you."

"I can eat out," the boy said.

"And you can talk to them."

"I talk to my friends, and they're boys."

"And, they can make you feel good."

"How?"

Randy's face reddened. "Um…well…um…" He glanced around as if searching for the answer in the air. When nothing appeared, he shook his head and finally replied, "You'll find out when you're older."

"I hear that a lot."

"Joseph Andrew Carmichael, I've called you three times already," a girl yelled from the second-floor window of a building across the street. "If you don't come do your chores, I'm telling Momma."

"See what I mean?" the boy groaned. "Bossy."

Randy chuckled. "Go ahead."

They watched the boy skate across the street. Once he sat on the stoop to remove the metal skates attached to his sneakers, Cass cleared her throat.

Randy peeped over his shoulder at her, apparently trying to determine whether he should turn around or walk away and face the consequences of his words at a later time.

She crossed her arms over her chest and tried to maintain a stern expression, despite the urge to laugh at his impish grin.

"What?" he asked. "Did I say something wrong?"

"Bossy?"

He shook his head. "I didn't mean you. No, sir…I mean, girl…um, ma'am."

"Cass."

"Yeah, that's right, Cass. No, I'd never call you bossy." He added under his breath as he faced her, "'Cause you look like you'd hurt me if I did."

She playfully smacked his arm. "I heard that."

"Ow, girl." He rubbed the spot she hit. "What do you do when you leave the club? Spar with Joe Louis?"

"I barely touched you."

"You hurt my feelings."

Cass rolled her eyes. "Please, spare me." She stooped to pick up a can before he could see the corner of her mouth twitch.

His laughter indicated he'd seen her smile anyway. "Let me get those."

Cass straightened and went to the curb to retrieve a

can of tomato sauce that had rolled into the street. "What brings you up here? We're not rehearsing today."

"I was takin' a stroll."

"That must have been a long walk."

"No, I only live a couple of blocks away."

She waited for a couple to pass before stepping back to his side. "You live in Harlem?"

"Yeah, why?"

"Man, don't you know you're white?"

He shrugged his shoulders. "The mirror tells me that whenever I look in it. And, in case I've been struck blind, Junior makes it a point of remindin' me every time he sees me."

Most of her life, Cass had watched white people do everything they could to keep as far away from coloreds as possible. The only time they allowed a colored to cross over into their territory was when one was working for them. Even then the colored had to complete the job and move on; there was no lingering. Yet Randy willingly crossed the line to live and work in a colored neighborhood, as if it was the most natural thing to do.

She shook her head.

"What's wrong?"

"I've never met anyone like you before."

"A funny white man?"

"Honey, you've got the white part down pat, and I'll take your word that you're a man, but as for the funny part…"—she snorted—"I don't suggest you quit your night job."

He placed a hand over his heart. "You wound me."

Ignoring his antics, Cass elaborated. "I've never

met someone as colorblind as you."

"I'm not colorblind. I see colors as clearly as the next person. When I look at us, I can see my skin's fair, and yours…" He focused on her legs for a heartbeat before continuing. "Yours is brown, like the color of nutmeg."

It was another second before he glanced up at her frown.

Cass made it a point to let everyone who worked at or patronized the club know there was a line she would not cross. She was a co-worker and an entertainer. She'd even go as far as being a friend and a confidante. Anything else, however, should not be considered.

Though she realized some white men ventured to Harlem to find colored girls to scratch their itch, Cass had not figured she'd have to worry about improprieties from Randy. She assumed his tastes would lean toward women with fairer skin—the kind he'd be able to walk down the street with and not cause a stir.

As she opened her mouth to set the record straight, Randy nodded as if he read her mind.

"I'm sorry. I was out of line."

His voice was solemn and his eyes reflected his sincerity. The somber change in his attitude was enough for her to give him a slight nod of her own.

He turned his attention back to the groceries. "I won't lie and say I haven't noticed that I don't blend in with the rest of the band. I realize I'm the lightest one on the stage. Hell, I'm the lightest one in the entire place. However, I don't make color a determinin' factor when it comes to where I live, where I work, or who I'm around."

"And it doesn't make you feel uncomfortable being

the only white person in the room?"

"It's not somethin' I think about, until someone else makes an issue of it," he said. He stood up, cradling her bag in one arm. "When I'm on stage, all I think about is the music. Off the stage, well, all I see is people, not colors." He took the can of tomato sauce from her hand and dropped it into the bag. "Where you headed?"

"What?"

"Where you headed?" he repeated. "I'll carry this for you."

"That's not necessary. I don't want to keep you from your stroll."

"If I carry it, you'll be the envy of every colored woman we pass."

Cass raised an eyebrow.

"How many colored women have the privilege of havin' a white man carry their packages?"

She chuckled.

"I got a laugh. That's a good sign. So what do you say?"

To avoid feeding hope when there was no chance, Cass did not allow men to walk her home. However, she saw a glint of loneliness in his eyes that reminded her of her first months in New York. New to the city, away from her family and friends, she would have given anything to have someone to talk to.

She did not know whether or not he had friends outside the club, but, in the two weeks he had been at The Big House, she had noticed he kept to himself, though that was not entirely by choice.

Many of the employees snubbed him, making it clear he would never be welcomed. Others, like herself and Florence, were usually too busy to give him anything other than a quick greeting before running off to help with preparations for the show.

Deciding there was enough activity on the streets that she didn't have to worry about him becoming too pushy when they reached her place, she smiled up at him. "I've always wanted to know what it felt like to have someone wait on me," she joked. "I just need to get a couple of apples."

"And another loaf of bread," Randy added, holding up the flattened one.

"And another loaf of bread. I'll only be a minute."

****

"Are you sure you don't want me to carry one of those bags?" Cass asked a half hour, one loaf of bread, and enough fruit to require another shopping bag later.

She walked backwards, successfully avoiding the people who walked past them.

"I'm sure. Just relax and enjoy yourself."

Shrugging her shoulders, she spun on her heels and faced forward. As they headed south on Lenox Avenue, she casually swung her purse, reminding him of a young girl with no cares in the world. Her two braids, lavender dress with white polka dots, ankle socks, and canvas shoes added to the look.

It was no wonder the boy had mistaken her for a girl rather than a woman. Dressed as she was, it was hard to think of her as the same beauty who stood on stage and belted out one song after another with her powerful voice.

"So how did you end up in Harlem?" she asked.

"A guy I knew in D.C. suggested I check if his aunt had a room for rent," he answered.

"You're from Washington, D.C.?"

"You can say it's one of the places I've been to."

"That's not an answer."

Randy never enjoyed talking about his life. There were very few people or places in his past he wanted to remember. The only two people he cared to think about with fondness were with him whenever he picked up the saxophone.

Cass waited a minute before she tried again. "Well, where are you from?"

"You're persistent, aren't you?"

"Just making small talk. What did you expect when you offered to carry my bags?"

He hadn't thought that far when he made the offer. It had been spontaneous, as was his meeting her in front of the grocery. When he told her he was taking a stroll, he had left out the part about not planning to take a stroll until he glanced out the window of the fountain shop and saw her pass by carrying the shopping bag. He had drained his cup of coffee, tossed two quarters on the table to cover his meal and tip, then hurried after her.

Every night, Cass entered the club through the back door and stopped by his dressing room to greet him. She only had time for a wave and smile before she began her nightly routine of discussing business with Luther, going over the program with Red, or helping someone get through a crisis by sewing on a button, mending a tear, or searching for a misplaced instrument.

He had been curious as to whether she was simply being polite or if her courtesy extended beyond the four walls of the club. But the opportunity to find out had not presented itself, since she always arrived five minutes before rehearsals began and left before he finished his set. Therefore, when he saw the chance that afternoon, he jumped on it.

"I was born in Alabama, but I've stopped at a couple of cities on my way to New York," he finally answered.

"Where have you been?"

"Washington, D.C.…"

"You've already mentioned that."

Randy glanced down at Cass out of the corner of his eye. "Sassy," he muttered.

"I've never heard of that city," she teased. She gave him a grin that would not fool a blind man into believing she was full of sugar and spice. "Where is it?"

Ignoring her comment, he continued, "I left home at eighteen and traveled to New Orleans. There I worked in a warehouse during the day and played in a couple of clubs at night. After two years, I headed to Florida before workin' my way up here."

"Why New York?"

"I heard stories about the city and decided to see if they were true."

"Is it everything you'd thought it'd be?" she asked as they parted to keep from being run over by a colored man who passed between them.

Since there was plenty of room to go around them, Randy knew the man had a problem with Cass and him walking next to each other. It was a reminder that no matter where he went, when he was not playing music everything was black and white.

Deciding the best way to deal with the aggressor was to ignore him, Randy stared straight ahead and continued walking.

"What about you?" he asked to divert her attention when she glanced over her shoulder and sucked her teeth. "Where are you from?"

Cass made an obscene gesture before facing forward.

"Piney Woods, North Carolina," she replied, displaying no fear of retaliation from the other man. "I spent sixteen years on a farm before moving to the city."

Randy braced himself for the curse and hurried footsteps that would precede the inevitable confrontation. But, after a few seconds, when he heard neither, he shook his head. The woman was too sassy and bold for her own good.

"Any siblings?" Randy asked.

"Five brothers. I'm the baby. What about you?"

"It was only me."

"Just you and your parents. They must have doted on you."

Randy's snort was his only reply. He was grateful Cass took the hint and moved on to another topic when he didn't elaborate.

"You said you've been playing the sax for eighteen years. That means you started when you were…"

"Ten." He was impressed she remembered the bit of information he had offered before his audition. "I started takin' lessons from a man named Sax. He'd worked in clubs in New Orleans until he married Miss Sylvia and settled down in Mississippi. It was because of his stories I headed to New Orleans after I left home."

"But I thought you said you were from Alabama?"

"My mother and I moved around a lot when I was young. We eventually settled onto a farm in Mississippi, not far from Sax."

"Red spent a couple of years in New Orleans before he came to New York. A couple of times he's mentioned a man named Sax who worked in a colored club with him. He said the man seemed to make music come alive when he played."

"That sounds like Sax. I used go over to his place and steal apples. One day, I was sittin' in a tree when he came out of his house. I was sure he was goin' to run me off his farm, but he acted like he didn't see me."

"Maybe he didn't," she suggested.

"No, he saw me. Kinda hard to miss a scrawny white kid sittin' in a tree outside your door. But he paid me no mind. He sat down on a bucket and played his sax. That music was so smooth, I climbed from the tree, sat in front of him, and listened."

"It's a good thing he didn't find out about the apples."

"He found out." Randy laughed as they turned down a tree-lined block with brownstones on both sides of the street. "I was so into the music, I forgot I'd stuffed apples in my pockets."

"I guess he wasn't too mad at you, if he taught you how to play."

"Actually he gave me a sackful to take home and told me I was welcome back anytime. I took him up on his offer and spent a lot of time hangin' around his place. Eventually, he offered to teach me how to play."

"Your parents weren't too bothered by you hanging with coloreds?"

"Where'd you learn how to sing?" Randy asked.

"No place," Cass replied. He was certain she noticed his deliberate change of subject, but she continued as if it didn't matter. "I always liked singing, but other than the hymns at church, I didn't have the opportunity until I moved up here."

"You've got talent. With your voice, you're goin' places."

Cass shook her head. "I don't think so."

"Why not?"

"I don't have the right look."

Though he was afraid of the explanation he would get, Randy couldn't help but ask, "They said that after hearin' you sing?"

"I went to one audition before ending up at The Big House. The manager had all the girls line up on stage. Then he went down the line, picked three, and told the rest of us we could go. Being naïve, I asked how he could make his choice without even listening to us. He told me what we sounded like didn't matter, it was our looks that counted. He could always teach a light-skinned girl to sing, but he couldn't lighten a dark-colored singer. He then advised me to go back to scrubbing floors, 'cause that's the only thing women as dark as me were good for."

Randy wished Cass's explanation had surprised him. No, actually, he wished she had never gone through that experience. Growing up in the south, he had seen how not only race but the skin's shade determined how people were treated. Light-skinned coloreds were treated with a bit more respect, and light-skinned children were doted on more than dark-skinned coloreds.

He had left home foolishly thinking there would be

no barriers in the entertainment business, since music saw no colors. But, going from club to club, he learned very few shared his philosophy. In fact, the entertainment industry perpetuated the belief that light-skinned coloreds were better by insisting on hiring those who could almost pass for white and flaunting them as the ideal beauty.

"I'm sorry," he said.

"Why?" Cass asked. "You weren't the one who said that."

"I know. I just feel bad that some people can be so ignorant."

"Thank you, but saying 'sorry' won't change a thing, especially when the one you're apologizing for feels no remorse. You don't hear me apologizing for Junior, 'cause it's not like he's sorry for anything he says to you." Cass stopped in front of a three-story brownstone. "Here we are. It's not a mansion, but it's home."

An elderly colored woman sat on a chair at the top of the stoop. She wore a blue floral housedress underneath her opened brown coat, and her gray hair was twisted into four plaits.

"Good afternoon, Mrs. Cooper." Cass waved. "How are you today?"

The woman did not answer or make any indication she heard Cass. She was so still Randy couldn't tell whether or not she was breathing.

"Is she okay?" he whispered.

"Yes. Mrs. Cooper's son owns the building. She sits out here when the weather's nice, but she never says a word. Her daughter-in-law thinks she's either deaf or senile."

"Yet you still talk to her."

"Why not?"

"But if she doesn't answer you—"

"It never hurts to be friendly." She reached for the bags. "I can take those now."

"I don't mind carryin' them up for you."

"No offense, but I don't know you well enough to invite you up."

Randy passed her the bags. He was not offended because she was cautious. If anything, it made him respect her more.

"No offense taken. I'll see you tonight." Randy reached into one of the bags and took out an apple.

"Hey."

He took a bite out of the fruit and smiled back at her. Shaking her head, Cass headed up the stairs.

Randy watched her step inside. Mrs. Cooper had not moved once since he arrived, but he tipped his hat to her and wished her a good day before heading back down the block.

Chapter 5

"Staring at them won't make them move on their own."

"It's worth a try." Cass sighed. She rolled her shoulders as she stared at the bags she had dropped on the floor in the dimly lit hall outside her apartment. She'd only carried them up one flight and her arms were protesting from the weight. At the store, Randy hadn't complained as she added items to the bag and, during the walk, he moved as if he were carrying nothing, giving her no clue to their heaviness. "Figured I'd try floating them inside."

"That'll be some feat, though not as spectacular as getting a white man to carry your bags. Where'd you find your butler? I think I'd like to get one of my own."

Cass glanced over her shoulder at Maia Mathers, who sat on the steps leading to the third floor. The woman wore an ankle-length multicolored skirt, a bright orange blouse, and no shoes. Strands of curly ash-brown hair escaped from underneath an orange wrap and framed her tan face. Large silver hoops hung from her ears, and ten silver bangles covered each wrist.

Maia preferred to embrace her African roots and her artistic side by dressing in what she called a statement of her individuality. She reminded Cass of a colorblind clown.

"Why?" Cass asked. "Amaad's not up to handling the job?"

"Having a white man serve us would be a major change, after all these years of us working for them," Maia said, ignoring the remark about her man.

"It's funny, Randy said I'd be the envy of colored women if I let him carry my bags."

Maia rolled her eyes.

"I don't know where you'd find one, since he's not my butler. Randy's the new sax player at The Big House."

Maia's eyes grew wide and her mouth dropped open. It was the first time she had heard the news. She had been on a reading tour for the past month and returned early that morning, when most people were still in bed.

"A white man's working in The Big House? I don't believe it."

"Help me get these bags inside, and I'll tell you everything," Cass replied as she opened her door. "Like you said, they won't move themselves."

She grabbed one bag and stepped into the living room. In the four years she'd lived there, she hadn't added much to the pre-furnished one-bedroom apartment. Her landlady had given her permission to replace any piece she was unhappy with, but Cass had not felt the need to waste the money when she had perfectly good furniture. Instead, she'd purchased a couple of yards of green fabric and reupholstered the sofa and matching armchair. A coat of stain hid the scratches on the base of the marble-topped coffee table, and the crocheted doilies under the lamps on the end tables added a touch of elegance. Area rugs woven from scraps her mother sent her were scattered over the hardwood floors throughout the apartment to muffle her footsteps when she came home late at night. The only luxuries she allowed herself were the radio on top of the bookcase by the door and the sewing machine located at the other side of the room, near the kitchen.

Cass placed her bag on the enamel-topped yellow dropleaf table. She never bothered to raise the sides, since the only person she ever had over for dinner was herself.

Maia followed her inside, kicking the door closed behind her. She dropped the bag next to the other, then reached inside and grabbed an apple.

"Go ahead, help yourself," Cass said. She stepped out of her shoes and kicked them under the table to get them out of the way until later.

"Thank you," Maia replied as she bit into the fruit. "I don't mind if I do."

"At the rate y'all are going, I won't have any for my pie."

"You're baking a pie? What time should I be back down?"

"Never," Cass said, though they both knew once the pie was ready she'd take half upstairs, as she did with the majority of the desserts she baked.

Cass placed the butter in the yellow icebox. Growing up, electricity and indoor plumbing were only things she read about in the few books she'd been able to get her hands on. Never, not in her wildest dreams, had she imagined herself living where she didn't have to go outside to use the facilities, draw water in order to wash dishes, or light a lantern in order to see inside at night.

Sweet Jazz

She closed the door and turned to the table. As an afterthought, she went back to the icebox, took the pan from underneath it, emptied the water into the sink, and then replaced the pan to catch the melting ice.

"Well?" Maia asked. She pulled a white chair with yellow trim from under the table, turned it around, and straddled it.

"Well, what?" Cass replied as she returned to unpacking her groceries.

"What possessed Junior to hire a white man?"

"You need to learn not to talk with your mouth full." Cass brushed a bit of apple from the front of her dress. "You're spraying food everywhere."

Maia swallowed, then opened her mouth wide. "See, empty. Now are you going to tell me, or not?"

Cass shook her head. Sometimes it was hard for her to believe the other woman was twelve years older than she was. On most days, Maia was laid back and downright silly, but, when the situation called for it, she could be outspoken, ready to offer advice, even when it wasn't asked for.

They had met six months after Cass moved to New York and, after a rough beginning, became best friends. It was Maia who suggested she audition at The Big House and shorten her name to Cass because it sounded more sophisticated and less country than Cassie Ann. Cass, however, got her fashion advice from other women.

"Junior didn't hire Randy," she answered as she arranged her fruit in the bowl in the center of the table. "Luther did."

"And Junior went along with it?"

"He made it clear he was against it, but as you

know, Luther makes the final decision when it comes to the entertainment."

"So, how did the ghost get hired?"

"His name's Randy," she stressed, gathering bags of rice, flour, meal, and sugar. She carried them to the counter by the icebox, dropped them on the enamel top, and retrieved the marked canisters from the overhead shelf.

Maia shrugged as she took another bite out of the apple.

"He came to the club and auditioned. He was good, so he was hired."

"And what about our musicians? None of them showed up?"

"There were plenty of coloreds who came to the club, but none of them could play."

"You mean to tell me there are no good colored musicians in Harlem?"

"I'm sure there are plenty of good colored musicians, they're just not breaking down the door to The Big House. The majority of the big shots in entertainment are white, and with them being barred from The Big House, good musicians aren't falling over themselves to work in the club. Those who are there are biding their time until something better comes along. Or, they don't care about making it big. They're simply happy to get paid for doing something they love."

"And, what about the ghost?"

Cass slammed the canister of rice down on the counter and spun to face her friend. "His name's Randy," she repeated as she crossed her arms over her chest. "You know you'd be up in arms if he called you out of your name. Why don't you give him the same respect?"

Maia raised an eyebrow. "A bit sensitive, aren't you?"

Night after night Cass listened to the same people who'd be insulted if he called them anything but their names refer to him by everything but his. She had mentioned it to several of the other employees at the club, with a few taking what she said into consideration. The others, particularly Junior and Angel, rolled their eyes at her and repeated whatever name they had used at that moment, with more emphasis.

Randy never showed any reaction. Offstage, he simple stared at his antagonist until the other person got bored and walked away. Onstage, when he was playing, he appeared to be in another world where no one could get to him.

"Well, what's *Randy's* story?"

Though she could live without the sarcasm, she'd take what she could get. "He just wants a chance to play the sax," Cass said.

"So, how did he end up carrying your bags home?"

"I was shopping when a boy bumped into me and knocked everything everywhere. Randy just happened by and offered to lend me a hand."

"He just happened by? How can a white man just happen by in a colored neighborhood?

"He told me he lives up here."

"A white man who works and lives with coloreds?" Maia shook her head. "He's got to be up to something."

"You're awfully suspicious of someone you haven't met," Cass said.

"When a white man suddenly appears in Harlem,

you should be suspicious. They don't come up here to make friends. They always have an agenda."

"Couldn't it be possible for a white man to be up here 'cause he wants a place to lay his head at night or a job so he can put food in his stomach?"

"I haven't met one yet."

"You haven't met Langston Hughes, but you believe he exists." Cass turned back to the counter and continued pouring rice into the canister.

"I've read his work. That's all the proof I need to know he's real."

"And I've spoken to Randy, and that's all the proof I need."

"His word? That ain't enough to go on. Anyone can say the right words when they want you to believe something."

"Don't remind me." Cass sighed and placed the canisters back on the shelf. "Remember, I've been there."

"Then you know you shouldn't take everything he says at face value. I'm telling you, I have yet to meet a white man who'll come to our neighborhood without an ulterior motive. You can't trust them further than you can throw them." She then muttered under her breath, "Of course, that could be said about some colored men I know."

Cass raised an eyebrow. "Are my ears deceiving me or did you take a jab at our men?" She dropped into the chair and placed the shopping bags on the floor to see Maia on the other side of the table. "Okay, out with it."

Maia stared at the mustard-yellow wall behind Cass before her shoulders slumped. "Nothing's wrong with your hearing."

Her inability to look Cass in the eye spoke of a relationship rift Cass had predicted from the beginning.

Maia had met Amaad the previous year and felt an instant connection to the man because they shared a deep understanding of the world and were very much into their African roots. She had only known him a week before she allowed him to move into her apartment, while he struggled to find his sound and spread his philosophy of coloreds uniting as one.

"What happened on the tour?" Cass asked.

Maia examined her fingernails. "The tour was fine. The audiences were receptive, and I even made some contacts."

"But…"

"Amaad and I couldn't come to an understanding about my role as his woman." She crossed her arms over her chest. "He felt I should play the part of the submissive, obedient colored woman who stood behind her colored man when he preached his message to every ninny who was willing to lift up her skirt. And I thought he should take his primitive, cockamamie ideas and shove them up his colored ass."

Cass threw her head back and laughed. "I take it he didn't appreciate your line of thinking."

"I wouldn't know. It was kind of hard to hear what he was yelling as I drove off."

"You left him behind?"

"I couldn't take his nonsense anymore, so I drove off when he was in the bushes taking care of business by a gas station in South Carolina. Unless someone was kind enough to give him some money or a ride, I expect he's only walked as far as North Carolina by now."

"How could you do that?"

"It was easy. I started the car, put my foot on the gas, and turned the steering wheel. And I got a good laugh watching him in the rearview mirror as he tried to chase after the car with his pants down around his ankles."

Cass stopped laughing and stared at the other woman. She was equally shocked by her friend's action, happy for the woman's newfound freedom, and fearful of what would happen if Amaad ever made it back to the city.

"Chile, he's going to be mad when he gets here."

"There's no need for him to come back here, 'cause I don't want his crusty feet crossing my threshold."

"He'll have to come back to get his things."

"No need. I left them outside for him."

"You threw his clothes out?"

"I'd never do that. I neatly packed them in a box and left it on the curb for him."

Cass shook her head. "There was nothing on the curb when I came in."

"Someone must have taken it." Maia shrugged her shoulders. "Oh, well, he should've come to collect his things sooner."

"Chile, I don't want to be in your shoes when he gets back to the city."

Her friend stuck out a bare foot. "What shoes?"

"You know what I mean. Your shoes, your skin, or anything that belongs to you, I don't want to be in them. That man's going to want a piece of your behind."

"I'll honor him with a piece of my mind, but he

lost all privileges to my behind when he chose to sleep with other women. Shoot, I wouldn't even give him the honor of kissing my behind."

"I don't think he'll want to kiss it when he gets back and finds his things gone."

"You know, I don't think he's even worthy of getting a piece of my mind."

"Are you listening to me?"

"No."

Cass sighed. "Now that you've got rid of the extra two hundred pounds, what are you planning to do?"

"I'm going upstairs, write a verse celebrating my liberation from that two-timing bastard, and then I'm going out and announce to the world that I am once again free. You care to join me?"

"I can't. I'm performing tonight."

"What a pity. There's no telling what kind of fun two single women could find in this city."

"Most likely the kind of fun two single women should not be finding."

Maia got up and swished to the door. "Dear, you're too young to be talking like that. You need to go out there and live."

Cass shook her head as her friend walked out without waiting for an answer. It amazed her how quickly Maia was able to move on after the end of a relationship. Instead of shedding tears over her loss, she brushed herself off before stepping out under the belief there was someone out there for her.

She, on the other hand, was unwilling to take another chance. Being burnt once was enough for Cass.

****

"Let me get that for you." Randy reached over the

gate and grabbed the bag from the woman who had been fumbling in her handbag, at the same time struggling to keep her shopping bag in her arms.

Amelia Greene screeched. She jumped back, releasing her hold on the shopping bag as she pulled her handbag to her body.

The woman frowned and glared at her tenant. "Young man, you nearly gave me a heart attack," she scolded. "You need to say somethin' before you go grabbin' a person's bag."

"Sorry, but I wanted to get it before it fell."

"That's okay, it wasn't like I needed those five years you just took off my life."

Randy winked at her. "I don't know what you're worried about. You have a lot of years ahead of you. What are you, twenty-four? Twenty-five?"

She walked up the stoop and opened the door. "I'm too old to fall for a line from a sweet-talkin' boy like you." She glanced over her shoulder at him and grinned. "But that doesn't mean I don't like listenin' to it."

Randy followed the plump, smartly dressed woman through the hall to the newly renovated kitchen and placed the bag on the red floral-trimmed, enamel-topped table. She removed her tan sweater and draped it over the back of a red vinyl chair before walking past the electric refrigerator to the stove. She took the lid off a cast iron Dutch oven that sat over a low flame and stirred the stew.

"Have you eaten today?" she asked.

"I'm all right," he replied. Knowing the direction the conversation was going to take, he took a step back.

"I didn't ask how you're doin'. I asked if you ate."

"I had a little somethin'."

Mrs. Greene eyed him with her hands on her hips. "What?"

"A bologna sandwich from the fountain shop, and an apple," he finally confessed.

"Boy, don't you take one more step toward that door." She waved the spoon at the table. "Sit down while I fix you a plate."

Not used to having someone fuss over him, he insisted, "You don't have to, Mrs. Greene."

"I know I don't have to. Now sit."

A frown she'd most likely perfected when raising her children had him removing his jacket and sitting at the table without further argument.

According to another tenant in the boarding house, twenty-six years earlier Mrs. Greene had left her husband to his pursuit of other female interests. She moved to New York to be closer to her brother, who had bragged about the opportunities in the city. Because of his big talk, she half expected the streets to be paved in gold, which she could pick up if she ever found herself in need of some money. What she found was the same struggles she had in the south as an unskilled, minimally educated colored woman with four children.

Determined her children would have a better life than she did, she worked two jobs to get by. What little money was left over after paying the rent and feeding and clothing the children she saved until she was able to purchase the brownstone. She stressed education and helped finance four years of college for each of her children, who took her lessons to heart and became successful businessmen and women with families of their own.

After her last child left home, Mrs. Greene could not be content to sit back and relax. Instead, she rented two apartments and two rooms in the brownstone. She also mothered those she felt needed mothering—from the struggling young woman trying to work and raise children on her own to the single men she felt were helpless without someone to take care of them.

Though he appreciated the meals, Randy felt guilty since he only paid for his room and she refused to take anything extra from him for the food.

"Eat this," she said, placing a bowl of oxtail stew with a slice of bread and a cup of milk in front of him.

"Thank you, ma'am," Randy replied.

Mrs. Greene watched as he stirred the stew a couple of times. Once he took a taste of the broth, she dropped into a chair across from him.

"Now, tell me, what mischief have you been up to today?"

"Nothin'."

"Like I'm supposed to believe that." She shook her head and smiled. "I raised two boys of my own, and though they turned out to be fine men, they were always into somethin' when they were young."

"Honestly," he insisted. "I went for a walk and ended up helpin' Cass carry her bags home from the store."

"Cass? She your gal?"

Randy chuckled at the thought. Cass was attractive, even in her socks and canvas shoes, looking as if she were ready to go outside and play. And, from what he had seen from watching her at the club, she was also outgoing and she had a good sense of humor. With qualities like that, there was no way she was available.

Even if she didn't have a ring on her finger—and he had checked—she had to have someone in her life.

"No, she works at the club."

A look of recognition appeared on her face. "Oh, that Cass." She nodded. "The sassy gal who sings at The Big House."

"You know her?"

"No, I never met her, but I've seen her show several times."

"I figured you knew her, 'cause you called her sassy."

"All I had to do was take one look at that child and I could tell she got a mouth on her. Her mother either went through a tub of soap tryin' to wash the sassiness out of her or else she stripped a tree bare to go after that girl's behind." Mrs. Greene pointed to her face. "You know, I got an eye for these things. I can tell what a person's like the moment I set eyes on them." She shook her finger at him. "Take you, for example. The moment I saw you, I knew you wouldn't last one day in this city if I didn't take you in."

"Ma'am?" He broke off a piece of bread, dipped it into the stew, and popped it into his mouth.

Mrs. Greene dropped her hand on the table. "Here I open the door and there's a white boy on my stoop askin' if I have a room to rent, like it's the most natural thin' for a white man to be livin' in Harlem. You were too serious for your own good. I knew if I turned you away, you'd end up with doors slammed in your face, or worse—lyin' in an alley, beaten and robbed of your money."

"You could tell all that by lookin' at me?"

"Yes. I could also tell you're a good boy who don't

need to be in no club takin' Junior's mess."

"The Big House isn't that bad." He took another spoonful of stew.

Mrs. Greene sniffed. "Not from what I saw." Three days after he got the gig, she'd stopped by The Big House for dinner and to listen to him play. Luther had taken the night off and Junior stood in as the emcee.

Before the show, Junior came on stage to introduce the individual members of the band, with the exception of Randy. The club owner did remember his presence during breaks in the show, when he took the microphone to tell some off-color jokes at Randy's expense.

Mrs. Greene, who had requested a table near the stage, became visibly upset by the performance. Midway through Junior's second routine she stood up and walked out of the club, just as her meal was being placed on the table.

When Randy got home in the morning, she was waiting up for him. She expressed her opinion of what she had witnessed and declared the experience had left her with such a bad taste in her mouth she would never step foot in The Big House again.

"Things aren't always like that at the club. You came on a bad night. Most nights, Luther's in charge and Junior ignores me."

"You don't need to be makin' no excuses for that man or anyone else there."

"They're all not that bad," he insisted. "Red's a cool guy. He's not bothered by me. Then there's Cass. She's a doll. If it wasn't for her, I wouldn't have this gig. She spoke up for me at the audition."

"If she's got that much pull in that place, then she

needs to get Junior to lay off the insults."

Twice Randy had overheard her fussing with Junior about his jokes. The club owner was not repentant and had told her if it bothered her so much, she could leave and take Randy with her.

Randy liked that Cass stood up for him, but at the same time he'd been worried she would be fired if she continued to press the matter. Unlike her, he had other options available to him, and when working at The Big House became unbearable at the club, he planned to seek out those options.

Because she wasn't two shades lighter, Cass wouldn't get past the front door of many of the more reputable clubs in the city. Though, in Randy's opinion, there was nothing wrong with her color, and any club owner unable to see that was blind.

"She's done a lot for me, and I'm grateful for it. But I'm sure there's only so much she can do before Junior kicks us both out of his club."

"That would be a blessin' for both of you."

"I'll be fine," Randy insisted as he pushed back from the table. "I don't want to be rude, but I need to get ready to leave for work. Thanks for the stew."

"It was my pleasure," Mrs. Greene replied as she stood. "Before you go, I want you to promise me somethin'."

"What's that?"

"You'll watch your back at that club."

"Thank you, ma'am. I will," he said, before strolling out of the kitchen.

"'Cause, boy, you bein' at that club is only gonna lead to trouble," she muttered under her breath as she gathered his dishes.

Chapter 6

The last note of "Moonglow" faded and the house lights flickered on. Several musicians stood and stretched. Others talked with each other or with the few patrons who remained.

Randy laid his saxophone on his lap and sat back. He rolled his shoulders to work out the kinks while he watched Cass, who sat in a corner with a pudgy man dressed in an ill-fitted striped suit.

After Cass's final song for the night, there had been a deviation from the regular routine. Instead of Luther leading the applause, Junior approached the stage, encouraging the audience to show their appreciation to the singer.

Though her smile did not fade, Randy noticed her posture became rigid. Cass, however, kept up appearances by taking his arm and allowing him to escort her off the stage. He led her to a table where he introduced her to a man who, by her current expression, bored her with his one-sided conversation.

For over an hour, Cass had tried to excuse herself. When her companion would not let her get a word in, she silently pleaded with Junior, who ignored the looks and subtle hand gestures beckoning him back to the table. When everything else failed, she rudely yawned in the man's face.

Instead of taking the hint, her companion poured

her another glass of wine. Rolling her eyes, Cass accepted the drink and took a sip. As she placed the glass back on the table, her hand slipped.

The man jumped to his feet, but not quickly enough to avoid getting splashed. Cass grabbed a napkin and wiped at the growing red stain on his gray suit. In her eagerness, she knocked his cigar out of his hand. Apologizing, she reached under the table to retrieve the stogie, which was in no condition to smoke when she handed it back to him.

Smiling, her companion lifted her hand to his lips and kissed the back of it before excusing himself. As he headed toward the lavatory, Cass slipped away from the table and headed backstage, with a less than amused Junior behind her.

With the floor show over, Randy stood and moved to the rear of the stage, where he always stored his case while he played. He quickly disassembled and packed his saxophone, then stepped off the stage. He had made it halfway down the stairs leading backstage when Junior's outrage filled the space.

Randy flinched at the profanity-laced tirade. Though he was far from a saint, he had never considered it appropriate to use rough language around ladies.

As he contemplated whether or not he should intervene, he heard the crash in the ladies' dressing room. The sound helped him make up his mind. If there was anything he did not tolerate, it was violence against women. At the first sign of a woman in trouble, he was ready to step in, even if his assistance wasn't requested or appreciated.

Randy reached the ladies' dressing room as the

door flew opened and Junior limped out. The club owner pushed past him and continued toward the stairs, mumbling curses under his breath.

Randy peered into the large room, where costumes hung precariously from hangers and over the backs of chairs. Cass sat with her head cradled in her hands at a dressing table that spanned the entire length of the wall at the far end of the room. A broken chair lay on its side in the middle of the floor.

He tapped on the door. "Hey, are you okay?" he asked.

Cass looked up. Her complexion was smooth and unblemished, and every strand of her thick, dark brown hair was tucked into its French twist. Her navy satin gown appeared intact.

"I was passin' by and I heard—"

"Junior throwing a tantrum," Cass said. She glanced at the overturned chair. "Serves him right if he broke his toe."

He stepped into the room. "It didn't have anythin' to do with the incident at the table, did it?"

"You saw what happened?"

"I've been watchin' you for the past hour. You didn't look like you were enjoyin' yourself."

She shook her head. "It's amazing how someone across the room can see that, yet the man sitting inches away from me thinks I'm having the time of my life."

"So were the drink and the cigar an accident?"

She didn't say whether her actions had been intentional or not, yet the glint in her eye told him it was not the first time a man had walked out of the club covered in wine.

"Junior thinks it looks good if I have drinks with

some of his acquaintances. I think he should go to hell. Unfortunately, neither one of us wants to bend to the other's will."

Randy chuckled. "I can't blame Junior. Several people have suggested I visit hell, but I'm not too eager to take the trip. I guess Junior and I have a lot more in common than he thinks."

"I'll be sure to mention that the next time I speak to him."

"You do that, and he'll take the trip just to spite me."

"Good. Then I won't have to entertain those bores he insists I meet."

"That bad?" Randy pointed toward a chair with a robe draped across the back.

She nodded and he sat down, placing his case by his feet.

"Have you ever had someone talk for an hour about how much money he's made in stocks? For all the airs he was putting on, the only stock he's ever been involved with was stocking crates in the back of a warehouse."

"Stockin' crates is honest work," Randy said.

Between gigs, Randy had earned money working in warehouses and factories. He had more respect for someone who performed manual labor than for the man who begged because he thought he was too good to get his hands dirty.

Watching Cass before the shows, he hadn't figured she'd look down at others because of their jobs. She did not prance around the club putting on airs, expecting everyone to cater to her. Instead, she lent a hand, no matter how lowly the chore. In fact, just that evening, she'd mopped up a spill outside the woman's bathroom instead of asking someone else to do it.

"I have two brothers who work in a factory. Two others work for the railroad," she said. "All they do is handle freight all day."

"Then what's the problem?"

"He was trying to be someone he's not." She shook her head. "I'd like to think I've grown past the stage where smooth talk would impress me."

She frowned, and Randy suspected she had been there, done that, and wasn't eager to experience an encore.

"You know, it can be intimidatin' to meet the star of the show," he joked, hoping he could coax a smile out of her.

"Intimidating?" Cass chuckled. "I'm no different than anyone else. I have to eat and drink in order to survive. When I go to the bathroom, I squat just like everyone else, and when I'm finished the air isn't always as fresh as it was before I went in."

"I don't think I've ever heard it put so…so…"

"Eloquently?"

"That's not the word I was searchin' for."

"How about poetic? Honest?"

"Honest, yes. Poetic, no."

"That's because I'm not a poet. However, I've been told I'm a bit too honest for my own good."

"For some reason, that doesn't surprise me."

The faint sound of "The Entertainer" drifted into the room. Like an eraser removing blemishes from a blackboard, each note slowly erased the tension from her face until her lips turned up in a smile and her eyes danced.

"They're jamming tonight," Cass said as she stood and started toward the door. "I might as well stay and salvage something from this night."

He jumped up and grabbed his case. "You're goin' up there with Junior?" he asked, catching up with her in the hall.

She dismissively waved as if the other man were of no consequence to her. "Junior's already left for the night."

"How can you be so sure?"

"'Cause he's that predictable. After his tantrum, he went back upstairs and made some excuse for me, like maybe I'd had too much to drink. He then offered to have the club pay for the suit. Finally, he suggested they get a drink at some afterhours dive, and they left with his bimbo-of-the-month trailing behind him."

Her assessment of what had happened confirmed the earlier incident was not the first time she'd accidentally spilt wine on a patron. She had a devilish streak, and he would remember to stay on her good side.

"Even if Junior wasn't predictable," she continued, "Red knows how much I like this song. He wouldn't play it and risk having me go upstairs if Junior was still there."

"You sure?" Randy asked, concerned about her safety. He had known too many men who didn't have a problem using their fists to put a woman in her place. He recognized the short fuse in Junior and wondered how much it would take before the other man exploded.

"I'm as sure as my name's Cassie Ann Porter," she said with confidence as she strolled toward the stairs.

Randy would have preferred her to head in the

opposite direction. However, who was he to stop her. He only hoped she knew what she was doing.

"If you're sure, Miss Cassie Ann Porter, I hope you enjoy yourself." He also hoped he would not regret doing nothing.

She stopped halfway up the stairs and leaned over the banister. "Aren't you joining us?"

"I don't think so."

****

Cass glanced at the gold watch she wore only during her performances.

"You're telling me you have somewhere else to be at three-fifteen in the morning."

For most of the musicians it was still early. Those who did not have someone to go home to, and a few who did not care that there was someone waiting for them, usually went out to eat after the show. Of course, since she had never pried into his love life and he could not bring his woman to the club, there was the possibility he did have someone he needed to get to.

"No, it's just that I've never been invited to join in," Randy replied.

So it wasn't a woman who kept him from joining them but the unfortunate ignorance of those he worked with.

With the exception of Eli and Red, who offered him words of encouragement and advice, the other musicians had yet to warm up to him. She had expected as much when he started working at the club but figured over time a few of them would give him a chance.

She, however, was determined he would not be excluded. "Never been invited? Who do you think you are? The king of New York?"

"No, but—"

"Man, we don't send out invitations to jam. If you want to join in, then you do."

"I don't know."

"Why? You can't jam?"

He squared his shoulders. "Girl, I can jam."

She knew she'd hit a nerve by questioning his skills. All the musicians at the club knew their stuff, and even the most modest ones refused to back down when challenged.

"Then put your reed where your mouth is and prove it."

As she expected, Randy accepted the challenge and followed her back upstairs.

Red had resumed his position in front of the piano, with Eli accompanying him on trumpet. The other musicians and the few chorus girls who remained were gathered in small groups, joking with one another and drinking beers.

Cass slid onto the bench beside Red and, without missing a beat, took over. She watched as Randy laid his case on a table and reassembled his saxophone. Except for a few glances in his direction, everyone else ignored him.

She played through the song once before Angel joined in on drums. Cass screeched as he began to improvise, bringing Red to her rescue. Laughing, she waved off the hecklers as she scooted over to make room on the bench for the pianist.

Randy grabbed a beer off the table and stepped onto the stage with his saxophone.

"That was good," he commented as he handed her the bottle. "Why'd you stop?"

Cass took a swig before replying, "That's the only song I know how to play—"

"I taught her 'cause she was about to wear my fingers to the bone pestering me to play it," Red added.

"I did not." She nudged the older man with her shoulder. "I can only play what Red taught me. Change one note and I get lost."

"Hey, you forget something?" Angel called out.

As far as Cass knew, Angel had not spoken to Randy since his first night at the club. Instead of holding it against the other man, Randy glanced over at the drummer and replied, "No, I thought I'd hang around for a while."

"You what?"

"You know, hang and jam." To prove he was serious, he moved next to Eli and placed the reed to his lips.

All conversation ceased as the audience stared at the stage as if he were performing a lewd act. Red and Angel continued to play, while Eli lowered his trumpet and nodded in time to the music. After five notes, the trumpeter raised his instrument and played five notes. Randy responded to the call with several notes of his own before allowing Eli his five-note call.

The two musicians continued their call-and-response, increasing the tempo until the music blended as one. Cass and Red added vocals with a call-and-response scat.

Caught up in the fun, she did not realize no one else had joined in until the improv was finished. As Eli high-fived Randy, Cass glared at the audience, who continued to stare at the stage with varying expressions of disgust and disbelief.

While the others remained silent, Angel stood up, dropped his sticks, and stepped from behind the drums.

"That was solid, but I've gotta cut out. I have something to do in the morning."

Cass didn't know what disgusted her more, Angel's reluctance to give Randy a chance or his refusal to be upfront. At least Junior was man enough to let a person know outright what he thought of him and didn't hide behind phony smiles and excuses.

"You sure you've got to go?" she asked as she stood.

"You don't think I know my own business?"

"I'm sure you know your business and it's very important." Bracing both hands on the piano, she leaned forward. "Well, at least to you."

"You know—" Angel took a step toward Cass.

Red jumped between the musician and the singer. "We don't want to keep you from whatever you have to do. We'll do this another time."

Angel glanced around Red and scowled at her. When she didn't flinch, he shook his head as if she wasn't worth the trouble.

"Yeah, another time," he repeated, backing away. "I'll see y'all tonight."

He stepped off the stage and swaggered toward the back. As he passed a table, he snapped his fingers and a tall, slender woman jumped up and followed behind him.

The other musicians and the chorus girls followed Angel's example, and within five minutes everyone had left, with the exception of Florence, Cass, and the three musicians on stage.

"Where did everyone go?" Luther asked as he

emerged from the kitchen pushing a cart of food.

"They had things to do," Red said, making excuses.

"Actually, it's my fault they're gone," Randy replied. "The others weren't into jammin' with an ofay."

Cass's eyes narrowed. "I'm really getting tired of that word," she muttered through gritted teeth.

"What are we going to do with these leftovers?"

"I don't know about you, but I plan to eat," Eli said as he hopped off the stage and headed toward the cart.

"You haven't lost your appetite with me here?" Randy asked.

"You chew with your mouth open?"

"No."

"Belch with every swallow?"

"No."

"Pick your teeth with your fingers?"

"Again, no."

Eli shrugged his shoulders. "Then you're not bothering me, *amigo*."

Cass smiled at Eli. He did not casually use the Spanish word for "friend" at the club. Only a select few were given that title.

A native of Puerto Rico, Eli had been the lightest musician in the club before Randy's appearance. He, however, had been accepted by the other employees, thanks to the African ancestor from whom he inherited his toffee complexion and curly, chestnut brown hair.

"You'll fix me a plate first?" Florence asked.

Eli winked at her. "*Sí, mi amor*." He stared at the dancer until Luther cleared his throat, forcing him to focus his attention on the food.

"Make that three people," Cass added. "Of course,

you need to move out of the way so people can get to the food."

Randy stepped to the left, bowed, and waved her toward the cart.

Cass rolled her eyes. "Some people have to be comedians. Remind me to sock you after I eat."

"Don't you think two fights are enough for one night?" Red asked, following her off the stage. "You want another man trying to take a piece out of your behind?"

"I like living dangerously," she tossed over her shoulder.

"Now who's she antagonizing?" Luther asked.

"No one important."

"Angel," Red offered.

"Like I said, no one important."

Florence laughed, despite the sharp glare from her father. "Don't encourage her." When she refused to compose herself, Luther sighed and turned back to the singer. "Cass—"

"Don't worry about Angel. He's not about to tangle with nobody and mess up his clothes."

"Maybe so, but that won't stop Junior," he scolded, as he dropped a generous slab of meatloaf on top of the pile of mashed potatoes on his plate. "He's got a temper, and you need to stop messing with him."

"And he needs to stop telling people I'll have drinks with them."

"He just wanted you to have a glass of wine and talk to the man."

"If it's that simple, then why didn't you sit with him?"

"Because I'm not the one everyone comes to hear."

"If I'm that important, then I should have a say in who I have drinks with."

"Cass—" he started, without glancing up from the glazed carrots he spooned onto his plate.

"Cass nothin'. Look, I'll smile at these men, say hi, and even shake their hands, but if you want me to have a drink with someone, make sure it's not some cat who feels he needs to impress me, 'cause they don't."

She grabbed the plate Luther had finished preparing and walked away. He stared at his empty hand, then at the singer, who sat down and dug into the food. After several seconds he shook his head and grabbed another plate.

"Okay, I'll talk to Junior," he said as he started dishing out more food. "But if you're bored, you could at least try to find a better way to excuse yourself. I'm getting tired of paying to get wine stains out of suits."

"Luther, I tried, but he wouldn't let me get a word in edgewise. He went on and on and on about all the money he had and the people he knew. Like I'm to believe he had lunch with Mayor LaGuardia to discuss the colored population in the city."

Eli glanced away from Florence. "He said what?" He laughed.

"That was after he offered me the use of his cottage in Florida this winter, so…how did he put it?" She propped her elbow on the table and tapped her forehead. "Oh, yeah, so my delicate voice wouldn't be subjected to the harsh New York cold."

"Cottage in Florida?" Red exclaimed. "I know that joker, and believe me, he don't have a cottage in Florida. He hasn't given his landlady the five dollars he owes her for last month's rent, and she's threatening to kick him out."

"That's not all," Cass continued. "He pulled out a wad of cash. Like I couldn't tell it was a couple of singles wrapped around some paper."

"I can top your story," Red said, as he pushed a table against the one where Cass sat, to accommodate everyone. "Not long after the club opened, some cat came strolling in here throwing money around like he could just step outside and pick it off a tree. He claimed he was some dancer who traveled all over Europe."

"What happened?" Cass asked.

"He was showing off on the dance floor, stepped on the gal's foot, and broke one of her toes."

"I remember that," Luther added. "She couldn't walk for two months after that."

"Instead of 'fessing up," Red continued, "he came up with all types of excuses, from his shoes being new and not properly broken in, to the dance floor being too slippery, to that gal doing some fancy moves he wasn't used to."

"What kinda moves?" Randy asked, as he placed his plate on the table next to Cass.

"All she was doing was trying to keep out of his way," Luther replied. "He moved like he had paddles strapped to his feet and the floor was covered in ice."

"If I recall correctly, he stomped on his own foot several times," Red said.

As they ate, the two older men continued to reminisce. Each story was wilder than the previous one, until Cass was laughing so hard she could barely breathe.

"And you thought you had it rough listening to these men talk?" Luther said, after telling an anecdote that had Cass leaning against Randy with tears rolling down her cheeks.

"I guess I shouldn't complain," she laughed as she dabbed the corner of her eyes with her napkin. "The worst anyone's ever done to me was bore me to sleep."

"That's about where I'm at," Eli commented as he pushed away from the table. "I thought we were going to jam."

Cass sat up. She glanced at Randy with a smirk. "You were supposed to show me what you can do with your reeds."

"Is that a challenge?" he asked.

"It's however you want to take it."

"I think that was a challenge," Eli said.

"Sounded like one to me," Red added. "What you think, Luther?"

"I'm always interested in hearing what my musicians can do."

****

After a few more minutes of ribbing, Red, Randy, and Eli climbed back onstage and started playing. Luther joined them on bass, with Cass and Florence providing the vocals.

They finally decided to call it a night at six. Luther and Eli piled the dishes on the carts and wheeled them back into the kitchen, while Florence and Cass disappeared backstage.

"That was a good session," Red said, as he gathered his sheet music.

"It was fun," Randy agreed. It felt good being a part of something, with everyone treating him as an equal. "But I'm sure you would've had more fun if the others hadn't left on account of me."

"You got to understand, kid. Some of these cats have had it rough."

"I understand more than you realize. And, before you ask, no, I'm not passin'."

Red nodded but didn't push for an explanation. "Give them a little time and they'll warm up to you."

By the end of his first week at The Big House, Randy had figured out who would accept him, who would tolerate him, and who would cause trouble. There wasn't much he could do to change people's opinions, and it would be best for everyone if he didn't try.

"Sorry if I don't share your optimism."

"Go on home and get some rest," Red said. "I'll see you tonight."

Deciding he'd repack his instrument in his dressing room, Randy grabbed the case. "Yeah, later."

At the top of the steps, Florence rushed past him with her coat and bag draped over her arm. "'Night, Randy," she called out over her shoulder.

He felt a twinge of jealousy when she disappeared into the kitchen after Eli. The couple seemed to spend most of their time together; if you saw one, the other was not too far away. Each night, they arrived at the club together, and most nights Florence waited until the band finished playing so Eli could escort her home.

Randy could not remember the last time he'd been in a relationship that lasted more than a couple of dates. He knew his outlook on life—on race in particular—had a lot to do with it. And though he one day wanted to settle down with a family of his own, he refused to compromise his beliefs in order to get that family.

With a sigh, he headed down the steps. As he

approached the ladies' dressing room, Cass's deep alto voice drifted out to him. He stopped by the doorway to listen.

She had changed back into the red dress, socks, and saddle shoes she had worn to the club. With her back to the door, she packed her purse as she sang "Dream a Little Dream of Me." Unaware she was performing for an audience, she let her hips sway in time to the song. Her movements were mesmerizing, awaking every part of him, even the part he would have preferred to remain flaccid.

He knew he should walk away, but his legs refused to listen to his brain. Instead of moving him away from the door, they carried him into the room. He told himself it was the song that drew him to her. All he wanted to do was make music with her.

As Cass began the second verse, he placed the saxophone to his lips. Startled by the sound, she spun around and glared at him. His attention dropped to the hands she placed on her hips. Though they were no longer swaying, he stared at her hips for two beats before slowly travelling up, taking in her small waist and modestly-sized breasts.

He eventually worked his way up to her full lips, turned down in a scowl that said she wanted to throttle him for scaring her. With no remorse, he cocked an eyebrow and continued playing. After a second the corners of those lips twitched until she was smiling. She shook her head before giving in to the urge to sing.

Her features relaxed as her body moved in time with the music. They focused on one another and continued their private performance, unaware they had attracted another audience until the round of applause at the end.

Cass appeared more than a bit peeved at being startled for the second time in less than five minutes.

"You two are good together," Red said as he leaned against the door jamb. "You should add that number to the show."

"Junior would burn the club down before puttin' a spotlight on me," Randy said, shaking his head. Though his desire to play sometimes took him to venues where he was not welcomed with open arms, he made it a point not to draw more attention to himself.

"Junior's not the only one who has a say in what goes on here."

"I'm not tryin' to start trouble."

Red frowned. "It's a shame to see such talent go to waste," he muttered under his breath before he strolled away.

"You're leavin' now?" Randy asked Cass, wanting to avoid any further discussion about the performance.

"Yes, I just have to get my purse," she replied, thankfully taking the hint and not pushing the topic.

"I'll walk you out."

"Hmm, a gentleman. Something we rarely see at the club." She grabbed a cream-colored sweater off the back of a chair before following him to his dressing room.

Cass stood in the doorway while he packed his saxophone. Once he'd shrugged into his coat and placed his hat on his head, he grabbed the suit he'd worn to the club, stepped out, and closed the door.

He led her outside and through the alley to the front of the club. A car sped down the street, its tires squealing as it turned the corner.

Seeing no other vehicles, Randy stopped beside her. "I'll wait with you 'til your ride gets here," he said, though he hoped the wait would not be long. The air was chillier than it had been when he arrived at the club, and with only her sweater to keep her warm, he was afraid she'd catch a cold if she was out there too long.

"My ride?" Cass laughed as if he told the funniest joke. "Man, the only women up here who get rides are royalty, some big shot's girl, or a woman who's expecting a nice payment when you're finished with her."

"Isn't someone comin' to pick you up?" he asked.

"Someone like who?"

"Your man?"

She stuck out a leg. "You see this?"

Even in the dark, he couldn't miss the shapely limb. He swallowed hard. "Yes," he croaked through a throat that had suddenly gone dry.

"This is how I get home."

Busy ogling her leg, he took several seconds before comprehension set it. He shook his head. "Girl, have you lost your mind?"

"What?"

"You're not walkin' home by yourself."

"Why not?" She shrugged her shoulders as if it were no big deal.

"Don't you know it's not safe for a girl—"

She cleared her throat.

"Oh, excuse me. It's not safe for a woman to be out here by herself at night. No matter how sassy she may be."

"It's not night. It's after six in the morning.

Sweet Jazz

Besides, I walk home by myself every night."

She had a point. It was no longer night and, by the time she arrived home, the sun would be rising. Also, it wouldn't be like she was out there by herself. People were getting ready to leave for work. But, still. He couldn't let her do it.

"I'm escortin' you home," he announced.

"You're sweet." She smiled up at him and patted his cheek. "But that's okay."

"I wasn't askin'. I'm walkin' you home. Like you said, I'm a gentleman."

Cass crossed her arms over her chest and snorted. "Trust me, I'm thinking of a couple of words to describe you right now, and gentleman isn't one of them. If you had said crazy, then you'd be close."

Randy placed his case on the ground, imitated her stance, and stared down at her.

"What?" she asked.

"Are you ready to go, or would you like a few more minutes to sass me before I walk you home?"

"And who said I'm going to let you walk me home?"

"The choice is yours. We can go together and have a nice conversation. Or you can ignore me and walk ahead, while I follow. Either which way, I'm goin' to make sure you get home safely."

"You're really sure of yourself."

"As sure as your name's Cassie Ann Porter," he replied, borrowing the line she had used earlier.

"I don't know what I'm going to do with you." She chuckled. Shaking her head, she turned toward Seventh Avenue. "Come on, I don't have all day."

"Wait a minute."

She spun around and threw up her hands. "Now what?"

"What about your coat?"

She glanced down at her dress. "I didn't wear one."

"Have you lost your mind? It's November. You need somethin' heavier than a sweater."

"Why? It was warm enough when I left home."

"Girl, you should've known the temperature would drop by the time you left the club. You're goin' to catch your death of cold out here in that thing."

"Not if you quit your spoutin' and come on."

Randy shrugged off his coat.

"What are you doing?"

"Makin' sure you don't get sick." He draped the coat over her shoulders. The hem, which stopped approximately two inches below his knees, reached her ankles.

"What about you?"

"Wear it until you get home. It doesn't matter if I catch a cold. I'm not the one who'll sound like a frog on stage." He picked up his case.

"I'll let you know I've never sounded like a frog."

"Let me guess. You have the voice of an angel?"

"If you keep it up, I'll whollop you so hard you'll see angels."

Randy laughed as they crossed the street. On most nights, he was home and in bed by six. Though he was beginning to feel the effects of staying up later than usual, he suspected, in the long run, he would not regret his decision to walk Cass home.

Chapter 7

Randy stopped at the corner of 135th Street and took a drag from his cigarette. As he exhaled, he closed his eyes and listened.

A car horn honked. A curse and the tapping of a shoe against the pavement expressed a pedestrian's impatience. A carriage wheel squeaked to a stop; teeth were sucked; sighs were blown.

One hundred and fifty-five seconds later, an engine roared as a car sped eastward through the intersection. A westbound car squealed to a stop. An exhaust pipe coughed before a truck headed north. More shoes tapped against the pavement.

Randy took another drag, then dropped the butt of his cigarette onto the pavement. He opened his eyes and joined the flow of people crossing the street. He continued concentrating on the sounds around him. For him, every movement had a distinct beat. He arranged them in his mind, turning the chaos into music.

His ability to hear music where others heard noise had caused him to be called many things—an optimist, a dreamer, a fool. He preferred to think of it as a gift that helped him get through life.

Lost in thought, Randy failed to notice Cass, who stepped from between the two buildings and into his path. She bounced off him, stumbled back on her black one-inch pumps, and dropped the book she had been reading.

"You need to stop running into me," she said as she stooped down to pick up her book.

"The last time, a boy bumped into you," Randy corrected. "Maybe you need to learn to step aside faster."

Cass straightened and placed her hands on her hips. Remembering how her hips had swayed when she sang in the dressing room a week earlier, Randy quietly groaned.

At the club, dancers wearing less than Cass had worn moved their hips more provocatively than she had, yet they had no effect on him, not like her innocent movement, which was burned into his mind and, like a movie, replayed over and over.

"Well?" Cass said, forcing him to focus on the person in front of him, not the memories.

"Well, what?" he asked.

"Why are you down here?" She pointed to the case he carried. "You have a side gig?"

"No, I'm here for rehearsals."

"We don't rehearse on Sundays."

"Angel told me last night we were rehearsin' today at two."

"Angel told you what? The only person who comes in at this time on Sundays is—"

"You need directions findin' your way away from here?" Junior asked as climbed from the back of a red Cadillac limousine. He walked over to the couple, ignoring the overly made-up, petite woman who struggled to climb out after him.

Cass huffed. "We're just talking."

"I don't pay you to stand out here and talk."

"You're not paying me no how. I'm on my own time."

"Then go somewhere else and talk. People see him standin' out here and they'll be thinkin' ghosts are welcome here."

Her eyes narrowed and she frowned up. With her arms crossed over her chest, Cass moved until she stood directly in front of Junior.

Hoping to ward off the impending argument, Randy touched her arm. "It's okay—"

"Ever since Randy started working here, he's shown you nothing but respect," she stated. "He's a good musician, he's always on time, and he's never given you any trouble, yet you always insult him. What does he have to do for you to be civil to him?"

"Leave," Junior replied with a straight face.

Cass's frown deepened. Her reply was interrupted when a black Buick pulled up behind the limousine. Eli honked as Florence stuck her head out of the passenger window.

"Hey, sorry we're late," she called out, waving toward the car. "Junior, we're going out to eat. You want to join us? There's plenty of room in the car for you and…" She hesitated with the name of the woman who stood a step behind Junior.

"No," Junior grumbled. "I'm choosy about the company I keep."

Randy glanced at the woman whose name had not been offered. She wore a fake-fur wrap over a tight, purple dress more suited for a street corner on a Saturday night than for a Sunday afternoon drive.

"Oh, well." Florence jerked her head toward the back of the car. "Come on, you two. Hop in."

Randy gently tugged Cass's arm. "Come on. Our ride's here."

She hesitated for a second before allowing him to guide her to the car.

"Next time find somewhere else to meet," Junior shouted. "There ain't no bus stop in fronta the club."

With a huff, Cass began to back out of the car. Knowing nothing good would come of the confrontation, Randy gave her a little push and climbed in behind her, forcing her to slide over on the seat. Florence pulled her head into the car as he closed the door, and Eli drove off.

"Thanks for the save," Randy said, once they turned left onto Seventh Avenue.

"No problem," Florence said. She shifted around in her seat to face the back. "Eli and I were coming down the block and saw you standing out there."

"The moment we saw Cass cross her arms, we knew it wasn't a good sign," Eli added.

"I was about to give Junior a piece of my mind," Cass said. Her bottom lip stuck out like a disgruntled child who didn't get her way. "That would've made me feel good."

"I'm sure it would've, but can't you forego that pleasure for just one day?" Florence said.

"Wouldn't it be easier to ask a bear to sing an aria?" Eli chuckled.

Cass rolled her eyes. "You just hush and drive."

"What were you doing over there today?" Florence asked.

"I left my book in the dressing room last night," Cass answered, holding up a copy of *Jane Eyre*.

Florence reached over the seat and snatched the

book. She flipped through the pages before shaking her head and tossing the book into Cass's lap.

"Boring."

"Reading's good for you. You should try it sometime."

"I resent that," Florence protested. "I read."

"The Sears catalog doesn't count."

Eli howled with laughter.

Florence punched his arm. "Oh, hush, and do like Cass said and drive."

"Don't upset the driver," Cass snapped.

"Don't tell me you still have a problem with cars," Florence said.

Randy noticed a tense frown had replaced Cass's pout.

"I haven't gotten used to them," she admitted. "Growing up, we got around with a wagon and a mule, or we walked. I didn't sit in a car 'til I was sixteen."

"There's nothin' to a car." Randy reached over and patted her hand. Her fingers slid around his and she held on tight. "It has four wheels, like a wagon."

"But I control a wagon. When I want to stop it, I pull the reins and the mule stops. I don't have to rely on a bunch of mechanical things that I don't understand."

"Then how do you get around the city?"

"Most of the time I walk."

"What about the other times?"

"I'll take a trolley if I have to, but I'm not too particular about riding the subway. Think about it…a train…underground. What if there's a cave-in?"

"*¡No hay problema!* I've been driving for years, and I've never had an accident." Eli looked back at her and smirked. "Except for that one time I ran into a parked car."

Cass tightened her grip on Randy's hand.

"Please tell her it was your first time behind the wheel and you haven't had an accident since."

Eli shrugged. "If you say so."

"Keep your eyes on the road," Cass snapped.

"The light's red," Eli insisted as he faced forward. "*¿Por cierto, dónde vamos?*"

Randy had learned a little Spanish while working in a Latin nightclub in Florida. An incident in New Orleans had taught him it was in his best interest to learn a few phrases when exposed to languages other than English. He'd also learned never to repeat anything unless someone he trusted translated it for him.

"I guess I'll head back home," Randy answered. "You can pull up to the corner over there and I'll get out."

"You don't want to hang with us?" Florence asked.

"I don't want to intrude." He actually liked the idea of going for a ride if it meant he would spend time with Cass.

"Intrude nothing," Eli said. "Man, if you think you're leaving me with these two, you're crazier than people say."

"My sax—"

"You can drop it off at your place, and then we'll grab a bite to eat."

The light changed. Before the oncoming traffic started to move, Eli made a sharp U-turn that made Cass shriek.

****

After some playful bantering, they had decided to

venture into Bedford Stuyvesant. The Brooklyn neighborhood was far enough from the watchful eye of Luther and anyone who would inform him of his eldest daughter's misdeeds. No sooner had they crossed over the Brooklyn Bridge than Florence lit a cigarette and slid closer to Eli.

Even though they had been seeing each other for two years, at the club they kept a distance of at least one foot away from each other. The distance grew to a yard when Luther was present.

At times, Cass envied the dancer's relationship. She longed to have someone look at her with the same admiration Eli had in his eyes when he stared at Florence. But then the memories of her past mistake came to mind and she nixed the idea of having what her friend had.

"Why were you down to the club?" Florence asked Randy after they were seated in a booth in the rear of a diner. She sat close to Eli, who enjoyed the freedom of draping an arm around the back of the booth without her father threatening to remove the limb. "Don't tell me you forgot your reed?"

"I was under the misimpression there was rehearsal today."

"Where'd you get that idea?" Eli asked.

"Angel," Randy and Cass said at once.

"It figures that joker would come up with something like that," Florence said. "That *puta*."

"Sweetie, you just called him a female whore," Eli said.

"Then I had the right word."

"I meant to ask Red," Randy said, "but he was meetin' with Luther. By the time they finished, we had to go onstage."

"You could've asked me, seeing as how I'd be at the rehearsal if there was one," Cass replied.

"Girl, every time I turn around, you're talkin' to this one or helpin' that one," Randy commented as he pulled out a pack of cigarettes and held them out.

Cass waved her hand to decline. "You need to jump in like everyone else."

"I'll remember that the next time."

"Angel probably won't try that prank again," Florence stated as she took two cigarettes.

"I hope he knows you're smart enough not to fall for that twice," Cass said. "You are smart enough?"

"Girl, you're much too sassy," Randy said.

"How do you like working at The Big House?" Florence asked. She passed a lit cigarette to Eli and took a drag off the other one. "I mean, aside from the practical jokers."

Randy shrugged his shoulders. "It's not much different than some of the other clubs I've worked at."

"Except for you being the only white cat in the joint," Eli stated.

"Nothin' new there."

"Is this some kind of preference, or what?"

"It's just a coincidence. My first gig was at a juke joint in New Orleans. Guy I was workin' with at the factory invited me to sit in with his band. Everyone at the joint, except me, was colored. Some of the white guys at the factory gave me flak for playin' with the band, and there were plenty of coloreds at the joint who didn't want me there."

"Then why'd you stay?"

"'Cause I wanted to play more than anythin' and

they were willin' to give me that chance."

"Man, I don't think I could do that."

"I won't lie and say it was easy. When another opportunity came, I took it. Until then, I grinned and beared it."

"If another opportunity came your way, you'd leave The Big House?" Cass asked, though she wouldn't blame him if he left.

With the majority of the other employees barely tolerating his presence and a few being outright hostile, she did not know how he'd managed to stick it out for as long as he had. For anyone, she imagined it would be only a matter of time before the bad outweighed the good and he had to move on.

"No one would mourn if I left," Randy stated. "Junior would hold the door open while Angel tossed my things out the door."

"Don't sell everyone at the club short," Florence said, crushing her cigarette in the ashtray. "You're not a bad guy, and some of us would miss you."

"And I'd miss a couple of y'all, too." He winked at Cass. "I don't think I'll ever meet anyone as sassy as Cass here, f'r instance."

"Amen to that," Eli said.

Cass playfully punched Randy in the arm. She'd miss his sense of humor. It was a rare person who could continue to smile when faced with ugliness.

But until the time came…

"Here's to surviving your stay at The Big House," she said raising her glass of orange juice.

"Hear, hear," Eli and Florence exclaimed, joining into the toast.

Chapter 8

"And let everybody present say Amen," Luther directed.

The first syllable was barely spoken before hands reached across the table for the platters of food. The diners had endured a ten-minute grace in which they were encouraged to remember everything for which they should be grateful. Then, in case their memories were faulty, Luther spent another ten minutes listing a few of the blessings they should give thanks for.

"That was some prayer," Eli said as he passed the yams to Florence, on his right. "If you ever get tired of running this club, you could take up preaching."

"If you ask me, that prayer was too long," mumbled Angel, who sat two chairs down from Eli, next to Red.

"Just reminding you to thank the Lord for your blessings," Luther said, as he carved one of the four turkeys prepared for the meal. At the other end of the four long tables set up to accommodate the diners, Junior worked on another turkey.

"Don't see why I need to give him thanks for anything."

"You watch that blasphemous talk, young man," Mother Hamilton reprimanded.

"No disrespect, ma'am, but everything I've got's on account of Junior hiring me," the musician replied.

"If the Lord hadn't blessed his mother those many years back, Junior wouldn't be here to give you a job."

"She's got a point, Angel," Red commented.

"So you just mind your manners and stop your blasphemy before he sees fit to strike you down where you sit. Nothing ruins an appetite quicker than a dead body at the dinner table."

Cass smiled as she passed Luther's mother the cranberry sauce.

The Big House's Thanksgiving dinner had been an annual tradition since the second year of the club's existence. After discovering many of the musicians had spent the previous holiday in their rooms eating cold turkey sandwiches, Junior organized the get-together so no one would be alone.

Though every employee had been invited, Randy was noticeably absent…at least, Cass had noticed his failure to appear. She was certain the others had not given him a second thought.

"You've outdone yourself, again," Mother Hamilton said after swallowing a bit of stuffing. "It's a shame I'm going to miss your Christmas dinner."

"You won't be able to make it?" Cass asked.

"No, dear. Unfortunately, since I'm spending Thanksgiving with Luther, I have to spend Christmas and New Year's in Maryland with Helen and her family."

"That seems like fair," Cass said as she grabbed a roll from the basket in front of her plate. "But why did you say unfortunately?"

"My daughter's a smart woman, a good wife, and wonderful mother. But, Lordy, the girl can't cook for nothing."

"You're going to miss the New Year's Eve party," Red said.

Mrs. Hamilton snapped her fingers. "I forgot about the party. What are you planning this year?"

"We'll have a special show followed by a party after midnight, with a buffet, music, and dancing," Luther answered.

"Red and I will do a duet," Cass said. "We haven't picked out a song, yet."

"You could do 'Ain't Misbehavin',' " Florence suggested. "I liked what you did to the song the other day during rehearsals."

Cass smiled. A week earlier, the band had spent several hours rehearsing new numbers. During a break, Red and she performed a silly duet, hoping to ease the stress of being at the club all day.

"Cass and Randy should do a number together," Red said.

The suggestion elicited the opposite response. Cass inhaled sharply and choked on a bite of potato. Luther reached over and patted her back as Eli passed her a cup of water.

When she had performed with Randy, she'd felt as if he had invited her into the world he escaped to whenever he played the saxophone. At that moment, it was only the two of them and nothing else mattered—no Junior or Angel or anyone else. But the mere suggestion that they do a number together would bring down a wrath neither one of them wanted to face.

"Have you lost your mind?" she hissed. She peeked down to the other end of the table at Junior. Thankfully, he was absorbed in another conversation and had not heard Red's suggestion.

"No, last time I checked, I had all my faculties."

"Then what do you have against Randy? I thought you liked him."

"I don't have a thing against the kid."

"Who's Randy?" Mother Hamilton asked.

"He's our sax player, Momma," Luther replied.

"So, what's wrong with the two of them doing a duet?"

"Junior doesn't like Randy."

"Why not?"

"'Cause he's white."

"And?"

"And nothing else."

Mother Hamilton placed her fork on the corner of her plate and folded her hands, a move Cass's mother used to perform. She and her brothers always referred to the gesture as the calm before the storm. Her mother started off composed before, depending on what displeased her, launching into a lecture or laying into a behind with a switch.

"You're going to tell me the only reason Junior does not like your sax player is 'cause he's white?" Mother Hamilton asked.

"Yes, ma'am," Luther said. "He wasn't too thrilled when I hired the boy. Until six weeks ago, there's never been a white man in this club."

"I'm aware of the club's policy, though I never agreed with it."

Luther stopped carving the turkey. "You didn't?"

"I never said anything 'cause this is your business and you need to run it as you see fit. I realized you wanted someplace where our people would be hired based on their talents, but I never felt it was right to exclude people simply to achieve that. You were only doing the same thing those other places did refusing us. I always hoped one day my son would run a desegregated club."

Angel stabbed his fork into his ham. "You sayin' we should welcome someone who's done us wrong?"

"Oh, the boy did something to you? Now, that's a different story. What'd he do?"

"Um…well, um…*he* didn't do nothin'."

"But you just said he wronged you."

"I didn't mean him. I meant the white people who look down on us because we're colored."

"You're telling me 'cause a few white people acted unchristian-like you should hate all white people? If we're going to think like that, then I should have Luther toss you out of here, 'cause some Negro about your age and size took my purse the last time I was up here."

"That won't be right. You can't judge me for what some other kid did."

"Isn't that what you and Junior are doing to that sax player?"

"I…I…," Angel stuttered.

"You shouldn't waste what precious little time you have hating people. What good has come from Junior hating that boy? Has it changed his past?"

"No, but—"

"Then why hate that boy for something he didn't do? If you're going to hate someone, do it 'cause that person did something to you."

"Junior can't help hatin' him. When he looks at the ghost he's reminded of all the wrongs the white folks done him."

"Boy, stop making excuses," Mother Hamilton

scolded. "I can't count how many times in my seventy years I've heard one person say he don't like another 'cause of the color of his skin. No matter how many times I hear it, it just don't make any sense. Maybe if people tried as hard to find excuses to like each other as they do to hate one another, this world would be in better shape."

For the first time in the four years Cass had worked at the club, words seemed to escape Angel. After a heartbeat he bent over his plate and began shoveling food into his mouth.

With a satisfied smirk, Mother Hamilton reached forward and spooned more stuffing onto her plate. Cass, however, had little faith the older woman's logic would change the way Randy was treated.

"Luther, what reason did you have for hiring that boy? You do it to get under Junior's skin?"

"No, Momma," Luther replied, picking up the carving knife. "I hired him 'cause I thought he was talented."

"And is he?"

"Is he what?"

"Is he white?" She sucked her teeth. "Sheesh, what'd you think? Is he talented?"

"Yes, he is."

"Then there's no reason why he shouldn't play while this gal sings," Mother Hamilton stated as if that settled the discussion. "Now, pass me some more turkey. I need to fill up on this food, since I won't taste anything like this until I come back up for Easter."

Cass glanced over at Luther as she passed the older woman the platter of meat. Though his expression was unreadable, she'd bet a week's salary he was

considering a number featuring Randy and her.
****

Randy's decision to arrive late in the afternoon for dinner and possibly avoid Junior had backfired. The word "ofay" followed by a few choice expletives and the phrase "blue-eye devil ghost" that greeted Randy when he stepped into the club indicated the other man had yet to leave.

Deciding a confrontation would not do much for his digestion, Randy turned back to the door. He failed to notice the pail someone had set by the wall, until his foot sent it bouncing across the floor. The clatter echoed through the venue.

"Not brave enough to stick around and find out what all the fussing's about?"

Randy glanced back at Cass, who stood in the doorway of the ladies' dressing room. "From the way he keeps spittin' out 'ofay,' I assume it's about me."

She placed a finger to her lips before peeking over her shoulder at the office. He was not sure who she expected to emerge, but when no one appeared, she rushed forward, grabbed his arm and dragged him into his dressing room. Inside the six-by-six-foot space, she pulled the string to turn on the overhead light, then, unexpectedly, closed the door.

Though she wore a long-sleeved green dress with a neckline a church matron would approve of, he could not help but be aware of the rise and fall of her chest.

"Are you goin' to tell me what's goin' on?" he asked, trying to divert his attention to something less intimate, before his body reacted to being so close to her.

"Luther wants me to sing a solo in the New Year's

Eve show—"

"What's the big deal?" he interrupted. "You do that every night."

"You're accompanying me."

"And? I always play when you're on stage."

"You don't understand. It'll just be the two of us."

The announcement effectively brought his body under control. "What the… Where the hell did he get that idea?"

"Red suggested it."

"That's just damn great," Randy muttered under his breath. "I can see Junior agreein' to that, over his dead body and after hell freezes over."

"Actually, he said that would happen once pigs fly. Now I figure, all we have to do is get a pig on an airplane—"

"It's not funny," Randy said, his tone harsher than he intended. "You see what I deal with every night. You put me in the spotlight, and he'll come down harder on me. Just 'cause I take his crap doesn't mean I'm a glutton for punishment. All I want to do is play the saxophone. Can't I be allowed that without havin' to put up with someone's crap?"

"If that's what you want, then leave," Cass said.

His head snapped back as if she'd slapped him. "What?"

She did not raise her voice, yet the coldness in her tone and her thicker accent belied her fury. "You've worked in colored-only clubs before, so you knew the deal when you first walked in here. You wanna play without havin' to deal with Junior's crap, then take your reed and go find some other gig. You plan on leavin' when somethin' better comes along, so why don't you do it sooner rather than later? Unlike the rest of us, you've places you can go where people won't treat you like you're beneath 'em."

Randy's shoulders slumped. What Cass said was true. He'd known it would not be easy before he first walked into The Big House. Hell, Junior and Angel let him know where they stood right from the beginning. But he had insisted on staying.

"Wait, Cass…" He reached for her arm when she opened the door.

Her gaze dropped to his hand, then rose. Her smoldering glare, speaking louder than words, indicated she did not appreciate being manhandled.

Respecting her space, wary of the consequences if he didn't, Randy released his hold on her.

"For the record, there are some people here who are in your corner," she said. "Hell, Luther's mother spoke up for you today, and she's never met you. So, I suggest you watch who you yell at before you find yourself facin' Junior alone."

She pushed the door. It swung open and slapped the wall behind it.

"Cass," Randy called out as he followed her out of the room.

Ignoring him, she marched toward the stairs, slipping past Luther, who was coming down them.

"Surprised to see you here today," the older man commented. He stood in the center of a step with a hand on the banister, blocking Randy from following her.

"Cass said you were servin' dinner."

"We ate dinner at three."

"I figured if I dropped by later I'd avoid Junior."

"No such luck. Junior takes these holiday

celebrations seriously. He's here two hours beforehand and at least an hour afterwards to make sure everything runs smoothly." Luther glanced up the stairs. "So, is there a reason why our lead singer looked like she wanted to hurt someone?"

"I snapped at her when she told me about the New Year's Eve show," Randy explained. He felt lower than dirt for snapping at the one person who'd had his back since he first stepped into the club.

"It's amazing how one number can have such an effect on so many people." Luther sighed. "I just got through listening to Junior rant and rave about it."

"I heard him. In fact, I think the entire city heard him."

Luther faced him. "Now, Red thinks Cass and you are good together. On the other hand, Junior believes both of you will go straight to hell if you do the number."

"Well, at least Cass," Randy stated. "He already thinks I'm a product of the devil."

"I'm interested in hearing what you think."

There was nothing for Randy to think about. Cass was easy to work with, even when she was sassing everyone. And he enjoyed the few times they'd spent together.

He foresaw only one problem. "At the moment, Cass wouldn't spit on me if I were on fire, much less perform with me."

"Spit on you if you were on fire? It sounds like some of her poetics is rubbing off on you."

"She has a way of rubbin' off on people."

"That she does. Anyway, if you have any hype, I suggest you go up there and smooth things over with her. You have less than six weeks to put something together," Luther declared as he continued down the steps.

"You mean Junior agreed to this?"

"No, he didn't. However, before he left to find someone to put a hex on me, I reminded him it's my stage. Now, go upstairs and convince Cass to work with you, else we won't have a closing number for the show."

Randy sighed. He wondered if he could make things right with Cass, not only for the show but their friendship. During his life, he'd had too few people in his corner. He'd learned to value friendships and would do everything in his power to maintain them.

"And, while you're up there, tell Cass to fix you a plate," Luther called after him. "I can't hear myself talk over your growling stomach."

****

"Chile, if you don't quit throwing those spoons, someone's liable to go upside your head with one of them," Mother Hamilton stated after another utensil was slammed into the sink.

Cass paused a second as she contemplated the threat. Deciding she did not want to see whether or not the other woman would follow through on the threat, she gently placed the precious serving spoon on the stainless steel countertop.

"Now, what's gotten into you, chile?"

"Nothing, ma'am," Cass answered.

"That noise didn't sound like nothing to me," the older woman replied.

Cass gripped the side of the stainless steel, double-basin sink, her shoulders slumped. As a colored woman, she knew what it felt like to be spurned because of the color of her skin. Down south, she had been denied entrance to establishments and segregated to less desirable sections in public venues merely because her skin was not light enough. Therefore, she knew it couldn't be easy for Randy to deal with the daily slurs and abuse he had to endure to pursue his dream.

She had figured Randy would eventually snap from the pressure of working somewhere he was not welcomed, but she'd never thought she would be the recipient of the outburst.

"Well?" Mother Hamilton asked.

Crossing her arms over her chest, Cass turned and leaned against the sink. "I just let someone get under my skin," she replied.

"Taking your anger out on those poor spoons is no better than Junior taking his frustrations out on that sax player," Mother Hamilton said as she transferred a slice of sweet potato pie to a plate. "Go find the source of your anger and give him a piece of your mind."

"I'll make it easy for you," Randy offered as he stepped into the kitchen. "I'm here, so you can throw whatever you want at me."

"I just got this chile to stop slamming things in here." Mother Hamilton waved the pastry server toward the door. "If you want to fight, take it into the next room."

"Yes, ma'am." Randy held the door open. "Cass?"

Uncertain if she wanted to hear what he had to say, she hesitated.

"Got to respect a boy who's brave enough to face an angry woman," Mother Hamilton said.

With a huff, Cass pushed away from the sink and marched past Randy.

"Though, if that boy had a lick of sense, he'd wait until she cooled down," the older woman muttered as the door swung closed.

Once everyone had their fill of food, the majority of the employees had dispersed in search of entertainment elsewhere. Those who remained sat in small groups around the dining room, in no hurry to go anywhere.

Randy pointed toward the stage, the one place everyone seemed to be avoiding.

"It was wrong of me to yell at you, and I don't know what got into me." Randy quickly jumped into an explanation, as if he expected her to walk off again. "Maybe it was temporary insanity, or the lack of food affecting my brain. But, whatever it was, it's no excuse. I'm sorry."

Despite the apology, Cass questioned his sincerity.

Sorry. As children, they were told to say "sorry" whenever they hurt someone. Whether or not they meant it, they complied to avoid further punishment. Eventually it became a habit, with the expectation of acceptance by the recipient.

As far as she was concerned, anyone could say "Sorry." Or "I love you."

"Okay, I see an apology won't work. I'm supposed to get on my knees and grovel."

She remained silent.

"All right. I guess it's on my knees, then."

"Don't you dare." Cass grabbed his arm before he could lower himself to one knee. "Didn't anyone ever tell you you're not supposed to bow down to anyone?"

"I figured an exception could be made for the woman who's done nothin' but help me since I first stepped foot in this club and who deserves to have my undyin' gratitude."

"Man, that's the biggest load of manure I've ever heard in my life. You need to work on your hype, 'cause your lines aren't working."

"I beg to differ."

She raised an eyebrow at him.

"You're talkin' to me again."

Cass threw up her hands. He was impossible, mainly because he could make her smile.

She stepped around him, hoping to make it back to the kitchen before he saw the corners of her lips twitch. He caught her around the waist before she made it to the door.

"Cass, I truly am sorry. I shouldn't have snapped at you. It was uncalled for."

The tenderness in his voice forced her to look up. His eyes reflected his sincerity, erasing all her doubts. There was no way she could stay mad at him. Wordlessly, she nodded her head.

"If it's all right with you, I'd like to do the number with you."

"Junior agreed to it?" she asked.

"No, but Luther said we're doin' it."

"That means you'll have to work closely with a sassy gal."

Randy smiled. "There's nothin' I'd prefer." His stomach growled loudly, as if it were putting in its two cents.

"Lord have mercy, what was that?" Cass stepped out of his arms. "Didn't you eat today?"

"No, the luncheonette was closed, and Mrs. Greene went over to her brother's house for dinner."

She took his arm and pulled him toward the kitchen. "I have a right mind to let you starve."

"If you do, there won't be a closin' number on New Year's Eve."

"We could freeze your body and watch Junior dance around it in joy."

"Girl, you're cruel. Now, are you goin' to offer me a plate, or what?"

Cass stopped just outside the kitchen door. "I'm thinking."

His devilish smirk was the only warning she received before he tossed her over his shoulder.

Cass squealed.

"Now what?" Luther sighed when he came into the room.

"I'm followin' your orders, sir," Randy replied as he pushed the door.

"And, that was?"

"To have Cass fix me a plate."

"Put her down or she's fixin' a frying pan upside your head."

"Nah, she's been forbidden to throw anythin' in the kitchen," Randy said.

"Forbidden? When has that ever stopped her from doing anything?" Luther mumbled as he followed the couple into the kitchen.

Randy placed Cass on a stool. She introduced him to Mother Hamilton, who insisted he sit while she prepared plates for them and they discussed the new act.

Chapter 9

Randy stood by the entrance of the living room and watched the boarding house's unofficial welcoming committee entertain his company. In her white blouse, red plaid skirt, ankle socks, and saddle shoes, Cass could have come over to play with the three girls who surrounded her, instead of to rehearse.

It had been a week since they agreed to do a number at the New Year's Eve show, and they had yet to choose the song. Meetings at The Big House had been interrupted by Junior, who seemed to find pressing matters that demanded Cass's immediate attention. The obvious attempt to keep them from working finally forced them to find another rehearsal space.

Randy had considered her apartment, but quickly nixed the idea. Each time he walked her home, she placed the gate between them when they arrived at her brownstone and never invited him upstairs. He respected the boundaries she set up and suggested the front room of his boarding house, instead.

In the afternoon, with most of the residents at work, they would have enough privacy to rehearse without disturbing anyone. At the same time, the room was open enough that Cass could be comfortable being alone with him.

"Who is this?" Cass asked, pointing to the brown rag doll Bessie Davis cradled in her arms.

"This is Suzy," the youngest of the three sisters answered. "She's my baby."

"And how old is Suzy?"

"She's one years old."

"I also have a doll," Estelle, the second oldest, added. "She's upstairs taking a nap."

"And what's her name?" Cass asked. She gave each girl her undivided attention when each spoke, as if they were the most important people in the world.

"Mary."

"Your babies have beautiful names."

"Did you have a doll when you were little?" Bessie asked.

"Yes, her name was Hannah."

"What happened to her?"

"One of my brothers decided to burn her at the stake. By the time Papa put out the fire, it was too late to save her. I cried for an entire day after I lost her, but Mama gave me an old box to put her in. I had a funeral for her and buried her in the woods behind our house."

"Boys can be so icky. I'm glad I don't have a brother," Estelle commented.

"I have five brothers, and I agree they can be icky."

"There's a boy in my class who's icky. He's always pulling my braids and sticking his tongue out at me."

"You know, sometimes boys do that when they like a girl."

"Yuck. I don't like him."

"You like someone else?"

"Ewww, no." Estelle wrinkled her face. "I don't like any boys. They're all icky."

"I wish I could tell you they're different when they

grow up, but they're not."

"Mariah, have you finished your homework?" Mrs. Greene called from down the hall to the girl sitting on the floor, staring at the group on the sofa.

The eldest sister glanced at the books spread out on the coffee table in front of her. She scribbled a quick note before closing her writing pad.

"Yes, ma'am," Mariah yelled back.

"I didn't have any homework," Estelle commented.

"Me neither," Bessie added.

"Of course, you don't have homework, silly. You don't even go to school."

"That's enough, Estelle," Mrs. Greene chastised as she stepped around Randy to enter the room.

"Yes, ma'am."

"Y'all get your coats and go outside. Miss Cass came here to rehearse, not play with y'all."

"Yes, ma'am," the girls said in unison. They gathered their things and raced out of the room and up the stairs.

"So, you're the famous Cass," Mrs. Greene said.

"Yes, ma'am." Cass stood and shook hands with the older woman. "It's nice meeting you. Thank you for letting us practice here."

"Don't mention it. When Randy asked if you could use the front room, I couldn't say no. He's such a fine young man."

"Accordin' to Cass, I'm icky," he replied, moving to her side.

"Call it payback for your 'bossy' comment a while back."

"I was only agreein' with that boy."

"And I was agreeing with Estelle."

Mrs. Greene laughed. "You two remind me of my youngest and his wife before they were married. Those two used to fuss about everythin'."

Cass shuddered. "Eww, I hope you're not suggesting I'd marry him. He's icky."

"And she's bossy," Randy added, pointing his thumb at Cass.

Mrs. Greene shook her head. "I'll leave you two to fuss, rehearse, or whatever you're gonna do." She chuckled as she returned to the kitchen. "Call me if you need anythin'."

Randy waved Cass toward the sofa.

"Would you like somethin' before we start?" he offered after she sat down on one end. "A snack or a drink?"

Before Cass could answer, Bessie ran into the room and around the coffee table.

"Since you don't have a doll, you can borrow Suzy while I'm outside playing," the girl offered.

"Thank you," Cass replied, taking the doll and placing it next to her on the sofa. "She can lie here and take a nap, and I'll watch her for you."

"Come on, Bessie," Mariah shouted from the doorway.

The child ran out, and a moment later the house seemed to shake from the force of the front door slamming.

"It seems like you've made a friend," Randy commented as he sat in a chair next to the sofa.

"Those girls are angels," she said, tucking the blanket around the doll. Though it was just a toy, she seemed to know how important the doll was to Bessie, and she was taking her babysitting job seriously. She would not have the girl come back and find her doll tossed in the corner like…well, like a rag doll.

"They are, and they're just as friendly as they can be," Randy replied. "I don't think they've ever met a stranger. They greet everyone who walks through that front door."

"Are they Mrs. Greene's grandchildren?"

"No, they belong to Mrs. Davis, who lives on the floor over me. Her husband passed away four years ago, right before Bessie was born. Mrs. Greene gave her a room and helped her out until she was able to get work. Now, she watches them when their mother's at work."

"That was generous of her."

"She remembers what it was like to struggle. She's one of those rare people who doesn't just toss a coin in the collection plate to say she helped and then goes home where she doesn't have to see or worry about those in need. She actually does something."

"It's good they have someone to protect them from people like you."

"People like me?"

"People who believe in corrupting children."

"I'd never corrupt a child," Randy protested.

"So you don't consider making a bet with Bill and Earl corrupting them?" Cass asked, referring to an incident a couple of weeks prior.

Cass had come out of the club in time to see him give the boys each a dollar, even though they had lost a bet with him. He had meant for it to be a lesson that there was no such thing as a sure thing. And though they had learnt their lesson, she had not appreciated his method of teaching. Luckily for the boys, she did not tell their mother. Instead, she made them write fifty times "I will not gamble" and she took the dollars away from them.

Though Randy did not have an irate mother looking to get a piece of his hide for teaching her children to gamble, he did not get off easy. Cass insisted he write "I will not gamble" a hundred times, and she did not return to him the money she took from the boys.

"I guess gambling's something every child should learn, along with reading, writing, and arithmetic," she said. "By the way, you still haven't handed in your punishment."

"My dog ate it."

Cass rolled her eyes and sighed.

"I'll admit maybe I could have found a better way to teach those boys the evils of gamblin'."

"You think?"

"But, darlin', gamblin's not as bad as you make it out to be."

She leaned forward, bracing her forearms on her knees. "Is that so?"

"Not if you consider that life's a gamble. Gamblin's a game of chance, and every day we take chances and pray the outcome's in our favor. For example, when crossin' the street, you're takin' a chance you'll make it safely to the other side."

"The more reason why we shouldn't take unnecessary chances."

"And who's to say what chances are necessary and what aren't? Should we only take chances when the odds are in our favor? Or only when luck's on our side?"

"You never know when Lady Luck's going to take a nap and leave you on your own."

"I know, but that could happen with anythin'." He pointed toward the window behind the sofa. "When you leave here, you're goin' to wait at the corner 'til the light changes. Then you'll strut across the street like you're a queen and the drivers are your subjects, stoppin' at your command. You're not goin' to worry about whether Lady Luck's asleep or not."

"I'm not so sure about that anymore. After talking to you, I may never cross the street again."

Randy chuckled. "All right, let me put it in a way that won't have you growin' roots on the corner of 139th Street. We're always confronted with chances. Sometimes the odds are for us and sometimes they're against us. However, we can't let others decide for us whether the chance's worth takin' or not. We have to make that decision for ourselves."

"And how do you make your decision?"

"I consider how much I have to lose if I don't take the chance and what the reward would be if I succeed."

"Like working at The Big House?"

He nodded his head. "Yes. Before I went to the audition, I knew the odds of me gettin' this gig were about a million to one, but I considered everythin'—what I had to lose and what the reward would be."

"What did you have to lose?"

"I could have lost out on a chance to play in New York."

"And was the reward everything you expected?"

"Yes, and more," Randy said. "I'm playin' the sax, plus I've made a friend."

"And what about the insults thrown at you every

night and being the butt of everyone's jokes? Is it worth it?"

"I'm not the butt of everyone's jokes. Like you said on Thanksgivin', not everyone's against me. I could name at least six people who haven't joined the pranksters' efforts to get rid of the ofay, and one of them is sittin' in front of me right now. Durin' my life, I've had less people in my corner when I was confronted with things worse than findin' my suit stuffed in the trash."

"When?"

He thought about his life before he met Sax. He had been alone even when he was with the one person who should have been there to protect him. Though years had passed and most of the scars had faded, he could not bring himself to talk about that.

"It's not important."

"Randy—"

"We've only a few weeks to get this number together, and we haven't chosen a song," Randy reached down and unsnapped his case. "I'm sure Junior would like nothin' better than for us not to come up with anythin', and I'd like to disappoint him."

****

"A nickel for your thoughts."

Cass looked down at the coin in Randy's hand, then up at him. "Isn't it supposed to be 'a penny for your thoughts'?"

"So you'll owe me four thoughts."

She shook her head and frowned.

"Was it somethin' I said?" he asked.

"It was more like something you didn't say."

They had worked for two hours in the front room

of the boarding house, until it was time to leave for the club. Because they had scheduled their rehearsal for the middle of the afternoon, Cass had brought her dress to the boarding house so she wouldn't have to go back home for it before coming to the club.

As they walked to The Big House, they talked about various things, from current events to Cass's promise to make dresses for each of the Davis girls' rag dolls. Randy, however, would not revisit the subject he'd changed from before they started rehearsing.

Cass had noticed he didn't like talking about his past. Though he talked about Sax and the clubs he worked in before coming to New York, he did not offer much more information about his personal life. When pressed, he would give short answers that sounded rehearsed or else he would change the subject altogether, like he did earlier in the afternoon.

"You're an interesting man, Mr. Randy Jones," she added, as she pulled him toward the club from the middle of the sidewalk, where people had to step around them.

"Umm, thank you, I think."

"That's when you're not being so secretive."

"Cass, I'm not—"

"You offered me a nickel for my thoughts. I'll do better than that." She opened her purse and pulled out a bill. "I'll give you a dollar if you answer one of my questions and not change the subject."

She looked up at him as he contemplated what he should say. For a second she thought he was about to satisfy her curiosity—and then Junior stepped outside.

"You forget how to find your way inside?" Junior asked. "Or you plannin' to move the show out here?"

"Neither. I was talking to Randy," Cass answered.

"Where have you been? I was expectin' you hours ago."

"Minding my own business on my own time."

"I need you inside, now. We have things to go over."

"I'll be there in a minute," she replied, knowing there was no reason for him to be looking for her other than his need to keep her and Randy apart.

"Make it quick," he ordered, before ducking back into the club.

Cass glanced up at Randy. His frown told her the moment had passed. Whatever he had planned to tell her would not be revealed that day.

Taking her hand, he placed the nickel on top of the dollar, then closed her fingers around the money.

"What's that for?" she asked.

"I offered it to you for your thoughts."

"And what about yours?"

"Maybe another time," Randy said, before disappearing into the alley beside the club.

Chapter 10

Downstairs, Mrs. Greene's grandchildren squealed as they tore paper from the boxes under the Christmas tree. Above Randy, the Davis girls made similar high-pitched sounds with each present they opened.

The noise had started at six with the not-so-quiet shushing of the children as they tiptoed through the brownstone to see what surprises awaited them. Even though their attempt to be quiet woke Randy, the other adults in the building slept through the racket, not rising until seven.

Though he'd had only two hours of sleep, Randy enjoyed the sounds of young people excited by life and not bothered by problems that should only fall on adult shoulders. Listening to them allowed him to relive the childhood he never had.

Once the presents were opened and the noise quieted to a low roar, Randy rolled over to get a couple more hours of sleep. But the second he closed his eyes, images of a sassy woman appeared in his mind.

Over the past several weeks, Cassie Ann Porter had worked her way into his subconscious like no other woman. Randy hadn't thought much about it when he woke up one afternoon with the memory of his dream still fresh in his mind. They had spent the previous day rehearsing; therefore, it seemed natural for him to picture them performing together on stage.

The next night he dreamt he was accompanying her on the sax. She stood next to him, idly playing with his nape. Her touch had been gentle, yet enticing enough that once the song was over, he reached up and pulled her down until he could taste her lips on his own. When he woke up, he attributed the dream as a normal male reaction to an attractive woman.

Two days later, when the dream became more intense, he finally had to admit there was much more to the dreams than going to bed after eating a heavy meal. It had gotten to the point where he had to jump under a cold shower every morning.

As Sax would have said, he had it bad.

After an hour, Randy rolled out of bed and shuffled next door to the bathroom he shared with the boarder who rented the room across the hall. He stripped off his pajamas and stepped under the shower to relieve the uncomfortable reaction to the images of Cass. By the time he returned to his room, he was able to contemplate the long day ahead of him.

With no family to visit and all businesses closed for the day, Randy had few options beyond cleaning his room or reading to occupy his time. Cleaning was immediately rejected, since he considered it something that only needed to be done when the mess became overwhelming. Until then, a light coating of dust on the furniture and a few clothes and papers left out did not mark the end of the world. He therefore settled for passing the time reading Zora Neale Hurston's *Their Eyes Were Watching God*, which Cass had forgotten when they left for the club the previous day.

Though he was not a big fan of reading, the book grabbed his attention and he managed to lose himself in it. He was so engrossed in Janie Crawford's life he didn't hear the knocking on his door until the visitor was pounding almost hard enough to punch a hole through it.

Expecting Mrs. Greene had come upstairs to invite him to dinner, Randy rolled off the bed to answer the door. He dropped the book on top of several newspapers scattered across the table as he walked by. Randy cracked open the door. Instead of the older woman, Cass stood in the hall with her purse draped on one arm and a shopping bag in her other hand.

"Yes, he's awake," Cass called over her shoulder.

"All that poundin' woulda woke the dead," Mrs. Greene yelled from downstairs. "Remember, I'm expectin' you for dinner."

"You heard that?" Cass asked.

Randy nodded.

"Good." After a minute she added, "I guess this means you can invite me in."

"Sorry." He stepped aside, and she walked into the room. "What are you doin' here?"

He was unsure what surprised him more, seeing her on Christmas or having her venture upstairs to his room. Though he felt their relationship had grown from co-workers to friends, he had yet to cross the line she had drawn between them. They never met anywhere more intimate than the living room at the boarding house, and the gate remained firmly closed between them at her apartment.

"You know how to make a girl feel welcome," she commented.

He left the door cracked open to maintain a sense of appropriateness with the children running around the building.

"That didn't come out right."

"I'll say."

"Sorry," he apologized, for the second time in less than a minute. "I was surprised to see you."

"How about I step outside and we try this again?"

"No reason for you to leave. There was nothin' wrong with your entrance. How about I step outside and try it again."

She smiled. "Momma said to never argue with a man who's trying to be logical, 'cause you'll only end up with a headache."

"Here, let me take your coat," Randy offered.

"That's more like it," she replied. She placed her purse on the table and the bag on the floor next to a chair.

He helped her off with her coat. As he hung it in the closet that was big enough to house a couple of suits and slacks, she glanced around the small room. Suddenly, the dust on the dresser in the corner, the unmade bed, the scattered newspapers on the table, and the jacket and tie draped on the back of a chair seemed more apparent. He should have opted to cleaned, earlier.

"Nice room," she commented.

"I'm sorry it's a bit messy." He walked to the table and gathered the newspapers into one neat pile. "Had I known you were comin' over, I would have straightened up a bit."

Cass shrugged her shoulders. "It looks fine to me. I don't believe it's my place to comment on the cleanness of someone's space, unless I plan to clean it, and I've enough to clean at home without taking on anyone else's mess."

"Girl, you're amazin'," he said, dropping the papers on top of the dresser. "Somehow you can make a compliment sound sassy."

"It's a gift." She beamed with pride over her talent.

Randy pulled out a chair. "Would you like to sit down?"

"No, I think I'll stand here and grow roots."

"Sit down."

"He's giving orders." Cass slapped the back of her hand against her forehead and dropped into the chair. "It's so…so manly. I think I'm going to swoon."

"Girl, you can try the patience of a saint," he replied, sitting across from her.

She smiled as she dropped her hand to the table. "I hope I'm not disturbing you."

"No, I wasn't doin' anythin'."

She picked the open book off the table and held it up.

"Okay, I wasn't doin' anythin' important."

She raised an eyebrow, which alerted him to his mistake. Cass had a passion for books. She always carried one in her bag, and whenever the Davis girls were not around to entertain her, she would be reading when he walked into the front room for rehearsals.

Besides reading colored authors like Zora Neale Hurston, James Weldon Johnson, and W.E.B. DuBois, she read bestsellers by George Orwell, Colette, and Sinclair Lewis. She also read classics by Mark Twain, William Shakespeare, and Jane Austen.

"How's this?" Randy asked, attempting to correct himself again. "I wasn't doin' anythin' I wouldn't mind puttin' down in order to entertain a lovely, intelligent lady such as yourself."

"It sounds like a load of manure." She slipped an envelope into the book to mark his page. He watched her caress the cover and made a mental note never to leave the book open. "So how are you enjoying it?"

"It's interestin'."

"I guess that's your way of saying you don't like it?"

"No, I've enjoyed what I've read so far."

"Let me know what you think of it when you've finished it," Cass said, pushing the book across the table to him. "I would also recommend *Jonah's Gourd Vine* and her short stories."

"I'll keep that in mind." He looked forward to having something else to talk with her about in the future. "So what brings you over? I thought you'd be too busy celebratin' with your family."

"You forget my family's in North Carolina. Before I left yesterday, Mrs. Greene invited me to join y'all for dinner."

"You don't have any relatives up here to watch you open your presents?"

She shook her head. "No."

"Every little girl should have an audience when she opens her Christmas dress and doll."

"I guess cruel little boys who pick on us sweet little girls don't need an audience to watch them pull coal out of their stockings."

"Sweet? Girl, you've got a devilish streak in you a mile long."

"Never mind, you. As for opening my presents, I did that before I went to bed this morning."

"This mornin'?"

"Yes, I didn't get in from the club until six."

"That's the time Mrs. Greene's grandchildren decided everyone here should wake up, whether or not they were ready."

"I'm not surprised. I could hear Mrs. Cooper's grandchildren beggin' their parents to let them open their presents when I got in." She smiled. "When I was a kid, I used to jump out of bed at five to see what Santa left me."

"When was that? Last year?"

Cass rolled her eyes.

"Okay, two years ago."

"Keep it up and I won't give you your presents."

"Presents?" he asked, his curiosity piqued.

"Yes. You left the club before we could exchange gifts."

Randy had known they were planning a celebration after the last patron left the club, but since his presence would not be welcomed and he had not expected to get anything, he departed the moment the band finished their last set.

"I had to go," he said without offering more of an explanation.

"That's okay, because I'm here as the official representative of Claus & Co." She reached into the bag on the floor by her feet and retrieved a bottle of champagne and an envelope.

"These are from the management of The Big House, with their compliments."

"Thank you." Randy reached across the table and took the bottle from her. "Somehow I knew Junior wouldn't forget about me."

Cass raised an eyebrow as if he had lost his mind.

"I can dream, can't I?"

She snorted. "Honey, you have to have a mighty powerful imagination to dream up that."

"I guess it's safe to say he had nothin' to do with this?"

"You better hope he had nothing to do with this, 'cause he'd be liable to poison you if he did."

"I'll thank Luther on Wednesday."

Cass reached into the bag and pulled out a small box. "This is from Red," she said, passing the gift to him.

"Red?"

"Yes, he always gives everyone in the band gifts."

Randy opened the box to reveal a silver lighter with his initials.

"I didn't get him anythin'."

"Don't go running out to buy him anything, either. Red didn't give that to you 'cause he's looking for something in return. It's his way of saying thanks for doing a good job."

He nodded as he closed the case.

"And this is from me." Cass placed a small wrapped box on the table. "I hope you like it."

Randy stared at the box, trying not to read more into the present then there was. She was generous and had most likely given presents to everyone at the club.

On second thought, he could not see her giving Angel anything but a piece of her mind. He did not know their history, yet he always sensed the animosity between the singer and the drummer whenever they were less than two yards away from each other.

"Well, open it. It's not going to bite," she said, pushing the box toward him.

"Are you sure?"

"What do you take me for?" she asked, trying her best to maintain a sweet, innocent expression...and failing.

"I told you, a sassy girl with a devilish streak."

She dropped her hands on the table and sighed. "Okay, I'll admit I was planning to get you a lizard, but the one I found ran away."

"Sassy," he mumbled, before tearing off the paper and opening the box. He pushed aside the tissue paper to find a blue necktie with gold stripes. He whistled. "This is sharp."

"I guess that means you like it?"

"Girl, you've got taste. You're sassy as sin, but you got taste."

"Put it on and let me see it."

Randy draped the tie around his collar, knotted it, then stood with his hands out for her to see.

Cass smiled and nodded.

"How's it look?"

"See for yourself," she said. She stood and directed him to the mirror on the inside of the closet door.

Randy stared into the glass. Instead of seeing his reflection, he saw Cass, who stood behind him. He admired her navy-blue dress, black jacket, stockings, and pumps. Though the outfit was simple, as was her French braid with a ribbon on the end, she appeared more sophisticated than the women who spent too much money and too many hours primping in front of a mirror before they considered stepping foot out of the house.

"Well, what do you think?" she asked, pulling him out of his stupor.

"Beautiful," he answered as he glanced at her reflection one more time. He reached for a package sitting on the end of the dresser next to him. "This is for you."

"You got me something?" She took the box back to the table. "What is it?"

"You have to open it to find out."

She rolled her eyes at him as she pulled off the lid. The inside of the box was lined with a pink crocheted blanket. Lying on top was a colored rag doll in a blue dress and blue ribbons in her two braids.

"Randy, she's pretty," Cass gasped as she lifted the doll out the box.

He had remembered the story she told Bessie when he saw the doll in the five-and-ten store. Several times he had worried the impulsive purchase had been too childish. Yet, he finally relented after Mrs. Greene saw the doll and assured him Cass would appreciate the thought behind the gift and it would be a nice accent on a bed.

Relieved she liked the gift, he could not keep from teasing her. "I figure every little girl should have a doll to play with."

"Ha, ha."

"Mrs. Greene made the blanket. She insisted on usin' it to line the box. Come to think of it, she also gave me the box."

"Sounds like you were planning to simply hand me a bag and say, 'Here, this is for you.' "

Randy's cheeks burned with embarrassment as he remembered his landlady's horror upon learning that was indeed how he planned to give Cass the gift.

"Did she give you the doll also?"

"No, that I bought myself," he said as he removed his necktie and laid it back in its box.

"Why don't you wear your new tie to dinner?" Cass asked, when he reached for his old tie draped over the back of the chair.

"I'm savin' it for a special occasion."

"Such as?"

He shrugged his shoulders before turning toward the mirror. He was so busy stealing glances at her he only succeeded in creating a twisted mess that almost choked him.

"Do you need some help?"

"No, I got it." From the way he was acting around Cass, he could scratch debonair off his list of personality traits.

"What's gotten into you?" She slapped his hands away and undid the knot he had made. "You're all tongue-tied and thumbs today."

"Not enough sleep?" he offered as he mentally scolded his body to behave while she stood close to him. She wore the simple scent of Ivory soap, which was more of a turn-on for him than the overpowering scent of heavy perfume.

"If that's the case, let's get you downstairs and fed so you can come back up here and go to bed." She finished her work to accomplish a more presentable knot.

His body would have reacted to the word "bed" had he not reminded himself that she would not be joining him.

"Are you sure you're not hurryin' downstairs so you can play with the other little girls?"

"What a charmer."

"I haven't even begun to dole out the charm, *ma chérie*." Randy led Cass downstairs, where she headed to the kitchen with the other women while he joined the men in the dining room.

****

"I can't believe you came out of your warm house to walk me home," Cass fussed, continuing the argument that started before they left the brownstone.

They had spent the rest of the afternoon with Mrs. Greene and her family until eight, when Cass announced she had to get home. And though she claimed it wasn't necessary, Randy insisted on walking with her.

"Sax always said if you treat a woman like a queen, she'll treat you like a king," Randy replied, placing a hand on the small of her back as they hurried across 125th Street. He cradled her gift in his other arm.

Though the streets were not as crowded as they normally would be on a Sunday night, they passed a number of pedestrians apparently looking for entertainment. Neither the cold nor the holiday kept some from their parties.

"Did he also teach you all those lines you're always spouting?" Cass asked.

"No, why? What's wrong with my lines?"

"They're lame."

"Girl, you know how to wound a man."

"I rest my case." She adjusted the red-and-white knit scarf around her neck against the wind. "By the way, before we went downstairs for dinner, you called me your cherries."

"Cherries?" He thought for a second. "Oh, you mean, *ma chérie*?"

"Yes, that's it. Why'd you call me that?"

"It's French for 'my darlin'.' I learned a little when I was in New Orleans…tryin' to charm the ladies."

She rolled her eyes. "It figures." It seemed all men were alike. Full of charm…and BS.

"Some men I worked with taught me a few phrases," he continued, ignoring her comment. "They told me the woman I had my eye on would get a kick out of it." With a shudder, he let out a whistle. "Boy, did she ever. I don't know what I said, but I got a kick right in my…well, where it hurts…a lot."

"Ouch, that doesn't pleasant."

"Trust me, it wasn't. Though guess I shouldn't have been surprised. Seems like a lot of people enjoy makin' me the butt of their jokes. At least I'm good for somethin'."

"That's 'cause you're too trusting. When you meet someone, you're quick to assume he's good and has your best interest at heart. Most people could care less about you."

Something a couple of the musicians at The Big House seemed to go out of their way to prove each night he was there. She had given up hoping they would accept him.

"What do you suggest I do? Become suspicious of everyone?"

"No, your innocence's kind of cute. It's what makes you special."

"Innocent and cute? Two words most men wouldn't use to describe themselves."

"Well, you are," Cass said. "But you need to be a bit more careful. Either that or hire someone to watch your back for you."

"Sounds like you're sellin' mob insurance. For a mere five dollars a week you'll find someone to look out for my best interests…or at least my butt."

"Be serious. You know I don't have any dealings with the mob."

"I know. Besides, I'm not interested in some big, hairy guy lookin' out for me when there's a cute little gal who's already doin' a fine job."

Cass threw up her arms. "There he goes with the charm again."

"You think I'm tryin' to throw you a line?" he asked.

"Well, aren't you?"

"You're too suspicious. Girl, I just paid you a compliment, that's all."

She stopped walking and crossed her arms over her chest. "And what do you expect for that compliment?"

Randy stopped and turned back to her. "A thank you."

"And?"

"That's it."

"Fine, thank you."

"If you get any more enthusiastic, you may actually sound like you mean it."

"I give up." She started walking. "First I'm too suspicious. Now my thank you isn't exciting enough. There's no winning with you."

If he were colored, she would have made it clear months earlier she was not interested. However, since he was white, she didn't feel she had anything to worry about and had never said anything to him.

It was the assumption he would not be interested in a colored woman, along with the extra people running around the house, that had made her feel comfortable enough to go up to his room that afternoon.

But considering the amount of time they spent together she thought maybe she needed to let him know where he stood…just to be on the safe side.

"Randy—"

"You've already said I'm naïve and innocent, so what else do you think of me?" he asked.

She briefly considered ignoring the subject change. Yet why ruin the pleasant afternoon they'd spent together by bringing up something he was most likely not entertaining?

"The words 'irritating' and 'aggravating' come to mind," she finally said.

Randy raised his eyebrows. "Really?"

"I could have used the word 'comical.' "

"You know how to make a man feel good about himself. If you keep it up, I may never get out of bed again."

Cass laughed as they stopped in front of her building. As usual, Randy reached over, unlatched the gate, then stepped aside. He did not make a move to follow her as she stepped through. Nor did he seem put off when she closed the gate and leaned forward.

Cass mentally shook her head. How could she have accused him of throwing her a line? He was simply joking around. There was no way he would be interested in her.

"You're also nonjudgmental and you have a good sense of humor." His most impressive qualities.

"Nonjudgmental?"

"Another way of saying colorblind," she clarified. She reached up and took the box from him.

"So you think I'm cute and have a good sense of humor." He wiggled his eyebrows.

"I did not say you were cute. I said your innocence is cute," she clarified. She felt a blush rise to her cheeks as she mentally agreed that he was attractive.

She debated whether his green eyes or his impish grin was his best feature. His eyes reflected his emotions, while his grin was a part of his charm.

As if he could read her mind, the corner of his lips turned up and his eyes danced. It was a draw. Both were equally his best physical features.

"We have an audience," he said, nodding toward the ground floor window where Mrs. Cooper sat staring up at them.

Cass waved at the elderly woman, who did not acknowledge the gesture. She noticed the woman wore the orange knit sweater she had dropped off for her before she left to visit Randy.

"It's good to see her at the window. She's been under the weather the past couple of days."

"Speakin' of which, go inside before you catch cold."

"And you had the nerve to say women are bossy?"

"You can tell me about it tomorrow at rehearsal. Now get."

"Thank you for the present." Cass ran up the steps. She stopped in front of the door and glanced at him over her shoulder.

Randy tipped his hat to her and smiled. As she stepped into the building he turned away, stopped, and looked back. He tipped his hat to Mrs. Cooper, and Cass added "gentleman" to the list of his positive traits.

Chapter 11

Ten minutes before he had to go on stage, Randy stood outside his dressing room and watched as the other performers rushed about, preparing for the show. Those who were ready stood around talking about the party that would take place in four hours, after they welcomed in the New Year.

Cass, who still wore a robe, stood outside the men's dressing room, sassing Eli, who threatened to pull her over his knee. She teased the musician, taking him as seriously as she would an older brother she was determined to torment, and laughed as if she didn't have a care in the world. A contrast from what Randy felt.

They had practiced every day in Mrs. Greene's living room, until Randy was sure he could perform the number in his sleep. Yet the second he stepped inside the club that evening he forgot every note for the song.

What had he been thinking when he agreed to do the closing number with Cass? In the ten years he'd been performing in clubs, he had never had the spotlight on him. He had always been content to sit in the shadows and play his saxophone.

At eight minutes until showtime, Luther came backstage to discover his lead singer was still walking around in a dressing gown. Instead of pleading with her to get ready, like he would do on any other night, he picked her up and carried her to the women's dressing room. Without knocking, he opened the door and deposited her inside, much to the dismay of the chorus girls, who were in various stages of undress and screamed for him to get out.

When Junior appeared and announced they had three minutes, Cass emerged from the dressing room. She wore a black strapless evening dress that hugged her in all the right places, with matching heels. Her hair hung loose, past her shoulders, with the right side pulled back from her face with a silver barrette.

Cass walked over to Luther, who was discussing the last minute details of the show with Red. She spun around in front of the men, showing she was ready. Though clearly relieved, Luther chastised her for worrying him. Like a young girl trying to pacify her father, she gave him a peck on his cheek.

Grabbing his saxophone, Randy headed toward the steps. As he passed the woman, she gave him the once-over. Nodding her approval, she grinned. He returned the smile and, thirty seconds before Junior announced the start of the program, Randy found his courage and no longer felt as if he were going out there alone.

For the next four hours they entertained the clientele who had paid seven dollars a person cover charge for the privilege of ringing in the New Year at The Big House. They moved from one number to the next with smooth transitions that could make the audience believe it was one big number. In what seemed like no time to Randy, the lights dimmed. The spotlight illuminated Cass, who stood at the front of the stage. She smiled and waved to several people while waiting for the room to settle down. Once there was complete silence, she began singing "Dream a Little Dream of Me" *a cappella*.

As she started the second verse, Randy joined in on the saxophone. She continued belting out the lyrics with no other accompaniment. At the end of the fourth verse, she stepped off the stage, into the arms of a gentleman who had been sitting at the first table on the right. Randy played his solo while the couple danced. Near the end, the man whispered in Cass's ear. She laughed and playfully swatted his arm before he helped her back on stage and returned to his seat.

Cass strolled across the stage toward Randy. He winked at her. She smiled back at him, snatched the white carnation off his lapel, and strolled back to the front of the stage. She repeated the third and fourth verse and then finished the song by humming a few notes softer and softer until the only sound was the sax.

A thunderous applause filled the room before the last note faded. Cass stood on the stage beaming at the receptive response. She bowed three times, acknowledging her appreciation to each dining section of the hall. Stepping to the side, she motioned with her hand in Randy's direction. He nodded.

Without his usual scowl, Junior stepped onto the stage, handed Cass a glass of champagne, and invited everyone to join him in ushering in the New Year. The chorus girls moved to the dance floor, while the audience rose to their feet. Shouting at the top of their lungs, they counted down the final ten seconds.

At midnight, the band played "Auld Lang Syne," while the other performers and the audience tossed confetti in the air and blew horns. Cass received a quick hug from Junior, followed by a warm embrace and peck on the cheek from Luther, who had joined them on stage. She then sauntered to the dance floor, where she passed out hugs and well wishes.

Once the song was over, the band began to jam and couples converged on the dance floor. Cass climbed onto the stage and began giving each member of the band pecks on the cheek.

Taking the change in the music as his cue, Randy headed backstage. Away from the crowd, he paused to enjoy the knowledge their number had gone well.

"Randy," Cass called out, running down the steps. She hurried toward him and threw her arms around his neck. He slipped an arm around her waist and held her close to him. He only had a few seconds to enjoy her touch before she pulled back. "They loved us."

"They loved you," he corrected. Though they had barely embraced, he missed the warmth of her body and the feel of her soft curves against him.

"No, they loved us. I was so nervous. I didn't want to say anything before, but Luther had said if the audience liked us, he would consider adding the number to the show."

Randy smiled at the irony. Though he did not have a say over who went on stage, Junior had hinted that if even one person complained about the number, Randy would no longer have a job. With one owner trying to put the spotlight on him and the other trying to get him out of there, they had God working overtime listening to their prayers.

"You were nervous?" he asked. "But you sing every night."

"I always get nervous before performing a new number. There are so many things that could go wrong.

Sweet Jazz

I could forget the words, miss my cue, or the audience could simply hate it. But they didn't. They loved us."

"You could've surprised me. Before the show, you seemed so sure of yourself."

"Trust me, I was a bundle of nerves on the inside. I didn't even eat dinner tonight."

"I haven't eaten either," he confessed.

"You didn't? Then what are you doing down here?" She grabbed his arm and motioned to the steps. "You should be upstairs attacking the food."

Randy laid a hand over hers. "I'd love to, but I'm goin' to get ready and go."

"Why? You have somewhere else to go?"

"I bumped into Junior earlier, and he made it clear this is a private party and outsiders are not welcome."

"Randy, you're not an outsider. You're a part of the club."

He shook his head. He appreciated her going out of her way to make him feel welcomed, but he had to face reality. No one, including him, would feel comfortable if he stayed.

"Cass, it's nice you want to believe that, but I only work here. I'm not a part of this club…this family."

She gave his arm a slight tug. "Come on. I don't see any reason for you to leave. You could stay on one side of the hall, away from Junior."

"Cass," the man in question called out from the foot of the steps. "There are people upstairs who want to see you."

"I'll be there in a minute."

"Hey, Junior, Happy New Year," Randy greeted.

Junior grunted.

Cass released Randy's arm and placed her hands

on her hips. "Junior, we're celebrating. Can't you be pleasant for a change?"

"I will once he leaves," Junior mumbled before heading back upstairs.

Cass sighed.

"It's all right. I think I'll make his night and leave."

"Do you have any plans?"

"No, I think I'll just head home."

"At least stop in somewhere and have a drink or something."

"I'll think about it," he said, though he could not think of anyplace he could go by himself and not feel like an outsider. At least at the boarding house he'd be able to sit in the kitchen and talk with Mrs. Davis and Mrs. Greene, who had not made plans for going out that evening.

"Cass!" Junior yelled again.

"I'm coming," she called back.

Before Randy realized what was happening, she grabbed his face and planted a kiss on his lips. Stunned by the action, Randy barely heard her wish him "Happy New Year." She said a few more things before rushing back to the party, but all he could think about was the feel of her lips on his and the havoc the simple gesture caused his body.

It took him a minute before he gathered his thoughts and went to his dressing room. He quickly packed his instrument, then slipped into his coat, placed his fedora on his head, and headed to the exit.

Outside, the sounds of various celebrations taking place in the neighborhood filled the air. He reached the top of the steps and noticed three large colored men blocking the way to the street.

"May I help you?" was all he managed to get out before one of the men grabbed him by the front of his coat and shoved him against the building. He was about to tell them in which pocket they could find his money when it dawned on him muggers did not wear suits that cost more than he made in three months.

A fist slammed into his gut with so much force he felt as if he had been ripped open. He doubled over, dropping his suit and sax case. His head felt light and his legs rubbery. Before he could fall to his knees, two of the men grabbed him and slammed him back to the wall.

They pinned him against the building as the third man used his face as a punching bag. With each blow, his vision became blurrier and the stars in his eyes became brighter. Blood dripped from his nose and the tear in his lip.

It seemed an eternity before he was released and permitted to slide to his knees. A punch snapped his head back. He hit the wall before crumpling to the ground.

A foot connected with his stomach. The kick was followed by another, then another. Covering his head, he curled up into a ball and prayed it would quickly end.

When the blows finally stopped, Randy waited until he heard fading steps before uncovering his head. Through the one eye he could open, he saw two of the men walking toward the end of the alley. The third frowned down at him.

"Stay away from our women," the last attacker warned, before delivering a kick to Randy's ribs.

Without another word, the man followed his

accomplices.

Unable to catch his breath to call out for help, Randy attempted to push himself up. The world spun and he fell back. He blindly reached out until his hand found his saxophone. Once he held the case, he stopped fighting consciousness and allowed his world to go black.

Chapter 12

The pounding woke Randy. He pressed the palm of his hand to his temple, which threatened to split open. He groaned at the unnaturally cheery voice singing his name.

Silently he cursed to himself. Cass would have been a sight for sore eyes—well, at least the one eye he could open. If he had known then the result of her innocent peck, he would not have let her break away as fast she did. Instead, he would have grabbed her and kissed her back, making it worth the beating.

Cass pounded on the door again. At any other time, he would admire her persistence, but at that moment, he wished she would go away and leave him to suffer in peace. His body had no desire to leave the soft bed he had managed to find his way to, after regaining consciousness earlier that morning.

"Chile, you break that door, and you're gonna pay for a new one," Mrs. Greene called upstairs. "Whatcha tryin' to do up there? Wake the dead?"

"I'm trying to wake these sinners so they don't miss service," Cass called back.

"Service?" the older lady snorted. "Lord knows the last time you've been inside a church."

"What the hell's goin' on out there?" The voice belonged to the rather large man who rented the room across from Randy's.

"And, good morning—oops, I mean afternoon—to you," Cass greeted.

"Someone should beat your butt for makin' that noise."

Demonstrating a speed he did not know he possessed, Randy stumbled off the bed to let Cass in before his neighbor decided to volunteer for the mission.

"Honey, you couldn't handle this," Cass sassed as the door opened and she was yanked into the dark room.

"You better handle your woman," his neighbor ordered, and slammed his door.

"What the hell was that all about?" Randy mumbled, pushing his own door closed. He shrugged out of his coat and jacket and dropped them on the floor.

"I'm sorry," Cass said, her voice dripping with feigned innocence. "Did I wake you?"

"Girl—" A hiss cut off the rest of what he was going to say as he sat down on the bed. He dropped his head into his hands.

"That must've been some party you found. The shade's down and you're still in the clothes you were wearing last night. Were you in bed with your coat and shoes on?"

He kicked off a shoe. "No," he mumbled under his breath.

"I don't care how hung over you are, we have work to do." She raised the shade, allowing the sun into the room. "So, I suggest you get up and—"

Cass's cheerful banter ceased when he raised his head. He did not need a mirror to tell him what his face looked like. Her reaction said it all. In a matter of seconds, her expression changed from happy to shocked to horrified.

"Shit, what the fuck happened to you?" she asked as she dropped her handbag to the floor. Her profanity confirmed just how bad his face looked. No matter what happened at the club, the strongest words she uttered were an occasional "hell" or "damn."

"Girl, you got a filthy mouth," Randy replied.

"I don't give a damn about my mouth. What happened to you?"

"Someone didn't like our new number. You know. Everyone's a critic."

"How can you joke like that?" She placed her hands on her hips. "Have you seen your face?"

"No, 'fraid to look into the mirror. Might break it. Seven years' bad luck, you know."

Cass rolled her eyes. "Funny. Real funny."

"I thought so myself." Randy smiled. At least he tried to force the corners of his lips to turn up. Giving up, he dropped back onto the bed. A sharp pain shot through his right side, and he regretted his action.

"Who did this to you? Did you talk to the police? What the hell were you doing fighting?"

"Trust me, I wasn't fightin'. It was more like me bein' held down and havin' the crap beat out of me."

Cass tugged on his arm. "Come on, you need to see a doctor," she insisted.

"Let me just lay here and I'll be fine." He closed his eyes.

"Lie there. Look at you. You're a mess. You need—"

"Damn, girl, don't matter whether you're colored

or white, all women are the same. You don't know when to shut up and let a man die in peace."

The second the words were out of his mouth, Randy was sorry he'd said them. With a huff she released his arm. Her pumps slapped against the bare floor as she stomped across the room. His door hinges squealed.

Randy opened his one good eye as the tail of her coat swung out of the room. Fighting against the sharp pain in his side, he tried to sit.

"Wait, Cass," he called out. A wave of dizziness forced him back down as the door slammed shut.

Randy cursed as he closed the eye that wasn't already swollen shut. At least his attackers had got what they wanted. With Cass never speaking to him, there was no chance of her lips ever touching his again.

****

Cass didn't know why she bothered. It wasn't like she didn't have enough to do so she had to fuss over a man who refused to take care of himself.

From his grimaces, it was obvious Randy needed a doctor, not the alcohol-drenched washrag she held. But, no, he was too stubborn to seek a professional.

She had a right mind to drop the cloth on his face, pick up her bag, and go home. Yet the purple and black bruises on his face, along with the crusted blood on his lip and above his eye, brought out the caretaker in her. She couldn't leave him in his condition, no matter how much he tried to push her away.

Trying not to jar the bed, she leaned over and dabbed at the cut over his left eye.

"Crap," Randy cursed. He opened his right eye and stared at her with disbelief. "I thought you left."

Sweet Jazz

"I went downstairs to get a washrag and some alcohol," she replied. She sat on the edge of the bed.

"Why?"

"Somebody's got to take care of you. It's obvious you won't."

"Look who's being funny now. Maybe you should add comedy to your routine."

Cass bit the inside of her lip to stifle a laugh at his attempt to roll his eye. "That's an idea," she said as she tried to clean away the dried blood around his lip. "We could do the act together."

"What'd we call ourselves? The Chocolate Twins? Coffee and Cream?"

"Which one would you be? Coffee?"

Randy let out a chuckle that turned into a groan. "Don't make me laugh," he said, holding his right side.

"I prefer Sweet Chocolate," Cass said. "Of course, I think Black and Blue would suit you better."

"You're a real comedian, all right. Kick a man when he's down."

"Now, honey, you know I'd never do that." She placed the washcloth on the bed next to his head and reached for his belt.

"What do you think you're doin'?" he asked, grabbing her wrists.

He had a strong grip for someone as battered as he was. There were callouses on his hand, which she suspected he'd gotten working odd jobs when he couldn't find a gig in a club. However, from watching how he held his saxophone, she'd seen how those same strong, rough hands could be gentle.

"I want to see why you're holding your side," she replied.

"Why are you undoin' my pants?"

"Easier to get your shirt out of them that way."

"Never mind my shirt." He released her wrists.

"Don't be shy. You don't have anything I haven't seen a thousand times before."

"A thousand?" Randy cocked his right eyebrow. "You have a side job I don't know about?"

"Okay, maybe not a thousand times, but I do have a couple nephews. I've changed their diapers, and I'm sure you have the same things they do."

"Girl, trust me, there's a difference between them and me," Randy said.

"Besides your skin color and the fact that they're more agreeable with a rash on their rear than you are right now, I can't imagine what."

"You're much too bold for your own good."

"How's this? I'll cover my eyes and you take the shirt off." Cass placed her hands on her face. Her fingers were spread apart and eyes wide open. "I promise I won't peek."

"Ouch." Randy grabbed his side as a laugh escaped. "Don't make me laugh."

She lowered her hands. "Sorry, but I had to do something. You're a miserable patient. Now about your shirt."

"Okay, okay, okay, you win."

"I can take it off?"

"No," he snapped, struggling to sit up. "I can take it off by myself."

"How?" She grabbed his arm. "You can't even sit up by yourself."

"Yap, yap, yap, yap, yap. Are you goin' to help me or keep flappin' your trap?"

"Rhyming? You're a poet now?"

He pulled off his tie but had trouble removing his vest with his shaky fingers. After a minute of watching, she lost her patience and pushed his hands away.

To his credit, he seemed to know when to give up and did not argue as she removed his vest and shirt.

"What did they beat you with?" she asked, examining the purple and black bruises on his arms.

"Their fists—"

"Fists did this?" She lifted his undershirt.

"When I fell to the ground, they kicked me. Careful," he groaned, when Cass touched a purple bruise on his right side.

"You should go to the hospital. You could have a broken rib."

"Nothing's broken."

"How can you be sure?"

"I've broken a couple of bones in my life."

"I never knew playing the sax could be so dangerous."

"It's not, but upsettin' a glass of milk in my house was. That could earn you a busted rib and arm."

Cass's head snapped up. "That's not funny, Randy," she said, though there was no hint of amusement in his eye.

"I wasn't jokin'."

She didn't mean to stare with her mouth hanging open, but it was hard for her to believe anyone could beat a child for a minor infraction like spilling milk. Sure, a switch was used by her parents on her and her siblings when they were younger. It was only for breaking rules—like lying, stealing, or causing danger to themselves or others—or to put a child back in her place when she got too fresh with an elder. Spilt milk was not considered serious enough to warrant a spanking…a lecture, maybe, but not a spanking, and certainly not a beating that resulted in broken bones.

"Randy—"

He placed a finger on her lips. "No, not now, Cass," he said, shaking his head. "I don't want to talk about it now. Maybe another time."

She reached up and covered his hand with hers. She wanted to ask him questions but was prevented when Mrs. Greene barged into the room.

"What's this I hear about you fightin'?" the older woman asked, showing no concern about finding Cass sitting on Randy's bed with him partially dressed.

"I wasn't fightin'," Randy insisted.

"You don't look like that from playin' pinochle."

"Trust me, I wasn't fightin'," he repeated. "I didn't even get to throw a punch."

"Then what happened?" Mrs. Greene asked.

****

Randy hesitated as he tried to decide what and how much he would tell the women. Without a doubt, Mrs. Greene would have plenty to say about him working at The Big House if he told them the truth. Cass would assume Junior was behind his attack and head off to confront the man. And though he also suspected Junior was involved, or maybe because of his suspicions, he did not want her in the middle of it.

"Well, what happened?" Mrs. Greene asked again, tapping her foot against the hardwood floor.

Knowing he wouldn't be able to dodge the older woman's questions, Randy gave the women a quick recap of what had transpired after he stepped from The

Big House. He left out the warning he'd received before the final kick was delivered.

During his explanation, Cass held his hand in her lap. He wondered what the punishment for that gesture would be. Hell, he'd probably earned another asskicking from her simply stepping foot in his room.

"You lay in that alley and nobody helped you?" Mrs Greene asked.

"Besides Randy, I'm the only other person who leaves through the back," Cass explained. "This morning, I left with Florence through the front."

He saw the guilt in her eyes and knew she felt somewhat responsible for deviating from the routine he suspected she'd started after he was hired.

He gently squeezed her hand. When she glanced at him, he shook his head to let her know he did not blame her for anything.

"Considerin' the circumstances, you don't have to worry about the rent this week," Mrs. Greene announced.

"I have the money. They didn't take anythin'."

"They didn't? Then why would they do this?"

Randy shrugged his shoulders. Mrs. Greene stared at him, her tapping foot the only sound in the room. It didn't take a genius to realize she didn't accept his response and knew he wasn't telling them everything.

"Lucky for you, we don't have to be back at the club until Wednesday," Cass said, saving him from further interrogation from the older woman.

"The way I feel, I may have to miss a couple of nights. With this lip, I won't be able to play even if I do show up."

"I have a liniment you could put on those bruises,"

Mrs. Greene offered, switching from the role of interrogator to caregiver. "I made a stew this mornin'. I'll brin' up a tray."

"Mrs. Greene, no—" he started, but she was already out of the room. "Damn."

"What's wrong?" Cass asked, placing her free hand on his shoulder to prevent him from going after his landlady. The move was unnecessary. He did not have it in him to chase after the woman.

"I don't want her to make a trip back up here for nothin'. I can't stomach anythin' right now."

"What you need is some rest. And a doctor," she muttered. He opened his mouth to argue, but she cut in, "But, since you refuse to see one, lie down while I go downstairs and tell her you'll eat later."

Cass released his hand and gently pushed him back. With a sigh, Randy obeyed. She always seemed to be going above and beyond for him, even after he acted like an ass.

"Hey, Cass?"

"Yes," she answered as she stood.

"I'm sorry for what I said before, about women not knowin' when to shut up."

She removed his other shoe. "Don't worry about it. We'll discuss it when you're better able to defend yourself," she teased, pulling over him the blankets that had been pushed to the foot of his bed.

He closed his eyes. "Thanks, you're all heart."

She chuckled as she left the room.

It didn't take him long to drift off to sleep. When he opened his eyes again, Cass was sitting in a chair by the window. The shade had been pulled down again, all but a crack to allow just enough light so she could see the coat spread across her lap. She sewed a last stitch before breaking the thread with her teeth and shoving the needle into a spool of thread, which she set on the windowsill. She then stood, held the coat out, and examined it. Nodding her satisfaction, she draped the garment over the back of the chair.

"I wish it was that easy to fix me," Randy said.

With a squeal, Cass spun around. "Good Lord, you scared me. How long have you been awake?"

"About a minute or two."

"Why didn't you say anything?"

"'Cause I enjoyed watchin' you." He tried again but was still unable to get his lips to turn up.

"I could throttle you for scaring me like that."

"Girl, could you at least wait until I recover from my last beatin'?" he asked as he struggled to sit up. "What are you doin' here?"

"You seem to ask me that a lot. Keep it up and I'm going to start feeling unwelcome."

"Trust me, that's the last thing you should worry about." He enjoyed having her around more than she realized. Just something as simple as sitting and talking made him feel welcomed, as if he was a part of something.

"I sat with Mrs. Greene for a while. When I came back up to get my things, I noticed your coat and decided to mend it. How do you feel?"

"Like I had the crap kicked out of me."

"Oh, poor baby. I know what would make you feel better."

"What?"

Cass yanked the blankets off him. "A shower and food."

Though the radiator under the window provided sufficient heat to the room, he missed the coziness of the covers. "You've got to be kiddin'," he grumbled as he reached out for the blankets. To his dismay, she pulled them off the bed. "I don't even think I have the strength to get out of this bed."

"Come on," she insisted, tugging on his arm.

"Is that an order?"

"Yes, it is."

"That kid was right," he complained as he slowly sat up. Every nerve in his body seemed to scream in protest. "Women are bossy."

She released his hand and moved across the room. "Oh, hush and go take a shower." She snatched the washcloth and towel from the rack on the outside of his closet door and tossed them on the bed next to him. "Mrs. Greene went out, but she left some food in the kitchen for you. I'll make you a plate."

"Whatever you say, boss."

She watched him, appearing ready to sprint to his side and catch him at the first sign that he would fall face first onto the floor. To his credit, he summoned the strength to not only get to his feet but remain there.

Randy picked up the cloth and towel and shuffled into the bathroom. As he closed the door, he avoided looking in the mirror. Having seen the results in the past of having a fist introduced to his face, he did not need to see his reflection to know he looked a sight.

The warm water eased some of the kinks in his muscles, and when he stepped out of the shower fifteen minutes later he felt a bit refreshed. Once he'd dried off, he glanced around and realized he'd forgotten to bring a change of clothes with him.

"Cass?" he called.

When she did not answer, he rushed to his room with his towel around his waist. She had switched on the lamp on the end of his dresser. The sheets on his bed had been changed and the blankets turned down. His coat hung on the back of the closet door, while the clothes she had helped him out of earlier were folded on his table.

He had just pulled on a pair of green pajama pants when Cass opened the door and waltzed into the room, carrying a tray of food. The rich smell made his stomach growl, reminding him it had been over twenty-four hours since his last meal.

"How was your shower?" she asked.

"Wet," he mumbled, determined to be difficult to avoid an "I told you so." He didn't think there'd be any living with her if she knew she'd been right.

She placed the tray of the table. "And you have the nerve to call me sassy."

"I learnt from the best."

Cass sucked her teeth as she picked up his shirt. She did not appear fazed by his state of undress as she helped him put it on.

"Be nice. I brought you a bowl of chicken and dumpling, some bread and butter, and a root beer. After you eat, I'll rub some of the liniment on your bruises."

She finished buttoning his shirt, then placed a hand on his chest, guiding him back to the bed. He grimaced as he lowered himself to the mattress.

"Are you sure you don't need a doctor?" she asked, her voice filled with concern.

"For what?" he replied. "All he'll do is clean my cuts and then tell me to go home and get some rest. It's the same thing you did. The difference is you're a lot more pleasant to look at."

Cass snorted as she carried the tray over to him and placed it on his lap. "Even battered and bruised, you're able to dish out the manure."

He reached for the spoon only to have her snatch it out of his hand. She reached behind her and dragged her chair close to the bed.

"Cass, this isn't necessary," Randy protested, sensing what she had planned. It was one thing for her to clean a cut, but feeding him? That was something he couldn't remember anyone doing for him since he could hold a utensil.

"Sit back and enjoy being waited on," she chided. "Besides, the more food we get in you, the quicker you'll heal and the sooner I'll get to fuss with you about your comment on women."

"I should have known there was more to this than simple concern about my well-bein'."

"Oh, hush and eat." She stuck a spoonful of stew in his mouth.

Chapter 13

Randy sat on the window ledge, playing "As Time Goes By." The swelling of his lip had gone down and, though it was a bit tender, it allowed him to play a medley of his favorite tunes.

Cass's laughter from below announced her arrival. She had stopped by every day since New Year's, sitting with him for hours, telling him stories about her life on the farm and anecdotes about The Big House.

He finished the song and left his perch to open the door, swinging it wide just as Cass raised her fist to knock.

"You were staring up at the clouds. I didn't think you saw me coming down the street," she greeted.

"I didn't. I heard you laugh and decided I better open the door before we have a repeat performance of Sunday."

"You mean you didn't like my wakeup call?" She pouted. "I'm hurt."

"Trust me, I'd love to be awakened by you every day, I just don't like havin' to save your behind from a whoopin'."

"And here I thought you liked helping damsels in distress."

"I don't mind helpin' damsels, but could you wait awhile? Let's say ten, fifteen years?"

"Speaking of helping, please take this bag. My

arm's getting tired." Cass held out a shopping bag.

"What's this?" he asked, taking the bag.

"If you invite me in, I'll be happy to tell you."

He stepped aside and Cass strolled into the room. She headed straight to the open window and closed it.

"I'm glad I came by. What are you trying to do? Catch pneumonia?"

"I wanted some air."

"You catch pneumonia, and you'll be laid up in a hospital room that's stuffier than here." She dropped her purse onto his unmade bed, shrugged out of her coat, and laid it on top. The day after his attack she had given up trying to keep his bed made, muttering under her breath that if he wanted to live like a slob then she'd let him. However, she made her declaration as she moved about the room, hanging up the clothes he had tossed on the back of a chair.

"How'd the show go last night?" he asked as he placed the bag on the table. "Did Junior threaten to find someone to take my place?"

"The moment he realized you weren't showing up, he put the word out that we needed a new sax player. He's probably holding auditions as we speak," Cass teased.

"The man's all heart. If I dropped dead on the stage, he'd start holdin' auditions before they got my body outa the club." Randy disassembled his instrument, wiping down each piece before placing it in the case open on the bed.

"Man, you're so full of yourself. Junior wouldn't wait that long. He'd start the auditions before your body hit the floor. That's after he danced around it several times."

"I bet you'd join him."

"No, I'd cry."

"You would?" He glanced over his shoulder at her.

"Of course I would. Just the thought of having to sit through auditions again is enough to bring tears to my eyes." She rubbed an invisible tear from her cheek and sniffed.

"You're all heart," he mumbled, turning back to his saxophone.

"Everyone sends their best wishes for a speedy recovery."

"Everyone?"

"Okay, Luther, Red, Eli, and a couple of the girls, including Florence."

"That sounds more realistic." Randy closed the case and turned back to the table. "Now, what's in here?" he asked, pointing to the bag.

"Open it and see."

He did as he was told. "Smells good," he commented as he pulled out four covered plates and a bowl.

Like a child ripping paper off a Christmas present, he peeled away the aluminum foil over the dishes. He uncovered a mountain of fried chicken, macaroni and cheese, collard greens, cornbread, and an apple pie.

"Mrs. Greene said she wouldn't be around today, so I brought you a little something. Now sit down and eat, so we can get you back to work."

A little something? There was enough food to last him three days.

Randy sat at the table while Cass reached into the bag and retrieved a fork. Ignoring the utensil, he grabbed a chicken breast and bit into it.

"Damn, girl," he said between bites. "This is good."

"It's Momma's recipe. She taught me everything I know about cooking." Cass sat in the chair across from him. She reached for a wing and picked at it.

"Tell her I said she taught you well."

Every day Cass received a note from a relative with news about life in North Carolina. She immediately wrote back with stories of her own. Sometimes she wrote the letters during their rehearsals. It was then he learnt she mentioned him in her correspondences.

He did not mind her including him. It made him feel like part of a family. Eventually, he began dictating a line or two of greetings to them.

"She'll be glad to hear that."

Randy picked the fork off the table and practically inhaled the macaroni and cheese that was still warm despite the journey from her place to his in the cold weather.

"Eww, didn't anyone teach you table manners?"

"This is good," he answered, without swallowing what was in his mouth.

"How can you tell, when you're shoving it down like that?"

"Trust me, I can tell." He took a chicken leg. "You can cook. You can sew. And you can sing like an angel. Why are you up here by yourself instead of settled down south with a man?"

"'Cause I wanted to see the world."

"Darlin', I hate to tell you this, but New York isn't the world," he said before taking a bite from the chicken.

"I know, but it's as far as my husband and I got,"

she said.

Randy gasped and choked on the food he had started chewing.

"That's what you get for eating like an animal," she scolded. She got up and walked around the table. He jumped up and backed away from her.

"Husband?" he shouted between coughs. Everything started to make sense to him—why he had never been invited to her apartment; why most nights she left the club after she finished a show; and why the men took exception to the innocent kiss.

"Yes, my husband and I—"

"Husband? As in stand before a preacher kinda husband?"

"Yes?" Cass answered. She took a step toward him. He took two steps back.

"As in united in holy matrimony kinda husband?"

"Yes, so?"

"As in big colored man tryin' to rip my heart out through my ass 'cause his woman's in my room kinda husband?"

Cass shook her head. "No, as in I was young and made a mistake but I grew up and corrected the situation. I'm divorced."

"Divorced?"

She nodded. "Yes, divorced." She stepped back to the table and sat down. "The marriage was an error in judgment."

Randy also returned to the table. "You were blinded by love?"

"More like blinded by the promise of adventure."

"You saw marriage as an adventure?"

"It wasn't the marriage but the things he promised

me. Don't get me wrong; there was love in my marriage. At least I thought there was. I thought he loved me, and I fooled myself into believing I loved him. But the reality was my head was more turned by the things he promised me."

Randy shook his head. "Come again."

****

Her marriage and how naïve she had been was not a topic she readily talked about. But she felt comfortable with Randy and knew he would not judge her for her folly.

"When I was a kid, I could only go to school until I was thirteen," she explained, deciding to start with her deepest desire, which her ex-husband had used to gain her trust. "There were no colored schools for older children in the town, and my family could not afford to send me away to continue my studies. But the few years I had of school were not enough to satisfy me.

"I once asked Grandma if she went to school when she was a kid. She told me no, 'cause the masters knew once the slaves got a taste of knowledge, they wouldn't be content with their situation and would want more. I didn't understand what she meant, until I was fourteen."

"What happened?" Randy asked, pushing the food away and giving her his full attention.

"One morning, I was in the field when some children walked by on their way to school. At that moment I was no longer satisfied picking cotton, feeding the chickens, or milking the cows. I knew there was more to life than that farm and the small town where my family did their shopping, and I wanted to experience that life."

"And you thought marriage was the answer?"

"At the time, yes. I was barely sixteen when I first met Henry. He showed up at church one Sunday wearing a fancy suit and with his hair conked. After service he bragged about his trips to Chicago, New Orleans, and New York. Little did I know he'd never been out of North Carolina. I later figured out he'd mentioned those places hoping I'd be so impressed I'd let him under my skirt."

"Did you?"

"Hell, no," she exclaimed, jerking back. "Daddy would've killed me if I'd been messing around with some man. And then he'd turn over what was left of me to Momma so she could finish the job."

"So Henry married you to get you in bed?"

Cass rolled her eyes and sucked her teeth. "Now, why would he marry me to get in my drawers when he could sweet talk a sillier girl who'd give him access after one hello? I'm not that special." That was something she had learnt after their marriage, when she realized she wasn't special enough for him to honor his vows.

Randy shook his head as if to disagree with her, but he did not elaborate.

"Henry married me to get his hands on the hundred dollars Grandma left me when she died. I had told him about the money one afternoon when he was walking me home from church. I should've known something was wrong, 'cause I barely finished telling him about it when he was asking me to marry him."

"So you got married and he got his money?"

"Yes and no. We got married, but he didn't get his hands on the money. My parents knew what he was all about, and they had expressed their dislike for him when he started walking me home from church services two months earlier. They said he was a sneaky, lying, con man who was up to no good. But, thinking they didn't know anything about big city folks, I refused to listen to them."

She glanced down at the table, running a finger over the smooth linoleum surface. If there was anything she was embarrassed about regarding the situation, it was her stubbornness in not listening to her parents' warning. She was ashamed to have ignored their wisdom, thinking she knew more than they did since she had more schooling and a little book knowledge.

"Knowing my parents would never agree to the marriage, I suggested we elope. I figured once we were married Papa would have no choice but to accept him. The next morning, Henry and a friend of his met me on the road, a mile from my parents' house. We drove to the next town, where a preacher married us in a short ceremony, with his wife as the second witness. Afterwards, we had cake and punch before returning to the farm."

"How did your parents take it?" Randy asked.

"When we got back, Papa came from the field and ordered Henry off the farm and me into the house. Feeling I was a woman 'cause I was married, I walked up to him and told him he couldn't throw Henry off the farm 'cause he was my husband. Instead of congratulating us, Papa called Henry everything but a child of God and declared that as long as I called myself Mrs. Scotts and chose to associate with trash, I was not to set foot back on the farm.

"Henry told Papa once I got my stuff, we'd leave, but my father refused to let me into the house. He insisted everything in there belonged to him, and since I was married, my husband could provide for me. When Henry mentioned the money Grandmother had left me, Papa said the money belonged to his daughter, not a lowlife's wife.

"At that, Henry changed from the wonderful, sweet-talking man I married to a foul-mouthed monster. He began using language I'd never considered thinking in my parents' presence, much less saying."

Looking back at it, she should have disassociated herself from Henry the moment the man disrespected her parents on their property. If he didn't have respect for his elders, what made her think he'd respect her?

"Papa had Momma get his shotgun from over the front door. Once he had that gun, he told Henry that he could either shut his mouth or have it shut for him. Now, I'm telling you, Henry may've been called many things, but no one ever said he was stupid. As soon as he saw that gun, he pushed me back into the car and told his friend to drive."

"How'd you end up in New York?" Randy asked.

"We stayed with his aunt for three months, before she kicked us out 'cause of Henry's drinking, fooling around, and laziness. That's when Henry decided we should head north, where one of his friends had moved a year earlier. I thought once we got here things would get better, he'd get a job, and we'd fine a nice place of our own." Cass sighed. "Things just got worse. He'd go out at night and not return until morning. He wouldn't hold a job, and whatever money we did have, he spent on booze and women."

"Why didn't you leave him and go back to your parents?"

"I guess I stayed with him 'cause I was hoping things would work out. Everyone had told me what Henry was about before I married him, and I wanted to prove them wrong. I even made excuses for him—he couldn't find anything up to his standards, and it's hard for a colored man to get ahead in this world. Meanwhile, I supported us with the money I earned as a maid. I paid for our room and put food on the table. I even gave Henry spending money, to keep him from going through my purse."

Cass glanced up, expecting a smug grin. Instead, he frowned. There was sympathy in his eyes.

"What finally made you decide to make him your ex?"

"I had the sense knocked into me."

Randy's frown became more intense and his eyes narrowed. "He hit you?" His voice deepened with rage.

"Only once, but that one blow was enough to get me thinking straight. I had come home from work one evening to find him sitting around, drinking with some hussy. It was bad enough he'd go out and spend the money I worked hard for, but when he decided to bring his women to the room I paid rent for, I knew I had to speak up.

"I snatched that drink out of her hands and ordered her out of my home. Henry told me I had no right to speak to his guest that way, so I reminded him who paid the rent. I also told him that once he started contributing money to the house he could invite over whoever he damn well pleased. Until then, no one was allowed into the room unless I invited them. That's when he backslapped me."

"What'd you do?" Randy asked. He had flinched

when she mentioned the slap, and his hands, which rested on the table, balled into fists. He appeared ready to get up and find Henry to retaliate for the incident that had taken place four years earlier.

"I grabbed the bottle of gin off the table and broke it upside his head."

"Good girl," he said, his shoulders relaxing slightly, though his fists stayed clenched.

"Momma raised all her children to know that no man should hit a woman. She wouldn't even let Daddy spank me. She oversaw my punishments. Daddy only laid hands on me to give me a hug. So if my own father wasn't going to hit me, I wasn't going to stand for another man to do it."

"What did Henry do? Did he hit you back?"

"I'm sure he wanted to strangle me, but I was still holding what was left of the bottle. I guess he thought better than to come near me again and settled for cussin' me." Cass chuckled. "All his little hussy could do was jump up and down and scream, 'Oh, Lawdy, you kilt him. You done kilt Henry.' "

Randy laughed at her high-pitched imitation.

"By then, a crowd had gathered outside our room 'cause it sounded like a war was going on in there. Henry was cussin'. The hussy was screaming. The landlady was there, threatening to call the cops. And I was yelling they should get an ambulance, 'cause if Henry came near me again, he'd need one.

"One of the other boarders finally convinced Henry and the hussy to leave, and the cops were not called. But the next day he got his revenge."

"How?" Randy asked.

"The next morning, I packed Henry's things. I

knew where that hussy lived, and I planned to take his things there after work and tell her she was welcome to his worthless behind. But when I got to work, I found out Henry had stopped by, told my boss I had quit, and collected all the money I was owed. Though I insisted it was a mistake, she refused to rehire me. She didn't want any part of what was going on between Henry and me.

"I left there and I went to the hussy's apartment, where I was told she'd left that morning for California, where her man was going to make her a star. Knowing Henry had no money of his own, I knew he went back to our room and took the money I'd stored in a jar in the closet.

"Of course, he couldn't stop there. I got home and was told he'd bumped into the landlady. When she told him she didn't appreciate the behavior displayed the previous night, he cussed her until she told him she was putting us out."

"So Henry left you with no home, no job, and no money?"

"So he thought. A friend had advised me to put aside some money where Henry couldn't find it. For once, I'd listened to someone, and I kept my savings in an envelope under a floorboard, under the bed. I had enough to get me a room somewhere else and tide me over for a couple of weeks until I got my job at The Big House."

"Have you seen him since that night?"

"I didn't, but I had the pleasure of seeing that hussy. Twenty-four months after she left with my husband, she came to The Big House looking for him, with one child on her hip and another one in her belly.

They had made it as far as Arkansas with the money they had taken from me. They must have been trying to live large, 'cause there had been enough money in that jar to make it to California and back.

"Now, I hadn't seen that man and I didn't know or care whose bed he was laying his head in at nights, I just wanted to be free of him. I had already filed for divorce and was waiting for my day in court."

"I've heard divorces can be hard to get."

"They are. I had to file for mine on the grounds of adultery. And even though Henry had up and left me two years earlier, my lawyer had warned me that without a witness to the adultery I might not win my case."

"Now, how'd they expect you to find a witness?" Randy asked. "They expected one of his women to go in front of the judge and admit to havin' an affair with your husband?"

"The hussy did."

Randy slumped back in the chair with his mouth hanging open.

"Every time that hussy walked into my life, good things happened for me. The first time I met her, you can say I saw the light, and the second time she helped me get my divorce."

"You're tellin' me she walked into court and told the judge she slept with your husband?"

Cass nodded. "She came to The Big House thinking she'd find Henry there with me. I told her I didn't know where he was, but I was sure he'd show up at the courthouse three days later. I knew he wasn't going to be there, but I was hoping she'd be stupid enough to show up looking for him."

"And was she?"

"Just as I figured, she waddled into the courthouse with her son and her swollen belly." Cass smiled as she recalled the scene. "When it was my turn, the judge asked where Henry was. I told him I didn't know but maybe she could help. He called the hussy up, and I just stepped back and let her ramble on about how she traveled all the way back to New York from Arkansas searching for Henry 'cause he needed to come home and take care of his children. She went on and on about how they had been together for three months before they left New York and then right up until two months earlier, when he went out to get a shoeshine and never returned to the room they were renting. She talked so much the judge was signing the papers granting me my divorce before she finished her story."

"What did she do when she figured out she'd been used?"

"I don't think she ever realized it. She was upset she didn't see him."

"How'd your family take the news of your divorce?"

"Joe wrote that they went out and celebrated for me."

The best surprise she received was a call from her father. He had walked to town to use the telephone at the store to tell her he was sorry things had not worked out. It had been the first time she had contact with either of her parents in four years.

"And you've been alone up here since then?"

"I've been on my own, but I wouldn't say I'm alone. I have my family at The Big House, and my friends."

"Would you ever…I mean, do you think…?"

Cass shook her head. "No, my experience with Henry convinced me marriage was not for me," she answered without hesitation. "Momma and Papa have been together for over thirty years, so I know successful marriages are not just fantasies. I just don't believe that's going to be a part of my reality."

Chapter 14

The clap snapped Randy back to reality. He glanced at the annoyed owner of the thin, smooth hands that were inches from his face.

"I'm sorry I'm so boring you have to daydream," Cass said.

"What makes you think I was daydreamin'?"

"No reason. You always sit around staring at nothing with a lost look on your face while I talk to myself." She snapped her fingers. "Oh, wait, I wasn't talking to myself, I was talking to you, but you weren't listening because you were daydreaming."

Unable to deny the accusation, Randy simply grinned. Taking advantage of Junior's week-long vacation out of the city, they were rehearsing at The Big House, which served as an unfortunate distraction for him. On stage, Cass was more alive when singing. She moved with the music, beginning with a slight sway of the shoulders, which worked its way down to her hips by the end of the song.

There was a natural sensuous flow in her movements that would drive any man crazy. He would be lying if he said watching her had not affected him. He'd have to be blind or like men for that to have not stirred something inside him, and since he was neither, he was glad the pants he was wearing were loose.

"I was wondering if you could dance," Randy

confessed, omitting he would prefer the dancing to be done horizontally, not vertically.

"Can I dance? What kind of a question is that? You've seen me dance."

"How do I know?" He cocked an eyebrow. "Maybe you dance like you play the piano. You only know one move."

Cass placed her hands on her hips and rolled her eyes.

"Well, can you?" he asked, wishing she'd move her hands somewhere else to get his mind off that part of her body.

"Of course I can," she responded, folding her arms under her chest. "What brought that up?"

The new placement of her arms wasn't exactly what he had been hoping for. It only succeeded in shifting his attention to her breasts. He mentally groaned.

Though he forced himself to look into her eyes, the image of her body was etched in his mind. How could a fully clothed—and modestly dressed—woman cause such a reaction from him?

"The way you sashay those hips around, I was wonderin' if you can also move them on a dance floor."

"I do not sashay."

Randy stood from the stool he had perched on during the rehearsal, walked to the edge of the stage, and placed his saxophone in its case. "Girl, the way you move, someone's liable to get hurt if one of those hips gets loose."

Cass threw up her hands, turned, and stalked away.

"Hey, watch it. You nearly took out my eye with those hips."

She grabbed a stack of sheet music off the top of the piano and stomped back toward him with her hand raised. In a quick motion, Randy straightened, caught her raised wrist with one hand, and slipped the other arm around her waist. He pulled her close and began swaying from side to side.

He knew he would be on the receiving end of another beating if someone walked in and found her in his arms, but, for the moment, it was a risk he was willing to take.

"Nice moves," he complimented. "Graceful." He spun around. "Coordinated." He dipped her. "And light on your feet." He pulled her up. "You have some potential."

"Some potential!" Cass pulled free and stepped back.

Randy shrugged. "It's hard to assess your dancin' without music."

"Sometime I'll have to show you what I can really do."

"How about tonight?"

"What?" Her smile faded as the suspicion rose to her eyes. Though he considered her a friend and hoped she saw him as one, she kept him at arm's length, as if she didn't trust his intentions.

"How about tonight?" he repeated. "We can go to the Savoy and you can show me what you can do, unless you're just talk."

As he expected when he issued the challenge, the suspicion was instantly replaced with a spark.

"Do you think you can handle this?" she countered.

"Girl, I can handle anythin' you can dish out."

"We'll see how much you can handle," she called

over her shoulder as she stepped off the stage. "I'll meet you at the ballroom at nine."

Randy leaned against the piano and watched her hips switch as she headed backstage. He knew he did not have a death wish when he woke up that morning, but sometime between leaving home and arriving at the club he subconsciously must have thought life was no longer worth living. It was the only explanation he could come up with for arranging to meet with the woman he had been warned to stay away from. Yet as he watched her walk away, hips slightly swaying from side to side, he felt it would be worth the consequences.

****

The Savoy Ballroom was one of the few integrated clubs in the city. Though the majority of the clientele were colored, it was not unusual to see whites dancing and socializing in the block-long venue. It was the main reason Randy had chosen the place for meeting Cass. Hopefully, they would be able to enjoy the evening without others judging them for being together, even as friends.

He leaned against the store next door to the Savoy. As two colored women passed by, the darker one glanced back over her shoulder to give him the once-over. She winked at him, then continued on her way.

Randy had lost count of the number of women, both colored and white, who had given him the eye or flirted with him in the few minutes he had been waiting for Cass. Some of them were pleasant on the eye, but one glance was all he could afford to give them. They had appeared either desperate—as in, "I'm out to get a man"—or curious—as in, "I wonder what it would be like to be with a white man?" And though both types guaranteed company between the sheets, he wanted to be more than a plaything for the desperate, curious, and bored.

He was also turned off by how hard the women worked at trying to catch his eye. Everything about them—from their dress to their gestures and words—was too calculated and rehearsed. When he looked at them, he couldn't help but compare them to Cass.

By contrast, the singer was not fussy about her appearance. She was well groomed but didn't spend all her time primping in front of the mirror. Her dress was simple and modest. Her skirts were not too tight, her hems fell mid-calf, and her necklines left something to the imagination. She did not wear makeup, except for the lipstick she applied before a show, and he thought that was more for moisture than beauty. Her hair, which no chemicals or hot comb touched, was worn in braids when she was not performing or in sleek, sophisticated styles when she was onstage, dispelling the myth nothing can be done with natural hair. And though she wore perfume when she performed at The Big House, she applied a light scent that did not announce her approach or linger hours after she walked out of the room.

Another woman passed by and ogled Randy. He looked past her and spied Cass strolling up Lenox Avenue. He pushed himself off the building and walked over to meet her.

"You wore your dancin' shoes," he greeted, pointing to her saddle shoes.

"I came ready to show you a thing or two."

"You sound sure of yourself."

"Honey, I'm always sure."

He placed a hand on the small of her back and led her to the entrance. After paying their admission and checking their coats, they walked up two flights of stairs to the hall, where the band was playing "Goody Goody."

Couples filled the dance floor, keeping pace with the music. The best dancers performed in the Cats Corner, on the northeast end of the floor, for a crowd of onlookers. Those not ready to work up a sweat gathered in booths and at tables.

"Dressed like that, you look like a schoolgirl," he commented, admiring her yellow blouse, green plaid skirt with suspenders, and green sweater. "Are you sure you're old enough to be out here with me?"

"I'm old enough, but I'm wondering how safe I am with you." He suspected she was only half teasing.

"You'll be safe. I'm the perfect gentleman."

"I know you will be, or else I'll have to show you a few moves my brothers taught me to protect myself."

"Knowin' you, I'm sure they were the ones needin' protection."

Cass pinched his arm.

"Ow, that's what I mean."

"Oh, hush," she said as she reached up and straightened his tie. "Nice threads." She stepped back and took in his dark blue suit, white shirt, and blue tie. "I especially like the tie."

"Thanks. It was a Christmas gift from a sassy girl I know."

"She has good taste."

"I'll tell her the next time I see her."

"Is that Cass I see in the Savoy?" a familiar voice pierced through the noise.

Randy glanced across the tables to where Florence sat in a booth with Eli. Across from them were two other women. He recognized the woman who had winked at him outside. Next to her sat a colorfully dressed lady he had seen at The Big House on several occasions.

"Chile, what are you doing here?" Florence exclaimed.

Cass tensed, though Randy wasn't sure who she seemed to regret bumping into.

****

"Why me?" she muttered under her breath. After a second, she motioned for him to follow her. A quick glance at the table told her what was supposed to be a pleasant evening was going to turn into a night she'd regret. She could only hope the fireworks would wait until later before they erupted.

"This is a dance hall, so why do you think I'm here?" she asked as they neared the booth.

"To pray for us heathens who dare to go out and have fun," Florence guessed.

"You shouldn't tease her," the flirtatious woman scolded. "She can't help it if the last time she went out Hoover was President."

"Joke's so funny I forgot to laugh," Cass said.

"So how did you get her out here?" Florence asked Randy.

"I came here to give this man a few dance lessons," Cass answered.

"You know, they've invented some new dances since the Charleston."

"A comedian you're not, Ruth."

The woman dramatically slapped the back of her

hand to her forehead. "There goes my dream of success."

"Randy, these are my friends, Maia and Ruth. Ladies…" She paused as she glared at Ruth. "And I use that term loosely, this is—"

"I know," Ruth interrupted. She eyed Randy like he was a fresh piece of meat and she was a tigress who had not eaten in a week. "You're the saxophonist at The Big House."

"Is there anyone in Harlem who hasn't heard about the white man who brought color to The Big House?" Randy asked, extending his hand.

Ruth reached out to take his hand. "Honey, I hate to be the one to tell you this, but you don't exactly bring color to anything. But I won't hold that against you."

"Down, girl," Cass said.

"I'm just being friendly."

"I've seen your type of friendliness."

Cass told herself she was not jealous of the other woman's attention to Randy. She was looking after his interests, though why she could not explain. Ruth could be a flirt, but flirting did not always lead to other things. Besides, Randy was a grown man who probably knew how to handle himself around the opposite sex better than she did. And even if her friends did end up together, it wasn't as if he would be cheating on Cass.

Ruth glanced from Randy to Cass. A smirk replaced her leer. "Oh, I understand."

"Understand what?" Cass questioned.

"I know when to back off."

"I don't know what you're talking about. Randy and I met here to dance…"

"Mmm-hmmm."

"…and he doesn't need to be attacked by some woman on the prowl."

"Sure."

"I'm just looking out for his best interests."

"The lady doth protest too much, methinks," Florence smirked.

Cass's cheeks grew warm. Randy and she were friends, and there was nothing written that said two friends of the opposite sex could not go dancing. Of course, leave it to others to read more into it.

From the grins on Florence's and Ruth's lips, her being with Randy was no big deal. She wouldn't be surprised if they showed up at her door in the morning or tackled her at the club to get all the juicy details. Not that there would be anything to tell, since she was certain Randy would not try anything, and even if he did she would make sure he didn't get far.

The scowl on Maia's face, however, said she was not pleased to see them together and, when she caught up with Cass, she'd have to set the record straight regarding the sin of coloreds mingling with whites.

"Does anyone want anythin' from the bar?" Randy asked.

Cass wondered how long Maia would be able to hold her tongue. The woman looked like it was killing her not to speak her mind.

Deciding her friend could wait, Cass nudged Randy in the ribs with her elbow. "I thought we came here to dance." She emphasized the word "dance" to stress to all present that was the only intention she had for the evening.

"We did, but I figured you'd want to talk to your

friends."

"Are you trying to back out?" she teased. "Listen, I'll make this easy on you. All you have to do is admit you can't handle this, and I'll spare you the embarrassment of going out there."

"Girl, the day I can't handle you is the day I eat my hat."

"Hmm," Cass said, strutting away from the booth. "The sooner we do this, the sooner you can enjoy your meal."

Randy followed her onto the dance floor, where they remained for two hours. When they returned to the booth, they were sweaty and out of breath.

"I'm impressed," Ruth said as Cass slid into the seat Florence and Eli had vacated.

"We sing. We dance. Maybe we should put together an act and take it on the road," Randy suggested, sliding in next to the singer. He lit a cigarette, then leaned back and draped an arm across the back of the seat.

"But who would pay to see a colored woman and white man perform together?" Cass asked.

"You never know. Anything's possible."

"Possible, my ass," Maia snorted. "It's easy for you to talk about what's possible, 'cause you're white. But it isn't that easy for us coloreds."

"That didn't take long," Ruth mumbled under her breath.

"Maia," Cass said. From the tone of her friend's voice, she could tell the eruption she had been praying would not take place was about to occur.

"No, she's right," Randy said. "I know coloreds don't have it easy, but is that a reason not to try? If everyone gave up on their dreams 'cause things were tough, nobody would get anywhere. That's why you have to fight for what you want."

Maia snorted. "What do you know about fighting? You've never had to face the same problems as me."

"And I'm not goin' to sit here and pretend I know what problems you have. I'm not a colored woman."

"You're damn right you're not."

He removed his arm from the back of the booth and leaned forward. "However, I will tell you I've had some fights durin' my life. I'm currently fightin' to be viewed as an individual and not classified as another white man who's against coloreds."

"You want us to believe that you're into the 'we're all brothers and sisters' crap?"

"I don't think we're all brothers and sisters, 'cause to be honest with you there are a few people I don't want to be related to. Particularly those who can't see past the color of a person's skin to give him a chance."

"And why should you be given a chance when so many coloreds are denied the same opportunities you can easily get elsewhere?"

"Do two wrongs make a right?"

"Where's the wrong in denying someone, who's obviously up here slumming, a job that could go to a colored who can't go downtown and get hired as anything else but a laborer?"

"Maia, that's enough," Ruth ordered.

"But I'm not finished speaking."

"But I'm finished listening," Cass said, wondering why everything had to go back to black and white. While they were on the dance floor, they had been two friends, enjoying each other's company, not a colored woman with a white man. She motioned for Randy to move. "I came here to have a ball. Sitting here listening to one friend instigate a fight with another is not my idea of having a good time."

"Cass, where are you going?" Florence asked, returning from the dance floor, dragging Eli behind her.

"Let's just say the welcoming committee went home for the night, and that's where I'm heading," Cass answered as she slid out of the booth. "Ruth, I'll speak to you later. Florence, Eli, I'll see you tomorrow."

****

Cass did not acknowledge Maia before storming off. Randy said his good-byes and hurried after her.

"I'm sorry about that," Cass apologized as they waited for their coats.

"I thought you didn't apologize for what others do."

"I don't. I'm sorry for putting you in that situation. I know Maia's opinion, and I shouldn't have taken you over there."

"You wanted to talk to your friends. Besides, everyone's entitled to her opinion, and it's not like she said somethin' I haven't heard before."

"Yes, but there's a time, a place, and a way to express those opinions."

Randy took their coats from the check girl and tipped her a dime. He led Cass to the side to make room for the couple behind them.

"I hope you weren't serious about goin' home?" he asked, holding her coat out.

It had been the first time since his altercation three weeks earlier that they had been together outside of work or rehearsals. He was not eager for the evening to end so soon.

She slipped her arms into the sleeves. "Why not? What else is there?"

"I haven't eaten since rehearsals," he said, referring to the sandwich The Big House's chef had made for them from the leftover meatloaf.

The thoughtful expression on her face gave him hope. "I'm kind of hungry myself."

"I know a nice place that serves the best catfish north of Virginia."

"Where?"

"Come on, you'll see." He slipped on his coat as he led her outside.

He adjusted the pea cap she had bought him a week earlier to replace the fedora lost in the alley on New Year's Day. He had found the hat in a box on his chair in his dressing room after the show. There was no note attached to the gift, yet he knew, without a doubt, who it was from. The previous day Cass had given him a lecture about going out in the cold without a hat on his head.

"Where are we going?" Cass asked, following him south on Lenox Avenue through the integrated crowd of people out to enjoy the evening.

It wasn't lost on him that the street would be the only time many of these people would be seen together. The majority of them were headed to destinations where one group or the other would be excluded. Lucky for them, during his time in the city, he had located places that were all-inclusive, where the workers were as colorblind as Cass insisted he was.

"You'll see," he replied.

"Why don't you just tell me where the hell you're

taking me?"

"Damn, girl. Wouldn't your mother have washed your mouth out for saying 'hell'?"

"Yes, and she'd have got you for that 'damn,' too."

"She reminds me of Miss Sylvia. One day, not long after I met her, she heard me swear. She grabbed me by my ear and marched me back to her farm. I swear it took me a week to get the taste of her homemade soap out of my mouth."

Cass laughed so hard she had to stop walking. When she reached out to grab a lamppost to keep from falling, Randy crossed his arms and glared at her.

"It's not that funny."

"Yes, it is." She ignored the curious stares from people walking by.

"I'm sure you didn't think so when your momma cleaned your mouth with her laundry soap."

"I never had my mouth washed out. I saw her do that to Joe, and I swore I'd never let her catch me cussing."

"So you're tellin' me your momma never got on you?"

"No, I didn't say that," she replied, trying to catch her breath. "She got to my behind on several occasions. The last time, I was fourteen. One morning Momma told me I had to help her scrub the floors. I hated scrubbing floors, and I wanted to go to town with my brothers, so somehow I worked up the nerve to tell her I was grown and didn't have to listen to her. For some reason, those words sounded right smart in my mind, but the moment they started tumbling out my mouth, I knew I'd made a mistake. I tried to stop talking, but my mouth wouldn't listen when my brain told it to shut up."

"I take it your momma didn't take too kindly to you assertin' yourself?" He smirked.

"Momma didn't move, bat an eyelash, or anything while I spoke, though Papa and my brothers, who were sitting at the table, got out of there and didn't return until suppertime."

"They didn't want to witness what was next?"

"No, they didn't. Hell, I didn't even want to witness it. When I finished talking, Momma didn't say a word. She just walked out the back door. That's when I knew I was in for it. Normally when I got too sassy, she'd send me out to get a switch off the hickory tree in the yard."

"What did you do when she left?" Randy asked.

"My first thought was to run for my life, but I knew she'd catch me. My second thought was to tell her I'd been possessed by some kind of spirit or something, but I knew that wasn't going to spare me from a whooping. So I made the first adult decision of my life."

"Which was?"

"I prayed to my maker and then accepted the consequences of my actions." Cass whistled. "Lord, were there consequences. Momma almost didn't let me live to regret the day I talked back to her. I'm not lying when I say she didn't bring back a switch but practically the whole tree. She applied that to my backside with such passion I had trouble sitting for a week."

"And it still didn't cure you of your sassiness," Randy commented.

Cass shook her head. "Oh, it cured me all right. I

haven't sassed Momma since. And, like I've said before, I've never let her hear me cuss."

"I should write your Momma and tell her you're long overdue for a cleanin'."

Cass started laughing again. "I just pictured Momma washing your mouth out."

Randy grabbed her hand and pulled her down the street behind him. "Come on."

"You never told me where we're going."

"If you'd come on, we'd get there."

"I have no other choice. You have my hand and I'm kind of attached to it."

Randy glanced back at her, without breaking his stride.

"Will you just tell me," she implored.

"Trust me."

****

Cass wondered when she would learn never to trust a man who said to trust him. Randy had dragged her to a…to a… She could not even think of a word to describe the place. Calling Cornbread 'n' Grits a dive would have been too kind.

Cass scrunched her face in disgust as she stared at the litter-covered steps that led down to the restaurant and the grimy window. She had been tempted to walk away, yet Randy smiled like a little boy so filled with pride at having done something special for a friend that she did not have the heart to refuse to go in with him. She just prayed the inside was better than the outside.

To her dismay, the interior was worse. The floor appeared as if a mop had never touched it, and the wall near the kitchen had enough grease on it to fry a whole chicken. She could tell what other patrons had eaten, from the spilled food not cleaned off the tables.

For the first time since she had learned to talk, Cass was speechless. She searched her brain to remember what she ever did to make Randy bring her to this place and tried to think of an excuse that would keep her from having to eat anything placed in front of her.

"I can't wait for you to try their catfish," Randy commented after their waitress had taken their order and disappeared into the kitchen.

"You've eaten here before?" Cass asked, wondering how anyone could have eaten there and lived to tell about it. At least the waitress had been nice enough to wipe down their table.

"At least once a week."

She did not reply as she scanned the room.

"I'll admit the atmosphere's not much, but the food's delicious. After one bite, you'll forget about everythin' else."

"But what will be doing the biting? Me or the things scurrying around this place?"

Randy laughed.

"It's not funny. If I die from eating this food, so help me, I'm going to kill you."

He laughed harder at her logic, and she pouted.

Randy reached across the table and took her hand.

"What are you doing?" she gasped as she tried to pull away.

With a strong but gentle grip, he held onto her hand and rubbed her palm with his thumb. The motion sent a shiver through her she had never experienced before. Though the touch was pleasant enough and a part of her didn't want him to stop, it was also too intimate, a reminder of why she did not hang out with men, even if they were simply friends.

"Relax, it's okay."

She had to set the record straight. They were friends and nothing more. She just wondered how he would handle her declaration.

Aside from his occasional compliments, he had never given any indication he saw her as more than a friend. Yet if he did and she made her view clear, would she lose his friendship?

Choosing the coward's way, she figured she'd try the one thing sure to get him to back off.

"Randy, I know you're blind when it comes to race and everything, but we're in public," she whispered, hoping someone as colorblind as he was would not want to cause trouble in a restaurant. "What will people say?"

"Nothin', since we're the only ones here."

Cass looked around and noticed the restaurant was indeed empty aside from them. Yet she continued to try.

"Okay, but what about the waitress? She could have the owner kick us out." Not like that would be a bad idea. It would save her from eating there.

"Mattie'll probably say it's about time I brought someone here with me."

"Mattie?"

"Our waitress. She also owns this restaurant. I'm sure she's watchin' us, with her husband."

Cass peeped over his head. Sure enough the waitress, a tall, healthy white woman, was peering around the kitchen door. Standing behind her was a colored man, who towered over her.

"I see her, but she's with a colored…" She glanced

back at Randy, who nodded his head. "You mean she and him, they're…they're married?" She'd never met a couple who dared to defy the social taboo of marrying outside their race.

"Well, not by a preacher, but they've been together long enough they consider themselves husband and wife. And they'll challenge anyone who says otherwise."

She glanced toward the kitchen again and watched as the man leaned forward and whispered something in the waitress's ear. When Mattie only shook her head, he wrapped an arm around her waist and pulled her into the other room. A giggle indicated she was not opposed to him handling her.

"If they feel that way, why didn't they get married?" she asked, turning her attention back to Randy.

He shrugged. "Before they moved to New York, they lived in Georgia, where their union was considered illegal. But even though they couldn't find someone to marry them, they stayed together. By the time they came up here, they felt God already knew what was in their hearts, so why did they need a piece of paper from the courts to tell them how they feel about each other."

"But what about what other people think?"

"I'm sure there are plenty of people who have strong opinions about their relationship, but that's not goin' to change their feelin's for one another."

"You want to hear strong opinions, get Maia started on mixing races, and she'll give you an earful."

"I kinda had the feelin' she's not open to white people."

"You're pretty observant."

"The two of you are so different. When you first met me, you were willin' to give me a chance. On the other hand, Maia looked as if she wanted to pour kerosene over me and light a match. How'd you two become friends?"

"I met Maia about six months after I moved to New York. One day Henry and I were in the market and he tried talking to her. Now, Maia likes men. In fact, I haven't known her to be without one long. But there are two types of men she won't deal with—some other woman's man and a man with a wandering eye."

"Don't forget white men."

"I figured that was a given. Anyhow, when Henry tried talking to her, she told him about himself, then left the store. The next evening, when I got home from work, she was waiting for me, so she could lecture me on the evils of allowing my husband to disrespect me by flirting with another woman in my presence. I listened to her, then thanked her for her concern before I walked away. But when Maia has something on her mind, there's no stopping her until she's had her say."

"You know, I could say the same thin' about a sassy little gal I know."

Cass sucked her teeth. "The next evening I came home to find her outside again. This time she wanted to know if I'd thought about what she said and came to my senses. I told her everything was all right between Henry and me, then excused myself. But she was persistent. The next night, she was out there again. This time I stood in front of her, looked her in the eyes, and told her our marriage was none of her business.

"Maia saw right through my tough-girl act and decided to take me under her wing. She would come around, check on me, and offer me advice so I wouldn't be too badly burnt when he screwed me over. She was the one who suggested I hide some money from him from each of my pays. When Henry left me, she helped me get my apartment and the gig at The Big House."

"I guess anyone who's willin' to put up with you and that sassy mouth of yours can't be all that bad."

Cass stuck her tongue out at him.

"Here you go," the waitress interrupted. She stood over them with two plates of fried catfish, string beans, hopping john, and cornbread.

"Thanks, Mattie," Randy said, releasing the hand Cass had forgotten he was holding. Though she had been surprised when he initially held it, she had to admit she missed the contact once he let go.

"Anything for my favorite customer." Mattie placed the plates on the table.

"I bet you say that to all the young men."

Mattie snorted. "Boy, don't flatter yourself. I don't need to be bothered with you young things when I've had that strapping man of mine for over thirty years. I'll leave you scrawny little things to the young girls like her."

Cass remembered walking in on Randy after his shower on New Year's. Though he was not as large as Mattie's husband, he could not be considered scrawny. He had a lean yet defined physique.

At the time, Cass had been concerned about Randy's well-being and had not given any thought to being in his room with him half-naked. But, as she reflected upon that day, or more specifically his body, her face grew flushed.

"It's about time you brought someone here with

you," Mattie continued.

Randy threw Cass a look that said, "I told you so."

"I saw that," the woman chuckled. "Don't worry, I remember what it's like to be young. I'll leave you two alone."

After Mattie returned to the kitchen, Cass peeked at her plate. The food smelled good and, to her surprise, the dish and utensils were clean.

"Go ahead," Randy coaxed. "Try it." When she did not move, he added, "It's not goin' to hurt you. Watch." He took a bite of his catfish.

Still apprehensive, she simply stared back and forth between the plate and him. He speared a couple of string beans on his fork and held it out to her.

"Go ahead. I promise they won't bite back."

She hesitated a second before allowing him to place the food in her mouth.

One bite. That was all it took for Cass to forget her worries. She not only finished her meal but polished off half his fillet and his cornbread.

"I'm glad you decided not to eat the utensils," Randy joked when she laid down her fork. "Let that be a lesson to you. Never judge a book, or a restaurant, by its cover."

"Are you finished with the 'I told you so's?"

"No, 'cause I haven't said it, yet."

Cass rolled her eyes.

"I told you so," he said.

"It was good. Thank you," she managed through a yawn.

Randy glanced at his watch and let out a whistle. "I think I need to get you home. It's past your bedtime."

"What time is it?"

"It's after two."

"What? You're not serious. Where'd the time go?"

"It flies when you're in great company."

"Ugh. I need to go," she announced, tossing her napkin on the table. "It's getting crowded in here, with that big head of yours."

He reached into his jacket and pulled out his wallet. "I'll walk you home."

"Randy, you're right around the corner from your house. You don't need to walk me home. You'll only have to come all the way back up here."

"I couldn't call myself a gentleman if I didn't insist on escortin' you home."

"Well, now that you insisted, you can stay up here and I'll find my way own way home."

"Or you can realize you're not goin' to win this argument and I'm goin' to see you home."

"Are you always so sure of yourself?"

"I haven't lost the argument yet."

An hour later, Cass stepped through the gate in front of her building. As she turned to close it, Randy squeezed through behind her.

"Come on, I'll walk you up," he said. He reached down to take from her hand the key she had fished out of her pocket.

For the second time that evening, she was at a loss for words. The previous times he had walked her home, he'd been content with saying good-bye to her outside. Escorting her upstairs made the evening more intimate, more than just two friends hanging out. It made her wonder what he expected from her after he'd paid for her admission into the Savoy and for dinner.

Outside her apartment, Cass waited as Randy

unlocked the door. Once the cylinder clicked, she reached for the key. His hand closed over hers as he stared down at her.

"Randy—"

"Shh," he whispered as he caressed her cheek with the back of his free hand. He was standing so close to her, she swore she heard his heartbeat. Or was that her heart? She was not sure whose heart it was, only that it was beating faster with every passing second.

His hand slipped from her cheek and hooked under her chin. He raised her face as he leaned down.

Randy's other hand slid around her waist. He pulled her closer to him. The pressure of his lips on hers sent chills through her. She forgot her worries and enjoyed the kiss.

She actually felt safe and comfortable with him, something she'd never expected to feel with a man. She wanted the feeling to last. Then she felt the twitch on her hip.

His growing hardness set off warning bells in her head.

With a gasp, she pulled her head back.

"I knew something wasn't right with the kiss you gave me on New Year's," he said.

"What was that?" Cass asked.

"It was too short." He leaned forward again, but she put her hands against his chest and turned her head.

"Randy, no," she pleaded.

"What's wrong?" he asked as he released her and took a step back.

"I'm not... I don't... I won't..."

He stared at her, confusion on his face.

"I have to go," she said, before slipping into her

apartment.

"Cass—" was all he had a chance to say before she closed the door in his face.

Inside, she listened to his footsteps on the stairs. Once the outer door closed, she let out a deep breath. Their relationship had just taken a new turn, and it was one she was not sure she could handle.

Chapter 15

It had been a tough decision. Kissing Cass would take them to another level, which, if things did not work out, would be the end of their friendship forever. Yet, once they were outside her building, he'd decided to take the chance.

Cass's reaction had puzzled him. She seemed to like the kiss enough at first, but something had her pull away from him and run. He spent the rest of the night trying to figure out what spooked her. It wasn't like she was a blushing virgin who didn't know what went on between a man and a woman, and he didn't think he had been pushy.

Unable to come up with a solution, he resigned himself to the idea he'd moved too fast and possibly destroyed the first genuine friendship he had. Yet when Bessie knocked on his door and announced Cass was in the living room, he figured maybe there was hope. Either that or she was a professional who refused to allow her feelings to affect the show.

By the time he had retrieved his saxophone and made his way downstairs, Cass had Mrs. Greene's sewing kit. She knelt in front of Bessie, who stood on a chair from the kitchen, and pinned the hem of the girl's dress. She refused to look at him when he entered the room and seemed to go out of her way to talk to the girls and avoid him.

Randy was determined to wait until the girls had left to talk to Cass, but after a half hour he became impatient as the fittings dragged on. Estelle chatted about her part in the school play, while Bessie begged Cass to make a matching dress for her doll. Mariah, eager to go outside and play with her friends, fidgeted and came close to getting stuck by one of the many pins in her dress.

He had no doubt in Cass's ability to handle the three hyper chatterboxes. However, he decided to help calm the girls by giving them a private performance so she could get done sooner rather than later.

"I'm finished," Cass announced as she climbed to her feet. "Go upstairs and take off the dress."

Mariah jumped down from the chair and rushed out of the room.

"And be careful of those pins," she called after the girl as she placed the pincushion in the sewing basket on the coffee table. "Okay, everyone's taken care of."

Randy stopped playing. "What about me?"

"You want a dress, too?" she asked, acknowledging him for the first time. "How about one with a high collar and lace?"

He glared at her.

"Don't you know you shouldn't cross your eyes?"

"Mommy says if you cross your eyes, they'll freeze like that forever," Bessie added, beaming with pride at her knowledge.

"I'll take my chances," he mumbled.

"Do you know how to play 'Pop Goes the Weasel,' Mr. Jones?" Estelle asked. "That's the song my class is singing at the show."

"I'm not sure. Is it the one that goes, London

Bridge is falling down, falling down, falling down?" He teased the girl.

"No." Estelle giggled. "That's 'London Bridge.' "

"Then it's the one that goes, Twinkle, twinkle little star, how I wonder where you are?"

"No, that's not 'Pop Goes the Weasel,' " Bessie announced. "Even I know that."

"Maybe if you hum a couple of notes for me, I'll recognize the song."

Estelle stood with her hands folded in front of her as if she were on stage at school and recited, "All around the mulberry bush, the monkey chased the weasel. The monkey thought 'twas all in fun…" She popped her hand on her mouth, before she finished with, "Goes the weasel."

"Oh, that song," Randy said. "I think I'm familiar with it."

"I wanna do that," Bessie declared. She dropped her doll in Cass's lap as she ran to her sister.

"I'll tell you what," Estelle said. "You can clap your hands."

"No, I wanna hit my mouth."

"We can't have everyone hitting their mouths. At school, some of us hit our mouths. Others stomp their feet, and some clap their hands."

Bessie crossed her arms over her chest. Her bottom lip protruded and trembled.

"I have a suggestion," Cass intervened, interrupting the impending tantrum. "Why don't both of you pop your mouths…"

"But…" Estelle began, but a frown from Cass stopped her.

"As I was saying, the two of you can pop your

mouths, I can clap, and Mr. Jones can stomp his foot."

"Mrs. Greene doesn't like anyone stomping in her house," Bessie said, her face beaming.

"I think I can do it soft enough so as not to upset her," Randy assured the girl.

"Then, are we ready?"

"Yes," the girls answered.

Cass, Estelle, and Bessie sang three verses of the song with Randy accompanying them on the saxophone. At the beginning of the last line of each verse, they each did their assigned parts.

At the end of the first verse, Randy decided to have a little fun and increased the tempo at each verse until the singers could no longer keep up. The girls dropped to the floor in a fit of giggles while he played through the song one more time. When the final note faded, the three singers applauded.

"We sang that song in my school play two years ago," Mariah said, trotting back into the room with her coat on. Her dress was draped over one arm. She held her sisters' coats in each hand.

"I hope they do that song when I go to school," Bessie announced. "But I don't think the way they do it will be as much fun as the way Mr. Jones does it."

"No, it isn't," Estelle agreed. "They try not to make anything too much fun in school 'cause they want you to leave. If you had fun and loved going there, they wouldn't be able to get rid of you in the evenings and everyone would fail on purpose so they would have to repeat the grade and they would never graduate. As long as it's boring, you'll get good grades so you can hurry up and get out of there."

"The wisdom of youth." Randy laughed.

Cass shook her head and smiled.

"Here's my dress, Miss Cass," Mariah said.

"That was quick." Cass took the dress and inspected it. "I hope none of the pins came out, in your rush."

"They didn't."

"Good." Cass placed the dress on the back of the chair with the other two. "Don't forget to tell your mother I'll bring them back on Monday."

"I won't," Mariah replied. She handed her sisters their coats before rushing out of the room.

Estelle and Bessie slid into their outer garments, then followed their older sister.

"Button your coats before y'all catch colds," Cass called after them.

"Yes, ma'am."

"And hold Bessie's hand when crossing the street."

"Yes, ma'am," Mariah called back.

Shaking her head, Cass moved to the window. Randy stood behind her as she watched the girls run to the corner and across the street. They joined three other girls who were playing jump rope.

"You've a way with children," he commented.

Cass jumped when she realized he was right behind her. She slid around him and moved to the chair with the dresses.

"You're not so bad yourself," she said as she began folding the clothes.

"I learned by watchin' you. You're very patient with them. I was impressed on Christmas when you sat on the floor with them and had a tea party."

"It's not hard to play with children. Unfortunately, once most people start smelling themselves, they think it's not hip to play. Then once they become adults they've forgotten how much fun it is to get down on the floor and sip air or roll a toy truck around."

"Smell themselves? You always have an interestin' way of sayin' things."

"I believe in being straightforward."

"So, how come you don't have any?"

"Any what?"

"Any children. How come you don't have a house full of them?"

****

Cass froze. It felt as if someone stabbed her in the heart and twisted the knife a few turns for the fun of it.

She had always wanted children she could encourage to explore the world and everything it had to offer. Unfortunately, it had not happened and, most likely, would not.

After a second, she dropped the dress and looked over at Randy.

"Cass, I'm sorry. I guess that was a bit too personal," he said. He moved toward the sofa. "I think I'll just sit over here and gnaw on my foot for a while before I pull it out of my mouth."

"It's all right." She sighed. "I always wished I'd have a houseful of children, but I guess it wasn't meant to be."

"I'm sorry, Cass. Look, maybe it can still happen. I'm not a doctor or anythin', but maybe you can have children. You should speak to your momma or someone. Maybe it was somethin' you did."

"It was. I spent more time trying to keep Henry from touching me than being with him."

"Well, that's the problem. Girl, you have to be with

a man to get with a child."

"I know that."

"Then why didn't you let him touch you?"

She walked over to the sofa and sat on the other end. "I didn't like being with him. It...it...well, it just wasn't any fun having a sweaty man on top of me while he did his business." The shocked expression on his face caused her to add, "It's not like he minded. He got what he wanted from some other woman...well, most of the time."

"What about the other times?"

"I did what I had to do."

"Which was?"

"Lay there until he relieved himself."

Randy scrunched his face in disgust. "Relieved himself? You make it sound like he was going to the bathroom."

"That's what it felt like." She glanced past him at knickknacks displayed in the cabinet behind him. She could not believe she was having this conversation. It wasn't something she ever talked to anyone about—not her mother or Maia or any of the women at the club. And especially not with a man.

Though the chorus girls gossiped, sometimes going into details that left Cass's face burning with embarrassment, she believed what went on between a man and woman was something that should be left behind closed doors. Yet, as usual, she felt comfortable confiding in Randy.

"Darlin', when you're with a man, it should be pleasurable. Both of you should feel something special."

"I did feel something—dirty and disgusting."

"Then what was the purpose of doin' it?"

"What choice did I have? It was my duty as his wife—"

****

Duty? Duty? Duty? The word echoed through Randy's mind, getting louder with every repetition, until he heard nothing but the word.

He had always thought Cass was ahead of her times. Whereas most women were raised to be dependent on a man, she was independent and thought for herself. She did not stand for a man to raise a hand to her and defended herself against any assault. Yet she still possessed archaic ideas when it came to sex.

"Darlin', weddin' vows say you should love, honor, and obey, in sickness and in health, for richer or for poorer, in joy and in sorrow…there's nothin' about you havin' to lay down for your husband."

"It doesn't have to be said. It's understood."

"It is? Says who?"

"Says everyone."

"Really? I don't say so."

She focused on him. "You're not married, so you don't understand."

"No, I don't understand. Maybe you should explain to me why you followed some unspoken vow when he couldn't even honor the vows he recited to you in front of a pastor, witnesses, and God. Unless I'm wrong, there's nowhere in the ceremony where a man says, 'I'll forsake all others, except on days of the week that end in the letter y.' "

"Why are you yelling at me?"

Why? Why was he yelling? Because of the absurdity of her statements. He took a deep breath to calm down before continuing.

"Why did you feel it was your duty to submit to your husband?" he asked, trying to keep his voice down.

"The morning after Henry and I were married, his aunt took me aside and told me that submitting to my husband in bed was part of my duty."

"Why did she tell you that?"

"She could hear me telling him to get off of me the previous night when he came to me. He didn't beat me or anything. He lifted my dress, removed my drawers, entered, did his business, then rolled over and went to sleep."

"He knew you'd never been with anyone before?" Randy asked.

Cass looked over his shoulder as she nodded. He realized the conversation was embarrassing her, but he couldn't let it go.

"And he didn't do anything to prepare you?"

"Prepare me how?" she asked.

"Kiss you. Touch you."

"No."

"It's no wonder you didn't enjoy being with Henry. He should have been gentle with you so your first time was special."

"Special!" Cass snorted. "Painful was more like it."

"The first time's usually painful for the woman, but things can be done to ease the pain. Did you tell his aunt?"

"I told her it hurt, and she said it didn't matter. A woman's not expected to enjoy it, only lie there and deal with it until her husband's finished."

"That's the biggest piece of crap I've ever heard.

You believed her?"

"Why shouldn't I?" She finally looked at him.

"Didn't you talk to your mother?"

"Not when I was married to Henry."

"What about before?"

Cass raised her eyebrows as if to ask him if he was serious. The gesture, however, was unnecessary, as he realized the absurdity of his question the moment he asked it.

"Are you kidding me? The most Momma ever told me was to keep my skirts down, my legs closed, and don't bring home any surprises before I was married."

Randy dropped his head in his hands and massaged his temples. Her answer had not surprised him.

As a child, no one had been concerned about discretion in his house, and by the time he was eight he knew what went on between a man and woman. It was not until later he learned sex was not a subject discussed, much less performed, in the open. All talk, and activity, was done behind closed doors, away from children, particularly girls.

Beyond the warning to never have some girl's daddy come looking for you, not much was said about what a boy could or should not do before marriage. More emphasis was placed upon a girl's behavior. "Good" girls did not talk about, think about, or engage in sex before marriage. Any discussions with a girl started with, "Don't get pregnant," followed by, "Do you understand me?" and concluded with, "That's the end of the discussion." It was not considered necessary to elaborate, since a girl was not supposed to have sex.

Randy sighed. "It's a crime we live in a society where girls are left in the dark, not knowin' what will happen to them," he mumbled. "For Christ's sake, we're livin' in the nineteen-thirties, not the eighteen-thirties."

"They expect us to learn on our wedding night all we need to know," Cass replied. "I mean, I pretty much figured it out by the time Henry had relieved himself."

Randy sat back. "Will you stop sayin' he relieved himself?" he shouted. "He wasn't goin' to the bathroom."

"Well, that's what it felt like," she shouted back.

Realizing tempers were flaring, Randy took a deep breath and tried to calm down. He did not want to fight with her. On the contrary, he wanted to carry her upstairs and make love to her, doing all the things her husband should have done.

He never understood how men like Henry called themselves men when they were not willing to take the time to make the women they had pledged to love feel special in and out of the bedroom. He had seen men use women with no thought to their feelings, and he wondered what guys got out of the experience besides the same physical release they could get using their hands.

"When we were at your apartment and you pushed me away, was it because you were afraid it would be the same like it was with Henry?" Randy asked.

"Yes." She started with a nod that turned into a shake of her head. "No."

"Which was it? Yes or no?"

"I don't know. When we were going upstairs to my apartment, I was nervous. I wanted to tell you nothing was going to…nothing could ever happen between us. Then you kissed me, and I felt…I don't know what I felt. It was strange, but good, and I was afraid if I didn't get away from you everything I didn't want to happen would happen."

Randy stared at her as he tried to make sense of what she said.

"It's confusing," she added.

After replaying what she said in his mind, he shook his head. "No, I think I understand. You're afraid of being with someone 'cause you think the experience will be like what you had with Henry. Darlin', you can't push every man away just 'cause you had a bad experience with one man."

"But it wasn't just one man," she whispered, hanging her head.

"What?!"

Cass held her head up. "I said, it wasn't just one man. I was with a man besides Henry." She quickly added, "It happened once, and it wasn't like I wanted it to."

"Someone forced himself on you?"

"No, it wasn't like that. I knew the person, and I agreed to go out with him."

"Who was he?"

"His name was Pedro. He began hanging around the club about two months after I started working there. He asked me out several times, but Henry hadn't been gone long, and I wasn't interested in going out with anyone, so I turned him down."

"What finally made you decide to go out with him?"

"One night he caught me between acts. You know how chaotic it can be backstage at that time. I was in the middle of helping two people while listening to

Luther's suggestions for the next act when Pedro asked me out again. With all the confusion, I agreed. By the time I realized what I'd said, he had slipped away and did not appear again until it was time to meet me."

"You could have told him no then, explained you made a mistake."

"I know, but I didn't want to hurt his feelings. Besides, I figured what harm could there be in one drink. After the drink, he walked me home and invited himself in. We sat on the sofa and talked for a while. When he started to get touchy-feely, I told him I wasn't comfortable with what he was doing, and he told me I was being rude."

"How the hell were you being rude?" Randy asked, while thinking, *Where does she find these jerks?*

"He paid for the drinks. Though I admit it didn't feel right giving it up for a few drinks. It made me feel like—"

"It wasn't right," Randy interrupted, not wanting her to finish the sentence. He could not blame her for her naïveté; instead, he blamed society. Good girls didn't need to be taught how to handle manipulative men, since they would never find themselves in those situations. According to the backward society they lived in, only an easy girl would find herself in that situation, and then an easy girl would know how to get out of it.

"Just 'cause a man pays for drinks does not give him the right to demand anythin' from you. Cass, I'm sorry you had to go through that."

"Not as sorry as I was. But the experience taught me that I shouldn't accept anything from a man unless I'm willing to offer myself, and since I don't care to share a bed—"

"You don't go out," Randy finished her sentence.

"Yes."

Randy slowly slid across the sofa to close the gap between them. "Then why did you accept my invitation to the Savoy?"

"'Cause we're friends, and friends don't… Friends are…"

"Safe?"

"Yes."

"Darlin', you had two bad experiences, but Henry and Pedro do not represent all men."

"I know, but I'm not willing to take the chance. The next man to offer me drinks could be just like them."

"Or he could be the complete opposite. He could be honorable and care about you. If you don't take the chance, you'll never find the happiness." He reached over and took her hand. "And everyone deserves a bit of happiness."

Cass looked down at their hands. "Why are you so concerned?" she asked softly.

"Because you're a friend," Randy replied. *And I don't want you to rule me out*, he silently added, knowing he was ready to take the next step beyond friendship.

Chapter 16

Randy glanced up from his book at the sound of wet shoes sloshing up the stairs. His shoulders slumped when Maia appeared, shaking raindrops from her umbrella onto the green wall. She stopped when she saw him sitting on the floor outside Cass's door, holding a copy of *Jonah's Gourd Vine*.

"What happened? You forgot how to knock on a door?" Maia asked.

"I was thinkin' if I sat here long enough, the door would open by itself," Randy answered. "Figured Cass and I could add a magic act to the show."

"You two are planning on doing more numbers together?"

"Luther's mentioned addin' another number or two."

Maia sucked her teeth as she started past him. "You people always have to be in the spotlight," she muttered under her breath.

Randy knew he should have let it go. It wasn't the first time someone had looked down on him with disdain, and it wasn't the worst thing anyone had ever said to him. But the anxiety of waiting had made him irritable, and he needed an outlet, or at least a distraction, to keep him from backing down from what he felt he needed to do.

Over the past two days, all Randy could think

about was Cass's confession. Though she had been hurt in the past and was willing to give up on relationships, he could not walk away. He wanted to take the next step and had finally gotten the courage to tell her how he felt. However, after waiting an hour, he had begun to worry whether his confession would move the relationship in the direction he wanted.

"I'm beginnin' to suspect you don't like me," he said as he stood, preparing for a confrontation.

"Perceptive, aren't you?"

"Is there any particular reason? You know, I kinda like to know why my presence disturbs people."

Maia stopped short of the steps leading to her third-floor apartment, whirled around, and studied Randy. Of course, he did his own scrutiny of the woman who was light enough to pass for his sister.

"Doesn't it bother you that you took a job from a colored man?" Maia asked, after a minute of scrutiny.

"I didn't take anythin' from anyone."

"If you consider all the places you could have gone and got a job, you took one of the few gigs available for coloreds when you came to The Big House."

"Like I said, I didn't take a thin' from no one. I showed up, auditioned, and after listenin' to Junior tell me how he felt about me, I was offered the gig by Luther. It's not like I woke up and said, 'Let me see what I can take from someone.' In fact, I knew before I went down there I probably wouldn't get the job because of my color."

"Then why did you go to the audition if you didn't think you'd get the gig?"

"If I was colored and had the talent, you'd think a club should hire me regardless of how dark I am."

"But you're not colored."

"No, I'm not, but shouldn't I be given the same consideration? Don't you believe in equality?"

"Of course I do. I believe coloreds should be allowed the same opportunities as whites."

Though he knew it would be like talking to a wall—some people were set in their ways and nothing that was said would change their minds—he could not let it go. "When you speak of equal rights, you should mean it for all people, not just coloreds. Equality won't be achieved until all people—whites, coloreds, Indians, Chinese, and all the rest—are considered for their talents, not the color of their skin."

"That's a lot of talk coming from a white man. You don't know what it's like to have a door slammed in your face because your skin's too brown or your hair's not straight enough or you have one drop of colored blood tainting the white blood flowing through your body."

"I know what it's like to have a door slammed in my face because my skin isn't brown enough."

"If you know that's going to happen, then why not stick to places that will accept you? Why do you have to force your way into our clubs?"

"I can say the same thing about you. If you know you're not gonna be accepted, then why bother tryin'?"

"Because it shouldn't make any difference what I look like."

"You contradict yourself."

He saw the cloud descend over her face and realized she was thinking about the contradiction. However, he could also see in her eyes that she was not about to admit he was right.

Maia shook her head. "You think you know what it's like because you're slumming in Harlem and you read Zora Neale Hurston. That doesn't give you any experience. All it gives you is some unrealistic view of what it's like to be colored."

"You're right. I don't know what it's like to be colored and not have my skin burn when I've been out in the sun too long. And I don't know what it's like to have to struggle to get a comb through my hair. But I know what it's like to have dreams, and I know what it means to struggle to make ends meet, just like everyone else who lives up here. You know how I know? 'Cause that's not what it means to be colored, that's what it means to live in this world in this day and age. As for your criticism of Zora Neale Hurston, I think you need to read her books and stop listenin' to her critics."

Maia rolled her head along with her eyes. "I read Hurston's work, and there's nothing an ofay can tell me about her."

"It seems like an ofay needs to enlighten you, 'cause you missed a lot when you read her books. Miss Hurston's characters are not unrealistic. They're everyday people you could meet in any town."

He held up his copy of *Jonah's Gourd Vine*.

"If you changed the skin color of John and Lucy, then I'd swear she was writin' about a preacher I knew in Mobile. He was always provin' how weak the flesh was, while his wife stood beside him despite his need to enter the sanctuary of every woman that beckoned."

In the dim light, he thought he saw a flash of recognition in her eyes, like she had lived through the experience, but just as quickly the look was gone. She snatched the book from his hand and threw it to the floor. The move, Randy reasoned, was out of frustration at losing an argument, and he held his ground.

"Your assertion that her characters are people you can meet is why she needs to stop writing that trash. She has people like you thinking all coloreds are uneducated hoodoo practitioners who can't speak properly and an educated colored person is a freak of nature," she argued. Randy, however, noticed how she jumped from one point to another when he hit upon a truth.

"People who believe that are narrow-minded fools, and it doesn't matter what they read, their opinions will never change. Anyone with an ounce of sense knows Miss Hurston's characters do not represent the entire colored race."

"Then I guess whites don't have any sense, 'cause that's what they think of us."

"What makes you an authority on what all whites think?"

"Experience. The white folks I've met don't think coloreds could amount to more than servants."

"So one person represents an entire race? If we use that line of reasonin', then it's safe to say the colored prostitutes I met in New Orleans represent all colored women…you included."

Maia's mouth dropped open, but she was too shocked for any words to come out.

"That's your argument, not mine," Randy said as the front door opened downstairs.

****

Cass sighed when she reached the second floor and saw Maia and Randy outside her door. Maia looked as if she was ready to lash out, and Randy appeared ready to forget he was talking to a lady once the blow was delivered.

Wet and cold, Cass was not in the mood to play referee and was tempted to walk back out and let them have a go at each other. However, her friendship with both of them forced her to stay. She knew if she left them together, one of them would be arrested—Maia for striking a white man or Randy for striking a woman.

"Randy, what are you doing here?" she asked, figuring he would be more reasonable and easier to deal with.

"I wanted to talk," he answered.

"About?"

He shook his head. "Nothin'," he replied as he stepped toward the stairs.

"But—"

"I'll see you tonight," he called over his shoulder.

Cass stared after him until the front door closed. She placed her bag on the floor, crossed her arms, and glared at Maia.

"What was that all about?' Cass asked.

"Don't you stand there and get snippety with me," Maia huffed. "He asked me a question and I answered it. It's not my problem if he can't handle the truth."

Cass sighed. "Why couldn't you have just passed by and leave him be?"

"You're acting like I started it."

"That's 'cause I know you. What do you have against Randy?"

"I see him for what he is."

"And what's that? A man who's trying to make a living doing what he likes?"

Maia snorted. "No, a white man sniffing around the

skirt of a naïve colored woman."

"I think you have him confused with the men you go out with."

"Trust me. I'll never confuse that ghost for one of the fine chocolate men I hang with."

"If they're so fine, where are they? I don't see Amaad anywhere around. Oh, wait, that's 'cause you left him in South Carolina 'cause you got tired of him sniffing around other women's skirts."

"That was low," Maia said, lowering her voice as her eyes narrowed. "You didn't have to go there."

"It's no lower than you walking around and passing judgment on a man you haven't even taken the time to know. Before you even met him you were saying he was up here slumming. What are you basing your assumptions on?"

"Because I know white men and how they operate. They sweet talk you to get up your skirt. Then if something happens, they're either quick to deny they've ever been with you or they'll accuse you of being with every man on the block."

Cass thought of Maia's parents. Her friend had been told that her parents' relationship had been consensual. But when Maia's mother became pregnant, her lover abandoned them. Though he admitted to being with Maia's mother, he claimed she slept around and suggested any number of men could be the father of her child.

"You're basing your assumptions on your mother's experience? What about your own experience?"

"Whose experience do you think I'm talking about?"

Cass flinched.

"Yes, that's right, I was with one. Instead of learning from my mother's mistake, I had to go mess with one. Everything was fine until I got pregnant. Then he took off."

"What happened?"

"I wasn't going to follow in my mother's footsteps, so I had someone take care of it for me. I'm telling you, that took a piece of my soul, and I don't want to same thing to happen to you.

"You managed to do fine after Henry screwed you over. I don't want to see you lose everything 'cause you fooled around with a slumming, two-bit con."

The last time Cass ignored advice on men, she'd ended up married to a lazy skirt-chaser. She was not eager to make another mistake. However, aside from his kiss after they had gone to the Savoy, Randy had never shown any interest in her. And, since their talk the other afternoon, she was certain he understood nothing could happen between them.

"Randy's not like that. Why don't you get to know him before passing judgment on him?"

"Because sometimes we need to trust what others tell us, to avoid unnecessary pain."

"Randy's been nothing but kind to me since the day I met him, and he sure hasn't been sniffing around my skirts."

"What do you call him taking you to the Savoy or walking you home? In all the years I've known you, you've never needed a man to walk you home. Now he shows up and he's walking you from the store, he's here on Christmas, and the other night after you hung out."

Cass tossed her hands in the air. "What? Your life

has gotten so boring without Amaad that you've taken to spying on me?"

"I'm not spying on you, I'm looking out for you."

"Then I'm going to make this easy for you. I already have a mother. She's alive and well, and though she's in North Carolina, she can still do a good job looking after me. So you don't need to worry yourself about my welfare."

"If my memory services me correctly, neither one of you were doing a good job looking after your welfare when you came to New York. And if it hadn't been for me—"

"Now who's treading in territory she has no business in?" Cass opened her purse and searched for her keys. "Thank you for your concern, but how about we do things this way—You worry about your man or the reason you lack one at this moment, and I'll worry about mine."

"Fine." Maia sighed as she marched away. "But don't say I didn't warn you."

Cass did not bother to call after the other woman. The conversation had been too long and only succeeded in adding a headache to her list of complaints.

She unlocked her door. As she reached down to retrieve her groceries, she noticed *Jonah's Gourd Vine* lying on the floor. She placed the book on top of her bag, stepped into her apartment, and kicked the door closed behind her.

She had made it halfway through the living room when there was a knock. She continued to the kitchen, dropped her bag on the table, then hurried back to answer the door.

"Hey," Randy greeted, appearing calmer than he

had been when he stormed out.

"Hey, yourself," Cass returned.

"I wanted to apologize for the way I left."

"Come in," she said, stepping aside.

He hesitated. "Is it safe to come in?"

"Yes, Maia's upstairs, most likely praying for my ungrateful soul."

"Good." Randy sighed as he stepped inside. "I don't think I have it in me to go another round with her today."

"She went a round with me after you left. I think she's had her fill of fighting today. Let me take your coat."

"Thanks." He passed her his umbrella, then shrugged out of the wet article of clothing and handed it to her.

"I was in the kitchen, about to unpack the groceries. Sit down in there while I hang these up," she called over her shoulder.

"You don't suppose she's upstairs resting up for a rematch tonight?" Randy asked when Cass entered the kitchen. She had taken off her coat and galoshes and was wearing a red knitted sweater and a matching pair of slippers.

"I wouldn't be surprised," she answered as she pulled the book out of the bag and dropped it onto the table in front of him. "She'd have plenty of support."

"I noticed she stops by a lot. I'm surprised Junior lets her in the door. I mean, with the exception of me, she has to be the lightest person to walk into the club."

She noticed him eying the bananas she placed on the table. She pulled one off the bunch and passed it to him. "That's because Junior and Maia have something in common."

"You mean their inability to tolerate the color white?" he asked as he peeled the fruit. He broke off a piece and held it out to her.

She took the piece of banana from him. "Yes," she answered, before popping the fruit in her mouth.

"Oh, I hadn't noticed."

Cass chuckled. "It's that common interest that gets Maia past the front door." She sighed. "You know, on Thanksgiving, Luther's mother said something I wish Junior and Maia had heard."

"What's that?" He stretched his long legs out and ate the rest of the banana.

"She said if people worked as hard to find excuses to like one another as they do to hate each other this world would be a better place."

"That's what Sax told me when I asked him how come he didn't hate me even though my skin was the same color as those who looked down on him when he went to town."

"Though, knowing them, those words will never change anything. Junior's always going to hate you and Maia will always be suspicious of you."

"Suspicious? Why?"

"She's convinced you're hanging around me, you know, walking me home and stuff, 'cause you're, as she likes to say, sniffing up my skirt."

"I hope you don't believe that, Cass. I see you home 'cause you're a friend."

"That's what I tried to tell her, but she wouldn't let me get a word in edgewise. She's so convinced you want to be with me."

"I do," he said, laying the banana peel on the table.

Cass froze, holding a can of pineapple juice. "What did you say?"

"I said, I do want to be with you."

She slammed the can on the table. After all these years, she would have thought she'd learned.

"Maia's right?"

"No, she isn't, Cass. I don't want you thinkin' I do things for you 'cause I'm playin' some game. Like I said before, I do those things 'cause we're friends. As for sniffin' up your skirt, that's for dogs. They sniff around 'til they find a female who's willin' to let them mount her."

"And that's different from men how?"

"I can't speak for other men, only for myself, and I can assure you I'm not a dog. I don't sniff around lookin' for someone to mount, to take my pleasure and then walk away when I'm done."

"And I'm to believe you why?"

"'Cause so far I haven't done anythin' to suggest otherwise."

"Randy, why are you telling me this?"

"'Cause you deserve to know the truth."

"Thank you for letting me know your intentions," she snapped, before walking past him toward the room where she had taken their coats.

Randy jumped to his feet. "Cass, I was lettin' you know what I want, not what I intend to do."

She spun to face him. "And what's the difference?"

"When I intend to do somethin', I plan to achieve a goal and I don't let anythin' stop me or get in my way. When I want somethin', I desire it, I long to have it, but that doesn't mean I'm goin' to get it."

"Then you had best turn your attention elsewhere,

'cause I'm never—"

"Goin' to give me a chance?" he finished her sentence. "Why, Cass? 'Cause you had a bad experience? You're goin' to judge all men by the actions of your husband or some man who conned his way into your bed?"

He slowly stepped toward her. Though tempted to flee into her bedroom and lock the door until he left, she remained still.

"You were raised in the south, where you've seen bigotry and hatred show their ugly faces more than once, yet the first time I walked into The Big House you didn't take one look at me and assume I was like the bastards who looked down on you," he continued as he stopped in front of her. "Instead, you gave me a chance to prove what kinda person I am before you judged me. Now all I'm askin' is for you to let me prove to you what kinda man I am."

Cass stared up at Randy and remembered the words she had spoken to Maia a few minutes earlier and realized they also held true for her. Just like the other woman should not judge all white people by the actions of a few, she should not judge all men by the actions of two.

It was sound advice, but hard to follow. Though she wanted to believe Randy was sincere, her mind told her to get his coat, throw him out, and forget he ever said anything.

"I'm not askin' anythin' today, except that you think about what I've said."

"How do I know this isn't some line you're running on me?" she asked.

Randy reached out and brushed his fingers against

her cheek.

"I can't tell you that. All I can do is ask you to trust me."

Cass shook her head. It was easier for him to ask than for her to do.

Chapter 17

"Ouch!" Florence jumped off the chair she had been standing on while Cass worked on her dress and grabbed an empty soda bottle off the table. "I'm warning you! If you stick me with one more pin, you're going on stage tonight with a lump on your head."

Cass stood and faced the woman rubbing her derriere. "I'm sorry," she apologized. "I guess I'm a little distracted."

"I'll say. You stuck me so many times I won't be able to sit for a week."

"I didn't stick you that much."

"Like hell you didn't. I haven't been this sore back there since Momma took a belt to my behind for upsetting the table and breaking all her good dishes when I was eight."

"I'm sorry," Cass repeated.

"Now, what's gotten into you?"

"I've got a lot on my mind."

"Like what?"

"Nothing," she lied.

"Tell that to my behind," Florence fussed.

"Stop whining and get back up there so I can finish pinning your dress."

"I'm not sure I want you anywhere near me. You keep mistaking me for a pincushion."

Sucking her teeth, Cass pointed to the chair. "Get

up there."

Florence climbed back onto the chair with the bottle in her hand.

"You can put that back on the table," Cass said.

"Hell, no. I'm keeping this with me so I can make good on my promise to clock you if you stick me again."

Deciding it would be easier on Florence's derriere and her own head, Cass knelt next to the chair and worked on the hem.

"So, talk to me," Florence said.

It had been a week since Randy stopped by, and though he hadn't mentioned it again, all she did was think about their conversation. Over the months they had known each other, she'd believed he was a decent man—smart, caring, with a sense of humor. And, though he was colorblind, he was not ignorant of the struggles coloreds faced on a daily basis.

She'd like to think that over the years she had learned to be a good judge of men, but there was still the lingering doubt. What if she was wrong? Was he truly a good man—like the one her mother married—or would he turn out to be like the others who walked into her life—sweet talkers until they got her where they wanted?

"I've told you. I've got a lot on my mind," Cass finally said.

"Men problems?"

Cass looked up from the hem and cocked an eyebrow.

"I've never seen a woman this distracted unless she's thinking about a man. So, am I right?"

"I guess."

"You guess? What kind of an answer is that? You're going to tell me you don't know what's on your mind?"

Cass sighed. "Fine, it's a man."

"Good. Now we got that cleared up, are you going to give this man a name?"

She hesitated.

"No?" Florence commented after a minute of silence. "I have to guess that, too? Then I think I'll take a stab and say it's a certain light-skinned sax player who goes by the name of Randy? Ouch, dammit!" Florence screamed as a pin was jammed into her leg.

Cass jumped back in case Florence decided to follow through with her threat. Luckily for her head, the dancer was too busy rubbing her sore leg to swing the bottle, though if looks could kill, Cass knew someone would have been measuring her for a coffin at that moment.

"That's it," Florence shouted as she stepped off the chair. She placed the bottle on the table and shrugged out of the unfinished dress. "I'm taking this thing off before you poke me so full of holes water will run out of me when I drink it."

"How did you figure out it was Randy?" Cass asked as she stood.

"It doesn't take a genius to figure it out. He's the only man you ever spend time with."

"We rehearse a lot."

Florence shoved the dress into Cass's hands. "That was some mighty fine rehearsing you were doing in the Savoy. When are you going to debut that act at The Big House?"

"Okay, maybe we're not always rehearsing."

The other woman nodded. "Mmm-hmm."

"But this isn't something I need you telling everyone."

"Are you kidding me? If this got around, Junior wouldn't hesitate to get rid of Randy for messing with one of the women at the club, even though he never seems to have a problem with Angel or anyone else chasing after us. Besides, I kind of like Randy. He's a cool cat."

"Thank you."

Wearing only her slip, Florence sat down in the chair she'd been standing on. "Now that we've cleared up the who, tell me the what."

Cass pulled out another chair from the table and sat down. "Do you think it's possible for him to be serious about all of this?"

"All of what?"

"Harlem, The Big House, him being friends with coloreds, you know, everything?"

"More specifically, can he be serious about you?"

"Well, I guess. Sort of," Cass replied, fingering the material she held.

"You enjoy being vague, don't you?"

"Okay, yes. Do you think it's possible for Randy to be serious about a colored woman and…I mean, wanting more than to see what it's like to be with one?"

"Anything's possible."

Cass tossed the dress on the table. "Thanks, that was a lot of help," she sighed, slumping back in her chair.

"Well, it's true. Anything's possible. I can't give you a definite yes, because I don't know what's in his mind. Only he knows that." Florence leaned forward, bracing her arms on her legs. "So what brought about the question?"

"Randy stopped by the other day and told me he wanted to be more than friends."

"And you're trying to figure out what's his angle?"

"Yes."

"You know, there is such a thing as being too cautious."

"I'm not being too cautious, I'm just trying not to get hurt."

"Which is fine, but after you've convinced yourself Randy only wants to experiment with you and you send him packing, then what? You'll have to come up with a reason why you can't be with the next cat interested in you. Eventually, you'll run out of reasonable excuses and come up with things like his shirt's too wrinkled or his hair's too curly."

"Be serious." Cass chuckled.

"I am, 'cause you will. Listen, instead of trying so hard to find excuses not to go out with him, why don't you figure out why you should give him a chance?"

"It's not that simple."

"Why not? 'Cause he's white?"

"Honestly, no." As strange as it seemed, his race had nothing to do with it. She knew it should be an issue, but it wasn't. "When I'm alone with him, I don't see a white man. I see someone I can talk to and laugh with. It's not until we're in public that I'm reminded of our differences. When Randy walks me home, I see how the colored folks look at us. The men glare as if they want to beat the crap out of him for simply talking to me, and the women roll their eyes at me as if I'm a prostitute. Yet Randy ignores them and continues his conversation like it's the most normal thing to see a colored woman and white man together. Before I know it, I've forgotten about everyone else."

"Then if it's not the color of his skin, what's keeping you from admitting you like him?"

"I haven't had the best of luck when it comes to men. The ones I've come in contact with were perfect gentlemen—until they got me in a position where they could take what they wanted from me."

"Let me ask you a question. When you went to The Savoy with Randy, who paid your admission?"

"He did."

"And when you left the ballroom, did you go somewhere else?"

"We went out to eat."

"And he paid?"

"Yes."

"And, after you ate?"

"He walked me home."

"When you got there, did he try anything?"

"He kissed me."

"And?"

"And nothing. He kissed me, and then I came inside by myself and went to bed." Then she'd spent the rest of the night dreaming of the kiss. It had been unexpected, but gentle, as if he wanted to take his time and savor the moment.

"So nothing happened that night. I guess since then he's tried to collect his payment for taking you to dinner and dancing?"

"No."

"Has he even hinted that you owe him, or acted like you stiffed him?"

"No."

"Then, Cass, the way I see it is if he was all about taking what he wanted, he would have tried by now."

"Maybe he's simply buying time."

"And maybe he's a decent man. You know there is such a thing as one."

Cass snorted.

"There are a few out there," Florence insisted as she sat back. "Now, the majority of the men at the club aren't examples of decent men, but if you pick through the weeds, you'll find some. Look at my father. In all my life, I've never seen him treat my mother with anything but respect. He's never laid a hand on her or cheated on her. Then there's Red. Before his wife passed away two years ago, we all saw how devoted he was to her. He came to the club, put in his time, and then went straight home to her. Not once did anyone ever see him look at another woman. And are you going to forget your father? From the way you talk about him, I can't believe he ever done your momma wrong."

Cass nodded. She couldn't remember a time when her mother shed a tear, packed her bags, or threatened to pack her father's bags because of something he said or did. Nor did she recall her mother ever wondering where he was, what he was doing, or who he was doing it with. That wasn't to say they never argued. They'd had their share of disagreements, but they always worked through their problems, together.

The memory of how happy two people could be together did not help erase the memories of her disastrous encounters with the opposite sex.

"But what if—"

"There are no what-ifs, just the excuses you're

making 'cause you're scared. I don't blame you for being cautious and not jumping into something with the first man who comes along and sweet-talks you. But, if you don't ever take a chance, you can end up letting a good man slip away. There's a chance Randy can turn out to be worse than your ex-husband. But, on the other hand, he could be the type of guy every woman dreams of—decent, loving, and totally devoted to her. I know that's what I'm looking for, though in a darker package."

Cass laughed.

"Think about what I said, but don't take too long making up your mind, 'cause no man's going to wait forever for a woman."

Florence got up and left the kitchen.

"Where you going?"

"To put some clothes on."

"But what about your dress?" Cass asked, holding up the unfinished piece.

"Humph. You've lost your mind if you think I'm going to get back on that chair and let you stick me again. We'll finish it when you can focus on what you're doing."

Chapter 18

"What devilment are the three of you up to now?" Cass asked as she stepped from the taxi she'd shared with Florence to The Big House.

Randy turned, hands behind his back, to face the woman who stood with her hands on her hips and a frown that reminded him of a stern school teacher. Bill and Earl, two of the neighborhood boys who hung around the club to earn extra money running errands, followed his example.

"What makes you think we were up to somethin'?" Randy asked with a straight face.

"I don't know. Maybe it's 'cause you're out here in the cold when you could be inside where it's warm."

"Don't you know the cold's good for you? It gets your blood flowin'."

Cass looked at him like he'd lost his mind.

"Well, that's what they'd tell me when I was younger, before handin' me a shovel and sendin' me outside to work."

She shook her head and rolled her eyes. "Bill? Earl? What are y'all doing out here?" she asked, focusing her attention on his partners in crime.

"Standing around," Bill answered.

"Talking to you," Earl added.

Cass slapped Randy's arm.

"Hey, what'd I do now?"

"Listen to how sassy these boys have become since you started working here."

"Me…sassy?"

"Yes, you. And, what do have behind your back?"

"My hands."

With an exasperated sigh, she walked into the club. Laughing, Florence winked at him before following her

Ten minutes later, he strolled into the ladies' dressing room, where Cass sat at a table sewing a button on a shirt. She did not look up from her work when he propped a foot on the chair next to her and leaned forward on his knee.

"How long are you goin' to ignore me?" he asked after a minute.

"I'm not talking to you."

"That sounds like talkin' to me."

She turned in her seat until her back was to him.

"You're actin' like a spoiled brat."

She glanced over her shoulder and stuck out her tongue, then turned her back to him again. When Randy chuckled, she spun around in her chair to face him.

"Don't you dare laugh at me. You should be ashamed of yourself. Teaching those boys to sass me."

"I didn't teach them nothin' of the sort," he protested as he straddled the chair. He leaned forward with his crossed arms on the back. "I'm innocent. Really."

"Sure you are."

"Would it help if I told you they realized they were out of line and they're sorry?"

"Yes, but that doesn't excuse you."

"What did I do?"

"Taught them your sassiness."

"Me? Girl, if they handed out awards for sassiness, you'd win top prize."

"I don't have the slightest idea what you're talking about."

"You ain't foolin' no one by battin' those pretty little eyes of yours."

She stuck out her bottom lip.

"And poutin' won't do you any good either." He reached forward and tapped the tip of her nose with a forefinger. "Admit it, you're sassy."

He saw the corner of her lips twitch. "Don't you have anything to do with yourself?" she asked, trying but failing to maintain a straight face.

"I do," he replied.

"Why don't you go do it?"

"I am. I'm admirin' a sassy little gal who I wouldn't have any other way."

"Why are you really down here?"

"I went out to mail a letter and decided to drop by and maybe bump into someone."

"Were you looking for anyone in particular, or did you just plan to bump into complete strangers?"

"Thought maybe I'd bump into Junior. It's been twelve hours since someone's called me an ofay."

"Junior's on his way over here," Luther announced as he strolled into the room. "If you wait around a couple of minutes, you'll get your wish."

"I was jokin'. I get enough of that." Randy stood. "I think I'll go and continue my walk."

"I figured you had something between your ears besides air."

Randy winked at Cass before strolling out of the room.

****

"You two have been spending a lot of time together," Luther commented after Randy left. He turned the chair next to her and sat down.

"We rehearse a lot," Cass replied.

"Rehearse? I didn't know you were planning on adding a dance to your number."

Cass cocked an eyebrow.

"Several people have mentioned that you not only perform well at the club, but you also dance well at the Savoy."

"Several people need to mind their own business." She glanced down at her sewing.

"Cass." Luther had a tone in his voice that reminded her of her father whenever he was about to dispense advice.

"We went dancing. What's the harm in that?"

"There's no harm, if that's all you plan to do."

"I don't know what you mean."

"I've noticed the way you look at him."

"How's that?"

"Like you're interested in being more than singing partners or friends."

Cass did not answer. She would not confirm or deny what he thought he saw, since she was trying to figure out what she felt for Randy. She enjoyed his company, he was easy to talk to, and she admired his thoughtfulness. She was also curious about what it would be like to be with him, whether being with him would be as special as he claimed or if she would be left feeling used again.

"I can also tell that Randy wants to do more than practice numbers with you. I wanted to talk to you because I don't want to see you hurt."

"Randy wouldn't—" she began, ready to defend him against anyone, even though she was not sure how he would treat her if she decided to be with him.

"I'm not saying he would purposely try to hurt you, but you have to remember he's not like us."

"'Cause he's white?"

"Randy seems like a good boy, but you have to understand this is temporary for him. When he gets tired of being the open-minded white man, he's going to move downtown where he belongs. And, when he does, he's leaving all this behind. He won't be inviting his colored friends to hang with him, and he definitely won't be taking any colored girls with him.

"I'm only telling you this because I care about you. I know you're a woman, but you have as much experience with men as a child does."

She could not argue with him about that. Cass would be the first to admit her experience with men had been not worth mentioning. Two men. Two bad experiences. Twice used and then discarded without a second thought.

Luther reached out and patted her hand. "I want you to think about what I said before you get too involved," he said as he stood up. "By the way, don't make any plans for tonight."

"Why? Is Junior inviting another associate to meet me?"

"You'll see," he said, walking away.

****

Staring down at Cass, Randy wondered at how quickly things could change. That afternoon she had been joking with him, but by the time he returned to the club that evening, she was distant. He had tried to talk to her, but she went out of her way to avoid him. When she was finally alone, it was time to rehearse.

Once they finished practicing, he waited until she had gone downstairs before he left the stage. He found her talking to Florence and Eli outside the men's dressing room. Without caring how rude he was, he grabbed her by the elbow and steered her away from the group, claiming he had to discuss a number. Ignoring her whispered protests, he led her to his dressing room, where he closed the door and stood in front of it, blocking her exit.

"What has gotten into you?" she asked.

"I should be askin' you that question, since you've been avoidin' me."

"I've been busy."

"And Junior and I are best friends." He leaned against the door frame and crossed his arms over his chest. "What's goin' on, Cass?"

"Nothing," she answered, shaking her head.

"Come on, it's me. What's wrong?"

She hesitated before letting out a sigh. "I have something on my mind."

"I thought we were friends."

"We are."

"So what is it? And don't say it's not me, 'cause if it wasn't, you wouldn't be avoidin' me."

"Would you believe it's me?"

"No."

"Then will you accept that I have a lot to think about?"

"About what we talked about last week?"

"Yes."

Though they had not spoken about their previous conversation, it gave him hope that she was thinking about it. He placed his hands on the wall on either side of her. Without giving her a second to think, he leaned down and covered her lips with his.

She tensed but did not push him away. Instead, she allowed him to trace the outline of her full lips with his. Despite his desire to devour her, he took his time. He wanted to move slowly and gain her trust instead of rushing her and losing everything.

His patience was rewarded when she began to relax and return the kiss. His hand slipped from the wall to her shoulder and made its way down, until it encircled her waist. Her arms slipped around his neck.

He held onto her, taking in everything—the feel of her in his arms, the light scent of coconut in her hair, the sweet taste of her lips, and her soft sighs in his ear. Once he was certain he'd committed everything to memory, he pulled back and saw the confusion and passion in her eyes.

"That's not helping," Cass murmured.

He was sure she was unaware that her fingers teased the nap of his hair—and of the effect her touch had on him.

"I was hopin' it would help sway things in my favor," he said, though it had backfired on him. He would need more than a moment to himself before he got back onstage, or it would be a long night.

"It added to my confusion."

"Cass!" a woman screeched from outside.

Forgetting how small the room was, she jumped back and banged her head on the wall.

"Oww, dammit," Cass hissed.

"Girl, we need to do somethin' about your filthy mouth," Randy scolded.

"I'll worry the hell about it later."

"Cass!"

Before he could stop her, Cass ducked under his arm and opened the door.

"You don't have to shout the roof off," she yelled back. "I'm right here."

Randy listened until her voice faded to the opposite end of the club before pulling his door closed and unzipping his pants. For once, he was grateful for having a room to himself, as it allowed him to deal with the aftereffect of the kiss in private.

****

All concerns regarding Randy were replaced with thoughts of revenge when Junior approached the stage during her last number. She considered stopping in the middle of the song and storming off. However, the plan was ruled out when she noticed Florence and three other chorus girls blocking the door that led backstage.

She finished the song while glaring at Junior as he stepped up next to her. He took her elbow to prevent her from leaving as he moved to the microphone.

"Ladies and gentlemen, before Cass runs off, I want you to help The Big House wish our star a happy birthday."

His words did not register until a cake was rolled into the center of the dance floor and the band played "Happy Birthday." Surprised, she allowed Junior to escort her to the cake, where the chorus girls gathered around her and sang.

"Are you gonna blow out those candles or let them set my place on fire?" Junior asked, once the song was over.

There was another round of applause after she blew out twenty-three candles.

"Red," Luther called over his shoulder to signal the band to play their next number.

"This is why you told me not to make plans for tonight?" Cass asked.

"You think we'd let your birthday go by without doing something?" he answered.

"But how—?"

"Did we manage this without you knowing? Careful planning."

"It wasn't easy, with you nosing around here," Florence added.

"Are you going to talk or cut the cake?" someone called out.

"The cake can wait," Luther replied. "I want to dance with the birthday girl first."

The cake was pushed to the side to make room on the dance floor. Once the song was over, she changed partners. Other couples joined them, and the party eventually turned into a jam session.

At three o'clock, Cass noticed Randy slip backstage. She was on the other side of the room, and by the time she worked her way through the crowd, he was gone.

The clock struck five before anyone started showing signs of slowing down. It was another hour before Cass stepped outside the club carrying a bag of presents and what was left of the cake.

As she started down the deserted street, a figure stepped from an alley. He walked toward her, and her mind yelled for her to run. She knew it would be the right thing to do…

"Why didn't you tell me it was your birthday?" Randy asked, disappointment in his tone.

Despite the high stakes, being with Randy felt right. Besides, she asked herself, what was the harm in talking to him?

"I didn't think it mattered. It's not like I even know your birth date."

"September 9th."

"Oh."

"I was born in Mobile, Alabama."

"I know that."

"My mother was two days tryin' to give birth to me."

Cass stared at him.

"I arrived at six fifty-three in the mornin'."

She did not reply.

"I came in feet first. That's probably why I seem backwards at times."

"Why are you telling me all this?"

"So, you'll never have an excuse to keep somethin' from me. Now, where was I? Oh, yes. There was no doctor, just a midwife. I think her name was Mildred."

"Okay, I'm sorry I didn't tell you it was my birthday. I didn't think it was important."

"Why? It's not like you're old enough to start hidin' your age. But then again, you probably have to so you can skip school and work in a club. How old are you anyway? Sixteen?"

"You know I'm twenty-three."

"I don't know nothin' of the sort. I can only go by what you tell me."

"If my birthday mattered so much, why didn't you

stay and have some cake?"

"'Cause I didn't want to ruin your good time."

"How were you going to do that? By getting drunk and dancing on the tables naked?"

"You know if I'd stayed everyone else would have left."

"I would have insisted they stay."

"So you could've listened to Junior curse me with every other breath he took?"

Cass sighed, knowing he was right. "Why'd you wait around?"

"To say happy birthday."

"You waited outside all this time just to wish me happy birthday? You could've told me that the next time you saw me."

"This is the next time I saw you."

"You're irritating."

"It's 'cause it's past your bedtime." He reached for her shopping bag. "Give me this so I can get you home and you can go to bed."

"Where I come from, a gentleman asks a woman if she'd like him to escort her home."

"And I also know where you come from little girls don't hang out in clubs all night."

"I'm twenty-three."

"You're twenty-three seconds from bein' tossed over my shoulder and carried home."

"What a charming invitation. Rudolph Valentino you're not."

"You can list all my faults on the way home."

Cass took him up on his offer. By the time they arrived at her apartment, she had listed his faults, many of them silly, along with the necessary steps to correct them.

"Explain to me once again how spinach will make me more sociable?" he asked as he unlocked her door.

"It's simple," she replied. "Spinach is healthy for you. Healthy people are happy people. Happy people are sociable people. So, if you have a healthy meal, which includes liver and spinach, you'll be happy and more sociable."

"There's no way I'd be happy if I ate liver and spinach. I'd be cursin' the person who served me that vile combination."

"It's not vile. You should taste Momma's liver. It's tender, and seasoned just right."

He placed her keys in her hand, though he did not release them. "I'm sure your momma can make good liver, but there's no way I'm goin' to eat it."

"I'm going to write Momma for her recipe."

"I'm not goin' to eat it."

"Seems like every time I make it, I leave something out."

"Girl, didn't you hear me? I don't like liver."

"I heard you. I'm just paying you no mind."

Randy sighed as he pushed her door open. "Go inside so I can go home and get some sleep before I come back here."

"Come back? Why?"

"To take you out to dinner. I have to celebrate your birthday properly."

"It's not necessary for you to make such a big deal over my birthday."

"I know it's not, but I want to. Besides, I thought little girls liked makin' a fuss on their birthday."

"If you don't stop calling me a little girl, I'll—"

Cass gasped when Randy leaned forward and kissed her behind the ear. A bolt shot down her spine and settled between her legs. The sensation wasn't unpleasant. It left her wanting him to do something to relieve the growing ache.

Was that what he meant when he talked about a man preparing a woman?

He licked the lobe before whispering, "Were you able to think about what was on your mind?"

Feeling his hot breath against her skin, she sighed. Unable to find the words to speak, she nodded.

"And?"

Cass shook her head. She took a step back to collect her thoughts. "I'm not sure," she finally said when she could form a coherent sentence.

"Are you really givin' it some thought, or are you just tryin' to put me off until I give up and go away?" Randy asked. "I'll tell you right now, I'm not goin' anywhere until you tell me no."

"I'm not trying to put you off. When I make my decision, you'll be the first to know."

Randy leaned forward. She expected another kiss that would leave her wanting more. In fact, she wanted him to kiss her like that. However, he disappointed her when he simply gave her a quick peck on the lips.

"Go inside," he said as he backed away. "I'll pick you up at three."

"Yes," she replied as she stepped into the apartment.

As she closed the door, she realized a little talking could lead to a lot of things.

Chapter 19

Cass crossed her arms and poked out her bottom lip. "You've proven you know where to find good food, and I trust you won't try to poison me. So why won't you tell me where we're going?" she complained.

"I told you. We're goin' downtown," Randy replied, trying but failing to avoid staring at the placement of her arms.

Even though she was wearing a thick wool coat, he could envision her round breasts hidden underneath. It was the last thing he needed to think about while riding downtown on the A, where he could do nothing about his body's reaction to her.

He forced his gaze to her face and silently groaned at the sight of her bottom lip poking out. She may have intended the pout to convince him to reveal her surprise, but all it did was tempt him to lean over and taste her lips, right there, throwing all propriety out the window.

"Where downtown?"

Randy finally settled on staring out the window behind her at the next car. "To a restaurant."

"What restaurant?"

"It's a secret."

With a huff, Cass dropped her hands into her lap. "Did I mention you're too secretive?"

"That was fault number eleven and two sixty-two,"

Randy replied, looking back down at her. Though her lip was no longer sticking out, it did not diminish his urge to kiss her. "You listed it twice."

"'Cause it's a really irritating fault."

"How come you never let me list your faults?"

"What faults?" she replied with a straight face that made him throw his head back and laugh. "Shh, you're causing a scene."

Randy glanced over his shoulder at the riders who shared the car with them. Several glared back at him, their contempt clearly written on their faces.

"So?" he asked, turning back to Cass.

"So? They're not exactly admiring the cut of your suit. Though I'm sure a few think your tie would make a perfect noose."

"They're jealous." He reached over, took her hand and raised it to his lips. "The women wish they looked like you, and the men wish they were lucky enough to be with you."

"Randy, behave yourself," she hissed as she snatched her hand back. "I don't want to be arrested for prostitution."

"Who'd mistake you for a prostitute?"

With the hemline of her skirt reaching halfway down her calf, her blouse buttoned up to her neck, and her practical beige coat and matching hat, Cass would be the last person anyone could accuse of prostitution.

"I'm sure that's the excuse they'd use to explain you with me."

"Cass, this is New York. It's not unheard of for coloreds and whites to associate with one another up here."

"You can take the person out of the south, but you

can't take the attitude out of the person. From the glares some of these people are giving us, a mixed friendship is not as socially accepted as you may like it to be."

"Then isn't it a good thin' that I don't have to, or care to, seek their approval to take you out."

He spoke loud enough for the woman sitting in the single seat across from them to hear. The blonde, whose hair was streaked with gray, had stared at them since she boarded the train at 59th Street. With a huff she redirected her gaze to the door.

Cass dropped her head forward and covered her face with her hands. "Oh, lordy, he's gonna get us lynched. They're gonna pull us off this train, find the nearest tree—"

"Okay, okay, I'll behave myself," Randy insisted, pulling a hand from her face.

She dropped her other hand into her lap and peeped over at him. "Do you promise?"

"Yes, I promise I'll behave myself. Now, come on." He reached up, grabbed a strap, and swung up from his seat.

Taking his extended hand, Cass allowed him to pull her up. He led her to the door as the train sped out of the 14th Street station. With no care as to who was watching, he slipped an arm around her waist. She tensed under his touch, but did not pull away.

Randy was not naïve enough to believe his feelings for Cass would change the way others looked at them. All some would see when looking at them was a colored woman and a white man. Some would care less; others would think she was easy or he was using her; a few would be outright hostile toward them. However, it didn't matter to him what others thought, as long as

Cass did not have a problem with the difference in color.

The doors opened at West 4th Street, and Randy led her off the train and out of the station. As they reached the street, the woman who had sat across from them on the train walked by.

"Some people need to go back to where they belong and stick with their own kind," she commented.

Just because he didn't care what others thought, it didn't mean he'd allow people to get away with saying anything they wanted.

"Then I wish you a safe trip back to hell, where you'll be with the other minions of Satan," Randy replied. He tipped his hat to her, before taking Cass's hand. They walked off in the opposite direction, leaving the woman standing in the middle of the sidewalk with her mouth hanging open.

"You can't talk like that to a lady," Cass scolded.

"Don't you dare call her a lady," Randy said. "As long as you're with me, no one's goin' to insult you and get away with it."

"I don't want you fighting because of me."

"Consider it payback for all the times you stood up for me at the club."

"And what if the next person who has something to say happens to be twice your size?"

"I'll admit I'm not much of a fighter, so while he's beatin' me to a pulp, I hope you can run in those pumps," he said, pointing to the black high-heeled shoes on Cass's feet.

"Then I'll pray no one else bothers us. It wouldn't be much of a birthday if I have to carry you back home and take care of you."

"Trust me, gettin' the mess beat out of me is no fun, no matter what day it is."

Luck was on their side and no one else harassed them as he led her down a maze of side streets to a brownstone.

"We're here," he announced, leading her down a flight of steps into the basement.

"Here" was a small club called Eden. Outside, there had been no signs or advertisements that would catch a person's attention and make them interested enough to go inside and give the place a try.

Inside, the lights were dim and it took a minute for their eyes to adjust to the darkness. Candles sat in the center of each table. In the front, a band played soft ballads. Yet it was not the atmosphere but the patrons that captured Cass's attention, Randy noticed.

In the front, two women held hands while enjoying a conversation. A couple of tables away, two men sat near each other, one with his arm thrown over the back of the other's chair. Besides the same-sex couples, there were couples of mixed races enjoying meals and the music.

"How did you find this place?" she whispered once they were seated. "Aside from the Savoy, I never knew there was a place mixed couples could gather."

"There are a few in the city, but not too many of them advertise, for fear of being raided for some trumped-up charge. They get their business through word of mouth."

She glanced around the room at the bare, unpainted brick walls and the concrete floor. He wished he could take her to a four-star restaurant, but when they went out, he preferred someplace that not only accepted him or her but both of them together. Unfortunately, the few he had come across would never make the society pages.

"Is that why the atmosphere is so…so…" she hesitated as if she was searching for the right words.

"Plain?" Randy said as he lit a cigarette. "They don't want to attract attention to themselves."

"They do a good job. If I were passing by, I wouldn't give this place a second glance."

"That's the point."

"But does it work in keeping the police off their backs?" she asked, looking back at him.

"From what I've heard, this place used to be raided regularly, but the police could never make any of the charges stick. All the licenses were in order, no illegal activity was permitted, and the atmosphere was so calm—no dancin', singin', or anyone talkin' above a whisper—the judge got tired of seein' the owners and he warned the police to leave this place alone. That was months ago, and the place has not been bothered since."

She nodded, seeming to accept his explanation. Yet instead of relaxing, she sat rigid in the chair and fiddled with the edge of her napkin.

"Hey, why so quiet?" Randy asked as he reached across the table and touched her cheek.

She glanced up. Worry lines creased her forehead.

"I was just thinking," she confessed.

"About what?"

"Us. You."

With no one around to judge who they were or who they were with, there was no worry about the day being ruined by someone seeking to give her opinion about them being together. However, her lingering doubts about his intentions continued to worry her.

Randy wished he could change the past, make it so she had never met her ex-husband. Maybe then she'd believe in "Happily Ever After" instead of waiting for impending doom.

However, had she not met Henry she might never have travelled from Piney Woods, North Carolina, to New York City, and she might never have met Randy.

"Talk to me," he said. He wanted to reassure her that what he felt for her was real and he had no intentions of breaking her heart. Yet he realized it would take more than one conversation in one afternoon to earn her trust. "You can ask me anythin'."

Cass hesitated a moment before she blurted out, "Have you ever been with a colored woman?"

Randy dropped his hand and leaned back in his chair. "Yes, I have. I met her in Florida. She frequented the club I worked at. You remind me of her. Sassy and smart."

"What happened?"

"Her family couldn't handle our differences." He rested his cigarette in the ashtray and reached across the table and laced his fingers through hers. "When it came to choosin' between them and me… Well, as you see, I'm alone."

"It's tough having to choose between family and the one you want to be with. You never know what the outcome will bring and whether you'll end up regretting your decision."

He knew she was remembering how she chose Henry and the heartache that resulted from her decision.

"I know, and I don't blame her. I couldn't ask her to give up everythin' for a life I knew wouldn't be easy.

I just wish the issue would have been somethin' more important than the color of my skin."

"This is so complicated," she whispered.

"Life is complicated," he added. "But we don't have to solve all life's problems right now. Instead, we should sit back, listen to the band, eat a good meal, and enjoy each other's company."

"And later?"

"Let's just take everythin' one step at a time...concentrate on the present and worry about later when later comes."

"You make it sound so simple," Cass said.

He shook his head. "I won't lie and say it's goin' to be easy."

"I wish you would."

"I can't, 'cause the lie would eventually be revealed for what it is, and that won't help build trust. Right now, all I can promise you is a special afternoon."

****

Randy had kept his word and made the afternoon special. After they ate, they went back uptown and saw a movie at the Lafayette Theatre. They then stopped by Cornbread 'n' Grits for coffee and cake before returning to her apartment.

"I can't remember when I enjoyed a Sunday afternoon as much as I did today," Cass said as she waltzed around the sofa.

"Are you sure you're twenty-three?" Randy asked, hanging up their coats in the closet by the door.

She stopped dancing. "Don't start that again," she sighed, placing her hands on her hips.

"You know, you shouldn't stand like that."

"Why not?"

"'Cause you draw attention to your hips."

"And what's wrong with my hips?"

A lecherous smile spread across his lips as he leered at her. "Nothin', from where I'm standin'."

She moved to cross her arms.

His eyes travelled up to her breasts. "And I wouldn't suggest crossin' your arms over your chest, either."

"Then where do you suggest I put them?" she asked, holding her hands up in the air.

Randy pushed the closet door closed behind him and strolled over to her. He took her arms and draped them around his neck. "Right here would be fine." He placed his hands on her waist and swayed from side to side.

"What are you doing?"

He cocked an eyebrow. "Dancin'."

"A moment ago you were teasing me for dancing around the room."

"That's 'cause you didn't have a partner."

Cass had to admit she preferred having a partner. After her experiences with Henry and Pedro, she'd never thought she could be comfortable with any man. However, she enjoyed being with Randy. He was easy to talk to, he made her smile, and, most importantly, she felt secure around him.

But how she could be sure she was not being set up? Yes, there were signs, but what if she missed them? Or what if he was skillful enough to hide them until it was too late? Where would she be then?

"You've gone silent on me," Randy said. "That's usually not a good sign."

Cass mentally shook herself. She did not want to think about the future or the "what ifs." She wanted to take his advice and focus on the now.

"What about the music?" she finally asked.

"You want music." He hummed a few notes of "I Only Have Eyes For You" before he asked, "Do you want me to sing, too?"

"I thought you couldn't sing."

"It's not one of my best talents, but for you, I can try."

Randy sang one verse. His rich tenor voice flowed through her, caressing every nerve. She could listen to him forever.

"That was beautiful," she critiqued, when he finished.

"I prefer to listen to you sing. Besides, I don't do that in public, so don't get any ideas for a new number." He stepped back, took her hand, and led her to the sofa. "And now, for the next part of the evenin'."

"What?" she asked as she sat on the edge. She watched him retrieve his case, which he had brought with him when he came by to pick her up.

"You'll see—or better yet, hear," he answered.

"You're full of surprises today."

He winked as he assembled his saxophone. Once it was ready, he played a medley of songs they had performed at The Big House. He finished with "Happy Birthday."

"Thank you," she said.

Randy placed the instrument in the case, then got down on one knee before her. He reached into his jacket and pulled out a small wrapped package.

"What's this?" Cass asked as he handed her the

gift.

"Open it."

She ripped off the paper and stared with wide eyes at the miniature black jewelry box with hand-painted flowers. The box had caught her eye at the novelty store two weeks ago when she'd dragged him in to make him buy a pair of winter gloves. "I can't believe you got this for me."

"I saw you admirin' it in the store, and I knew you'd never buy it for yourself," he replied. "I went back the next day to buy it, though I wasn't sure at the time when I'd give it to you. Look inside."

Cass opened the box. Inside the small black velvet pocket was a pair of gold teardrop earrings.

"They're beautiful. But you shouldn't have."

"Why not?"

"It's too much."

"I said I was goin' to make this day special."

He reached up and replaced the earrings she was wearing with his gift.

"How do they look?" she asked.

His fingers traced the edge of her lobe. "Beautiful," he whispered.

Cass saw the desire in his eyes. His hand slipped behind her head. Slowly he pulled her to him, until he could trace the outline of her lips with small pecks.

"Open your mouth," he whispered.

Cass complied and was rewarded with a new sensation as his tongue slipped into her mouth. She had never been kissed like this before. Henry never did anything beyond entering her, while Pedro had slobbered on her, reminding her of a dog.

The thought of Pedro brought to mind his

statement on showing gratitude. She thought about the dinner, the show, and the gifts Randy had just given her. He had never demanded anything from her in the past, but then, he had never spent so much on her, either.

The realization of what they were doing and what it could lead to struck her. She abruptly pulled back from him.

"Randy, I don't think…" She braced herself to scramble away in case he pounced.

To her surprise, he slid onto the sofa and took her hand.

"I'm sorry—"

"Shhh," he whispered, placing a finger on her lips. "Don't apologize."

"It's just that—"

"I understand, you're not ready," he whispered, pulling her head to his shoulder. "I promise I'll wait 'til you are."

Chapter 20

Cass and Florence sat at a table in the corner, whispering to each other like two girls sharing secrets in church. Randy wondered what mischief they were up to.

Though she was not having drinks with anyone, she had returned to the dining room after changing into her street clothes. The creases in Luther's forehead reflected his surprise in the deviation in her routine. Frowning, he had spent the past hour alternating glances between the singer and the musician.

As the band packed up the equipment, Luther walked around and critiqued individual musicians on the evening's performance. Once he finished talking to Red, he walked away without a word to Randy.

Randy closed his case and headed in the same direction.

"Hey, Luther," he called out before the club's co-owner stepped inside his office. "You got a moment?"

Luther stopped. "Yes."

"You seemed a bit preoccupied. Was there somethin' wrong with my performance?"

"It was fine. Actually, I'm trying to find a way to work in a couple more numbers with Cass and you."

Randy nodded, accepting the explanation. Any changes in the show that gave him more time in the spotlight would result in an outburst from Junior.

"Can't wait to hear Junior's response when you tell him."

"He won't be pleased, that's for sure. But I've gotten positive feedback from our clientele regarding the two numbers you do with Cass. You two are good together."

"Thank you. You know, Cass is easy to work with."

"Yes, I know."

"And, speakin' of Cass, I think I'll go see what that sassy gal's up to tonight."

He turned back to the stairs, but stopped when Luther called out, "She's a good girl."

Though Cass was a grown woman, Randy realized Luther watched over her as if she were one of his daughters. And, as a surrogate father, he would have concerns about Cass's welfare and about anyone who became involved with her. But nothing the other man said would change how he felt about Cass.

"I don't know what she's told you about herself, but she hasn't had much experience with men. What little she's had wasn't good. I know what she does and who she does it with is none of my business, but I don't want to see her hurt."

"You don't have to worry about her, sir," Randy replied, giving the man as much respect as if he were Cass's real father. "Hurtin' Cass is the last thing on my mind."

"Not many people start off with the intention of hurting another, but it happens. Usually, it's because people don't stop to think about the consequences before they leap into something."

"Since I first came to The Big House, Cass has

been good to me, which is somethin' I can't say about many people here. I have no intention of repayin' her kindness by hurtin' her. We're friends, and I'd never do anythin' to jeopardize that."

"Then maybe you shouldn't try to be more than friends."

Randy knew nothing but saying he would leave her alone would satisfy Luther. But he refused to lie to the man. Unless she said she wanted nothing to do with him, he had no intention of leaving Cass alone simply to pacify someone else.

"Thank you for your concern, but the decision's Cass's to make," Randy replied.

Luther nodded and walked into his office. Randy headed back to the dining hall to retrieve his saxophone. He scanned the room and noticed Cass's absence. Since she had not passed him downstairs, while he was talking to Luther, he knew she had not retrieved her coat and left the club. Instead of searching her out, he decided to change his suit.

Distracted by the conversation he'd had with Luther, it took a second before Randy realized his case was lighter than it should be. He placed it on the table, opened it and stared at emptiness.

His saxophone had once belonged to his mentor and, as one woman in New Orleans had found out, it was not something anyone messed with. He'd been in that city less than twenty-four hours when, coming from an audition, he was approached by a lady who expressed an attraction to musicians. Young and inexperienced, he agreed to have drinks with her. The next morning, he woke up in an alley, relieved of his wallet and saxophone.

Sweet Jazz

He spent the day searching the seediest neighborhoods for the woman. When he finally located her that evening, she was in the process of trying to convince another sucker she was attracted to him.

Carrying a two-by-four to appear more intimidating, Randy approached the couple and claimed she was his wife. The other man believed the lie and hurried away without an argument.

Under normal circumstances, Randy would never have considered striking a woman, but at that moment, he had been prepared to beat a confession out of her. Luckily, he did not have to toss aside his morals. Once backed into an alley, she had eagerly offered to return the instrument.

Since that day, Randy was more protective of the saxophone, only letting his guard down when he was in the club. He had reasoned that despite their feelings toward him, his fellow musicians would respect his instrument. That was, he realized, everyone but one.

Acting as if there was nothing out of the ordinary, Angel leant against the wall near the kitchen entrance, talking to Eli. He casually smoked a cigarette like he had been in the same spot all the time.

To a complete stranger, Angel was the epitome of innocence. But Randy was no stranger. He had been the victim of too many of the other man's pranks and knew better.

"Okay, you've had your fun," Randy called out as he walked across the room. "Where is it?"

The drummer continued talking, ignoring him.

"Hey, I asked you a question." Randy stopped in front of the two musicians.

"What?" Angel asked.

"Where's my sax?"

The darker man straightened. "Search me," he replied. He turned to walk away, showing he was not intimidated.

Randy grabbed Angel by his jacket and shoved him against the wall.

"What the—"

"Hey, man," Eli said. He pulled on Randy's arm. "*¡Cálmate!*"

"I will not calm down," Randy yelled at the trumpeter before facing Angel. "I'm only gonna ask one more time before I start beatin' the truth out of you." He slowly enunciated each word: "Where the hell is my sax?"

"Yo, ofay, I don't have your damn reed," Angel protested as he tried to pry Randy's hands off his jacket.

"Let him go, Randy," Luther yelled, rushing into the dining room.

"Not 'til he tells me what he did with my sax."

"What's going on out here?" Red asked as he walked out of the kitchen with Cass and Florence behind him. "And Randy, what the hell was your saxophone doing in the garbage?"

Randy looked at the instrument the pianist was holding. A strand of spaghetti still clung to the bell.

Taking advantage of his distraction, Angel slipped out of his grasp and introduced a fist to the fairer man's face.

Randy staggered back. He regained his balance, rushed forward and slammed his fist to Angel's stomach. He was preparing to throw another punch when two sets of hands pulled him back.

Sweet Jazz

"Enough," Luther shouted. "You know one of the rules of the club is no fighting."

Doubled over in pain, Angel grunted. "He started it," he said, wasting no time in placing the blame. "Can his ass."

"Fine," Randy said, shaking free of Luther and Eli. "You've been tryin' to get rid of me since I got here."

He grabbed his saxophone from Red, pulled off the spaghetti and flicked it at Angel. He then walked to the table where he'd left the case. With both items in hand, he headed downstairs to his dressing room.

"Randy?"

He closed the case, then looked at Cass, who stood outside his door. He knew he would regret it in the morning, but he was too angry to deal with her. They could curse him, ignore him, play pranks on him…but they crossed the line when they laid hands on his instrument.

"Not now, Cass."

"But, Randy—"

"I said, not now," he barked before grabbing his coat and case. He marched past her and out of the club.

****

"What the hell's your problem?" Cass yelled as she rejoined the group in the dining room.

"You better watch your tone with me," Angel warned. He sat on a chair, clutching his stomach as one of the newest chorus girls hovered over him. "I ain't takin' any of your lip."

"And I'm not backin' down like one of your ninnies who's afraid of her own shadow."

"Hey!" the girl gasped.

Angel sucked his teeth. "I don't have to answer to

you," he said, pushing the other woman's hand away.

"You're right," Luther said. "You don't have to answer to her, but you do have to answer to me, and I want to know what happened."

"Why y'all gettin' down on me?" Angel asked. "I was the one attacked, and I have a witness. I was standin' here talkin' to Eli when that ofay came over here beefin' about his damn sax, like I had it."

"You did," Cass accused.

"You saw for yourself that I didn't have it."

"Then you knew where it was."

"You don't have proof."

"I see you're not denyin' it."

"Cass," Luther said. His tone was soft in an attempt to calm her down.

"You gonna fire him?" Angel asked. "This is The Big House, not baseball. The rules are one strike and you're out."

"I know."

Cass shook her head. "No, Luther, you can't."

"But Cass, you know the rules."

"I don't give a damn about the rules."

"Young lady…"

"Luther, you have to be fair. For five months, Randy's put up with everyone's crap. The other night he had to walk home without his coat 'cause someone thought it'd be funny to hide it. He's not treated with respect by most of the people who work here or who come to see the show, yet he's always kept his cool. In fact, he's held it together longer than any one of us would've if forced to work under these conditions. It wouldn't be fair to fire him 'cause someone—and I won't mention any names, Angel—went too far."

Florence and Eli mumbled their agreement, while Angel cursed under his breath.

"If anythin'," Cass continued, "the person who hid the sax should be fired for instigatin' the fight. There's not a person who works here that doesn't know you respect another's instrument. Hell, most of the instruments here are owned by the club, yet if someone looks at, let's say, the drums, too hard he's told to back off."

Luther nodded. "You make a good argument."

"What?" Angel exclaimed, shooting out of his chair. "I had a fist in my stomach and he gets to return? If that ain't a double standard, nothin' is. If it had been any one of us Negroes, we'd be out of here before our fist hit our target. But let the ofay start a fight and we have the welcome mat dry cleaned before rollin' it out for him."

"Angel, there's no double standard here. Cass made a valid point. Randy was reacting as any one of you would if you found out someone had been messing with your instrument. But since you feel so strongly that justice be served, I'm willing to fire Randy—"

"Luther, no—" Cass started to protest, but the older man held up a hand signaling he was not finished.

"I'm willing to fire Randy," the club's co-owner repeated, "as long as the instigator also leaves."

"What?" Angel yelled. "Hell, what kind of sh—"

"The person who hid that boy's sax instigated the fight, so he should share the consequences. I can't have troublemakers working here."

"And what if you don't find the person responsible? No one's gonna step forward and confess, knowin' he'll be tossed ass first outta here."

"I'm not going to conduct an investigation to find the guilty party, because it'll be more trouble than it's worth. So either the guilty party steps forward and they both go, or no one's fired."

Angel slammed a fist on the table before pushing past the chorus girl and stomping out the front door cursing. Despite his dismissal of her, the young woman followed behind him.

"Thank you, Luther," Cass said, relieved the prankster had not won.

"Don't ever let it be said I'm not fair," the older man replied.

"You'll never hear it from me."

"I'm sure you'll tell Randy he still has a job, but I expect him to be here at five on Wednesday so I can talk to him about his outburst."

"Yes, I will," she said, before heading back downstairs to retrieve her coat.

She had originally meant to surprise Randy and take him out for a late-night drink after his set. And, though the evening had not gone as planned, she was grateful she had deviated from her routine that evening.

Luther was a fair man, but she could not say for sure whether Randy would still have a job had she not been there to argue his case. At times she felt it would be better, at least for him, if he left. However, his departure should be his decision, not something forced upon him.

Cass felt calmer by the time she stepped out of the club. She was eager to tell Randy he had not been fired, but she assumed he had gone somewhere to get a drink. Not in the mood to search all the afterhours dives in Harlem for him, she decided she'd drop by his place in the morning to give him the news.

She left the alley at the same moment Randy turned the corner. He appeared calmer than he'd been when he stormed out. She sauntered toward him, meeting him halfway. In the streetlight, she could see his left eye was beginning to turn purple.

"I'm sorry I snapped at you," he said when she stopped in front of him.

"Trust me, it wasn't the highlight of my evening."

The corners of his mouth turned up slightly. "If you're not too upset at me, I'd like to walk you home for one last time."

"I'm not upset, and, yes, you can walk me home whenever the mood strikes you."

"It may be hard, seein' as how I no longer work here."

"Unless you're quitting on us, you'll be around."

"But Angel said—"

"Angel says a lot of things, but he has no authority here. Luther didn't fire you. He said it wouldn't be fair to fire you and not the person who took your sax, seeing as how that person instigated the fight. Unless someone steps forward and admits to it, your job is safe."

"Thank you, Cass."

"For what?"

"I know you had a hand in Luther's decision."

"Luther's a fair man," she said. "By the way, he wants you here at five on Wednesday to talk to you."

"I guess I shouldn't be surprised. He couldn't let me off that easy."

"You have three days until you have to face him," she said, taking his arm. "Until then, don't worry about it."

As they walked, Cass recounted the conversation that had taken place after he left.

"If Junior had been there instead of Luther, I wouldn't have had a chance," Randy commented as they entered her apartment. He took Cass's coat and hung it up while she headed to the kitchen.

"Luther tries to do right by everyone."

"Different experiences breed different kinds of people."

"I disagree," she said as she chipped away at the ice in the icebox. "Each experience we face produces several different lessons. We choose what lesson we'll take from it."

He strolled into the kitchen and leaned against the wall, watching her wrap ice chips in a towel.

"Luther once told me he knew a colored woman who spent six months in jail after some money went missing from her employer's purse. There was no evidence to convict her and she never confessed, but that didn't stop them from throwing her behind bars. When they later discovered it was her employer's daughter who took the money, they released her, but without a word of apology.

"From that experience, Luther could have decided all whites deserve his disdain, but instead he chose to remember everyone deserves a chance. Whether it's a chance to follow his dreams—"

"Like playin' the sax," Randy commented.

"Yes, or whether it's a chance to prove his innocence."

"That's a good lesson." His voice, huskier than usual, forced her to look up. He stepped in front of her and cupped her cheek. "Do you believe in givin' someone a chance?"

His eyes said he was no longer talking about race. What lesson would she take away from the story? That all men should not be trusted, or each one should be given a chance to prove himself?

Randy tipped her head up. As he leaned forward to kiss her, a little voice screamed at her to push him away. The rest of her body begged her not to stop. Her body was more insistent, until it drowned out the other cries.

Deciding to judge the man for who he was, not for who others were, she dropped the icepack and slipped her arms around his neck.

Randy rested one hand on the small of her back. His other hand slipped to her breast and caressed her until her nipple hardened.

Her little voice made one more attempt to argue. It finally gave up when his hand moved from her back to her thigh. She felt a quiver between her legs as she waited for him to continue. But his hand moved no further.

Randy kissed a path from her lips to her neck. He gently nibbled on the skin as she squirmed beneath his hand.

"Do you trust me?" Randy whispered in her neck.

Unable to find the words, she nodded. But he refused to move.

He pulled back, took her face in his hands and looked her in the eyes. "Do you trust me?"

Knowing he wanted the verbal confirmation, she whispered, "Yes."

Cass saw his reluctance in his eyes. Proving she was serious, she took his hand and led the way.

In the bedroom, he kissed her. Her arms wrapped around his neck as if she were hanging on to him for support. His hands rested on her derriere, pulling her to him and allowing her to feel his growing arousal. Unlike before, instead of running, she moved her hands to his rear and tried to pull him closer.

The movement seemed to be the last confirmation he needed. He broke the kiss as he reached back to pull her arms from around him. Gently he pushed her back until she sat on the edge of the bed. He then dropped to his knees in front of her.

Taking his time, he stroked her legs until he had pushed her dress above her knees. He reached underneath the fabric, and unfastened her stocking clips. The tips of his fingers teased her legs as he slid her stockings down her thighs to her calves and finally her feet.

Once her stockings were off, he stood up, removed his jacket, and dropped it on the floor. His tie and shirt quickly followed.

"Randy, your clothes are going to get wrin—" She stopped. His frown said the condition of his clothes was the last thing on his mind.

As he finished undressing, she admired his slim physique and the muscles, which, though not overly defined, attested to the manual labor he was not too proud to perform between gigs. His pale skin was smooth, except for a raised three-inch scar over his left breast.

She was impressed by everything she saw, until he hooked his fingers into the waistband of his shorts and pulled them down. Dread took over.

Cass remembered when she had tried to remove his

shirt on New Year's Day. He had told her she was too bold for her own good. But, staring at him standing out, straight and proud, her courage faded away.

Her mouth opened as she stared, and her previous apprehensions returned. Henry had always worn clothes in her presence and always took her in the dark, under the covers. Pedro had already been lying on her when he opened his pants and immediately tucked himself back in once he was done. Therefore, having never seen a naked man before, she had never realized he could be so endowed. It was no wonder relations with Henry had been uncomfortable, and she was sure, despite his insistence, the experience would be no different with Randy.

"You know, I'm goin' to feel rather foolish if you reject me now," he teased, trying to lighten the mood.

He held his hand out to her. She hesitated a second before taking it and allowing him to pull her to her feet.

"Look at me."

Cass slowly lifted her head. Her eyes locked onto his. She stared until she once again saw Randy…the man she trusted…the man who had been tender with her up to that point…the man who would not hurt her.

Randy reached behind her and unzipped her dress. He peeled it from her body until it dropped in a pool around her feet. Her underwear soon followed.

Cass's first instinct was to cover her body. No one had seen her naked since she'd learned how to bathe herself when she was six. Like Henry, she'd made it a point to dress and undress in private.

Randy did not give her a chance to hide. Taking her hand, he pulled her back to the bed. She lay down and waited for him to pounce. But instead of mounting her, he stretched out beside her.

"I want to take this slow," he whispered as he caressed her breasts.

He leaned over and flicked his tongue over her nipple. Her shudder seemed to urge him on. His tongue stroked the nipple, carefully tasting the bud until it was hard.

Randy's hand moved slowly down her body. Every touch sent a shock through her, awakening every nerve. Now she understood what the women at the club talked about when comparing notes on their lovers.

His hand slipped between her legs. The first touch made her body jerk with pleasure. Her eyes closed and she gasped. She could not believe the same hand that had made a man double over in pain could give her so much pleasure.

"That's it," Randy encouraged. "Enjoy it."

One finger slid into her vagina. The others continued to stroke her. Cass felt a pressure building inside her. With each stroke, the pressure increased, and though it was incredible, there was an urgency to make it go away.

When she felt she could not take any more, her body became tense before a wave coursed through her. She gasped out loud. Her body trembled.

It took a minute before she had the energy to open her eyes. Randy, with his head propped up on one hand, stared down at her. Knowing he watched her, her face flushed with heat, but he did not give her time to think about it as he leaned over and kissed her deeply.

As their tongues stroked each other and their hands caressed their bodies, he settled between her legs. She felt him, rigid and hot, searching for her opening.

Expecting discomfort and pain, she tensed. Though he had managed to introduce her to a pleasure, she knew he could not prevent the inevitable pain.

Slowly he stroked himself against her, until she squirmed underneath him. He then took himself in hand and directed himself to her opening. When he found what he was searching for, he pushed his hips forward. He hissed as he slipped inside her.

It was tight, but he stopped to give her time to adjust. She realized how much effort he was putting toward making sure she enjoyed the experience, and with every passing second he earned more and more of her respect.

When she started squirming again, he pulled out a little, then pushed forward again, inching in a bit further. He continued until he had entered her fully.

"Are you okay?" he asked through clenched teeth.

Cass responded by wrapping her legs around his waist. She raised her pelvis and wantonly ground herself against him until he groaned.

Having his answer, Randy began thrusting without any more hesitation. Though he must have been eager to get relief, he did not forget there was someone else in bed with him. As he moved in her, he kissed and stroked her, until she tightened her grip on his waist. With one hard stroke he sent her over the edge as he trembled with release.

Once he was spent, he slipped out of her and rolled to his side. Leaning over, he captured a nipple between his teeth. He nipped the bud before laying his head between her breasts.

Breathing hard, Cass lay under him, unable to believe the pleasure she'd experienced was from the same action she had known countless times from Henry. If Randy had not demonstrated it, she would never have believed being with a man could feel so good.

She glanced down at him. His eyes were closed, but his ragged breaths on her breasts told her he was awake. She trembled as one last shiver coursed through her body.

Randy sat up and pulled the afghan lying across the foot of the bed over them. He returned to his previous position, wrapping his arms around her waist and holding her.

Shaking her head in disbelief at the consideration of the man with her, she leaned forward and placed a kiss on the top of his head.

"Thank you," he murmured as he nuzzled her breasts.

"No," she whispered before closing her eyes and enjoying the comfort of the man on her, "thank you."

Chapter 21

Randy could count on one hand the few times things had ever been right in his life. Most of his childhood was forgettable—he had not known happiness until he met Sax. His adolescent years were filled with turmoil, while adulthood was spent following a dream, which left him feeling at times more beaten than successful. But lying in bed next to Cass felt better than right.

He leaned over her and traced a trail of kisses from her temple to her full lips. With a sigh, her eyes fluttered open.

"What time is it?" Cass yawned.

"I don't know. Sometime after noon," Randy guessed from the shadows in the room. He was too busy working his way down to her breast to glance at the clock on her nightstand next to her.

"What are you doing?"

"I'm lonely," he whispered.

Rubbing the sleep out of her eyes, she rolled over to face him. "You should be tired."

He leaned back and reached out to play with a wild strand of hair that had come loose from her French twist.

"Your hair is softer than I thought it'd be," he commented as his fingers searched for the hairpins that kept her twist in place.

"It takes plenty of time and patience to get it that way," Cass said.

"I've heard there are things colored women can use to make their hair easier to comb."

Cass shook her head. "I learned the hard way to appreciate what I have."

"How?" he asked as he pulled a hairpin out and dropped it on the bed, behind her.

"When I was thirteen, I was jealous of this girl who lived in town. She wore the prettiest store-bought dresses, while I had to wear homemade ones. Her father drove a car, while my father used the mule and cart. And it seemed she always got whatever she wanted, while I could only look through the catalogs and dream. But what I envied most of all was her straight hair. It bounced when she shook her head, then fell back into place like she'd just run a comb through it. It didn't matter that my braids reached down my back while her hair barely touched her shoulders—I wanted hair like hers.

"I used to beg my momma to let me get my hair straightened. I even offered to pay for it myself, but she refused. She said all that fussing was not natural and it would make my hair fall out. But, at the time, I figured what did she know, she never had her hair straightened.

"Well, a couple of days before graduation, a classmate offered to straighten my hair with a hot comb. She said she had watched her momma, who was a hairdresser, and there was nothing to it. I thought she knew what she was doing, and I really wanted my hair to look special for the ceremony, so I agreed.

"After school, we went to her house, where she washed my hair. She then put a metal comb on the stove while she greased my scalp and hair. Since, like I said, momma never straightened her hair, I didn't know you shouldn't let the comb get too hot."

"What happened?" Randy asked as he combed her hair with his fingers.

Cass rolled her eyes. "What do you think happened? When she put that hot—and I mean hot—comb to my head I smelled something burning and I saw a good chunk of my hair fall to the ground."

"What did your mother do when she found out?"

"She marched me back to my friend's house and, with the money I'd earned from picking cotton, made me get a haircut to make it look neat. By the time the girl's mother was finished, I had about a half inch of hair left on my head. I also had a scab where the hot grease had melted onto my scalp."

"I guess you got that special look for graduation." Randy laughed.

She pinched his leg.

"Hey, don't pick at me. I didn't burn your hair."

"Oh, hush. Aren't you tired?"

Randy smirked as he reached out to cup her breast.

"Tired, no. Hungry, yes."

"Umm," Cass moaned. "Hungry for what?"

"Well, now that you ask," he said as he lay back and put his hands behind his head, "I could go for some grits, eggs, and bacon. And I'd like the newspaper with that."

Cass's mouth dropped open and her eyes narrowed. "Oh, I'll bring you a newspaper, all right." She shot up and slid toward the opposite end of the bed.

He laughed. "Come back here." Before her feet could touch the floor, he reached out, grabbed her by the waist, and pulled her back down. Her protests were interrupted as he rolled on top of her and kissed her.

They made love, then fell asleep again in each other's arms. When he woke up three hours later, his stomach demanded food. He slipped out of the bed, careful not to wake Cass.

Though it was late March, the apartment was warm. After a quick shower, he pulled on his shorts, then wandered into the kitchen to satisfy his stomach.

He was wiping up the last of his eggs with a piece of toast when Cass emerged from the bedroom, wearing a baby blue terrycloth robe. Her hair was pulled back in a single braid.

"Where are your clothes?" she asked as she knotted the robes belt.

"I'm wearin' them." He pointed to his white cotton shorts before pulling her onto his lap.

"Underwear does not count. You don't wear it out in public."

"Actually, I do. I make it a point to put on a clean pair of shorts every day."

"You know what I mean. You wear something over them." She took a strip of bacon off his plate.

"Of course I do. I can't have just anyone lookin' at me. That privilege is reserved for special, sassy, little gals like yourself."

She took a slice of toast. "I guess I should feel honored."

"Do you want me to fix you breakfast?"

Cass shook her head. "No, I'm fine," she replied as she picked up a spoon and ate the rest of his grits. "You're not a bad cook. You should do this more often."

"Kinda hard, seein' as how I don't have a stove in my room."

"You need to work on your jokes, 'cause you're far from funny."

He placed a hand over his heart. "Ouch, you know how to hurt a man."

"Better you learn the truth now, before you decide to become a comedian and embarrass yourself."

He played with the fine hairs at her nape. "I suppose I should say 'thanks.'"

"You can say it by cooking dinner for me."

"For you, I'll cook a feast."

"You're going to end up spoiling me."

"Every woman deserves to be spoiled and, girl, as long as you're with me, you're goin' to be treated like a queen."

She dropped the spoon on the empty plate. "You don't need to make promises, Randy. In fact, please don't. It'll be easier."

"What'll be easier?"

Cass shook her head as she started to slide off his lap. He held her waist to prevent her escape.

"Cass?"

"Randy, we're friends, and I don't want anything to change that."

"Is this a nice way of tellin' me you're sorry about last night?"

"No." With a small smile, she shook her head. "I'd never trade last night for anything."

"Then what's wrong?" He wondered if she had reconsidered because of the difficulties of being with a white man.

"When you make promises, you build hope for

things that may never be. I don't want to be hurt again."

He nodded his head. He should have realized one night together would not erase all her doubts about men. "I'd never hurt you," he said, though he knew it would take more than words for her to fully trust him.

"You say that now, but—"

"But it sounds like you're tryin' to find an excuse to push me away. I know you're afraid of gettin' hurt. Last night, you took a huge step. Now I hope you'll give me the chance to prove it wasn't a one-time deal." Cupping the back of her head, he pulled her down for a kiss.

He did not expect his kisses to magically dispel all the doubt from her mind. It would take time. But as far as he was concerned, she was worth the time and the effort. She was a rare gem. She saw past his physical appearance to know the man underneath, and he was not about to lose that.

Randy pulled back. It was a boost to his ego to hear her whimper at the loss of contact.

"Cass, I don't want to argue with you." He worked on the knot in her belt. "I just want to carry you back to your room, pull off this robe, remove your—" He stopped when he opened her robe and discovered she had nothing on underneath it. "Where are your clothes?"

"In the bedroom," she replied as she moved one leg over his hips to straddle him.

He felt a familiar twitch. "And you had the nerve to complain about me walkin' around in my underwear?"

"My robe covers a lot more than those shorts."

He slid the material off her shoulders and let it fall to the floor. "Not anymore," he murmured before kissing her again.

She shifted until he was pressed against her opening. He shuddered as he felt her heat through his shorts. His intentions of carrying her to the bedroom were forgotten when she started grinding against him.

Without breaking the kiss, he reached around her and pushed the plate to the side. Placing his hands underneath her, he stood and set her on the table.

"Randy, what are you doing?" she exclaimed as he straightened.

He did not answer as he pushed his shorts down as far as they would go without bending over. As he returned to her, he was grateful he had thought to pull down the shades and close the curtains when he came out of the bedroom earlier.

****

"Miss Cass, look what I'm making."

"Suzy's wearing the dress you gave her."

"Can you make one for my baby, too?"

The Davis sisters converged on Cass the second she and Randy walked into the living room.

"Mariah, watch those needles," Mrs. Greene scolded, folding the sweater she had been knitting. "Bessie and Estelle, mind your manners. Miss Cass don't need you jumpin' all over her."

"It's all right," Cass said, slipping out of her coat. She handed it to Randy before kneeling in front of the girls. "Now, let me see what you're making, Mariah."

"But, I..." Bessie started.

"Mariah got to me first, so I'll look at her work first."

The youngest girl folded her arms and dropped her head.

"Bessie, look at me." She held her head up; there were tears in her eyes.

"Do you think you're being fair to Mariah? She got to me first. How would you like it if you spoke to me but I ignored you and talked to your sisters?"

"I wouldn't like it," Bessie whined.

"Then you should give your sister the same courtesy you'd want."

Bessie nodded.

"Good. Now go upstairs and wipe your face while I talk to Mariah."

"Yes, Miss Cass," Bessie replied before shuffling from the room.

"Well done," Mrs. Greene praised.

"Thank you," Cass said before turning back to the eldest sister. "Now, Mariah, show me what you're making."

Mariah handed her knitting project to Cass. "I'm making a sweater for my baby. Mrs. Greene's showing me how. She knits all kinds of stuff and she doesn't even use a pattern."

"That's impressive."

"Let me show you," Mariah commented.

"So, what mischief have you two been up to?" Mrs. Greene asked.

"Nothin' much," Randy answered with a shrug. He glanced over at Cass, who bit her lip and blushed.

"I see." The older women, not missing the silent communication between the couple, pushed up from her chair. "Come help me in the kitchen," she ordered as she walked past Randy.

Knowing he could not hide anything from his landlady, he followed her down the hall, bracing

Sweet Jazz

himself for a lecture on fornication.

"Tell me you didn't get with *that* girl," Mrs. Greene said when they entered the kitchen. Her emphasis on the word "that" made him wonder what she had against Cass. Whenever she was over, his landlady seemed to welcome her.

"What's wrong with Cass?"

"There ain't nothin' wrong with her, but if you haven't noticed, she's colored and you're white."

"It's funny how people constantly feel the need to remind me of that," he replied, a bit surprised she was not lecturing him on the sin of sex.

"Maybe if you open your eyes and act like you can see, we wouldn't feel the need to remind you all the time."

"How am I supposed to act? Am I supposed to avoid others? Treat them like they're beneath me?"

"There's nothing wrong with you associatin' with other races, but lordy, you take it to a whole new level. You live in a colored neighborhood, work in a colored club, and now you're messin' with a colored girl."

"I don't see where I'm doin' anythin' wrong."

Mrs. Greene picked up a serving spoon and shook it at him. "That's 'cause you ain't usin' the sense the good Lord gave you. Boy, do you really expect people to accept the two of you together? You bein' with a colored girl is only gonna lead to trouble."

Randy wanted to deny the statement, but the not-too-subtle warning he'd received on New Year's to keep away from Cass came to mind.

"You're a nice young man and Cass is a nice girl, but just 'cause you two can look beyond the surface to see the person that's within don't mean others are gonna do so. White people ain't gonna open doors and welcome her 'cause she's with you, and coloreds are not gonna tolerate you 'cause y'all are together."

"I realize that."

"Then why are you with her?" his landlady asked as she opened the oven and pulled out a rack with a roast. "I hope it ain't 'cause you had some itch you needed scratched and you heard colored girls are fast."

"Hell, no."

Mrs. Greene straightened and frowned.

"Excuse me," Randy apologized for his outburst.

She nodded her acceptance, before she reached down for the pan.

"I would never use Cass like that. She's always been nice to me."

"Then don't you think she deserves more than the trouble y'all bein' together is gonna cause?" she asked as she slammed the pan on top of the stove. "If things were different, I'd say go for it, but in this day and age, all you're doin' is askin' for trouble. Maybe in fifty, seventy-five, a hundred years, it won't matter who you're with, but for now, it does. If you wanna repay her for her kindness, then be her friend, buy her flowers, or take her out to supper, but don't, for her sake and yours, don't invite this trouble."

****

"What's bothering you?" Cass leaned forward on the table she shared with Randy at Cornbread 'n' Grits.

"Nothin's botherin' me," Randy answered. "Why'd you ask?"

"'Cause you've been awfully quiet since we left your place."

"It's nothin'."

She reached across the table and touched his hand. "Is it what Mrs. Greene said?"

"You heard?"

"Yes." She nodded. "I was heading to the bathroom and I heard."

"How much?"

"Most of it," she admitted.

"Didn't your momma tell you eavesdroppin' wasn't nice?"

"I wouldn't call it eavesdropping."

"Then what would you call it?"

"Finding out information I wouldn't have learned if I hadn't heard it for myself."

"You were eavesdroppin'."

"Whether I was or wasn't is not the issue." Cass sighed as she interlaced her fingers with his. "What Mrs. Greene said should be considered."

"You agree with her?" He had been afraid of how Cass would take what she heard. She had never seemed bothered by their differences before, but once faced with the ugliness, would she be able to handle the differences, or would she choose a simpler road?

"I agree that race is going to be an issue, and it's something we can't ignore," Cass said.

"But you know our difference doesn't bother me."

"But what about everyone else?"

"If it bothers them, they can look the other way."

"I wish it was that easy," Mattie said, as she placed two plates on the table. "In the past thirty-three years I don't think a day's gone by when I haven't encountered someone who can't seem to focus on anythin' else but me and Paul. The looks are the easy part. It's those who have opinions they feel the need to express that make it difficult. I've been called everythin' from a whore to a devil worshiper, and that's just my family.

"When my momma found out Paul and I were together, she beat the mess out of me, and when I refused to stop seein' him, my papa kicked me out the house. My friends stopped speakin' to me 'cause they thought I was a whore. We both lost our jobs 'cause the hotel thought we had low morals, and we were arrested more than once for bein' together."

"You went through all of that but stayed together? Why?" Cass asked.

"I loved my family and friends, but they didn't make me feel special. At least, not the way Paul did. Yes, it's been rough, but I was able to manage 'cause I wasn't facin' those tribulations alone. Paul's been by my side through it all."

The front door opened and a colored man and white woman entered. They crossed the dining room and took a table in the far corner of the restaurant.

"Like I said, it wasn't easy, but if I had to do it over again, knowin' what I do now, I'd make the same choice," Mattie said. "Take your time, reflect upon everythin', decide on what you can and can't handle. Then follow your heart, not other's wishes."

****

Randy rolled over on his side, taking the covers with him. The realization that something was wrong pulled him out of his slumber. As his mind cleared, it occurred to him that Cass wouldn't have let him get away with stealing the covers. She would have tugged on the blanket until he rolled toward her, threw an arm around her waist, and pulled her closer to him.

Leaning up on his elbows, he stared at the empty

spot next to him. Outside, the first rays of sun appeared in the morning sky. The clock on the nightstand next to him said quarter to seven, much too early for Cass to be up.

Rubbing a hand over his eyes, Randy climbed out of bed and shuffled into the living room. Cass was curled up in the corner of the couch fingering the dress on the rag doll that decorated the furniture. "Stardust" softly played on the radio.

Randy sat on the opposite end of the couch. When she made no indication of being aware of his presence, he reached over and touched her foot.

"Are you okay?" he asked.

"What are we doing?" she replied.

"Until a few minutes ago, I thought we were lyin' next to each other, enjoyin' each other's company."

Cass glowered at him. Sighing, he reached over and gently pulled her leg.

"Come here," he urged as he turned and placed a leg on the sofa.

She crawled over to him and settled between his legs. He wrapped his arms around her as she leaned back against his chest.

He realized what she was going to say before she spoke. Whether he wanted it or not, it was a conversation they eventually had to have. They could not pretend they would be accepted as a couple. There would be so many against them, and they needed to consider whether they could deal with it before they got in too deep.

"Randy, there's so much to think about. Look at the problems we'd have to face."

"I know, but like Mattie said, we must take the

time to think about everythin'. We can't expect to make a decision overnight."

"But can you honestly say you're ready to deal with the consequences of being with me?"

He thought about the beating he'd taken in the alley. Though the bruises had healed, the warning was still in his mind. Yet what he felt when he was with Cass was more powerful than the threat.

"Yes, I am."

"But what about—"

"Cass, do you remember the night I took you to the Savoy?"

"What about that night?"

"I told Maia if people gave up on their dreams then they wouldn't get anywhere. They must fight for what they want."

"I remember."

"Well, darlin', my dream has always been to find a pretty, sassy gal, who despite knowin' me and all my faults wouldn't mind bein' with me." He reached up and stroked her face. "I always wanted someone I could talk to, who makes me laugh, who makes me want her every time I look at her. Now that I've found her, I can't give her up and settle for second best 'cause society says her skin's too dark and mine's too light." He kissed the top of her head. "You're my dream and I'm willin' to fight for you and deal with whatever society wants to throw at me, 'cause if I didn't then I don't deserve you."

Chapter 22

"Lay back and go to sleep," Randy suggested when Cass yawned for the third time in five minutes.

"That's what I was doing when you woke me up and dragged me out of bed," she snapped.

"You're not a morning person, are you?" Eli chuckled as he switched lanes.

"No, I'm not. That's why I work at night and sleep during the day."

"What'd you do when you were growing up? I'm sure your parents didn't let you sleep all day."

Cass snorted. "I got up. Then I grumbled to myself whenever they were out of earshot."

Randy laughed at the answer that had not come as a surprise to him. A week earlier, he had awakened Cass to suggest they go to an early movie. That day, he'd learned her sassy wit leaned more toward biting sarcasm when she was awakened before noon.

He reached across the seat and patted her knee. "Go to sleep, Cass. We still have a couple of hours 'til we get there."

"I want to see where we're going. By the way, where did you say we were going?"

"Nice try, but we didn't say," Eli answered. "*Es una sorpresa.*"

"Didn't I tell you I hate surprises?"

"You don't hate surprises," Randy insisted. "You

hate not knowin'."

"Same thing."

"Close your eyes and I promise I'll wake you when we get there."

"And there is where?"

"Where we'll be when we get there."

"You might as well give up," said Florence. She opened one eye and peeked over the seat. "They're not going to tell us anything."

"They're aggravating." Cass crossed her arms and glanced out the window. Once the gentle bouncing of the car rocked her to sleep, Randy rested her head on his chest.

That morning, after the band had finished playing, Randy and Cass joined Florence and Eli for an early breakfast at an all-night diner. When they finally arrived at her apartment, it was after six.

At ten, he woke her to tell her he was going home to change and requested she be dressed when he returned. She responded by rolling over and pulling the blanket over her head.

An hour later, she was still curled up under the blanket. He made the mistake of trying to wake her like Sleeping Beauty and ended up back in bed, minus his clothes. When they emerged from the brownstone at noon, Eli and Florence were waiting for them in the car.

With many people still in church for Easter service, the traffic on the road had been light when they started. As they approached their destination, the traffic became heavier, and the city was overwhelmed with visitors. Still, Randy was able to direct Eli to the neighborhood he recommended for leaving the car.

Once they were parked, he reached over and patted

Cass on the knee. She was slow to open her eyes and rub the sleep out of them, while he climbed out and ran around to open her door.

"Where are we?" she asked, stepping out of the car. She scanned the block lined with rowhouses.

"Washington, D.C." Randy replied.

Cass turned back to him, her eyes wide with surprise.

"Randy, please tell me you're not kidding."

"I'm not," he insisted. "We're in D.C."

Florence squealed and threw herself onto Eli. Cass simply stood with her mouth open.

"Well, say somethin'. Do you like your surprise?"

"Randy, stop teasing me. You know I do. When did you plan this?"

"The moment you showed me the article about today's concert. I figured the only thin' better than listenin' to a broadcast of Marian Anderson is bein' there to see her in person." He took her hand. "We need to get going if we want to reach the Lincoln Memorial before the concert starts. I figured we could walk down there, unless you want to hop on a streetcar."

"I prefer walking," Florence said.

"What about you?" Randy asked Cass.

"I want to see the city."

"I was hopin' you'd say that."

Despite the cold, the two couples took their time strolling through the city, passing the U.S. Capitol and the Smithsonian. However, it was the look of awe on Cass's face as they stood in front of the Library of Congress that made the trip worthwhile for Randy.

By the time they reached the National Mall, the crowd extended from the Lincoln Memorial to the

Reflecting Pool. The audience began moving forward as people walked onto the platform.

Secretary of Interior Harold L. Ickes gave a brief speech introducing Miss Anderson. Randy was disappointed their position only allowed them to hear. Yet when he looked down at Cass's smiling face, he realized she got her joy just from being present.

Once the introduction was made, Marian Anderson stepped up to the microphones and began with "America." Throughout the concert, Randy thought about the similarities between the singer entertaining the audience and the one standing next to him. Others had tried to silence both women because of the color of their skin, and both continued despite the obstacles they faced. But, unlike Marian Anderson, Cass would not be heard by a vast crowd, because the same prejudices that kept her out of venues where she could be discovered was also preventing the right people from finding her.

When the concert was over, the audience moved forward to extend well wishes to the contralto. Seeing the possibility for confusion, Randy grabbed Cass by the arm and maneuvered them through the crowd.

"That was beautiful," Cass exclaimed as they strolled toward the Washington Monument.

"You want to grab a bite?" Randy asked, eager to show her more of the city.

"Sure, but are you going to tell me you know a desegregated restaurant outside of New York?"

"You'd be surprised," he replied, leading them back the way they had come.

****

"Look what the cat done dragged back in here," a robust colored woman announced as they walked into the Panama Lounge.

"It's good to see you, Bertha," Randy greeted, giving the woman a hug.

"What are you doing down here?" Bertha asked. "Don't tell me they've already chased you out the Big Apple."

"No, we drove down from New York to see Marian Anderson." Randy introduced everyone. "We'd like a table, if you got one."

"You willing to play for your meal?"

"Don't worry, I brought a band with me."

Bertha slid off her stool and grabbed four menus. "In that case, follow me."

The club, located in the basement of a drugstore, had a tropical theme, with palm trees in the corners and bright yellow tablecloths. The décor did not impress Cass as much as the clientele, who chose to ignore society's rules and did not view integration as a sin.

"How do you find these places?" Cass asked once they were seated.

"I lucked out when I came to D.C." Randy nodded toward the door where Bertha was greeting another couple. "Her brother owned the boardin' house where I rented a room. He gave me the tip about the auditions."

Cass did not know whether Randy had a higher power looking over him or if he was simply lucky. Whatever it was, she would be grateful it helped him locate venues where they could be together.

"Hey, man, don't you work for The Big House?" a colored man called from across the room.

Randy raised his eyebrow at his companions, before turning toward the other diners. "Yeah, we do."

"I told you, Ida." The man tossed his napkin onto

his plate. He stood and motioned to the colored woman and white man sitting at the table with him. "I was just telling Willie about you. Ida and I caught your act the other night, and I liked what I heard," he said as he approached them.

"Thanks, umm—"

"Daniel, Daniel Fields." He pointed to the couple standing behind him. "This is my sister, Ida, and this here is Willie Hawke."

Randy reached out and shook hands. "It's nice meetin' you. This is Cass, the other half of the act."

Daniel looked her up and down, his brow wrinkled in disbelief. "You're their canary?"

"Yes, I'm the lead singer." Cass shook his hand.

"I hope you don't get offended, but you look a lot older on stage. Here you look like…well, like…"

"I'm not old enough to work in a club?"

"Yes."

"Don't worry, I'm not offended." Cass smiled at Randy. "You wouldn't believe how many times someone tells me that."

"And this is Eli and Florence," Randy continued with the introductions. "Pull up a table and join us."

"No, we were just finishing up here," Willie replied. "We need to get going. We have a long drive back to New York and an early morning meeting about a gig."

"You're in a band?"

"Willie Hawke's Band," Cass said, once recognition set in. "There was an article about you in the newspaper. It said you spent a year touring throughout the U.S. and France."

"We got back to the States two weeks ago."

"That's the kind of adventure I was looking for when I left home."

"Travelin's fine, but after a while, you can't wait to get back to your crib," Daniel said.

"But to see different states…a different country…"

"Eventually, it all begins to look the same. The accents are different, but the experiences… Well, let's just say not much changes from place to place."

"And on that note," Willie jumped in, "we need to get going."

"It was nice meetin' you," Randy said.

"Likewise." Willie reached into his breast pocket, pulled out a card, and passed it to Randy. "This is where we hang when we're in town. Drop by sometime and we can jam."

"Thanks, I will."

They spoke for a couple more minutes before Willie once again insisted they leave.

"It must be nice living someplace like Paris," Cass commented, once the two couples were alone again.

"I guess I wouldn't mind visitin'," Randy said.

"I heard they don't care about race over there."

"Don't fool yourself. I'm sure they care about race over there as much as they do here."

"How do you know?"

"Down south, they say the same thin' about the north. Coloreds are told there are no Jim Crow laws up here and the races get along. But once you get here you realize though there are no official laws on the book, there's still plenty of segregation. There are certain neighborhoods in the city you wouldn't take a stroll through unless you were wearing a maid's uniform or certain places you wouldn't dare stop for a drink. At least, not if you wanted to live to see tomorrow. Hell, we already know there are certain places I'm not welcomed."

"That's what Daniel meant when he said not much changes from place to place?" Florence asked. "Though things may be a little better, we shouldn't go somewhere and expect it to be much different or we'll be sorely disappointed?"

Randy nodded.

"So I guess moving to Paris would be out of the question," Cass mumbled, "'cause as long as we decide to ignore what society says is normal, we're going to have to deal with people who decide to put their two cents in whether or not it was asked for?"

"Exactly."

Cass sighed. "Sometimes it seems like it would be easier to follow the rules."

"But easier does not always spell happier."

Chapter 23

The pounding woke Randy from his nap. Thinking Cass had forgotten her key, he pushed off the sofa and shuffled to the door to let her in. He was halfway across the room when the running water in the bathroom reminded him she was in the shower.

He cursed under his breath, then apologized to no one when he remembered what day it was. Shaking his head, he started back to the sofa.

The profanity-laced tirade in the hall stopped his retreat. He listened as a belligerent man gave a detailed description of what he planned to do when he got his hands on his victim.

"There's no need for that kind of language," the younger Mrs. Cooper called from downstairs. "Especially on Sunday."

"Mind your own damn business," the man yelled before calling the landlord's wife a name that did not equate with the church-going woman.

Unwilling to stand by and listen to a woman being verbally assaulted, Randy turned back.

"Shut your mouth," he yelled as he ripped open the door.

"Go to hell," was the reply.

Randy glanced down at Mrs. Cooper, who was standing on the steps that led to Cass's floor. Even though a deaf person across town could tell by the racket where the man was, she pointed up to the next level.

Randy headed upstairs. Out of the corner of his eye he saw Mrs. Cooper duck into the apartment, most likely to tell Cass that her man was about to be beaten to a pulp.

A stocky colored man, who, with one punch could probably bring Randy to his knees, stood outside the apartment one flight up.

"The lady asked you not to use that language in here."

"I don't give a damn what that frumpy old cow has to say," the other man replied before he again pounded on the door in front of him. "I told you to open up, bitch, before I break down this door and beat your ass."

"No, Amaad," Maia shouted from the other side. "I have nothing to say to you."

"I got plenty to say to you about the crap you pulled. It got my ass thrown in jail for four months."

"That's not my concern. Leave me alone."

"She doesn't have anythin' to say to you, so maybe you should leave," Randy suggested.

"I don't need to go anywhere. I live here. This is my apartment."

"This isn't your apartment. I pay the rent here, not you," Maia screamed.

"That's a laugh," Amaad shouted. "You get me arrested, and now you're kicking me out? Where the hell am I supposed to go?"

"I don't care. Just leave."

"Fine, be that way." Amaad kicked the door. "I don't need your ragged ass. Just give me my things."

"You don't have anything here."

"What do you mean? I left my clothes here. Where's my things?"

"I put it out."

"You what?" Amaad started pounding on the door. "Open this door so I can break your neck."

Randy had hoped he could defuse the situation without laying hands on Amaad, the only excuse the other man needed before he pummeled him. The weak door, however, could not take much more abuse.

Taking advantage of the other man's distraction, Randy grabbed Amaad and slammed him against the wall. He then stepped in front of the door and braced himself for the inevitable blow.

Amaad took a step forward, then stopped. He looked at Randy as if he were seeing him for the first time.

"What the…?"

The unfinished sentence and the shock on Amaad's face told Randy he didn't have to worry about retaliation. Cass had told him how the other man had talked of standing up to "the white man," but in real life he apparently did not have the guts to face one head-on, even when provoked.

"The lady asked you to leave. She doesn't have anythin' that belongs to you, and she doesn't want to hear anythin' you have to say," Randy said, "so do us all a favor and leave so we can go back to enjoyin' our Sunday afternoon."

"Oh, I see," Amaad whispered under his breath before shouting at the door, "You couldn't handle a colored man, so you've found yourself a white man." He stepped back as Randy took a step forward. Though he was not about to fight, the man continued to talk trash. "Her high yella ass thinks she's something."

The door behind Randy opened. Maia rushed out of her apartment and around him to face her ex-lover.

"For your information, I don't need no ofay to protect me. I can take care of myself," she yelled.

"You finally show your face once he appears. Go hide behind him and see how long he's going to protect you. Once he gets tired of your yella ass he won't even remember your name." Amaad continued down the steps.

"Why don't you go find one of your nappy-headed ninnies and leave me alone?"

"Better dealing with them than some ofay-loving zebra," Amaad retorted before slamming the front door behind him.

"Ofay-loving?" Maia stood tall as if she was preparing for an attack. "That bastard better never show his face around here again after insulting me like that."

"You're welcome," Randy said.

Maia spun around and rolled her eyes. "No reason for you to get all snippety. No one asked for your help. I don't need a white knight rushing in to save the day."

Randy flinched as if had been slapped. He nodded his head, then started back down the stairs. He had known there was no limit to how ignorant people could be, but it still stung when he was reminded.

"Hell, no," Cass muttered as she ran past him up the stairs. She grabbed Maia's arm before the other woman could march back into her apartment. "You need to learn how to be more gracious."

"I told him—"

"I heard what you told him. But if it hadn't been for him, Amaad would have busted down your door and kicked your butt all over Harlem."

"Why do you care what I say to some ofay?" She glanced at Cass in her bathrobe and then at a stocking-footed Randy. His hair was uncombed and he had stubble on his chin. "He stayed the night? You're sleeping with him."

"That's none of your business," Cass stated.

Maia snatched her arm free. "How could you sleep with him? He's a ghost, for God's sake."

"Don' you dare put Randy down," Cass said in a low voice, her accent getting thicker. "He's proven himself to be a hell of a lot better than the messes you drag home."

"Oh, he's better because his skin's lighter."

"No, he's better for a lot more reasons. For one thin', he's got a job and he's not moochin' off me."

Maia's hand swung forward. Cass grabbed the other woman's wrist before the palm connected with her face.

"I don't suggest you try it, else there's gonna be a down-home ass-whoopin' in this hallway."

Randy grabbed Cass by her arm and pulled her off Maia. He ushered her back down the steps. There had been too much arguing, and he just wanted to put the incident behind him.

"So that's it, huh?" Maia called after her. "You're going to choose that ofay over me, and after everything I've done for you."

Cass whirled around. Randy grabbed her about the waist, lifted her off the ground, and carried her back to her apartment.

"Fine, then. Go ahead and be a white man's whore. But mark my words, you'll be sorry."

Randy walked into the apartment and kicked the door closed before setting Cass on her feet. Knowing her need to speak her mind, he stood in front of it in case she decided to go out and finish her argument with Maia.

"Why'd you do that?" Cass screamed.

"'Cause I didn't want you gettin' into a fight over me."

She snorted, throwing up her hands. "Not that," she said as she paced in front of him. "Why'd you go out there and help Maia? Look what it got you."

She stopped and glared past him at the door. Randy sighed. He had known all too well what his interference could get him. Without a word, he stepped around Cass and headed toward her bedroom.

****

Ignoring the argument in the hall between Maia and Mrs. Cooper, Cass followed Randy. She stepped into the bedroom as he plopped down on the bed and dropped his arm over his face.

"I don't know whether to call you stupid or brave for going after Amaad," she said from the doorway.

"Many people seem to have that problem," he replied from under his arm.

With a sigh, Cass walked to the bed. She leaned over and placed a kiss on his forehead.

"What's that for?" he asked as his arm slipped to his side.

"Being you. Always a valiant knight in shining armor, despite the rewards."

"I don't like seein' a woman treated bad by a man. Though you'd think I'd have learned by now not to stick my nose in other people's business."

"What?"

He stared at her for a minute before taking her hand and placing it under his shirt. She fingered the raised scar on his chest, she had never asked about.

"Randy—"

"It was a birthday present from my mother. She gave it to me while I was tryin' to protect her from her ole man."

Cass stared into his eyes. They always reflected the sincerity of his words and she trusted they would never lie to her. But…his own mother?

"I can't believe that."

"I have the scar to prove it."

"But you're her son."

"My mother cared about three things when I was growin' up—booze, men, and herself. I didn't fit into any of those categories, so as far as she was concerned, I was a nuisance she couldn't get rid of."

Randy pulled Cass down until she was lying on him. He closed his eyes as his fingers absently played with her single braid.

As she waited for him to continue, she listened to the laughter coming from the children playing outside. She knew his story would not be as happy as theirs. She had waited months for him to tell his story, and now that he was about to, she wasn't sure she wanted to hear it.

"My mother got pregnant when she was fifteen," he finally sighed out. "I never knew my father. In fact, I don't think she even knew who my father was. The man she hoped was the father didn't want to have a thin' to do with either of us. But then, he wasn't the only one. I can't count the number of times she said she never wanted me. She told me she tried drinkin' quinine and gin and takin' hot baths, but all that did was make her sick enough that the doctor was summoned.

"When the doctor told her parents she was pregnant, her father kicked her out the house. She didn't have anyone who would take her in, so she hitched a ride to Mobile, tellin' her companions she was a widow. When she got there, they took her to the preacher, whose wife took pity on my mother, took her in, gave her a job as a housekeeper, and even accepted me after I was born.

"We lived there for about four years, and durin' that time my mother acted like the perfect lady. She went to church on Sundays, helped the preacher's wife, visited the sick and elderly, and helped other women with their children. She even took care of me. Her act was so good, no one would have ever believed she wasn't a widow, not even if the Lord had come down and told them personally.

"One day the preacher's wife came home early from runnin' errands and found me in her garden, tramplin' her flowers. She carried me into the kitchen, where her husband was ministerin' to my mother with his pants down and her skirt up around her waist. Needless to say, my mother grabbed me and made a very quick exit out of town.

"We spent the next couple of years goin' from town to town with my mother hookin' up with men until they either found someone younger or were tossed in jail. She didn't work. She barely took care of herself, and she didn't care enough to look after me."

Bracing her arms on his chest, Cass leaned up to look at him. "How'd you survive?"

"Once in a while she met someone who cared enough to feed me, but most of the time I had to fend for myself," he replied without opening his eyes. "I scrounged for scraps and stole what I needed to get by. Occasionally, someone took pity on me and fed me."

"That's awful."

"On the one hand it was, and on the other, things were not that bad."

"How can you say that? No child should have to fend for himself."

He gently pushed her head back to his chest. "I know, but I fended for myself 'cause I was bein' ignored. Things were worse when my mother or one of her men acknowledged my presence. It usually meant I was bein' used as a punchin' bag. I guess you can say I actually learnt how to be a ghost, 'cause as long as I wasn't seen or heard, things were okay for me."

Cass remembered New Year's and Randy's declaration that spilt milk could lead to broken bones in his house. It disgusted her that a mother... No, she would not refer to the woman with the same title as her mother. A mother protected a child. She didn't hurt, or allow others to hurt, her children.

"I was ten when my mother met Adam. She brought him home one day, said they were married and we were movin' to Mississippi. That's where I met Sax."

"Didn't your mother mind that you were spending time with Sax?" Cass repeated the question she had asked not long after meeting him.

"If she knew, I don't think she cared, 'cause my bein' over there meant I wasn't at home in her hair."

Randy paused. She reached for his free hand and

gentle squeezed. She did not expect the gesture to make the story easier to tell, but she hoped it would at least give him a little comfort.

He moved his hand from her neck to her shoulder and embraced her. "My mother gave me this scar on my fourteenth birthday." His voice cracked. He took a ragged breath before he continued. "Every year since I'd met them, Sax and Miss Sylvia would do somethin' for me on my birthday. That year she made me a cake and they gave me a shirt as a present. They wanted me to stay for supper that night, but foolishly I insisted on goin' home to see if my mother had gotten me anythin'."

"It wasn't foolish to hope your mother got you something," she reassured him.

He snorted. "For me it was. She'd never gotten me anythin' before. Not for my birthday. Not for Christmas. Never. I'd be lucky if she said 'Happy Birthday' on her way out to get drunk. But every year I kept wishin' that birthday would be different.

"Anyhow, when I got home, Adam and my mother were in the kitchen. I sat with them for a while, droppin' hints as to what day it was. Finally, Adam asked if I had problem. I told them it was my birthday, and he asked what the hell did I expect, a present? He then slugged me so hard I went sailin' across the room and into the wall. For some reason, my mother jumped to my defense and told him not to hit me. So he started hittin' her.

"Because she'd taken up for me, I decided to return the favor. I pulled him off her and the two of us started goin' at it. When I finally got him pinned to the floor, I turned around to see if my mother was all right. That's when she plunged a knife into my chest.

"I thought she'd made a mistake and the knife was intended for Adam, but when she dropped to his side and yelled for me to get out, I knew it wasn't me she was tryin' to protect. When I didn't move, she got up and pushed me outside, then slammed the door in my face."

Cass forced back the bile that rose to her throat. How could the woman turn against her own son?

"I don't know how long I stood there, waitin' for her to come out and help me. Eventually, I gave up and stumbled back to Sax's house, though I honestly don't know how I managed.

"When Miss Sylvia answered the door, I was standin' with the knife still stickin' out my chest. The last thing I remember before passin' out is her scream. I didn't come to until a week later. By then, Adam and my mother had packed their things and vanished."

"What'd you do?"

"I ended up livin' with Sax."

"They took in a white boy?"

"Everyone in the town knew my mother's reputation and thought I was no better than her, so they didn't want to have anythin' to do with me. Miss Sylvia wrote to my grandmother, but Grams was too frail to look after me. Instead of lettin' me become a ward of the county, they offered to let me stay with them. Miss Sylvia told anyone who had anythin' to say against it that I was better off bein' raised by a colored family then thrown out on the street like a dog."

"How long did you stay with them?"

"Four years, until Sax died. After the funeral, Miss Sylvia decided to sell the farm and move in with her daughter. Before I left, she gave me Sax's horn. She apologized for not havin' anythin' more to give me, but I think she had already given me a lot."

"Do you still see her?"

"I write Miss Sylvia at least once a week, and I try to go down and visit her once a year."

"What about your mother? Did you ever see her again?"

"Once, about six years ago, at Gram's funeral. By then Adam had left her, but not before knockin' out her two front teeth. She could barely hear in her right ear from a beatin' she took from another man. She still drank, and she was into drugs. She was a mess, but she didn't seem to care. I haven't seen or heard from her since then."

"I'm…" She paused to clear her throat. "I'm sorry, Randy."

He brushed a tear from her cheek, leaned forward, and kissed the top of her head. "Don't be. I've stopped cryin' long ago over what she did or didn't do for me. I've found better uses of my time, like makin' sure the woman who took me in doesn't ever live to regret knowin' me."

Cass shook her head. As far as she was concerned, Miss Sylvia would never have regrets. Thanks to the older woman, the boy who had suffered so much had definitely grown into a man anyone would be proud of.

Chapter 24

"Everyone, can I have your attention," Luther shouted as he walked into the dining room. A photographer followed him.

The dancers ignored their boss and continued their conversations.

He cleared his throat and tried again. "Ladies."

Cass looked up from the book she had been reading despite the constant chattering going on around her.

"He might as well give up," Red mumbled from his seat next to Cass. "Nothing can hush those gals."

A shrill whistle cut through the noise, stunning everyone into silence. They glanced toward the kitchen door, where Florence stood with her thumb and finger in her mouth, preparing to whistle again.

"You were saying?" Eli beamed with pride. "*Esa es mi mujer.*"

Luther frowned. "Thank you, Florence, for that rather unladylike display."

The dancer shrugged her shoulders. "It got their attention."

"Anyway." Luther sighed, turning his attention back to the women. "I asked you to come in today for promotional photos. I need you in your costumes. Florence will tell you which outfit to change into first. Please hurry. The photographer doesn't have all day."

As if unaware of the meaning of the word hurry,

the women resumed their conversations as they strolled backstage.

"I'll see what I can do," Florence said before following the others.

"Sounds like you got your work cut out for you today," Red called out.

"I don't know why I put myself through this every year," Luther grumbled.

"Don't know why you told them to hurry," Angel said. He sat on the edge of the stage with a lit cigarette dangling between his fingers. "Those chicks are so busy spoutin' they ain't gonna move if their asses were on fire."

Cass glowered at the drummer. "With a mouth like that, it's a wonder any woman lets you kiss them."

"It ain't their mouths I'm interested in."

"You're a pig."

The drummer grunted.

She jumped to her feet and slammed her book on the table. "That's it," she yelled. "I'm not getting on stage with him."

Luther stepped forward and placed a hand her shoulder. "Cass, calm down. Angel, stop harassing her." He sighed. "Can't you two be in the same room for one minute without going at each other's throats?"

"Sure, as long as he does me one favor—" Cass started.

Angel snorted. "Over my dead body."

"That's the favor."

"You need to learn to respect a man."

"You start acting like one and I'll consider it."

"I'll show you a man—"

"I hope you don't plan to whip out that little thing

in your pants, 'cause it won't prove a thing. My brother's baby has the same thing you do, and he ain't no more of a man than I am."

Angel hopped off the stage but stopped short when Eli stepped between them.

"Angel, sit down," Luther said, pointing toward the drums. "Cass, not another word."

Cass and Angel opened their mouths.

"Not another word from either one of you, else I'll decide which one of you I can do without. The loser will find him or herself out of a job."

Not willing to test Luther, Cass sat back down with a huff. Showing the same unwillingness to gamble with his job, Angel snapped his mouth shut. He hopped back onto the stage and moved toward the drums.

"Okay, listen up, you guys. I want to get some pictures of the band while the women get ready," Luther announced. "You might as well do a number. You can rehearse and get your picture taken at the same time. We'll save the posing for later."

The musicians assembled on stage with their instruments.

"Cass, go change. We'll need you in a few minutes. And where's your partner?" Luther asked, eyeing the empty seat in the front row.

"I don't know." She shrugged her shoulders. "I haven't seen Randy all day."

"Red, I thought you told everyone to be here at three."

"I was busy," the pianist replied. "I asked Angel to do it."

"Angel?" Luther said.

Angel shrugged his shoulders. "I must've forgotten

about him, seeing as how we don't share a dressing room. You know how it is, out of sight, out of mind."

Luther frowned at Cass to ward off any remarks from her.

"Sorry, Luther," Red said, glaring at the drummer. "I wasn't thinking."

"I don't have time to go looking for him. We'll have to take the picture without him."

"Good. We don't need that ghost in the pictures anyway," Angel mumbled.

Luther grabbed Cass by the shoulders and turned her in the direction of the door leading backstage.

"Go change," he said, before calling over his shoulder, "someone move that extra chair and stand off the stage, and then spread out so we don't have an empty space in the picture."

Cursing under her breath, Cass headed downstairs. She entered the dressing room full of dancers in various stages of preparation, walked to the farthest corner, and dropped into a chair.

"I hope you're not planning on looking like that for your picture," Florence said as she powdered her cheeks.

"Why?" Cass asked.

"If looks could kill—"

"I could only be so lucky. Unfortunately, Angel is still breathing."

Florence tossed the makeup brush onto the table. "What did he do now?"

"He didn't tell Randy to be here this afternoon."

"It figures he'd do something like that today," Florence said, adjusting lapels on her floral silk robe. "However, I wouldn't be surprised if Junior was behind this. He can't do anything about Randy working here, but he can make sure Randy's face isn't on anything dealing with the club."

"Junior's not sneaky," Cass said, shaking her head. "If he didn't want Randy here, he would've just come out and said so. Angel's the sneaky one. He'll do something and then play innocent."

"Between the two of them, it's a wonder Randy hasn't quit by now."

"He has something stronger than hatred that makes him stay."

"His attraction to a certain sassy singer?"

"No, his love for music."

"Stop selling yourself short," Florence commented, reaching for her mascara. "He could leave and easily find a gig elsewhere, but he's not going to easily find another sassy gal who'll stand up for him."

Cass shook her head as she began to undo her braid. She did not believe Randy would put up with the abuse dished out to him night after night in order to be near her. There were far too many other women out there. As Angel, Junior, and many of the men who worked at The Big House had proven, it was too easy to jump from one woman to the next when the relationship got too complicated or they needed a change.

She refused to fool herself into believing she was not a complication. They had talked more about his life with Sax and Miss Sylvia and the trouble he'd endured living with a colored family. The white people in town had scorned him, treating him with the same hatred they would coloreds. Young men hollered insults at him from their cars or, if they found him on the road alone, used him as a punching bag. But no matter how much he had faced, she knew a person could tolerate hatred for only so long.

Randy being with a colored woman opened the doors to more hatred, from both coloreds and whites. Eventually, he'd get tired and decide it would be easier to find a fairer woman.

"No, he's dedicated to his music," Cass mumbled as she slipped out of her chair to search for her hairbrush.

After locating the brush, Cass twisted the sides of her hair, leaving the back loose. Once she'd changed into a silver gown and heels, she returned to the dining room.

As the band rehearsed, the photographer took pictures from various angles. After several numbers, she joined them on stage. Her heart was not into the music and it was difficult to do anything more than mumble the lyrics. After a half hour, Luther stopped her in the middle of a song and called the dancers out to rehearse.

Once the rehearsals and photographs were over, Luther dismissed everyone for supper, telling them to return at a quarter to eight for the evening's show.

"Cass, I have to tell you, with all honesty, that was the worst performance you ever gave," Florence commented as they walked down the steps.

"I'm still upset with Angel," Cass replied. "That jokester needs to get a taste of his own medicine."

"Daddy used to tell us 'whatever is begun in anger ends in shame.' "

Cass stepped off the stairs and spied the drummer hovering over one of the dancers he had backed against a wall. "But he never said whose shame," she muttered,

Sweet Jazz

as the devil started whispering in her ear.

Florence reached for Cass's arm. "What are you going to do?" she asked, panic in her voice.

Cass dodged her friend and hurried toward the couple.

"...we could have a couple of drinks after the show," Angel finished propositioning the young woman.

"Angel, didn't you already ask Julie out for drinks after the show?" Cass asked.

His head jerked in her direction. "What? I did no such a thing."

"Oh, then it must've been Maria. No, Karen...ummm..."

"Cass," he growled.

"No, that's not it. I can't seem to remember who it was. What's the name of your woman of the week?"

The dancer curled her upper lip in disgust, sucked her teeth and pushed past him. She marched into the dressing room, slamming the door behind her.

"You know, come to think of it, it wasn't you who asked Julie out," Cass said. She shrugged her shoulders. "Oh, well, sorry."

Angel grabbed her arm as she moved to walk away. "What the hell was that for?" he shouted.

"I was just trying to be helpful. It was an honest mistake," she smiled, before her eyes narrowed and she hissed, "Just like the one you made when you forgot to tell Randy about this afternoon."

"You did that 'cause of some ofay?" He tightened his grip on her arm, but she refused to flinch.

"No, I did that 'cause you're an ass."

"I have a right mind to beat your butt."

"Go ahead and try it," Cass dared.

"Angel, you raise one finger to her and you're out of here," Luther warned as he stepped out of his office with Florence and Eli following behind. "Now let her go."

Angel shoved her arm away from his as if it disgusted him to touch her.

"What is this all about?"

"Woman gettin' all in my business 'cause that ofay wasn't here this afternoon."

"Cass?"

"I made one simple mistake," she replied, feigning innocence.

"What is with you two?" Luther asked. "I know there's never been any love lost between the two of you, but lately you can't be in the same room without going at each other's throats."

"Blame it on the ofay," Angel answered. "She's been actin' all funny since she let him in her drawers."

Cass's mouth dropped open.

"Surprised I know? I bumped into your friend—oh, I mean ex-friend—Maia, and she told me about that ofay walkin' around your apartment all comfortable like he lived there."

"What Randy and I do in private is no one's damn business but our own."

"I figured you didn't like men 'cause you were always turnin' down the cats tryin' to talk to you, but to find out you prefer ofays… Would've thought better of you if you liked women."

"Okay, you two," Luther barked. "I'm tired of breaking up fights between the two of you. One way or the other we will have peace in this club."

"I was over here mindin' my own business—" Angel began.

"I don't care who started it, I want peace. Either you figure out a way to achieve it, or I will," Luther ordered before walking off.

"Best way to achieve it is to fire the ofay and his whore," Angel mumbled before he stormed off, shoving Eli aside with his shoulder.

****

Randy turned west on 133rd Street and noticed Florence and Eli walking away from The Big House instead of toward it. Before he could call to the couple, someone called his name.

He stared at the passenger hanging out of the rear window of the taxi before recognition set in.

"Hey, man, you're a hard person to find," Daniel Fields greeted as Randy jogged toward the car.

"Never knew I was lost," Randy responded.

"You got a sense of humor. Must come in handy workin' here, you know, with the jokes and everythin' at your expense."

"It helps me get by."

"Listen, I'm not gonna keep you. Our band recently lost our sax player."

"What happened?"

"He ran off with our singer. Don't expect to be seein' them around anytime soon. She was the wife of our trombonist. Anyway, Willie's lookin' to replace them, and I remembered your act." Daniel passed Randy a business card. "We rehearse downtown at Bleecker Street. You should drop by and let Willie hear you. The gig will require some travelin', but all expenses will be paid."

"When should I come down?" Randy asked.

"Tomorrow, around three."

He slipped the card into his coat pocket. "I'll think about it."

"You should, man. Someone with your talents shouldn't be wastin' his time in a hole in the wall, not gettin' the respect he deserves." Daniel looked at his watch. "Listen, I got to go. Think about it."

"I will," Randy agreed as he stepped back from the curb.

Eager to tell Cass the proposition, he hurried into the alley. He stopped short at the sight of the singer pacing outside the back door, already dressed for the show.

"If you want to offer free concerts outdoors, I suggest you find a better venue," Randy teased. "It doesn't look like you're attractin' much of an audience back here."

She stopped midway between the entrance to the club and the alley. Her eyes were narrow and her lips were pursed in a tight frown.

"Okay, we're not in the mood for jokes tonight," he said, placing his saxophone case on the ground. "Any particular reason why?"

"Angel," Cass mumbled before giving him the highlights of the afternoon's events.

Since their fight, just hearing the man's name made the vein in Randy's temple pulse and his fists tighten. As he listened, he fought the urge to search for the other man and beat him to a pulp for insulting her.

Once she'd finished, he pulled her to him and held her tight.

"The best part about leavin' this club will be the

beatin' I give Angel for everythin' he's ever done to you."

Cass snorted into his chest. "Nice dream, but I wouldn't waste my time worrying about something that might not happen for a while."

"It may happen sooner than you expect."

She pulled back and stared up at him. "What?"

Randy released Cass and picked up his case. "Come inside," he said, taking her hand.

"What's going on?" she asked, as he led her through the back door.

"Do you remember Daniel Fields and Willie Hawke? We met them when we were in D.C."

"Yes, what about them?"

"I just bumped into Daniel outside. The band's sax player ran off with their singer." Randy pulled the light string in his dressing room and scanned the closet for anything out of the ordinary. Satisfied everything was in place, he pulled her inside and closed the door.

"What does that have to do with us leaving?"

"Don't you see? They want us to audition."

Cass clapped her hands over her mouth. "Are you serious?"

"Would I joke about somethin' like that?"

"When? Where?"

He pulled the card Daniel gave him out his pocket. "This is the address. We should be there tomorrow at three."

"I can't believe this," Cass shrieked. Without looking at the card, she jumped into his arms. "I can't wait to tell Junior and Angel about themselves."

"Whoa, let's not get ahead of ourselves." Randy pulled back from her and slipped the card back into his pocket. "We should wait 'til we have the gig before we burn these bridges."

"I suppose, but I'm dying to give Angel a piece of my mind."

"Girl, you keep givin' him pieces of your mind, you're not goin' to have much left for anythin' else."

"It'll be worth it. Oh, but…"

"But, what?"

"What number should we do?"

"We should do one of the numbers we've been working on. Give them something new."

"And I don't know what to wear."

"I have a suggestion."

"What?"

"How about clothes?" Randy pulled her back to him. "I don't want anyone but me seein' you without them."

She draped her arms over his shoulders. "You're sounding a bit possessive," she said as her fingers grazed his nape.

"I'm selfish. I don't like sharin'," Randy whispered before he pressed his lips against hers.

He had only meant to give her a quick peck, but as soon as their lips touched, their mouths opened and their tongues got into the act. As they tasted each other, he discovered he wanted…needed…more. He became more adventurous and kissed a spot behind her ear that was particularly sensitive.

She sighed and she gripped his head. The sound urged him on. He backed her against the wall and pressed his hips forward. As he ground his erection onto her hip, his trembling hands searched for her zipper.

"Randy," Cass whispered as he opened her dress. "You don't have a lock on your door."

"I know," he said as he peeled the front of her dress from her body.

"Anyone can walk in on us."

He pushed the straps of her slip and bra off her shoulders. "No one's here, remember? You said everyone went out for supper. They won't be returnin' for at least an hour and a half."

"But, still…"

The plea in her voice was stronger than Randy's needs. Though he wanted nothing more than to make love to her, he knew he could not become like her ex-husband and put his needs before hers. As much as it pained him—and pain him it did—he sighed as he stepped back.

She quickly pulled her clothes back into place. Once she was dressed she glanced up at him, concern written over her face.

"I'm sorry, Randy, but even though I'm sure everyone knows about us, I don't—"

"Want to give them a show," he finished her thought.

Cass nodded.

He reached out and touched her arm. "Come here."

"Isn't that where we were a minute ago?"

"Okay, then, maybe you should stay over there," he said, dropping his arm to his side.

"Are you upset?"

"About what? That you're a lady who's willin' to show some discretion, despite my attempts to corrupt you? Cass, if I wanted a woman who's willin' to drop her drawers anyplace and anytime, I'd be comin' on to the women Angel chases after."

She frowned.

"I like that my gal has higher standards. Half of Harlem doesn't know what you look like and the other half can't tell stories about where you've been caught and who you've been caught with."

"But what about—" She glanced down at his groin.

"I'll survive. It was a constant state I lived in before you would have me. What's a couple of nights?" Randy asked, referring to his habit of spending Sunday to Wednesday at her apartment. The other nights, he returned to the boarding house after escorting her home.

"You mean a couple of hours."

"What?"

"You don't think I'd leave you hanging, do you?"

"Darlin', I'm not exactly hangin' right now."

"You know what I mean." She reached up and tapped his cheek. "I'll see you after the show."

****

"Cass, isn't it kind of late for you to be out?" Eli commented as he strolled into the ladies' dressing room with his arm draped around Florence's shoulder.

"She's been doing a lot of things out of the ordinary lately." Florence smiled at Randy, who leaned against a table while Cass gathered her things.

"Speak for yourself," Cass returned, looking from the trumpeter to the dancer and back.

"I think I've earned the right to do a few things out of the ordinary." Florence held out her left hand and wiggling her fingers.

"When did this happen?" Cass asked, rushing forward to examine the other woman's engagement ring.

"Sunday morning, after the show," Florence answered. "Eli proposed when we got back to my place."

"*Imagine esto*. We're outside when I dropped to one knee like they do in the movies and asked her to marry me," Eli reflected. "But instead of following the script and saying yes, she screamed loud enough to wake half the neighborhood. Before I knew it, I had people running out of buildings ready to rip off Eli Junior and his two friends."

Randy shuddered. "Ouch."

"*Exacamente*," Eli agreed. "Luther was leading the mob. I had to do some mighty fast explaining."

"When Daddy found out what really happened, he threatened to take a strap to my behind for all the commotion I caused."

"Why didn't you say anything earlier?" Cass asked.

"Like I have time to do anything but work when I step into this place," Florence remarked.

"When's the wedding going to take place?"

"June 26th," Eli answered.

"And until then, you're going to keep your distance from my baby," Luther commented as he walked into the room. He glanced from the musician to the dancer and frowned. "Is there something wrong with your arm, boy? If so, I can help."

"No, sir," Eli replied. He removed his arm from around Florence's neck and ran his hand over his head before dropping the limb to his side.

Luther glared at his future son-in-law for a second before turning to Randy, who was standing beside Cass.

Randy raised his arms. "Look, no hands."

Chuckling, Cass elbowed him in the ribs.

"I hire a musician and I get a comedian."

Randy dropped his hands. "What can I say? I have many talents."

"I need to see you two up front," Luther said, before walking out.

Randy looked down at Cass. She shrugged her shoulders and shook her head. She was certain Luther did not want her to have drinks with anyone, since there had been no patrons in the club when Randy and she came downstairs. Besides, Junior had left midway through the show, and Randy's presence had also been requested.

With a jerk of his head, Randy placed his hand on her lower back and led her out of the dressing room. Florence and Eli followed them upstairs, where Luther was talking to the photographer who had taken the publicity photos earlier.

"Marty stuck around for the show, and after he saw your act, he wanted to get a few pictures of the main attraction," Luther said, explaining the photographer's presence. "You up to taking a few more?"

"I don't know—" Cass began.

"Go ahead. You're still dressed," Randy said, glancing down at the outfit she still wore after the evening's performance. She wanted to give Randy the pleasure of removing it entirely from her body when they got home.

He lifted her hand to his lips. Though she was certain everyone at the club knew about their relationship, Cass's cheeks burned at his first public display of affection at The Big House. She felt even warmer when Luther cleared his throat.

Randy smiled as if amused by Luther's reaction. Though he didn't release her, he lowered her hand and escorted her to the stage. "Go ahead," he said. "You know I'll wait for you."

"No, he wants both of you on stage," Luther clarified.

"Say what?" Randy said. The expression on his face spoke of the confusion Cass felt.

"The two of you make a good couple," the photographer said.

Though Cass knew he was talking about the performance and not their relationship, it felt good to have someone acknowledge Randy's presence.

"What do you say?" she asked, giving Randy's hand a slight tug.

He hesitated a second before allowing her to pull him onto the stage with her.

"Where do you want us?"

"Over there," Marty replied, pointing toward a stool center stage.

Randy sat on the edge of the stool with one foot on the lower rung and the other foot on the floor. Cass stepped back until she was settled between Randy's legs. He wrapped his arms around her waist, and she placed her hands on top of his.

"Hold that pose," Marty said.

They spent the next hour posing for the photographer. He positioned them until he found poses in which they were relaxed, showing their comfort with each other.

"That was fun," Cass commented as the two couples stepped outside the club.

"I love how Marty works with us," Florence said.

"He tries to make you comfortable, so the pictures look natural, not like you're scared of the camera. He's agreed to shoot the wedding."

"Where are you having the ceremony?"

"The ceremony and reception will be at The Big House."

"It's nice to have a father who co-owns a club. You can have the wedding of your dreams for a fraction of the cost."

"That depends on the entertainment."

"Aren't you going to have the band play?"

"Yes, but we also wanted Randy and you to perform a few numbers," Florence said. "I know it'll be your night off, and I'm willing to compensate you…" She paused when she realized Randy and Cass had stopped walked.

"I believe we've just been insulted," Randy said.

"I believe so," Cass agreed.

"How?" Eli asked.

"To suggest we'd take money to perform at your reception."

"We'd be honored to do a couple of numbers," Randy said. "All you had to do was ask."

"And name your firstborn after us," Cass teased.

"Okay, I'm willing to ask, but I won't name any of my babies after you," Florence stated. "Might jinx them and I'd end up with a child sassier than you."

"I resent that."

"As well you should," Randy said. "There ain't no one sassier than you."

Cass jabbed him in the ribs with her elbow.

"Ow! Or more dangerous."

"If you're working that afternoon, Junior won't

Sweet Jazz

have an excuse to throw you out the club," Eli said as they continued toward the corner.

"Damn, for a minute, I forgot about Junior," Randy mumbled. "I don't want to cause any problems on your weddin' day."

"Please, you won't be a problem," Florence said. "Junior'll probably be so busy walking around acting like it's his party, he won't give you a second thought."

"Are you sure?"

"Sure as my name is Florence Jean Hamilton."

"I need more reassurance than that."

"Then how about, as sure as I am that Cass is the sassiest women you'll ever meet."

"Okay, now I'm convinced."

"Keep it up and you'll be kissing yourself goodnight tonight," Cass said.

"Darlin', you're sassy, but you know I wouldn't have you any other way." Randy raised her hand to his lips.

"Isn't he Mr. Romantic," Florence sighed.

"I hope you don't want me to act like that," Eli said.

"And have Daddy try to knock your lips to the back of your head? Sweetie, I love your face the way it is." Florence stopped when they reached Eighth Avenue. "Did you want to get a bite to eat?"

"No, we need to get home," Randy said. "We have a big day ahead of us."

Despite the late hour, they talked for another minute before Eli suggested the women continue their conversation in the afternoon and pulled Florence around the corner to his car.

"We should've joined them," Cass said as they

crossed 133rd Street. "I'm hungry."

"So am I," Randy said.

"Then why'd you tell them we need to get home?"

"Because I'm hungry for two things, but we don't have time to satisfy both, if we're goin' to get any sleep before the audition."

"I guess I'm willing to forego food for now," Cass replied, taking his hint, "as long as you make it worth my while."

"Darlin', it'll be worth it."

Chapter 25

The back door to the club was open when Randy and Cass arrived. They walked in and followed the music downstairs to an auditorium in the basement.

Willie Hawke sat at the piano, leading a diversified group of fifteen musicians in an original number. Ida Fields leaned over the piano, tapping her foot in time to the music.

"How was that?" Willie asked when they finished the song.

"Benny Goodman couldn't have done better," Ida replied.

Willie motioned to her with an index finger. She leaned forward and gave him a peck on the lips.

"It's a guaranteed hit," Cass said.

"Hey, you made it," Daniel exclaimed. He stood and stepped from behind the drums.

"It was an opportunity we couldn't pass up," Randy said.

"You really liked the number?" Willie asked, walking over to the couple.

"They're going to be dancing to it at the Savoy," Cass predicted.

"Come meet the band."

Willie introduced Randy and Cass to the rest of the band. Though she smiled and joked with each person, Cass twisted the strap to her bag around her hand, a sign she was nervous. Unlike most days, when she chose an outfit in less than five minutes, she had spent an hour that morning fussing over her clothes before finally deciding on a navy dress and black pumps.

"I caught your act the other night," the bassist said. "It was solid."

"Thanks," Randy replied.

"I grew up in Harlem, and I remember when The Big House opened. Back then, there were only a handful of clubs that would allow coloreds in the front door. It was a big thing to have a club that catered only to coloreds. How'd you get your gig?"

Randy draped an arm on Cass's shoulder. "A certain little canary spoke up for me," he said, glancing down at her.

"I couldn't let him get away," Cass said, patting his chest.

"The Big House is about to lose him," Daniel said as he returned to his seat.

"We'll first need to hear something," Willie said.

"Anythin' in particular you want to hear?" Randy asked.

"Anything you want to play."

Randy placed his case on a chair. "In that case, Cass and I wanted to do a number we've been workin' on."

"Cass and you?" Willie asked.

"Yeah, we figured we'd do a number together. Unless you want us to audition separately."

"No, whatever you prepared. The floor's yours."

Cass walked to the microphone and waited until Randy nodded, indicating he was ready. They performed "What a Difference a Day Makes," staring at each other as if they were the only ones in the room. Cass loosened up like she did on stage at The Big House. She ignored the strap to her bag. Her body slowly…sensually…moved to the music. And Randy enjoyed every movement.

They lost themselves in the song, forgetting others were present, until several of the musicians applauded when they finished.

"You two are good together," Ida said.

"Thank you," Cass said. "To be honest, I was a little nervous. It's been several years since I've auditioned for anyone."

"You did fine." Willie hesitated before offering, "Ida can take you upstairs and get you something to drink."

"Yes, please."

"Do you want anything?" he asked Randy.

"No, I'm fine."

"I'll be back in a minute," Cass said, following the other woman out of the room.

"You two make a good couple," Willie commented.

"Cass may be sassy as sin, but she makes a great partner."

"Until I heard you two, I hadn't considered a duet, but I think I like the idea of adding a couple of duets to the show. I'm going to keep that in mind when we audition singers. We'll find someone you'll feel comfortable working with."

"What do you mean? You're not hirin' Cass?"

"No, we weren't interested in her."

"But I thought you were lookin' for a singer and saxophonist."

"Well…yes…we are."

"Was it her singin'? We could do another number. She was a little nervous, but once she relaxes—"

"No, she's a fine singer."

"Then what?" Randy asked, realizing the man had trouble meeting his eye.

"She doesn't exactly have the look we need."

Randy frowned. He wanted to believe he had heard wrong. He glanced around the room, but when no one would look him in the eye, he knew his ears had not deceived him.

"You're not hirin' Cass 'cause she's colored?"

"No, it's not that," Willie insisted as he moved back to the piano, placing a good distance and the instrument between them. "She doesn't have the right look. You know, audiences want women who are more exotic looking. Like I said, it's nothing personal, but this is a business, and you've got to give the audiences what they want. I mean, hell, if appearances didn't matter, I'd put Ida on stage. She sings just as well as that gal of yours, but no one's going to pay to see a dark-skinned woman."

"And you don't have a problem givin' in to this behavior?" Randy glared up in the direction the women had taken. "Basically, all a dark woman's good for is servin' you coffee and warmin' your bed?"

"Hey, man, that's my sister you're talkin' about." Daniel threw his sticks to the side and stood. "Have a little more respect."

"And, how much respect are you showin' her by standin' here and listenin' to this?" Randy walked over to the table and packed his saxophone in the case.

"I think I understand," Willie said. "You're loyal to

Sweet Jazz

that gal for helping you get your current gig, but you've got to think about your career. You're not going to get far dragging her around with you."

"No, it's not just loyalty. It's being true to what I believe. I was raised to believe in equality, and I'd be a damn hypocrite if I talked about all races being equal and then joined a band that refused to hire someone because she's too dark."

"Funny you don't consider yourself a hypocrite working in a club that denies your own race entrance."

"They at least took a step forward when they hired me."

"Randy, I know you said you didn't want anything, but I brought you a soda, anyway," Cass announced as she came down the steps with Ida.

With his case in his hand, Randy walked over to her, snatched the bottle out of her hand, and passed it to Ida.

"What was that for?"

"Come on," he said, grabbing her wrist.

"Don't be so quick to judge," Daniel called out as the couple started up the stairs. "Sometimes you have to conform to get ahead."

"You keep tellin' yourself that," Randy responded, curling his upper lip in disgust, "and maybe one day you'll believe it."

He marched out, dragging Cass behind him. Outside, he did not slow down until they were in front of Washington Square Park, where Cass finally managed to free herself from his grip.

"Randy, I swear, you're acting like a mad man," she said. "What's gotten into you?"

"We'll talk about this later," he snapped, ignoring

the two men who stared at them as they walked by.

"No, we're going to talk about this now."

"Cass, come on."

"I refuse to go anywhere with you until you stop acting crazy. Now, are you going to talk to me?" She placed her hands on her hips and tapped her foot.

Randy stared at Cass. Talk? He didn't want to talk. He wanted to scream at the injustice of it all. One's too light. The other's too dark. It seemed as if everything always came back to race. He wished it could be like it was when they were alone, when nothing else mattered but them.

"Fine," she said, turning on her heels.

"Cass, where are you goin'?" he called after her.

"Back to the club. Maybe someone there will tell me what's going on."

"No, wait," he said as he rushed to catch up with her. He grabbed her wrist and pulled her to a stop.

Cass spun to face him. "Well?"

"We didn't get the gig."

"What?"

"I said…"

"I heard what you said. You're actin' this way 'cause we didn't get a gig?"

"It's not 'cause we didn't get the gig, but why."

"Huh."

Randy took a deep breath. He dreaded telling her the truth, but knew the truth was better than any lie he could make up to spare her feelings.

"Cass," he started, hoping to ease the blow. "We didn't get it 'cause they didn't want you. They're lookin' for a singer who's…well, who's…" He could not bring himself to finish the sentence.

"Lighter?"

His shoulders slumped. "Yes. When Daniel told me to come down, they only wanted to hear me play."

"They told you that when I went upstairs with Ida?"

"Yes."

Cass snatched her arm from him, turned, and started back in the direction of the rehearsal hall.

"Where you goin'?"

"Back there to tell them you've lost your cotton-pickin' mind," Cass called out over her shoulder.

"What?"

"I'm not letting you lose this gig because of me."

He couldn't believe her. He'd lost his mind? What about her? Did she seriously think he'd go back and work with them?

Randy waited for Cass to turn around and tell him she was joking. When she crossed the street, he realized she was serious and went after her.

He grabbed her by the shoulders and turned her to face him. "I'm not lettin' you go back down there."

Cass's eyes narrowed. "You're what?"

Realizing how it sounded, Randy softened his tone, while rewording his statement.

"I will not go back there."

As he had hoped, the change defused the eruption, though a shake of her head indicated the argument was not over.

"Randy, will you think for a second? This is your chance to get out of The Big House, to make it big."

"I'm not goin' to work with a band that'll deny a person a chance because she's too dark."

"Stop thinking about us for a moment and think

about you."

"Cass, if I was to take that gig, there'd be no us. How could I play with them and then look you in the face, knowin' what they stand for. Hell, I wouldn't even be able to play my sax, the sax that was owned by a colored man who taught me to look beyond the color of a person's skin and see what's on the inside." He sighed. "The very first day I walked into The Big House, you threatened to quit if I didn't get the gig. Did you mean that?"

"Yes, I couldn't have stayed there knowing someone with your talent was denied a chance 'cause he was not dark enough for the management's taste."

"Then what kinda man would I be if I took this gig knowin' they'd deny someone with talent an opportunity just 'cause she's not light enough? Not the kinda man who deserves to have you."

****

The disappointment over the audition stayed with Cass throughout the rest of the day, and by the time she walked into The Big House that evening, she was in a foul mood and ready to pick a fight. Unfortunately, the dancers gathered in the dressing room were not obliging. The second she stepped into the room, everyone became mute. They dispersed in various directions in an attempt to appear busy, as if they had not been talking about her moments earlier.

Cass had heard the women before she entered the dressing room. Bea's loud shrill filled the whole backstage area. But, as with most gossips, no one was willing to say to her face what they were thinking. This left her in need of another outlet for her frustrations, since she refused to attack without being provoked.

Ignoring the other women, she walked over to her usual corner and hung her dress on the hook on the wall. She knew they were waiting for her to leave so they could continue their conversation, but the little devil inside her convinced her to deviate from her normal routine of rushing out to discuss the show with Luther. Instead, she sat down and unbraided her hair.

"Damn place is quieter than a funeral parlor," Florence commented, breaking the silence as she sashayed into the room.

"You better not let your father hear you cussin'," Cass said.

"Please, I swear all the time."

Cass raised an eyebrow.

"So, most of the time it's in my head, but I still do it." Florence sat on a chair next to the singer. "Why's it so quiet?"

"Probably 'cause I won't leave so they can finish talking about me."

"The gossip mill is working again?"

"It was until I walked in. Then it shut down." Cass laid the brush she had been using on the table. "Strangest thing is, at this moment I admire Angel and his courage to tell me to my face what he thinks about me. At least when he called me a white man's whore, I knew where he stood. Better than having someone smile in my face and then call me 'massa's little gal' behind my back." Cass leaned back in her chair to look at the woman sitting at the other end of the table. "Those were your exact words, right, Bea?"

The dancer's head snapped up. She glared indignantly at Cass.

Florence stood. "Why don't we go outside and talk,

so they can finish their gossip."

"I kind of preferred to stick around and see how long they can hold their tongues before they explode."

"Come on," Florence insisted, tugging on Cass's arm. "We need to talk to Daddy about the show, anyway."

The attitude outside the room was no different. Small groups huddled together became silent when Florence and Cass passed by. There were stares but no one brave enough to speak his mind.

Cass wished Angel, who she suspected had started the rumors, were there. Not one to hold his tongue, he would have said something aimed at her within minutes of her arrival, giving her the excuse she needed to lash out verbally. Unfortunately for her, the musician had traded days with the other drummer earlier in the week in order to have the night off to visit with family.

Her wish was short lived. As she approached the office, Junior's rant greeted her. She knew he could always be counted on to speak his mind, which would lead to an argument. Yet, as she stepped into the room, he stopped in mid-sentence and glared at her from across the room. Luther sat behind his desk. Stress lines creased his forehead; it was one of the few occasions his expression was readable. Red, who occupied one of the two chairs in front of the desk, glanced back to see what silenced the other man.

"I always thought I could expect more from y'all than this," Cass said, staring back at Junior, with her hands on her hips. "I never figured y'all would be cowards, too afraid to tell a woman to her face what you're thinking."

"Cass, it wasn't like that," Luther said.

"Sure sounded that way from outside."

"You wanna know what I'm thinkin'?" Junior asked. He then answered his question without waiting for a reply. "I'm thinkin' after all these years I never figured you'd be some white man's whore."

"I've never been any man's whore."

"Then you're tellin' me the stories about you bein' with that ofay ain't true?"

"I'm telling you that who I may or may not be with is my business and no one else's."

"Typical answer I'd expect from a whore."

"I always considered a whore to be someone who finds a different partner in his bed each night. You know, someone like Angel…or maybe you."

Junior took a step toward her. "You better watch your mouth," he threatened.

"Why? You don't like the truth? The way I figure, you should look at your own whorin' ways before you go around pointing your finger at someone else."

"My grandfather fought in the war so we wouldn't have to be slaves to the ofay. Here we are, seventy-five years later, and we still have Negroes who aren't satisfied unless they're answerin' to a ghost."

"Junior, I never realized 'til Randy started working here that there's no difference between you and the reddies down south. Both of y'all are filled with hate."

"Don't you ever compare me to those devils."

"I don't have to. You do every time you open your mouth."

"If you don't like what I have to say, then you can leave. I don't want your kind workin' in here, no how."

"No one's leaving," Luther interjected.

"You don't have to worry, Luther. I wouldn't give

him the satisfaction."

"You keep talkin' big and you're gonna be sorry." Junior pushed past her and stormed out of the room.

"Does anyone else want to say something?" Cass asked, crossing her arms.

Luther's shoulders slumped. "Cass, like I've told you before, I don't want to see you get hurt."

"And he's going to hurt me 'cause he's white?"

"It's a reality you have to face, but yes. Sooner or later he's going to get tired of all of this, and when he does he'll leave. Maybe he'll even try taking you with him, but he's not going to find it easy with a colored woman tagging along behind him. After the door's been slammed in his face several times, he's going to distance himself from everything that's preventing him from getting what he wants, and that will include you."

Cass sighed, remembering their audition. Randy had refused the gig because Willie did not want her, but she had to wonder how many jobs he was willing to lose out on because of his loyalty to her.

Chapter 26

The front door slammed as the Cooper children ran out of the building, waking Randy. From the shadows cast around the room, it was after noon, time for him to get ready for work. He groaned at the thought of having to leave the bed and the woman by his side.

For three days they had stayed in her apartment, away from the prejudices of society and the stress of The Big House. They'd spent their time making love and lying in each other's arms while they talked. When they needed time to themselves, one moved into the living room while the other remained in the bedroom.

Since Luther did not pay him to lie around, Randy rolled out of bed and headed to the bathroom. After a shower, he returned to the bedroom in his shorts and undershirt.

He quietly slipped on his pants so not to wake Cass, who had her back to him. When he sat on the edge of the bed to pull on his socks, the mattress shifted with a movement from her, and he felt the air on his back as she raised his undershirt. He shivered as she ran her tongue down his spine.

The responsible thing to do would have been to stop it before it started, but he could not pull away from her mouth. He closed his eyes and relished the feel of her kisses on his back as she reached around and caressed his chest. His undershirt inched higher and higher, until he finally assisted her and pulled it over his head.

"You know, the plan is for me to get dressed," Randy groaned.

"Mmm-hmm," Cass moaned in his ear as her hands traveled down to his pants.

"I need to go home and get some clean clothes for work."

"Okay." She pulled open his zipper.

"You remember work, don't you? It's what we do to make money…"

Her hand slipped inside his pants. "Yes."

"So we can pay the rent and buy food."

"Sure," she purred as she wrapped her hand around him.

"Aw, hell," he groaned as he rolled over onto her.

Two hours later, Cass lay on her side, caressing Randy's back as he made a second attempt to get dressed.

"If you keep that up, I'll never get out of here."

"I don't want you to go."

"Darlin', there's nothin' I'd rather do than stay in bed with you, but that's not what Luther's payin' us to do."

Cass dropped back onto the bed with a sigh. "It was fun while it lasted."

Randy stood and reached for the bathrobe lying at the foot of the bed. He tossed it over her to keep from getting distracted.

"You make it sound like we won't see each other again," he said before pulling his undershirt over his head.

Cass sat up. "I don't mean it like that. I just prefer

spending time with you, alone, without people sticking their noses into our business," she said as she slipped her arms into her bathrobe.

"I know." He had wished the same thing more than once over the past month. After a night of dealing with other people, it was a comfort to have someone he could go home to. The only problem was it was not his home. After a couple of hours, or, if they were lucky, a couple of days, he had to return to the boarding house. "It doesn't have to be that way."

"What are you saying?"

"We could have more time together, just the two of us," Randy said as he pulled on his shirt.

"Sure, if we lived on a deserted island."

He leaned back onto the bed. "Or we could get married." He had not planned on making the suggestion. Yet even though it had been spontaneous, it felt right.

Cass stared at him for minute before falling back onto the bed laughing.

"What's so funny?" Randy sat up.

"You are," she gasped. "Get married?"

"What's wrong with getting married?"

Cass stopped laughing. "Randy, be serious."

"I am being serious. What's wrong with us getting married?" he repeated as he stood up. "It's not like it's illegal up here."

"I can't marry you."

"Why?"

Cass sat up. "It's just a step I'm not ready to take now…if ever."

He frowned. "With me or with any man?"

"Any man."

Randy had thought Cass had gotten over her fear of getting hurt. Her comment, however, told him otherwise. Even after the time they'd spent together, Henry was still haunting her. He didn't know whether he was more angry at her for not putting the past behind her or at her ex for hurting her so badly. But with Henry nowhere to be found, he took his anger out on the only other person available.

"I think I'd felt better if it had been me," he mumbled as he slipped into his shoes. "At least then I'd know you were judgin' me for me and not what some other man did."

"Randy, you need to understand—"

"I do understand. You were hurt by your ex-husband and you simply want to be cautious. But when are you goin' to stop judgin' every man by what he did?"

"It's not that simple."

"Hell, like I don't know that. I've been tryin' my damnedest to prove to you that I'm not like Henry, but no matter what I do, you still compare me to him."

"What do you expect me to do? Jump into something without thinking? That's what got me mixed up with Henry."

"There's such a thing as bein' too careful. You can't go through life tiptoein' around, tryin' not to get hurt, else you may miss out 'cause you didn't take a chance." He walked out of the room.

Cass jumped off the bed and followed him into the living room. He snatched his coat out of the closet, grabbed his saxophone, and opened the door.

"Cass, I'm willin' to fight for you, but I'm not willin' to fight with you," he stated before walking out.

Chapter 27

Randy buttoned his pants before opening the door to his dressing room.

"We need to talk," Luther said, his tone as grim as the lines creasing his forehead

Randy had been expecting the other man to show up, after witnessing his frown midway through the performance. Though he had dreaded the inevitable conversation, the look on Luther's face said he did not have a choice.

"The numbers you've been doing with Cass have been off the past couple of days," Luther continued. "Tonight's number was the worst. I've just spent the last hour trying to talk to Cass, and she said there's nothing wrong between the two of you."

"We're fine," Randy lied.

"Not from what I heard tonight. I don't know what's going on with you two, and I don't want to know the details. I just want the two of you to work it out."

"We will."

"You better. If there's another performance like the one you had tonight, I'm going to be forced to cut your numbers."

Without waiting for a response, Luther walked away. Randy was surprised the other man had not pushed for more information. He had been certain

Luther would at least promise him bodily harm for breaking the singer's heart.

Randy stepped back into the room and closed the door. It had been three days since he'd stormed out of Cass's apartment, and her rejection still stung. But at the same time he missed her teasing and the few moments they shared before each show. When he held her, even for a few seconds, he did not feel alone. Instead, he understood what Mattie meant when she said she was able to deal with what was thrown at her because she didn't have to face it alone.

Deciding it was time to talk to Cass, Randy finished dressing. As hasty as his suggestion had been, expecting an answer right then had been even hastier.

Walking out on her had been more foolish. He had acted as a child, throwing a tantrum because he didn't get the answer he wanted. He shouldn't have made it an all-or-nothing decision. Having the few days they spent together each week was better than not being together at all.

Randy opened the door; Cass's laughter greeted him. The sound ripped through him, leaving an ache in his chest more painful than any beating he'd ever received.

It was obvious she had moved on and, unlike him, with no regrets or remorse. He no longer wanted to talk. He needed to get out of there.

"Hey, Randy," Eli called out as Randy turned toward the back door. "You want to join us for a drink?"

He stopped and glanced over his shoulder at Cass. Her smile slowly faded. Their eyes locked for a second before he shook his head.

Sweet Jazz

"I'll pass," he said before he walked out.

****

"What the hell was that all about?" Florence asked.

"Nothing," Cass said as she turned to walk away.

Cass had seen the hurt on Randy's face. She was ashamed she was the cause of his pain, yet she did not know what to do to make things right.

She enjoyed spending time with Randy. He had kept his word and made every moment they were together special. But at the same time she feared he would change. She didn't want to get hurt again, not that she was doing a good job of preventing it.

Florence grabbed Cass's arm before she could take more than one step.

"What do you mean, 'nothing'? That didn't look like nothing. Come to think of it, your performance has been off. Did you have a fight?"

"We're okay, really."

Florence glanced at Eli. "Umm...hon..."

"Yeah, you go ahead," Eli replied to the unspoken request. "We'll do this another time."

"What are you two doing?" Cass asked.

"We're going to have a drink and talk," Florence answered as she tugged on Cass's arm. "Thanks, hon. I'll call you in the afternoon."

"You don't have to cancel your plans 'cause of Randy and me," Cass protested as Florence pulled her upstairs.

"On the contrary, you need someone to talk to. Since your mother's in North Carolina without a phone and Maia's not speaking to you, that someone is going to be me. So now talk."

They went into the dining room, where a few of the

musicians, including Angel, were hanging around. The drummer glanced over his shoulder at her and smirked. He was having too much fun with her misery.

It hadn't taken long for gossip and speculations about her relationship to begin. It would be nice if people got lives of their own and left hers alone.

Cass sighed. "Fine, but not here."

"How about the joint down the block," Florence suggested.

Cass nodded.

They walked in silence to a small bar in the back room of a restaurant. Payoffs had officials turning a blind eye to the illegal business and the prostitutes who frequented the establishment hoping to pick up one last client or two before calling it a night.

The women felt safe entering the bar, as the owner, and many of the clientele, recognized Florence and knew the consequences of bothering her.

"Hey, Zeke," Florence called out as they walked in, "can we have two beers?"

"You know your father's gonna have my head if he finds out you've been in here," the bartender said as he placed two bottles on the bar.

"We won't be long," Florence insisted. "We just need a private place to talk for a few minutes."

"There's no one over there," he said, nodding to the dark corner in the back. "Just make it quick."

Florence dropped a couple of coins on the bar. "Thanks, Zeke," she said as she picked up the bottles.

They walked across the cracked linoleum to the corner, though they could have sat anywhere and been assured privacy. Mostly everyone they knew avoided the dive, citing higher standards.

"Okay, so what's going on?" Florence asked as they sat on chairs with foam peeking out of torn red vinyl seats. She pushed a beer across the sticky table to Cass.

"Randy asked me to marry him," Cass confessed.

"He did? Congratulations." Florence held up her bottle.

"I didn't say yes."

Florence's mouth dropped open. She stared at Cass for a minute. "You said no?" She spoke slowly as if trying to comprehend a negative response to a proposal.

"Not exactly."

"What do you mean, 'not exactly'? You either said yes or no."

"I laughed at him," Cass replied, before taking a swig of her beer.

"You what?" Florence slammed the bottle on the table. "Have you lost your everlovin' mind? Why'd you do that?"

"'Cause it…us…everything's going too fast."

"Is it really, or are you just trying to find another excuse to keep him at a distance?"

"I can't jump into anything. I don't want to be hurt again."

"It doesn't sound like you're doing a good job of it. If you weren't hurting, you wouldn't sound like crap onstage."

"That's 'cause I miss him, even though it's only been three days," Cass confessed as she slumped back in her seat. "Before, I used to look forward to seeing him every evening. Even when he didn't stay overnight, we had our talks when he walked me home. But now…"

"It sounds like you're in love."

Cass snorted. She stared past the other woman at the faded, striped wallpaper peeling from the wall.

"Don't sell the feeling short."

"I thought I was in love with Henry, and look where that landed me." She dropped her gaze to the deep scratches in the tabletop. "Alone, in the city."

"Randy and Henry are two different people. Your feelings for them are totally different."

Cass took a swig of her beer. The excitement she'd felt with Henry, had not been for the man but the stories he told her. All week long she would look forward to Sunday, when he would walk her home and tell her stories of his travels.

With Randy, it was different. She was content around him, even when they were not saying anything. And, when he was not there, she missed his presence.

"You see what I mean?" Florence asked.

Cass nodded.

"Then you need to talk to him."

"Too late for that," Maia taunted. She staggered toward their table.

"Cass and I are trying to have a private conversation," Florence said.

Maia dropped into the chair next to Florence. "And here I thought I was being helpful by bringing you the latest news on your man."

"We're not in the mood to hear anything from you tonight."

"Not even that he's moved on?" Maia said, pointing in the direction of the bar.

Randy sat in the shadows at the far end. A thin, pale blonde stood at his side, one arm draped around his

Sweet Jazz

neck. Her other hand was hidden by the bar, but her arm moved as if she was stroking something.

He stared across the room at Cass, determination, as if he had something to prove, written on his face.

His companion stepped back and tugged his arm. He finished the drink sitting in front of him before sliding off the stool. He did not take his eyes off Cass as he picked up his case. With his free arm draped around the blonde's shoulder, he walked out of the bar.

During the sixty seconds it took for the scene to play out, Cass's heart shattered.

"Yep, he sure moved on very quickly," Maia smirked. "Just as I predicted, he got tired of your dark ass and found someone whose color was more to his liking."

"Maia, since it's obvious you've been drinking," Florence said, reaching over and pulling the bottle out of the other woman's hand, "I'm going to give you the benefit of the doubt and say it's the alcohol talking."

"Why? 'Cause I dare to say 'I told you so' to this traitor?" Maia leaned across the table. "You're not so uppity now that he's shown you exactly where you stand with him."

Without a word, Cass picked up her bottle and poured the remaining contents over her former friend's head.

Maia jumped out of her seat with a shriek that brought everyone's attention.

"Stay outta my damn business," Cass said slowly, enunciating each syllable. Disappointing the spectators who were waiting for a fight, she stood up and marched out of the bar, with Florence following.

"I guess you were right. He wasn't going to wait

forever."

"I'm sorry," Florence said. "I can't believe he did that."

She sighed. "It doesn't matter."

"Come on, I'll hail a cab, and we can go back to your place."

Cass shook her head. "Thank you, but I think I'd rather be alone."

"Are you sure?"

"Yes, I'll be all right," Cass said.

Florence stuck her hand out. An approaching taxi screeched to a halt in front of them.

"Call me if you need to talk," she said before climbing into the back of the car.

Cass waited until the taxi pulled away before turning in the opposite direction. She stopped and stared at Maia, who was standing by the door with a satisfied smirk on her face.

Holding her head high, Cass walked away, determined to hold in her tears until she reached home.

****

Randy did not see her hand move, but he felt the crack of her palm against his face. He could not blame her for striking out. Even hookers had pride, and he had bruised hers.

He had not been looking for company when he wandered into the bar. He had planned to drink until he could no longer feel the pain in his heart and had managed to down three shots before the blonde slid onto the stool next to him.

He ignored her attempt at small talk, hoping she would take the hint and go off to find another john. But she had been persistent and bold. After a few minutes, she slid off her stool and planted herself by his side. Under the pretense of admiring his suit, she placed her hand on his leg and stroked his thigh.

Though his body had reacted to her caress, inside he felt nothing but disgust for her. Aside from the woman in New Orleans, who had stolen his sax, he had made it a point to avoid women like his mother—those who were only looking for a good time and didn't care who they found it with.

He didn't want a one-night stand or to be a woman's play toy until someone else came along. He wanted someone who was willing to make the commitment to spend the rest of her life with him and him alone. Randy had thought Cass was that person. But with the ghost of Henry hovering between them, there was the possibility she would never be willing to take the chance.

Even so, Randy had not wanted anything to do with the blonde and had been about to ask her to leave him alone when Cass walked in. Seeing her with Florence had reminded him of her laughter, the pain she'd caused him, and her ability to move on while he was miserable.

A voice inside him had told him to show her—prove to her—that he could also move on. So, despite knowing the right thing to do, he had accepted the blonde's invitation to find a more private place for them to be together. Yet, as he walked out, the pain on Cass's face erased every desire he had to prove his point.

His hurt turned to anger toward himself. He had insisted he was not like Henry and would never hurt her, but at the first sign of trouble he became what she feared.

They had made it only as far as the alley across the street before he pushed the blonde away from him. He pulled out a five and told her to find her companionship somewhere else.

The remark earned him a slap he was sure would leave a mark, but he would not apologize. At least, not to her. He was saving his apology for the woman who owned his heart.

Randy dropped the money on the ground and hurried out of the alley. He returned to the bar, where instead of Cass, he found a drunken Maia, who was more than happy to inform him that he lived up to her expectations of him.

Ignoring her, Randy left and started toward Cass's apartment. Two blocks away from her street, he spotted her. She held her head high, a demonstration of strength for anyone who might be watching. She had too much pride to let others see just how much she was hurting, but he knew the truth. The image of the pain on her face as he left the bar was burnt into his mind, and he knew a simple apology would not do.

Keeping a distance of a half block behind her, he followed her until she reached her building. There her mask began to crumble. Her hands trembled as she reached over the gate to open the latch. Her shoulders shook and her head fell forward. Covering her mouth, she hurried up the steps and into the building.

He quickened his pace and slipped through the front door in time to hear the muffled sob—final evidence of the pain he had caused her. He stopped, unable to move, afraid of facing her.

Chapter 28

Cass groaned as he repeatedly called her name. She did not want to face anyone and considered pretending she was not home. But the realization everyone in the building knew she was always home by three in the afternoon convinced her to crawl off the sofa before her visitor took it upon himself to come upstairs to check on her.

Besides, it was no use hiding. She was sure half of Harlem knew her business, if Maia had a say in it.

She dragged herself into the bedroom and stuck her head out of the window.

"I'll be there in a minute," she called down.

Normally, a shout from Mr. Jackson sent her running downstairs to see what he had from her family, but that day even the idea of a package from down south could not make her move faster.

When she was young, her mother's kiss cured everything from nightmares to a scraped knee. A hug from Daddy put a smile on her face even after she missed the word that would have made her the spelling bee champion at school. And a peppermint from one of her brothers made her forget her dresses were not as fancy as those worn by the girls in town. But at this moment, such little comforts could not cheer her.

Outside, Mrs. Cooper sat on a chair near the door. Mr. Jackson, a man with a caramel complexion and curly reddish-brown hair, stood on the third step, like a lovestruck boy, waiting for Cass. It was no secret he'd had his eye on the singer since she moved into the building. And even though she had never done anything to lead him on, he fawned over her whenever he had the chance.

"Good afternoon, Miss Porter," he greeted. His grin practically covered his entire face. "I was about to come upstairs. What's wrong? You feeling poorly?"

"Maybe a bit under the weather," she replied.

"I'm sorry to hear that. But, even sick, you look lovely."

"Thank you, Mr. Jackson." She tried, but failed, to force a smile on her face.

"You know, my mother made chicken soup that was so good you felt better just from smelling it. Before she passed on, she gave me the recipe. I could make you some and bring it over."

"No, that's all right. Thank you for offering, but after a little rest, I'll feel better."

"You sure? It won't be a bother."

"I'm sure."

"Well, then, I best be finishing my route," he said as he backed down the steps. "If you need anything, don't hesitate to call me. You know I live just three blocks over."

"Excuse me, Mr. Jackson?" Cass called out when he stepped onto the sidewalk and turned to leave.

"Yes?" he answered with a hopeful tone in his voice as he turned back.

"Did you have something for me?"

"Oh, yes." He scampered back up the steps and handed her the small package he was holding. "You got some mail from your family. I know how much you love to hear from them, so I wanted to hand it to you personally."

"Thank you, that means a lot."

"You have a good day, and I hope you feel better," he said as he backed down the steps again. He glanced over his shoulder at her as he continued his route.

Cass sighed as she turned back toward her building.

"Lovely, my ass. Men will say anything to flatter a woman. You look like hell."

"Huh?" Cass stopped and stared down at Mrs. Cooper.

"You heard me. You're a mess."

Since Cass was certain the older woman did not keep up with the latest slang, she knew Mrs. Cooper did not think she looked good. She could not argue that fact. Even without a mirror, she knew she was a sight. Her two braids were unraveling, her beige dress was wrinkled, and her house slippers were worn.

"I'm feeling a little under the weather," she lied.

"More like you've been up all night crying over that man of yours."

Cass was too shocked at the accuracy of the older woman's statement to deny it. "How?"

"Only a girl crying over her man could look as bad as you do," Mrs. Cooper said. "Besides, I heard you two arguing the other day. Just 'cause I don't speak don't mean I can't hear."

"Why don't you talk?" Cass asked.

"I only speak when I have someone with sense to talk to, and there are too few of those around here. But this ain't about me. What were you two up there arguing about?"

"He asked me to marry him."

"And?"

"And I'm not ready to take that step."

"You're not ready? You've done played house with him but you're not ready to set up one with him?" Cass opened her mouth to respond, but Mrs. Cooper continued, "That man's over here so much an idiot could figure out what y'all are doing upstairs. And don't try and pretend you're rehearsing. I'd sooner believe you're holding a revival up there, 'cause there ain't that much rehearsing in the world."

Cass had never known the embarrassment she felt at that moment. Her face became so warm she was afraid it would combust. Talking to Mrs. Cooper was like talking to her grandmother, and there were some topics one just didn't discuss with an elder.

"Why aren't you ready to marry him? Is it 'cause he's white?"

"No, ma'am."

"Good, 'cause that would be the silliest excuse I'd hear. I've heard that gal who lives over you talking about how wrong you are for being with that white man."

"Many people seem to agree with her."

"Many people seem to know a lot when it comes to other people's business, but they can never seem to get themselves together. That gal's quick to judge your man 'cause of the color of his skin, yet she fails to see his character's ten times better than those deadbeats she's always dragging home."

Cass nodded.

"So if it ain't 'cause he's white, then what's

Sweet Jazz

keeping you from marrying him?"

"I've already been down that road before, and…well…I just don't want to get hurt."

"And what makes you think he's gonna hurt you?"

"People change."

"Well, that's a given. People change all the time. If they didn't, then they'd be no better than the day they were born. You expect him to change for the worse?"

Cass shrugged her shoulders. "My ex-husband did."

"You're basing your assumptions on what another man did. Chile, that's just as silly as judging him for the color of his skin."

"But—"

"You need to judge each man as an individual, not compare him to what others have done."

"I don't want to be hurt again."

"You're sure doing a fine job of protecting yourself. Right now, you look like you're having the time of your life," Mrs. Cooper said sarcastically.

"I'm not looking to make the same mistake twice."

"That's the smartest thing to come out of your mouth since you came out here. Listen, your first experience should have taught you what to look out for when it comes to choosing a man. Pay attention to the signs, but don't try looking for things that are not there."

"How can I be sure I'm seeing everything?"

"There's no guarantees. You could look out for the signs and he could still end up being a bastard. On the other hand, he could be genuine and 'cause you were too cautious you could lose a decent man. Is he good to you?"

Cass nodded. "Yes."

"And does he make you happy?"

"Yes."

"Then you need to stop focusing on things that haven't even happened yet and go talk to him."

Cass wished she had done it four days earlier. "I think it's too late for that," she sighed.

"Why do you say that?"

"He's already moved on and found someone else. I saw him leave the bar with her this morning."

Mrs. Cooper sucked her teeth. "I don't know what you saw, but that man's been with no one. He's been sitting across the street, staring at your window, ever since you got home."

Cass looked to where Randy sat on the steps leading up to the building directly across the street from hers. She held her breath as he slowly rose to his feet. With his case in hand, he crossed the street without taking his eyes off her.

Randy stopped two steps below her and stared. The shadow on his face, his unkempt hair, and the wrinkled clothes made him look as bad as she felt. However, instead of gloating over his misery, she mourned for his pain.

"Well, don't you two have anything to say to each other?" Mrs. Cooper asked after a minute.

"You look awful," Cass muttered.

"So do you," Randy replied.

"Lord, if that's what passes for courting today, I'm glad I'm too old for this nonsense," Mrs. Cooper mumbled. "Why don't you two get somewhere else and stare at each other or act like rabbits or whatever you're gonna do, and leave me be. Ain't like I got that much time left on this earth, and I sure have better things to do than watch you two stare at each other like a couple of ninnies."

Cass nodded. She stepped back into the building. Without a word, Randy followed her upstairs. Inside the apartment, he set his case down by the door and then shoved his fists into the pockets of his coat. His eyes focused on the rag doll she had dropped on the sofa before calling down to Mr. Jackson.

She had been ready to toss the doll in the garbage that morning when she walked into the room and saw it sitting in the corner of the sofa. However, the moment she picked it up, she felt comforted by holding something Randy had given her. She'd curled up on the sofa and held the toy while listening to the radio.

After a minute, Randy glanced down at her. She saw hope in his eyes, probably from the knowledge that she still caressed his gift. The hope eventually faded to a plea for her to say something.

Cass did not know where to begin. A part of her wanted to salvage what dignity she had left and throw him out. But another part wanted to run into his arms and beg him to never leave her. Neither part came close to winning.

"Randy, I don't know what to say," she admitted, finally deciding honesty was the best route to take.

"I know it may not count for much," he said softly, "but I'm sorry."

His voice was filled with remorse, though she was uncertain what caused the emotion—her response to his proposal or his actions.

"I was hurtin' last night, and I set out to prove a point—which, I know now, was wrong. With one stupid action, I disappointed the only three people who ever gave a damn about me."

"Three people?"

"You, who, despite your fear, took a chance with me, and Sax and Miss Sylvia, the two people who taught me better than that."

"Why'd you do it?"

Randy shrugged him shoulders. "Does it really matter now?"

"That's not an answer," she screamed. She needed to understand why. After all his talk about being patient, why would he walk away with another woman? Even if she had pushed him away, couldn't he at least spare her from seeing him with someone else?

"What do you want me to say? That I did it 'cause I love you and it hurts that you don't love me back the same way? That I heard you laughin' at The Big House and thought you had moved on, and I wanted to prove I could also move on? That the memory of how you looked at me when I walked out that bar will forever be etched in my mind, and I realize how stupid I was? I told you not to judge me by the actions of your ex, but when everythin' is said and done, I turned out to be no better than him."

His eyes reflected both his pain and his sincerity. Her heart ached for him, but she could not rush things.

"You really hurt me," Cass confessed.

"I know, and I'm sorry."

"So where does this leave us?"

"That's up to you." He stepped forward and reached out to brush a hand across her cheek. "I want to tell you I'll never do somethin' like that. Hell, I'll never do anythin' to ever hurt you again. But actions speak

Sweet Jazz

louder than words, and if you give me the chance, I would spend the rest of my life showin' you how much you mean to me."

Cass reached up to touch the hand on her face. Once again he left the choice up to her. But instead of trying to decide whether or not she should trust him, she had to decide whether she could also forgive him.

Randy bent forward and gently brushed his lips across hers before backing away. At the door, he reached down for his case. Then, without a word, he slipped through the door, leaving her more confused than before.

****

Randy had considered calling in sick that evening but at the last moment decided to go to The Big House and, figuratively, face the music. He had made a decision, in front of people who already had low opinions of him; therefore he had to suffer the consequences of his actions.

He walked into the building and felt every eye on him. He was used to the looks of hatred from the majority of the employees at the club. However, the scorn from those who had previously welcomed him was almost more than he could bear, especially without the support of the one person who had been always in his corner.

Though most chose to throw occasional glances in his direction and loudly whisper snide comments that carried throughout the backstage area, Florence did not appear as if she would be content until she had confronted him.

The situation was only avoided when Eli pulled her toward her father's office, reminding her that the problem was between Randy and Cass and it was up to them to work it out without outside interference.

Feeling more alone than he had ever felt in his life, Randy sequestered himself in his dressing room until he heard voices above him, indicating the band was gathering on stage for rehearsals. He waited another five minutes before heading upstairs.

Cass stood by the piano, talking to Red. She did not look up or make any indication she noticed him, until he passed by. Without breaking eye contact with the pianist or pausing in her conversation, she held out several sheets of paper.

He took the papers and moved toward his seat. He barely had time to sit before Cass stepped to the microphone.

"I want to try a new number," she announced.

Perplexed, Randy looked at the papers she had handed him. It was the sheet music for "Stormy Weather." He glanced at her, wondering what she was planning. They had tried several times to work on the song, but each time she nixed the idea, saying something did not feel right.

She gave a slight nod of her head. Trusting her, he placed the reed between his lips and played the introduction.

Cass kept her eyes on him as she started off softly, barely above a whisper. He, however, heard the catch in her voice. He looked beyond her, at Luther and Junior, and realized they also heard the emotion. Her voice became stronger, stopping everyone in their tracks. They stared as she poured her heart out in the song.

Just when he thought nothing could make him feel worse than the look on her face at the bar, her voice tore through him. He not only heard her pain but felt it.

Her eyes glistened with tears that hovered at the brim yet refused to spill over. The other women were not as strong. By the time Cass hit her last note, they were weeping, if not for her pain then for memories of their own hurt.

They finished the number but continued to acknowledge no one but each other. She had spoken, and he gave her a slight nod to indicate he not only heard her, but he understood.

"So, what do you think, Luther?" Cass asked, without taking her eyes off Randy.

"You captured the feeling of the song," Luther admitted. "Though I think we may want something a bit less emotional for the show."

Cass nodded. She stared at Randy for another beat before stepping off the stage and heading downstairs.

Randy did not see Cass again until she set foot on stage for that evening's performance. Though her show was better than the previous nights, she still lacked the spark that made people dance in their seats.

He heard the murmured speculations of the role he played in her lackluster performance. Tongues began flapping hard when Cass announced she was deviating from the usual show and performing her final number for the evening *a cappella.*

Without waiting for the hush to die down, she began singing "Can't Help Lovin' Dat Man of Mine." She stared straight ahead as she belted out the lyrics, sending a message that was sure to have the gossips working overtime the next day.

Disgust was written on Junior's face, while Luther's brow wrinkled with concern. But she had made her point and, once the song was over, received a roaring round of applause, led by Florence.

Cass acknowledged the audience with one bow, before turning the show over to the band and heading backstage. Randy impatiently performed for the next hour, eager to meet up with Cass. The band had barely finished the last number before he was off the stage, rushing to the ladies' dressing room.

His shoulders drooped as he stared into the empty space. He knew it had been too much to hope she would wait for him. Though she had publicly announced, through song, her feelings for him, he realized she still needed time. What he had done could not be made right in one night.

As he headed to his dressing room, he decided to give Cass space and time. It was his pushiness that had made her run, and if he did not tread carefully, he could lose her forever.

When he finally emerged from the shadows of the alley, a figure stepped out from a doorway. Dumbfounded, he stopped and watched as she moved closer to him.

"You waited for me?" he asked when she was standing directly in front of him.

"I needed to make sure you found your way home tonight," Cass announced.

Randy was at a loss for words. But knowing actions spoke louder, he dropped his case and suit, reached out, and pulled her toward him. She did not resist the embrace or the kiss that followed.

Chapter 29

Something was not right. Randy presented Cass with a box of chocolates and the line, "Sweets for the sweet," and instead of a sassy comeback, she simply took the candy and said, "Thank you."

He was ready to call a doctor, but reason took over. What was he going to say? "Send an ambulance, there's something wrong with my girl. She didn't sass me." If they sent someone over, it would be to cart him off to an institution.

"Hey," he called across the room as he hung up his jacket.

"Mmm," was her response as she walked to the kitchen. A bag of groceries sat on the table.

"What's wrong?"

"Nothing."

"Cassie Ann Porter, don't give me 'nothin'.' "

She made a sound that was between a chuckle and a snort. "You sound like my mother."

"I've been called many things in my life, but I've never been called a colored woman."

"I didn't call you a colored woman. I said you sound like my mother."

"Your mother's colored and she is a woman."

Cass sighed. "You're impossible."

Something was definitely wrong. She'd given up too easily. Walking up behind her, he gathered her in his arms and kissed the top of her head. "What's botherin' you?"

"Nothing," she insisted while trying to stifle a yawn.

"Nothin'?"

"I'm a little beat, that's all," she confessed as she let out the yawn so hard Randy was surprised her face didn't split in two. "Okay, maybe a lot. There's nothing I'd rather do right now than climb into bed and sleep for a week. So there, are you happy? You managed to drag out my deep dark secret."

Okay, it wasn't that big an emergency. She had some of her sassiness left. "Why aren't you in bed?"

"'Cause I had to go to the post office and the grocery store. The food's not going to walk over here by itself."

"Makes you wish you had a magic wand. One wave and, presto, instant groceries."

"Sounds good, but I'd prefer one that'd make Junior disappear."

Since her public declaration of her feelings for Randy, Junior had made it his personal mission to keep the couple apart. He began asking that she meet with him to discuss club business in the afternoon, when Randy and she normally rehearsed. After her performance, he would insist she mingle with the patrons, arguing it was good for business. Several times he requested she go in on her nights off.

This left little time for her to take care of personal business and sleep. It also limited the amount of waking time she could spend with Randy. But, as the saying went, "where there's a will there's a way," and the desire to see Cass made Randy find the time.

After finishing his set, he would wait outside the club to walk her home no matter how late she left. He also made it a point to show up at her apartment to walk her back to The Big House in the evenings. Even on his nights off, he escorted her there and back.

"You had a meeting this afternoon?" Randy asked, though he already knew the answer.

"Mmm-hmm," Cass answered as she leaned back against him.

"He's goin' to run you ragged."

"Maybe he figures if I'm raggedy enough, you'll leave me alone."

"Not goin' to happen." He added with concern in his voice, "You need some rest."

"Don't worry about it. I'll rest tonight."

"Why?" Randy leaned back and glanced down at her. "You don't have to play nice to his friends?"

"That and I have the night off."

"But it's Saturday."

"It doesn't matter. Before I left the club, I told Luther I'm not coming back tonight."

"And he agreed to that?"

"He wasn't thrilled, but I'm sure Junior was. He probably figured that me not being there works in his favor."

"How's that?"

"If I'm here in bed and you're at the club working, then we obviously won't be together."

"I guess he thinks he won this round."

"I don't care what he thinks right now." Cass stepped back, out of his arms. "I'm going to take a hot bath and go to bed as soon as I put these groceries away."

Randy grabbed her hand and pulled her out of the kitchen. "Forget about those."

"I have to put the food away," she insisted, slipping her hand from his.

"They can wait."

"But my meat—I don't want it to go bad."

"Wait here." He went into the kitchen, opened the icebox, shoved the entire grocery bag inside, and closed the door. "Come on," he said, taking her hand.

Randy led her into the bedroom and gently pushed her until she sat on the edge of the bed. He then left the room. When he returned, she had kicked her shoes off and was curled up on the bed.

"Cass," he called. "Hey, girl, wake up."

She rolled over, took one look at him, sans clothes, and burst out laughing.

"What's wrong with you?"

"You."

"You sure know how to make a man feel good about himself."

"I'm sorry. I didn't expect to see you without any clothes," she gasped.

"Keep it up and I'm goin' to dunk you in the tub. Head first."

"You ran a bath for me?"

Randy nodded.

She stopped laughing, though she continued to smile as she reached up with one hand and tickled his nap. "You're a sweetheart."

"And what do I get for my efforts? You laugh at me."

"I'm sorry. It's the sleep. Yes, that's it. I'm tired. You know I wouldn't laugh at you any other time."

"Sure you wouldn't." He poked out his bottom lip.

"I'm sorry. I really am." She pulled him down and kissed his lip. "Forgive me?" she asked when they pulled back.

"I don't know. You hurt my feelings," he teased, though his body was already showing it forgave her.

"How can I make it up to you?"

A lecherous grin grew on his lips. "I could think of a few things, but first, let's give you that bath you wanted." He slid off the bed.

"You're not going to toss me in head first, are you?" she asked, sitting up.

"As temptin' as that may be, I think I'll spare you, this time."

Randy led her to the bathroom. Steam rose from the bathtub, filling the room.

"A bubble bath," she sighed as he unzipped her dress.

"Don't ever let it be said I don't know how to take care of my girl."

"But what happened to your clothes?"

"You'll see." He pushed the dress down her body until it fell around her feet.

"You know, you don't have to climb into the tub to fill it. You can reach over the side, put the stopper in, and turn on the faucet. When it's full, you turn off the faucet."

"Very funny," he said as she slid her slip off.

"Or did you fall in while filling it?"

He glared at her as he removed her bra. "Keep it up and I may reconsider that dunkin'."

Cass pursed her lips, but her eyes continued to tease him. She leaned back on the clawfoot tub and held out a leg for him to remove her stockings. Once the hosiery was on the floor, he stripped off her garter belt and panties.

When she was free of her clothing, Randy took her hand and helped her into the tub. The satisfying sigh she emitted as she slipped into the water encouraged him to slide in behind her. Without any prompting, she leaned back against his chest and allowed him to wash her.

He took his time, caressing her, listening to her purrs, until he could no longer take it. Dropping the washcloth into the water, he tilted her head back to reach her lips. As they kissed, his hand moved between her legs. He stroked and played with her until she shuddered from an orgasm.

Before she could catch her breath, he lifted her to position himself at her core. He then lowered her until her warmth surrounded him. The fullness of him inside her, the upward thrusts of his hips and the stimulation from his hands, brought her to another orgasm.

Her muscles tensed, and she moaned. Her reaction spurred him to move harder. His thrusts became more urgent, until he could no long hold back. With one last deep push, he joined her in a realm that could be described as euphoria.

It took Randy a minute before a contented sigh from Cass brought him back to his senses. She was relaxed, against his chest.

"That's why you had to get undressed," Cass whispered.

He drew in a quick breath as she traced a circle around his nipple with her tongue. "I don't suggest you do that," he sighed.

"Why not?"

"'Cause we might end up stayin' here all night."

"What's wrong with that?"

"Unlike you, I have to work tonight," he replied. He nudged her forward so he could stand.

Cass whimpered as he stepped out of the bathtub and grabbed a towel. He shook his head. Though he wanted to, he was not getting back in.

Pouting, she leaned back and folded her arms over her chest. He laughed at her as he dried himself off and wrapped the towel around his waist.

"Girl," he said softly, as he leaned over the side of the bathtub to stroke her cheek, "I'd do almost anything in my power for you, but I can't give in to you this time. If you don't get some rest, you're liable to fall asleep underneath me, and what do you think that would do to my ego?"

She splashed the water in his direction, reminding him of a spoiled child who did not get her way. With another chuckle, he kissed her before stepping back to retrieve her towel.

"Come on," Randy beckoned.

Cass rose and he wrapped the towel around her. He picked her up, carried her into the bedroom, and laid her on the bed.

"Roll over," he said as he opened the towel.

She did as she was told, while he grabbed a bottle off her nightstand. She took a sharp breath as he squeezed cold lotion on her. He did not torture her for long, but warmed her as he massaged the cream into her skin.

As he worked, Randy watched her drift off to sleep, with an occasional sigh escaping from her. When he was finished, she whimpered as he moved off the bed. Yet the second he covered her with a blanket, she curled up and went back to sleep.

Randy stared at Cass. He longed to climb under the covers and simply lie with his arm around her. However, the increase in movement outside announced the return of workers for the evening, and he knew it was past time for him to leave for the club.

He returned to the bathroom and emptied the water out of the tub. Cass's clothes, which lay on the floor, were soaked from the waves of water that had splashed over the sides during their lovemaking. He hung the wet articles over the shower rod, then quickly mopped the floor.

Once the bathroom had been restored to a presentable state, Randy gathered his own clothes from behind the door and dressed. Finally, he looked in on the sleeping woman, placed a kiss on her forehead, and left for his nightly lesson in patience and tolerance.

When Randy returned to the apartment eleven hours later, the vein in his temple throbbed and his shoulders were tense. He had a cramp in his hand from the tight grip he'd kept on the handle of his case.

In all the nights he had been performing at The Big House, that night had been the most trying of all. When he arrived at the club, the door to his dressing room was missing. It had taken him twenty minutes to find the door and another fifteen minutes to place it back on its hinges.

Rehearsals had taken thirty minutes longer than usual. Luther had to leave early because of a family emergency, and Junior took advantage of his partner's absence to criticize every note Randy played. When

Sweet Jazz

Randy refused to take the bait and thanked the club owner for pointing out his flaws, Junior muttered under his breath that white trash would always be white trash no matter how uppity they tried to act. He then proceeded to call him every name in the book and some that had yet to be printed. This also failed to get the desired response out of the sax player, who then had the pleasure of returning to his dressing room to see the words "Ofay, go home" painted on the door.

By then, Randy was entertaining the idea of giving them their wish. It was only Red's visit, minutes before they were scheduled to go on stage, and his words of encouragement that made him stay.

The performance had not been made easier by several men, probably paid by Junior, heckling him throughout the night. At times it got so bad he had the undesirable urge to shove his saxophone where the sun did not shine. He had only managed to restrain himself because he did not want to tarnish his instrument.

Randy placed his case by the door and tossed his suit on the couch. He kicked his shoes off and left them in the middle of the floor. As he took off his jacket, he noticed the covered plate sitting on the table in the kitchen. He debated for a moment between food and sleep, before his growling stomach reminded him he hadn't eaten since the previous afternoon.

Without turning on the light, Randy moved into the kitchen. He lifted the dishtowel off a ham sandwich and a slice of chocolate cake. His stomach growled again. Ignoring it, he headed to the icebox to retrieve the beer Cass had started keeping there for his visits. Once he removed the cap and took a swig, he sat down to enjoy his meal by streetlight.

When he was finished, Randy placed the dish in the sink and threw the bottle in the garbage. He then headed to the bathroom, where he stripped down to his shorts. After hanging his clothes on the hook behind the door, he headed to the bedroom.

He pulled back the blanket. Cass, lying with her back to him, had put on a red nightgown some time during his absence. Disappointed he would not be able to feel her bare skin against his while they slept, he contemplated removing the gown. However, knowing she needed her rest, he nixed the idea and eased his way under the blanket, trying not to wake her.

"I hope you hung up your clothes and washed your dish," Cass mumbled as soon as his head touched the pillow.

"Girl, please have mercy on me," he groaned.

She rolled over and laid her head on his chest. "You had a rough night?"

"Rough doesn't begin to describe it."

"What happened?"

"Luther wasn't there, so Junior was in rare form tonight. Did you know the part in my hair is not straight?"

"He criticized your hair?"

"Among other things. Seems my crooked part is bringin' down the class of his club."

Cass leaned up on an elbow and looked down at him. "Are you serious?"

From the moonlight, Randy saw the disbelief on her face. He chuckled.

"You're teasing me."

"Okay, so he didn't criticize my hair, but he did attack practically everythin' else."

"Poor baby," Cass cooed as she kissed his forehead. The small gesture helped ease his headache. "But that still doesn't excuse you from leaving my apartment a mess."

"Girl, is there anythin' I can do to get your mind off those chores?"

"Yes, you can go hang up your clothes and wash the dish."

He reached up and cupped the back of her head. "Oh, hush," he mumbled as he pulled her to him.

When they broke from the kiss, Cass was lying on top of him. Supporting herself on her arms, she looked down at him.

"Okay, tell me what happened," she said.

Randy placed his hands behind his head. "I would, but you seem to have this weird obsession with my suit and plate."

"Smartass."

"I learned from the best."

"Shut up and tell your story."

He tapped the tip of her nose with his forefinger. "That, my dear, is physically impossible."

Cass rolled off him.

"Come back here," Randy said, reaching out and pulling her back on top of him.

"Are you going to tell me what happened?" she asked.

"If you'll be quiet, I will."

Cass mimed locking her lips.

"Now where was I?"

"You were saying Junior attacked everything you did."

"That does not sound like quiet."

She rapped his hip.

Randy laughed before he told her an abbreviated version of the events of the evening. Feeling the profanity was not worth repeating, he left out the choice words Junior used to describe him.

"I can't believe Junior would go through so much trouble to make you miserable. If he'd put in half the effort to like you, he'd see you're a decent guy and a good musician."

"I'd simply settle for him toleratin' me and not takin' his objection to us bein' together out on you."

"Don't worry about me. I can take care of myself."

Randy shook his head as he thought about the club's co-owner. There had been something in his eyes that went beyond intolerance, and it worried him. Hate was a powerful emotion that could make a man capable of almost anything.

"I wish it was as simple as you tellin' him to go to hell. When people are strongly against somethin', things can get very ugly."

"I don't think Junior would do anything stupid."

"Cass, dear, you just be careful."

She stared at him for a moment before laying her head on his shoulder.

"Promise me?" he added with concern in his voice.

She did not say anything, but nodded her reply.

Chapter 30

Cass momentarily forgot the words to "As Time Goes By" when Florence stepped from the foyer on the arm of her father. Dressed in a full-length white gown with a veil over her face, the dancer inspired a series of oohs and aahs from everyone in attendance, with the exception of the groom. Eli stood center stage with his mouth hanging open, mesmerized by the vision of his bride.

As Luther escorted the bride down the aisle, Cass's brain switched into autopilot, allowing her to continue the song the couple had chosen for the wedding march. Once she finished, Randy escorted her off stage to watch the ceremony.

"Are you all right?" he whispered in her ear, after they sat down.

Her nod turned into a shake as he wrapped his arms around her and held her close.

"Growing up, we didn't have much. Therefore, the most I expected for my wedding was a small ceremony in the front room of my parents' house, with my family present, and maybe a new dress made by my momma. Instead, Henry and I stood in the preacher's front room with two witnesses I didn't know. I wore my brown everyday dress because I didn't want my parents to be suspicious when I left the house."

She watched as Luther presented the bride to the

groom before taking a seat next to his wife.

"When I look at Eli and Florence, I realize not having a new dress or my parents there wasn't the worst part of the day. The worst part was that Henry didn't look at me the way Eli just looked at Florence. He was impatient, like he had somewhere better to be."

"Are you sorry we agreed to be here?"

"No, I'm happy for Florence. It's just, well—"

"You wish it was you?"

Cass nodded. "Kind of selfish of me, isn't it?"

****

Randy kissed her cheek as he squeezed her hand. "Darlin', there's nothin' selfish about wantin' true love."

That was what he had longed for since he discovered it existed. In his early years, all he knew was arguments, suspicion, and infidelity, thanks to the men his mother paraded around the house. But after witnessing with Sax and Miss Sylvia what a committed relationship looked like, he had wanted to experience it for himself.

The ceremony was brief. After the couple was pronounced man and wife, Randy and Cass returned to the stage, where she came alive. Their performance included a selection of numbers they performed at the club, along with arrangements they had yet to debut.

They performed for two hours, until Luther suggested they take a break and let the band earn their pay. The beaming bride hugged them as they stepped off the stage.

"When I asked you to do a few numbers, I didn't expect you to put on a show," Florence said, passing each of them a glass of champagne. "Now I really feel guilty for not paying you."

"Consider it a gift from Randy and me."

"A free show plus the towels you gave us. That's too much."

Cass frowned up at Randy. "You told her."

"I didn't, I promise," he protested, before admitting, "though I may have told Red." When she sighed, he quickly added, "But I only did it 'cause he was lookin' for suggestions for what to buy them."

Florence laughed. "I still think we should give you something for your performance. How about a picnic in Central Park when Eli and I get back from Atlantic City? We'll provide the food."

"It's a deal," Cass agreed.

"Florence," Luther called out as he approached the group. "Marty needs a couple more pictures of you with your bridesmaids."

The dancer sighed. "I don't think I've taken this many pictures in my entire life. Listen, you two, go sit down and get something to eat. I'll catch up with you later."

Florence maneuvered through the crowd to join the bridal party at the foyer that had been covered with purple and white orchids for the event.

"You two did a fine job up there," Luther commented.

"Thank you, sir," Randy replied.

"You make a fine team. I'm going to hate to see you go."

"We aren't going anywhere other than that corner to eat," Cass said, pointing to the empty table in the corner. Though the bride and groom had wanted them to sit near the front with the other performers, they insisted on sitting in the back to avoid any tension their presence would cause.

"The two of you have too much talent to be wasting it here at this club. Now, I know things didn't work out with Willie Hawke—"

"How'd you know about that?" Cass asked.

Luther laid a hand on her shoulder. "Young lady, you forget, I know everything about everyone who works for me."

"Don't be upset, Luther."

"Only one I'm upset with is Willie for not recognizing what he let slip through his fingers. But his loss will be someone else's gain. Just remember, after you two make it big, don't forget who first paired you together."

"There'll always be two front-row seats reserved for you at all our shows."

"I'll settle for a promise that you'll return to perform at our New Year's Eve show."

"Anything for the man who gave me my start," Cass promised.

"Good." He squeezed her shoulder. "Now you two go do as Florence said and get something to eat."

Randy escorted Cass around the huddles in the dining room to their table as Luther acknowledged a guest who wanted to congratulate him for gaining a son-in-law.

"I think Luther's finally warming up to the idea of us being together," Cass noted as she sat down.

"I wouldn't count on it, darlin'," Randy replied as he moved his chair closer to her. "He doesn't see anythin' wrong with us workin' together, but he'll always have his doubts about my commitment to you.

He probably won't believe I'm serious until our fiftieth wedding anniversary."

Cass sighed. "Isn't there anyone who's not against us?"

"It doesn't matter who accepts us and who doesn't. As long as we don't have any doubts, then everyone else can go to hell."

"I don't think I've ever heard anything so beautifully said." She leaned over to kiss him, not caring who saw them.

****

In their own little world, they were oblivious to everyone around them, until a short cough invaded their universe.

"I'm sorry to interrupt," Luther said, though his tone indicated otherwise. "I don't mean to disturb you."

"You're not disturbing anything," Cass said, a bit flustered from the kiss.

"Speak for yourself," Randy groaned under his breath.

She slipped her hand under the table and pinched his leg. "Behave," she scolded.

"I forgot to give these to you." Luther set an envelope on the table.

"What is it?" Randy asked, taking the package.

"Pictures that won't be used to promote the club. I figured you may want them for a photo album."

Cass leaned over to glance at the pictures Randy had pulled from the envelope. She examined the twelve eight-by-ten photos and realized she already had what she'd been wishing for. In each photo, Randy stared at her with the same love Eli had expressed when he saw his bride.

Chapter 31

"Dang pumps," Cass mumbled as she stumbled on the last step.

"Someone's had a bit too much to drink," Randy teased, catching her arm.

"No, it's these shoes."

"I've seen you walk in those pumps many times without stumblin'." Randy backed her against the wall. "So either you're a bit tipsy or you're lookin' for an excuse to get close to me."

Cass's arms snaked around his neck. "Do I really need to resort to tricks to get you?" she asked.

"Hey, *nada de eso*," Eli commented as they leaned together for a kiss.

Randy backed off and Cass groaned.

"Yeah, none of that," Florence repeated. She stood at the threshold of the women's dressing room with Eli. "Can't you two keep your hands to yourselves for one minute?"

Cass raised an eyebrow. "I could ask the same of you. That's a nice shade of lipstick, Eli."

The newlywed groom wiped his thumb across his mouth to remove the evidence of his impatience to start his honeymoon.

"What are you two doing back here?" Florence asked, trying to act nonchalant despite the blush that colored her cheeks.

"We're gettin' ready to go," Randy answered.

"Why? The party's not over yet," Florence said.

"The band's planning to jam for a bit," Eli added.

"We know," Cass said. "But with the guests trickling out, it will be only a matter of time before Junior doesn't have anyone to divert his attention from Randy."

"Though if you want to stay, I could disappear—" Randy began.

"Don't even bother to finish that sentence. I'm not going out there without you. I just have to get my bag, and then I'll meet you at the door."

"I'm sorry you can't stay longer," Florence said, walking with Cass to the dressing room.

"What are you apologizing for? If anyone should be sorry, it should be Junior."

"Eli and I are leaving in the morning for Atlantic City. But remember, when we return, we're taking you guys out."

"I won't forget."

Florence hugged Cass. "Thank you for helping to make my day special."

"It's my pleasure."

As Florence hurried out of the room to rejoin the party, Cass checked her hair. Satisfied everything looked right, she grabbed her bag and headed out the door.

She had started down the hall when Junior stepped out of his office and called her. With a sigh, Cass went over to him.

"What do you want?" she asked, not bothering to hide her aggravation.

"Go back up and mingle," he ordered, before

turning back into his office.

"Have you lost your mind? I'm not working tonight."

"Don't argue with me, just get your tail upstairs."

"No."

Junior stopped in his tracks, most likely surprised that she, or any woman for that matter, would not obey him.

"What'd you say?" he asked, as he spun around to face her.

"I said, 'No.' I'm on my own time and I'm not going to meet anyone."

"You'll do as I say."

"Or else what? You'll fire me?" She sucked her teeth as she turned away. She dismissively waved her hand at him. "Junior, I'm going home. I'll speak to you on Wednesday."

Junior reached out and grabbed her arm. His face was twisted and she could smell the liquor on his breath. "Who do you think you are, tellin' me what you're gonna do? You got a white man, so you think you're all that?"

"Let go of me," she said slowly, giving him his first and only warning.

"Or what? You're gonna call your ghost?"

Cass kicked him in the shin for her answer. He responded with a back slap. The force propelled her out of his grip. She hit the floor three feet from him.

"Damn, b—" was all Junior managed to get out before Randy's fist slammed into his face, knocking him back into the office.

Florence who had been heading upstairs, rushed to Cass's side. She tried to pull the singer up while, at the

Sweet Jazz

same time, she dragged her across the floor, away from the fight.

Junior staggered to his feet and charged forward, swinging both fists. Randy dodged the blows before landing one of his own to the older man's midsection. He followed through with an uppercut to the chin that sent Junior flying back onto his desk.

Randy stood with his fists raised, ready for Junior's next move. The older man attempted to push away from the flat surface where he'd landed. With a grimace he grabbed his left side and fell back again.

"I should've had them kill you on New Year's," he panted. "Next time I won't make the same mistake."

"You lay a hand on Cass again, and there won't be a next time," Randy threatened.

"Get the hell out of my club."

"With pleasure," Randy said as he marched away. Without slowing down, he grabbed Cass's hand and pulled her behind him.

"Yeah, that's right, take your whore with you."

Randy stopped, but Cass refused to release his hand. "Come on," she said, tugging on his arm. "He's not worth it."

He glanced down at her for a second, before continuing toward his dressing room. Florence stood outside the door, holding his case.

"Randy, Cass, I'm going to talk to Daddy and—" Florence started as she handed him the saxophone.

"Don't bother," Cass interrupted. "I'm sorry for ruining your day."

"Don't be. Like you said, Junior's the one who should be sorry."

They stepped outside and made their way through

the crowd of people out in search of a party. Even without the stares and whispers, Cass realized they were a sight. She felt the tenderness around her eye each time she blinked. But, determined to put as much distance as possible between them and The Big House, she ignored her discomfort and those around her.

They were three blocks away before she spoke. "What was that about New Year's?" she asked.

"You already know what happened," Randy answered after a minute.

"No, I know the conclusions you let me draw. You weren't mugged, were you?"

When he did not answer, she snatched her hand from his. He looked down. She had stopped walking and was staring at him with her arms folded over her chest.

"What really happened?" she insisted.

Randy sighed. "That night when I left the club, three men jumped me in the alley. Before the last one kicked me in the head, he warned me to stay away from you. Though I never had proof, I always suspected Junior saw the kiss you gave me and sent those men after me."

"Why didn't you tell me?"

"'Cause I didn't want you to think any of it was your fault."

"And even after they warned you, you still—"

"I couldn't stop wantin' you," Randy said as he reached out to her.

Cass allowed him to pull her to him. She wrapped her arms around his waist and laid her head on his chest.

She had been a fool to compare Randy to Henry.

Sweet Jazz

Before he had found out about the money her grandmother had left her, her ex-husband had been willing to walk away and find another girl, because her parents objected to him. He had been unwilling to fight for her, to prove how much she meant to him, even after they were married.

Randy, on the other hand, had already been through a lot before they became a couple. Yet instead of running away he continued to want her, and, no matter what happened, he didn't give up on them.

Cass heard the approaching car as Randy tensed. He reached behind him, took her hand, and began moving down the block again.

Though she had seen the car before they started walking, she asked, "We're being followed?"

She glanced back. The driver cruised behind them with the headlights off. Randy pulled on her hand until she looked forward. "I'm afraid so."

"You want to try and run?"

"No, I want you to run back to the club and get help."

"What about you?"

"I'm goin' to keep them from followin' you."

"Not by yourself."

"Cass, I want you to do as I say. I can't fight them and worry about you at the same time."

"Then don't worry about me and concentrate on what you're doing."

"I'm sure they won't want to do the two-step. You need to get out of here." He passed her the case. "Do you think you can run with this?"

"Yes."

Randy squeezed her hand before letting it go. He

dropped his arm around her shoulder and continued walking. When the car was in line with them, he gripped her shoulder and spun her around.

"Go," he shouted. "Run!"

Cass tucked the case under her arm and broke into a run. Randy followed her as the car came to a stop. The doors opened and five colored men jumped out. Three converged on Randy, while the other two went after her.

She moved as fast as she could, but the longer-legged man quickly gained on her.

"Drop the damn case and get out of here," Randy yelled before one of the men struck him from behind.

Instead of following directions, Cass gripped the case with both hands and slowed down. As soon as she sensed her pursuer was directly behind her, she spun around and slammed the case into his head. Stunned, he staggered back. The second blow brought him to his knees. One last blow and he hit the ground unconscious.

Cass looked up at the second man gaining on her. Behind him, Randy was not faring as well in his one-against-three fight. He had managed to land a few blows before two of the men restrained him and the third punched him.

****

A sharp pain shot through Randy side as his attacker's fist connected with his ribs. There was no question the damage would be greater than what he had sustained on New Year's. However, he was determined not to go down. Until Cass was safe, he had to stay upright and alert.

Through the haze threatening to take over, Randy

Sweet Jazz

watched as Cass swung the case at her second pursuer. The man, who was bigger than her first assailant, was prepared for the assault. He raised an arm to block the blow and knocked the case out her hand.

He grabbed her arm and yanked her toward him. Taking advantage of the momentum, she raised her leg as she came forward. He grunted as her knee connected with his groin. Releasing her arm, he cupped himself as he dropped to his knees.

As she reached for the case, another car pulled up. Before it stopped, Luther jumped out and grabbed her second pursuer by the collar. He introduced his fist to the man's face with enough force to knock the man unsecious.

Luther released the man, allowing him to drop to the ground. He grabbed Cass by the shoulder and pushed her toward the car.

"Get in."

Distracted by Luther's arrival, the man on Randy's left loosened his hold. Randy yanked his arm out of the other's man grip and rammed an elbow into his stomach. Before the man could recover, Red and Eli hopped out of the car and engaged the two restrainers.

With the attack coming from only one direction, Randy was able to block a punch aimed at his face and throw a punch of his own. The other man's head snapped back. Cass gasped when the assailant stumbled back and the light from a streetlamp illuminated Angel's face.

Taking the fight to another level, Angel reached into his pants pocket, pulled out a switchblade, and lunged forward. Randy jumped back as the blade sliced across his midsection.

Ignoring the blood forming from the cut, Randy dodged another swipe. He moved to the side, and Angel followed. Their dance moved them away from the fight.

Randy stumbled on his next step. He managed to catch himself as Angel lunged toward him one more time. However, he did not know how long he would be able to avoid the other man. He was praying for a miracle when Luther cursed.

"Cass, get back here," the older man yelled, a second before the saxophone case struck Angel in the back of the head.

Randy was not too proud to accept the assistance of a woman in a fight. He was grateful for any help he could get, especially when it momentarily distracted his attacker.

Forgetting about his intended target, Angel spun around, swiping at Cass. She was saved when Luther grabbed her arm and dragged her back to the car. The distraction was enough for Randy to move in and bring both fists down on Angel's temples.

Angel turned toward Randy. The sound of bone breaking echoed around them as Randy's fist hit the drummer's face.

Randy flexed his hand as Angel crumpled to the ground. The blow had bruised his knuckles, but at least the bones in his hand didn't suffer the same fate as the other man's nose. He lifted one foot to step forward, but stumbled back. Eli caught him before he joined the other men on the sidewalk. The wail of approaching sirens hastened their movements.

"What were you thinking?" Randy grumbled as he was shoved into the back seat next to Cass.

Though he was grateful for her assistance, it didn't

mean he wasn't going to give her hell for running toward danger instead of away from it. She shook her head. The danger to herself had not been her main concern.

"As long as we're together, we'll fight together," Cass stated before kissing the knuckles on his injured hand.

Chapter 32

The apartment was not Randy's idea of a dream residence. He had always imagined when he moved in with a woman it would be in a three-bedroom house on a farm where there would be plenty of room for his offspring to run around. He had also dreamt of carrying his new bride over the threshold and straight to the bed they would share for the rest of their lives. Instead, he dragged himself into the one-bedroom basement apartment barely able to carry himself, much less the two large suitcases in his hands.

He dropped the bags onto the floor. His broken rib and the pain the movement would cause him was the only thing that kept him from joining the luggage. Deciding the other bags could wait until after he rested, he shuffled to the bed, then eased himself down onto the soft mattress. Sweat dotted Randy's forehead from the strain of driving four hours from New York to D.C. and then carrying in the bags.

"Poor baby's tired," Cass cooed. She set his saxophone case next to the suitcases before placing her hands on her hips. Her expression became stern. "I told you we shouldn't have made the trip until after you had a chance to heal."

Randy had wanted nothing more than to stay in bed, but Junior's words had haunted him. It would only be a matter of time before the man sent someone else

Sweet Jazz

after them. He had been surprised when Luther, Red, and Eli had shown up to help with the fight. Though their gesture had proven he was not alone, he would not take a chance with Cass's safety. Therefore, despite his injuries and after only a day's rest, Randy had bought a car, packed their belongings into the trunk and the backseat, and placed some distance between them and the city.

"It was better to get you out of New York before Junior found you. It's bad enough you have that bruise under your eye. I didn't need someone tryin' to relocate your nose to the other side of your face...or worse."

He shifted until he could lean back against the wall, with his feet hanging over the side of the bed. Cass watched as he tried unsuccessfully to kick his shoes off without untying them. After a minute she mumbled under her breath about the stubbornness of men, as she walked out of the room.

He closed his eyes and listened as she moved from room to room, exploring the apartment at the boarding house he had stayed in during his previous time in the city. The landlord, whose only concern was the rent, had no problems with the unmarried mixed couple sharing the apartment. He not only welcomed Randy back but gave them a heads-up that the Panama Lounge was looking for a new act.

Cass had displayed no reaction when Randy requested one apartment. She'd simply asked about the rent and then proceeded to pay the man for two months in advance.

She returned to the bedroom, took a foot, and removed his shoe.

"My brother Joe works for the railroad and makes

frequent trips to D.C.," Cass said as she dropped the shoe on the floor. "We'll need to invite him over for dinner the next time he's up this way."

Randy moved his foot onto the bed as she untied his other shoe. "I'd like to meet your family, but could we do it in, let's say, a week or two, after I wake up. Figure by then I should be able to defend myself if he takes exception to you bein' with me."

"I think Joe will like you. If anything, he may not appreciate something I say and threaten to turn me over his knee."

"Girl, I beg of you, please try not to get into any trouble. Your knight in shinin' armor's too tired to fight off a fly."

She dropped the second shoe onto the floor. "I always thought my knight in shining armor would be tall, dark, and handsome. Well, you are tall, so one out of three ain't too bad."

"Get over here." He reached up and pulled her down onto the bed, making her squeak.

A sharp pain ripped through his side from the jostling of the bed. Ignoring the discomfort, he leaned forward to kiss her. When they pulled away from each other, he held her as she curled up next to him.

"Even after I meet your brother, I should probably write to your parents."

"Why?"

"I figure I should inform them that you're goin' to change your name to Mrs. Cassie Ann Jones."

She lifted her head and stared at him. "Since when?"

"And we'll eventually have to go down to Piney Woods so I can meet them in person," he continued, ignoring her question.

"Randy—"

"And I'd like to take you to Mississippi to meet Miss Sylvia."

Cass placed her hand over his mouth. "Randy, will you let me talk?"

He reached up and moved her hand. "Not unless you're sayin' the one word I want to hear."

"But—"

"That's not the word."

Randy knew he was taking a chance suggesting marriage again. They had not discussed the subject since their previous fight, but his feelings had not changed. He wanted to spend the rest of his life with her, even if it meant waiting another month, another year, or ten years until she was ready to make the commitment.

****

Cass saw the determination in his eyes. He wanted her, not just for the moment. His actions had proven he was in the relationship for the long haul. He was willing to deal with nasty looks and uninvited opinions of people who did not believe they should be together. He would also face the rejections due to his association with her as well as the daily sass he would get from her.

Before they left New York, they had made the rounds to say their good-byes. Once again, Luther expressed his concern about Randy's commitment to the relationship, while Mrs. Greene had worried about the challenges they would face.

Mattie reminded them that practically every day would be a struggle. However, she insisted if they were truly committed to each other, they would be able to handle whatever society threw at them.

Though Cass was no longer worried about Randy's commitment, she couldn't help but ask one more time, "Are you serious?"

"I've never been more serious in my life." Randy reached up and touched the bruise that marred her face. "I'm not goin' to pretend it'll be easy, but then again, nothin' worth havin' comes easy."

No, it didn't, she thought, but… "We can face the challenges, together," she said as she took his hand in hers and settled back against him.

A word about the author…

Ursula Renée wrote short stories in high school and poetry in college. She began writing novels while recuperating from orthoscopic surgery.

When she is not writing, she enjoys drawing, photography, and stone carving.

Visit Ursula at www.ursularenee.com.

Thank you for purchasing
this publication of The Wild Rose Press, Inc.
If you enjoyed the story, we would appreciate your
letting others know by leaving a review.
For other wonderful stories,
please visit our on-line bookstore at
www.thewildrosepress.com

For questions or more information
contact us at
info@thewildrosepress.com.

The Wild Rose Press, Inc.
www.thewildrosepress.com

To visit with authors of
The Wild Rose Press, Inc.
join our yahoo loop at
http://groups.yahoo.com/group/thewildrosepress/